Birnam Wood

Also by Eleanor Catton

The Luminaries
The Rehearsal

Birnam Wood

Eleanor Catton

GRANTA

Granta Publications, 12 Addison Avenue, London W11 4QR

First published in Great Britain by Granta Books, 2023

Copyright © Eleanor Catton, 2023

The moral right of Eleanor Catton to be identified as
the author of this work has been asserted in accordance
with the Copyright, Designs and Patents Act 1988.

All rights reserved. No reproduction, copy or transmission
of this publication may be made without written permission.
No paragraph of this publication may be reproduced, copied
or transmitted save with written permission or in accordance
with the provisions of the Copyright Act 1988. Any person who
does any unauthorized act in relation to this publication may be
liable to criminal prosecution and civil claims for damages.

A CIP catalogue record for this book is
available from the British Library.

1   3   5   7   9   10   8   6   4   2

ISBN 978 1 78378 425 7 (hardback)
ISBN 978 1 78378 427 1 (trade paperback)
ISBN 978 1 78378 426 4 (ebook)

Typeset in Adobe Caslon by Patty Rennie

Printed and bound by CPI Group (UK) Ltd, Croydon, CR0 4YY

www.granta.com

MIX
Paper | Supporting
responsible forestry
FSC
www.fsc.org   FSC® C171272

for Steven Toussaint

THIRD
APPARITION

Be lion-mettled, proud; and take no care
Who chafes, who frets, or where conspirers are:
Macbeth shall never vanquish'd be until
Great Birnam wood to high Dunsinane hill
Shall come against him.

MACBETH

That will never be.
Who can impress the forest, bid the tree
Unfix his earth-bound root?

I

THE KOROWAI PASS HAD BEEN CLOSED SINCE THE END of the summer, when a spate of shallow earthquakes triggered a landslide that buried a stretch of the highway in rubble, killing five, and sending a long-haul transport truck over a precipice where it skimmed a power line, ploughed a channel down the mountainside, and then exploded on a viaduct below. It was weeks before the dead could be safely recovered and the extent of the damage properly assessed; by this time the temperature was dropping, and the days shortening fast. Nothing could be done before the spring. The road was cordoned off on either side of the mountains, and traffic diverted – to the west, around the far shores of Lake Korowai, and to the east, through a patchwork of farmland and across the braided rivers that flowed down over the plains towards the sea.

The town of Thorndike, located just north of the pass in the foothills of the Korowai ranges, was bounded on one side by the lake, and on the other by Korowai National Park. The closure of the pass created an effective cul-de-sac: cut off from the south, the town was now contained in all directions but one. Like much of small-town New Zealand, the local economy depended for the most part on the commerce of truckers and tourists passing through, and when the rescue teams and television crews finally packed up and drove away, many Thorndike

3

residents reluctantly left with them. The cafés and trinket shops along the highway frontage began, one by one, to close; the petrol station reduced its hours; an apologetic sign appeared in the window of the visitor centre; and the former sheep station at the head of the valley, described by its real estate listing as the town's 'greatest-ever subdivision prospect', was quietly withdrawn from sale.

It was this last that caught the attention of Mira Bunting, aged twenty-nine, a horticulturalist by training, and the founder of an activist collective known among its members as Birnam Wood. Mira had never been to Thorndike, and she had neither the intention nor the means to purchase even the smallest patch of land there, but she had earmarked this particular listing when it had first appeared online some five or six months prior. Under an alias, she had written to the realtor, registering her interest in the proposed development, and asking if any of the subdivided plots had sold.

The alias, June Crowther, was one of several that Mira had developed over time and maintained on rotation. Mrs Crowther was imaginary; she was also sixty-eight, retired, and profoundly deaf, for which reason she preferred to be contacted by email rather than by phone. She had a modest nest egg in shares and bonds that she wished to convert to real estate. A holiday home was what she had in mind, somewhere rural, which could be shared among her daughters while she was living and bequeathed to them after she was gone. The house must be new – after a lifetime of repairs and renovations, she was done with all of that – but it need not be purpose-built. A smart prefab would suit her fine, a cookie-cutter sort of place on a cookie-cutter sort of street, as long as the neighbours were not too close, and she was free to choose the colours. All this the farm at Thorndike might have promised; some four months after the landslide on the pass, however, Mrs Crowther received an email from the realtor explaining that owing to the change in circumstances, his client had decided not to sell. It was possible the property would return to the market at a later date; in the meantime, he wondered if Mrs Crowther might be interested in another of his listings nearby – he attached a link – and wished her all the best on her house-hunting journey.

Mira read the email twice, wrote a courteous but non-committal reply, and then logged out of the fake account and called up a map of Thorndike in her browser. The farm, situated in the south-east corner of the valley, was roughly trapezoidal in shape, much narrower at the bottom of the hill than at the top, where it backed on to national park land. One hundred and fifty-three hectares, she remembered from the realtor's listing, with a perimeter of perhaps eight or ten kilometres. It was not far from the site of the landslide; she switched to satellite view to check, but the image had not yet been updated. The road over the pass still wound smooth and glittering, tacking back and forth as it ascended, interrupted here and there by the grey gleam of sunlight glancing off the roofs of trucks and cars. It occurred to Mira that the image might have been captured mere moments before the quakes: the motorists pictured might now be dead. She told herself this experimentally, as if testing for a pulse; it was a private habit, formed in girlhood, to berate herself with morbid hypotheticals. Today she could not muster pity, so as penance she compelled herself to imagine being crushed and suffocated, holding the thought in her mind's eye for several seconds before exhaling and turning back to the map.

A windbreak of arrowy poplars threw a toothy shadow over the driveway and up to the house, which was set far back from the road – high enough, she figured, to clear the height of the trees along the lakefront and so command a view across the water. Above the house was a kind of natural terrace, formed by the seam of limestone that divided the more wooded upper paddocks from the open pasture that adjoined the road. Mira enlarged the image and scanned the paddocks one by one. They were all empty. A rutted track showed the owner's habitual route around the property, and from the angled shadows in the dirt she could see that several gates were standing open. The realtor had not disclosed his client's name, but when she typed the address into a separate tab, a news article came up at once.

Mr Owen Darvish, of 1606 Korowai Pass Road, Thorndike, South Canterbury, had recently made headline news. He had been named in the Queen's Birthday Honours List and was shortly to be created Knight Companion of the New Zealand Order of Merit, for services to conservation.

Intrigued, Mira forgot about the map for the moment, and read on.

Chivalric titles had been abolished in New Zealand in the year 2000, only to be reinstated nine years later by a moneyed politician desirous of a knighthood of his own. It was embarrassing whichever way one felt about it: the monarchists could not celebrate, as the resurrection only proved the Crown could be politically compelled, and the republicans could not protest, because to do so would be to suggest that there was something sacred about a monarchic code of chivalry in the first place, that ought to be beyond a common politician's reach. Both parties felt disgruntled, and both received the twice-yearly Honours Lists with the same peevish cynicism, concluding, jointly, that all the knighted intellectuals were sell-outs, and all the knighted businessmen were bribes. Owen Darvish, it seemed, was a rare exception. The news of his elevation had come so soon after the landslide on the pass as to give the impression that the knighthood had been offered as a kind of consolation to the Korowai

region at large, and *that* was a kind of chivalry with which neither monarchists nor republicans were prepared to find fault.
Darvish had even offered up his house to Search & Rescue to
use as their base of operations in the days after the disaster. 'I
take my hat off to those guys,' was all he said about it. 'They're
heroes, they really are.'

Mira read on.

She learned that Darvish had begun his working life forty
years ago at the age of seventeen, clearing his neighbours' fields
of rabbits at a rate of a dollar a head. He was a very good shot,
and his two most treasured possessions, both presents from his
father, were his .22 air rifle and his skinning knife, which had
a fixed blade and a boxwood handle, and which he'd since had
mounted, together with the rifle, in a special presentation case
in his front room. In those early days, he'd skinned the carcasses
himself and sold the dressed meat as pet food to kennels and dog
owners nearby. The pelts had been a tougher prospect. Eventually he'd found a scour plant willing to take them, in batches, to
process into felt; but as the plant had insisted on invoicing, Darvish, now aged nineteen, had taken the decision to incorporate.
He'd hired an accountant, leased an answer-phone service, and
bought a tin of yellow paint from the hardware store. On the
doors of his truck he'd stencilled the words *Darvish Pest Control*.

As the son of a slaughterhouse worker, Darvish knew first-
hand that large numbers of healthy livestock had to be prematurely butchered each year on account of a broken ankle or
a broken leg. Rabbit warrens laid waste to good pasture; they
were also an introduced species, along with possums, rats, and
stoats, which shared their taste for the shoots of native plants
and the eggs of native birds. The extermination of these pests
was one of the few instances of common ground between
conservationists and industrial farmers in New Zealand, and

Darvish, as he expanded operations, steered a middle course, courting clients on both the left and the right. Mira read that over its lifetime Darvish Pest Control had held contracts with all of New Zealand's major agricultural industries, as well as with iwi and rūnanga, town councils, and departments of state; but it was a recent partnership with the American technology corporation Autonomo, included on the S&P 500 Index, that Darvish hoped would be his crowning achievement. Autonomo, from what Mira could gather, was a manufacturer of drones, and with its help Darvish Pest Control had just embarked upon an ambitious conservation project aimed at monitoring native wildlife populations that were under threat. It was early days, Darvish said modestly, but he believed the scheme had the potential to rescue a number of endemic species from near extinction – including, he dearly hoped, the critically endangered orange-fronted parakeet, which he confessed was his favourite bird.

Mira was scowling. It annoyed her, almost as a matter of principle, that anyone of this man's age, race, gender, wealth, and associated privilege should have used his power – allegedly – for good, should have built his business – allegedly – up from the ground, from nothing, and should possess – allegedly – the very kind of rural authenticity that she herself most envied and pursued. Even more annoying was the fact that she had never heard of the orange-fronted parakeet, which she now searched for, still scowling, in a separate tab. Like all self-mythologising rebels, Mira preferred enemies to rivals, and often turned her rivals into enemies, the better to disdain them as secret agents of the status quo. But because this was not a conscious habit, she experienced only a vague feeling of righteous defiance as, unable to dismiss Owen Darvish, she told herself instead that she disliked him.

The picture on the government website showed a clean-shaven, open-collared man of middle age, with a wide, capable mouth, a strong jaw, and an amused expression; the citation below it praised qualities of ingenuity, tenacity, and fair-minded pragmatism, casting him as a perfect exemplar of what New Zealanders flattered themselves to describe as the national temperament. In interviews, he played expertly to type, fielding questions in a manner that was bluff and self-effacing, and asserting, when asked about his politics, that he had none at all. Mira could not find a single article dispraising him. He presented as a patriot – in other words, as a staunch, self-sufficient, adamantly informal man, doting in his enthusiasms, nostalgic in his routines, and innately suspicious of all partisan displays – though tolerant, perhaps, of a little recreational churchgoing in his wife.

She – Jill, soon to be Lady Darvish – looked a little like Mira's mother: slim and rangy, with a tanned complexion and silver hair in a pixie cut. She had posed for the local paper with her arm around her husband's waist, pulling back to grin at him admiringly, her other hand resting on the broad muscle of his chest. 'The Knight Is Ours' ran the delirious headline, though the reporter had taken pains to qualify that it was Jill, and not the soon-to-be Sir Owen, who was the true Thorndike native: the farm had been her childhood home, bequeathed on the death of her father five years prior. The point was minor, but Darvish clearly knew his country well enough not to minimise it further. He performed the necessary reassurances that Thorndike was without question the best place he'd ever lived; extolled the many holidays and baling seasons that had brought them back here, over the years; made no mention of their plans to subdivide the property; and confessed, in a play of chagrin, that his wife's old man was surely laughing at him somewhere, for, despite his best efforts, the farm could not yet be declared pest-free. In fact – deftly steering the interview back to its proper subject – he had been shooting rabbits in the upper paddocks when he had received the call from the office of the governor-general informing him of his impending change of state.

'Bloody ruined my shot,' he told the paper. 'Phone went off, I jumped a mile. I was so mad I almost didn't answer it.'

'And bunny got away,' his wife put in.

'So she owes me a dollar.'

'The Queen?'

'The Queen herself. She owes me a dollar, a carcass, and a pelt.'

Mira had found what she was looking for. Her knee had started to bounce underneath the table, and she felt excitement rising in her chest. Returning to the government website, she read that the investiture of Owen Darvish was to take place at Government House in Wellington in three weeks' time. She noted down the date, then closed her laptop, picked up her cycle helmet, and walked out of the library.

Five minutes later the yellow circle labelled 'Mira' pulled out into the street and began traversing slowly north. Shelley Noakes reduced the scale of the map until her own circle, a gently pulsing blue, appeared at the edge of the screen, and watched the yellow disc advance imperceptibly upon the blue for almost thirty seconds before turning off the phone and throwing it, suddenly and childishly, into the pile of laundry at the end of her bed. Mira would not be home for half an hour at least, but already Shelley's heart was beating fast and the skin of her throat and breast had mottled. She stood up, breathing deeply, and tempted herself with the thought that perhaps today was not the day to broach the subject after all . . . but then she heard Mira's voice in her head telling her that there was a voice in her head, and that the voice was her mother's.

Shelley's mother was one of the pet topics of conversation at Birnam Wood, having estranged herself to Mira early in their acquaintance by referring to the collective as a 'hobby', and to her daughter's involvement with it as a 'phase'. Mira had taken such instant and lasting umbrage at these remarks that Shelley had begun to fear there must be something wrong with her, that she herself had taken no offence at all; and although she had now given more than four and a half years to Birnam Wood, she did not consider this to be a reproof of her mother's early lack of faith in her, for she felt more surprised than anyone that she had stuck it out so long. Mira could not understand this. She was not given to casual self-deprecation, and was convinced that Shelley had been either bullied or brainwashed out of a more natural self-belief; the irony, of course – which Shelley had only fully grasped in retrospect – was that a gently deprecating sense of humour was actually one of the things that Shelley most liked about herself, and one of the things, it had to be said, that she most loved about her mother.

Mrs Noakes was a recruitment consultant who believed that the world's population could be divided into those with a gift for sales and those with a gift for service; most people, she was fond of remarking, were employed against their type, and if they would only take a good honest look at themselves and determine into which of the two categories they fell, they might save the rest of us a lot of fuss and bother. When Mira had first heard this, she had laughed. Listing, with no small relish, all the ways that selling was a service, and all the ways that services were sold, she had dismissed the maxim as vapid neoliberal bullshit, adding, with careless perspicacity, that Mrs Noakes appeared to compete with her children in several arenas, but most particularly on the issue of job satisfaction, a hard-won prize for the women of her generation, and one that she was unwilling, perhaps, to share.

Shelley could recall it almost word for word. She had been twenty-one years old to Mira's twenty-four, and never in her life had she heard any adult criticised so openly and calmly, without any of the usual forms of obeisance – the ritual admission of the speaker's likely ignorance; the ritual deference to all opposing points of view – that for her were so thoroughly ingrained that they inhibited her thinking as severely as they did her speech. She had sought out Mira's friendship with a fervour that approached infatuation, transforming herself, though she would not realise this until years later, into a more perfect image of the person that Mira had told her that she already was: more benighted, more repressed, and more continually in conflict with a mother whose every utterance, she came to discover, incarnated no less an enemy than the spectre of late capitalism itself. Cast virtually since birth in the role of the family peacemaker, and praised throughout her adolescence for having cost her parents not a single night of sleep, Shelley had lived for as long as she could remember in perpetual dread of being dislikeable – a fate even more terrible than being disliked, for it encompassed not only her relationships with others, but her private judgments of herself. It was only under Mira's influence that she learned, if not to overcome this terror, then at least to direct the blame for it elsewhere.

She returned to the pile of laundry and checked her phone again. The yellow circle had crossed the avenue that marked the border of the central city and was drawing level with a planted flag that on Shelley's map was labelled SITE FIFTEEN. It slowed as it approached the turn-off and seemed to be on the verge of stopping. 'I went already,' Shelley said aloud, and as if Mira had heard her, the circle seemed to change its mind, and carried on, picking up speed again. Shelley had a creepy feeling. She shut off the screen a second time and plugged the phone into the wall to charge, stabbing the cord into the socket with more force than was necessary, and willing herself not to touch it again before Mira got home – not even if she heard it buzzing.

Shelley had been deciding between a diploma in library information studies and a diploma in high-school teacher training when she had first encountered Mira planting seedlings in the dirt. She was only fifteen credits short of the three hundred and sixty needed to complete her bachelor's degree, majoring in English and specialising in twentieth-century genre fiction, for which she had accrued twenty-three thousand dollars in debt; but within a fortnight she had dropped her final paper, *Popular Teen Fantasy and its Representation on Film*, blighting her academic record with the first failing grade of her life, and placing both diplomas, for the time being at least, out of reach. Her mother could not comprehend it, and flouted her own dictum by prescribing a few months' work in the thankless world of retail to set her daughter back on a sensible path; she was unable to accept that Birnam Wood might answer what she saw as Shelley's natural gift for service, for she could not see what higher purpose a frankly illegal scheme of trespassing and botanical vandalism could possibly hope to serve, either for Shelley or for anybody else. Or so she was imagined to believe. At Birnam Wood 'Shelley's mum' had become a kind of shorthand for the many evils of the baby-boomer generation, a despised cohort of hoarders and plunderers from which Mira's own parents, who had recently separated, always seemed mysteriously to be exempt.

(Nor was Shelley's dad of any interest to Mira as an adversary. He was a mortgage broker with an irritable disposition who was always, in the family parlance, 'in a rage' – an infirmity openly encouraged, as Mira pointed out, by his wife, who indeed devoted an unusual proportion of her daily conversation to reminding her husband of the many kinds of people in the world whom he disliked. That this list, which included vegans, slow walkers, loudmouths, ostentatious breast-feeders, people of indeterminate gender, buskers, bad drivers, and the unwashed, covered in one way or another the entire membership of Birnam Wood, Mira did not appear to find insulting. She saw Shelley's father as a creature of his wife's devising, not an autonomous adult, but a hapless pawn designed by Mrs Noakes for the solitary purpose of throwing her own, more vivid personality into greater relief – a plainly narcissistic exercise of which she, Mira, could not remotely see the appeal.)

Only years later had Shelley thought to place the long and penetrating conversations of the early months of their friendship in the context of Mira's parents' separation, which dated, she eventually learned, from the morning of the day that she and Mira had first met. From Mira's brief account of the scene – it had taken place over breakfast, her father standing behind her mother's chair and massaging her shoulders tenderly as she relayed the news – it would seem that her parents had arrived at their decision so amicably and mutually, and with such happy consciousness both of the wonderful years they'd spent together and of the exciting possibilities that now lay ahead, as to make redundant any further examination of either the meaning of their choice or its potential consequences for anyone involved. Mira could talk about other people's relationships endlessly – she freely confessed that she liked nothing better – but when she talked about her own, it was always in a tone of brisk, semi-exasperated satire that gave the impression she had exhausted the subject a long time ago and felt no impatience to revive it. For the first few months of their friendship, all that Shelley had known about Mira's parents had been that they were former hippies who had each stood for their local constituency – her mother for the Green Party, her father for Labour – in subsequent elections, without success; and that Mira's mother had a son from a previous relationship, Mira's half-brother Rufus, who was the lead guitarist in a touring rock band and whom Mira's father apparently adored. They sounded wonderfully enlightened, and the fact that Mira saw them only intermittently Shelley took as further proof of the psychological maturity that Mira found wanting in everybody else. She began to feel embarrassed that her own family convened each week for their parochial Sunday lunch, where invariably the conversation centred on, and was directed at, the dog – and she was even more embarrassed whenever Mira asked to tag along. Mira always behaved politely and engagingly at the table, praising the cooking and helping with the washing-up; she barely mentioned Birnam Wood except to narrate the odd family-friendly anecdote in the humorous and confidential mode of speech that she always used when speaking to adults. But to Shelley the occasions were unbearable, every detail an appalling indictment of her family's mediocrity, every word spoken an appalling desecration of Mira's deeply held beliefs. She was still too much in Mira's thrall to suspect her of any emotion so ordinary as loneliness, or so shallow as envy; and it was a relief, walking home, to return to the central theme of their friendship by cataloguing, freshly, all the many ways in which Shelley's mother was in need of reform.

If Mrs Noakes knew how unsparingly she was anatomised, then she possessed more fortitude of character than either Mira or her daughter ever diagnosed, for despite her initial resistance to Shelley's sudden change of course, and despite her frequent sharing of career vacancy advertisements 'just to give you a sense of what's out there', Mrs Noakes had really come around to Birnam Wood; in fact, it pained Shelley to admit, when her mother spoke about it now, it was with real pride and admiration. The political rout of 2016 had brought with it a new mood of deference towards the radically unforeseen. Around the globe, forecasters had been chastened and experts maligned; in their place had come the disruptors, the technological imperialists, the metadata millenarians and stokers of popular feeling who had managed, invisibly and hitherto impossibly, to manufacture the authentic, the world's most influential brand. A new vocabulary had come into force: Birnam Wood was now a start-up, a pop-up, the brainchild of 'creatives'; it was organic, it was local; it was a bit like Uber; it was a bit like Airbnb. In this new, perpetually unsettled climate, Shelley's defection from the conventional economy had gained, she knew, a kind of retroactive valour, and even Mira – seditious, independent-minded Mira – suddenly seemed to be just the sort of trendy big-talking renegade one could imagine being contracted by the government as a black-ops adviser, writing inflammatory blogs and newspaper columns that defended unorthodox opinions and debated the right to free speech. Agitation had lost its juvenile cast: it had been made urgent again, righteous again, necessary again. An aura of prescience now permeated Birnam Wood.

And Shelley wanted out. Out of the group; out of the suffocating moral censure, the pretended fellow feeling, the constant obligatory thrift; out of financial peril; out of the flat; out of her relationship with Mira, which was not romantic in any physical sense, but which had somehow come to feel both exclusive and proprietary; and above all, out of her role as the sensible, dependable, predictable sidekick, never quite as rebellious as Mira, never quite as free-thinking, never – even when they acted together – quite as brave. She wanted out with a force of feeling that was as abrupt and absolute as when she had first known she wanted in, and when she probed the conviction, she found that she could not explain the reason for her disenchantment any more clearly than she could explain what had so powerfully attracted her to Birnam Wood in the first place – and even more: she found that she did not *want* to explain it, did not want to understand it, did not want to subject to scrutiny that awful buried certainty that whatever she did or said, however she acted, whatever life she chose, she would always be wrong, ill-intended, ill-prepared, and incomplete. On a dark and shameful level of her consciousness Shelley knew that the drastic course corrections in her life – her *phases*, to use the word that Mira so deplored – did not owe to any sudden clarities of vision or vocation, but to this smothered and ever-present sense of dread. She had tried to escape it by joining Birnam Wood, and she was trying to escape it now, but she would never escape it, because she could not feel the difference, could not understand the difference, between running towards something, and running away.

Her phone buzzed, and she looked over to read the notification that had lit the screen, craning from where she stood so as not to break her promise not to touch it. The message was a promotional email from a hotel where she had once logged on to the lobby WiFi. *Last Chance to Save!* read the subject line. Shelley's heartbeat had surged again. Miserably, she put her hand to her throat to quell the pounding and stared at the device until the screen went dark and the image was replaced by a hash of oily streaks and fingerprints marking all the places she had scrolled and tapped and liked and pinned and maximised and minimised and forwarded and binned and sent.

To break up with a friend was difficult enough, but she and Mira shared far more, and had committed far more, than ordinary friends, and for all that Shelley had tried to reassure herself that she desired nothing more exotic or exceptional than an independent income, a chance at self-fulfilment, and a change of scene, she knew – and she felt sick even to acknowledge it – that Birnam Wood would likely not survive without her. After five years of operation the collective was still nowhere near the point of self-sufficiency that they jokingly referred to as 'breaking good'; without her contributions, that dream would recede even further. Mira would have to take over the accounting and schedule planning, fields in which she was almost comically unskilled. She would have to find a new flatmate, and possibly a new flat. She would have to train Shelley's replacement, not just over months, but over years, for each season brought its unique challenges and opportunities, and each crop behaved in a different way – and all of this, Shelley thought in disgusted outrage against herself, all of this would take up time that Mira did not have to spare. The project would be forced to downscale, members would lose interest and disband, and Mira's ambitions would be crushed. Feeling despicably, preposterously selfish, Shelley went outside to turn the compost heap and rehearse what she was going to say.

Officially the group cultivated eighteen plots of land around the city, some in the gardens of care homes and preschools, one bordering the car park of a surgery and dental practice, and most in the yards of rented student flats. In exchange for access to their space and use of their mains water, the hosts received half the yield of every crop; the rest of the harvest went to the members, either to consume among themselves or to pack in boxes to give to the needy or to sell on the side of the road beneath a sign that claimed, with some creative licence, that

the produce was home-grown. In accordance with their charter, they spent any income they earned only on seeds, soil, and
whatever equipment could not be bartered or salvaged from the
tip. Nobody received wages, and all assets were commonly held;
membership, as a result, was almost entirely a part-time affair,
and even Mira, who stayed perpetually enrolled at university in
order to draw down the student allowance and yearly bursary
for course-related costs, was occasionally obliged to seek temporary employment.

Several times Shelley had raised the possibility of launching
a subscription service – a monthly box of produce, collated from
all their growing sites and delivered door to door – so as to
afford the group a little more stability in planning, but despite
general interest it had never come to pass. The problem was
not just that they had never quite reached that point of critical
mass where their income would finally exceed their many costs
and liabilities; it was that breaking good, for Mira at least, had
always meant more than simply breaking even. Her ambition
for Birnam Wood was nothing less than radical, widespread,
and lasting social change, which would be entirely achievable,
she was convinced, if only people could be made to see how
much fertile land was going begging, all around them, every day
– and how much more could be accomplished in the world if
everybody simply pooled their knowledge and resources – and
how arbitrary and absurdly prejudicial the entire concept of land
ownership, when divorced from use or habitation, really was!
The difficulty, of course, was in knowing whether it was better
to raise public consciousness through protest, and risk putting
off those very people who were yet to be converted to the cause,
or to risk accusations of hypocrisy and try to change the system
from within – and here Mira never really gave a settled answer.
Temperamentally, two factions existed within Birnam Wood:

the ideologues, who were combative and self-conscious, and who cherished revolutionary aims; and the do-gooders, who were more reliably hard-working, but who were also, in a way, more hard work, being more fixated than the ideologues on the ways in which any breaches of protocol ought to be policed. Mira didn't fall wholly into either contingent, but the fact that the ideological faction had dwindled over the years was a source of great shame and consternation to her, and sometimes Shelley wondered if her patent lack of interest in the financial viability of Birnam Wood was her way of reassuring herself, even unconsciously, that she had not sold out.

Mira had a peculiar relationship with money. She was uninterested in profit and at the same time obsessed by growth, and she opposed most mainstream economic policy not only on moral terms, but also on the grounds that it was imaginatively limiting. Unusually for someone of her politics, she was untouched by depression; her convictions were of the sort that required a sparring partner, rather than of the sort that required a cure. She could be impulsively, even alarmingly, generous, and never seemed to second-guess (as Shelley did) the things she sold or gave away; but she was also wildly inconsistent. That the university, for example, had never once made contact to ask the reason for her continued non-attendance she saw as proof of a rapacious business model that in her opinion had so utterly debauched a university's fundamental reasons for existence as to justify almost any act of civil disobedience against it; but that she herself had effectively come to treat that institution not as a hallowed place of learning, but as a financial instrument, she considered to be merely fitting. She was untroubled, or at least claimed to be untroubled, that her student record showed only failures for the last three years; and although her student loan was now in excess of a hundred thousand dollars, she avowed that the debt did not remotely worry her, because she had no intention of ever paying it back.

In any case, a great deal of what they needed could be got for free – if not from the natural world, then by raiding skips and recycling bins, by making collections of unwanted household junk, and simply by asking for donations. Shelley had learned from Mira the particular clairvoyance of the scavenger, whereby discarded items now appeared to her only in the form of something else. Old window screens were shade cloth; flattened cardboard and carpet offcuts were weed matting; plastic bottles, when sliced in half, became little cloches to fit over seedlings to keep them warm. Any receptacle could be a seed tray, and anything reflective could be propped against it to maximise the light. She had discovered over the years that the more peculiar her requests, the more eager people seemed to meet them: clippings from hair salons for slug repellent; old tights to fit over the heads of cabbages and cauliflowers to protect them from pests; wool to drape cat's-cradle over plantings to deter the birds. Every windowsill of the tiny flat that she and Mira shared was occupied by rows and rows of seedlings, and they recorded each successive planting in the open-source folder shared among the members, that kept track of all the interlocking schedules of weeding, watering, and cultivation, advertised what jobs needed doing, recorded where tools were being stored, and disclosed how any income had been spent.

That was the official face of Birnam Wood, the one they wore when recruiting members and soliciting prospective hosts; in truth, however, a great deal of what they harvested had been planted without permission on public or unattended lands. They chose hardy perennials, fast-growing annuals, or – if the ground was tilled enough – root crops that might from a distance be confused for weeds, and sowed them along verges and fence lines, beside motorway off-ramps, inside demolition sites, and in junkyards filled with abandoned cars. To avoid detection, they tended these guerrilla plantings in the very early morning, or, when in daylight, wearing high-vis, to give the appearance of an authenticated scheme. Water posed their biggest challenge, being too heavy to transport in any volume. A twenty-litre water-cooler bottle strapped to the back of a bicycle was too memorable a sight to risk with any regularity, and although they had experimented with drip irrigators fashioned out of finely perforated plastic vessels, these also had the disadvantage of drawing the eye. They had better luck collecting rainwater, dredging ponds and rivers, and tapping private spigots and irrigation booms, where, in the event that they were apprehended, they took care never to identify themselves – or Birnam Wood – by their real names.

Shelley was not a natural liar, and no matter how minimally or justifiably they trespassed, she could never fully shake the dread of being caught. This was rare, but when it happened, all of Mira's reasonings – that they were only reaping what they themselves had sown; that they were giving to the soil, and to the air, at least as much as they were taking from it; that a good proportion of their harvest was destined for the needy; and – in anarchistic moments – that, after all, the landowners had committed theft on a far greater scale, simply by virtue of being landowners – deserted her, and she became too mortified even to speak; it would fall to one of the other members to deploy one of several plausible fictions they had devised in order to be able to stall an inquisitor for long enough that they could get away.

And they did more than trespass. Their plantings occasionally choked out local competition, or became so prolific as to be expensive to remove; sometimes, they returned to a site to find it had been doused in weedkiller or burned. They took cuttings from suburban gardens, leaf litter out of public parks, and manure from farmland. Mira had stolen scions from commercial apple orchards – budding whips of Braeburn and Royal Gala that she grafted to the stocks of sour crab-apple trees – and equipment out of unlocked garden sheds, though only, she insisted, in wealthy neighbourhoods, and only those tools that did not seem to be in frequent use. But she prized her freedom too highly ever to risk it very far, and she was careful to conceal any patently criminal activity from the wider membership of Birnam Wood, whose good opinion she was anxious to retain. That, Shelley thought, as she forked the compost and released the sweet vegetal stink into the air, had been her own most valuable contribution to the group, over the years; through the sheer unlikelihood of her allegiance, she gave Mira the only kind of credibility she lacked: the ordinary. In playing the supporting role not as a disciple or a fanatic, but as a foil, she not only tempered Mira's image, she ensured – she had ensured – that the hidden face of Birnam Wood stayed underground.

She heard a crunch of gravel behind her and turned in surprise, for even with a tailwind Mira could not possibly have made it home so soon. But the person coming down the driveway was a tanned, bearded man of around thirty, slightly round-shouldered, his long hair swept back from his forehead and his thumbs tucked under the straps of his backpack. He was wearing a tartan scarf and a misshapen woollen coat, both of which looked emphatically second-hand.

'Hi,' he said. 'I'm looking for Mira? Bunting?'

Shelley stared at him. 'Tony?'

'Oh shit,' he said.

He was shorter than she remembered, and his tan made his blue eyes seem bluer.

'Shelley,' she reminded him, 'Shelley Noakes.'

'God,' he said. 'I'm really sorry. I guess it's been a while.'

But his face was flushed: it was plain that he still did not recognise her, and that he was now desperately searching his memory for even the smallest piece of information about her, because the name hadn't helped. To prompt him, Shelley said, 'You left right after I joined up' – kindly, for in fact they had overlapped by several months. 'Few years ago now – yeah, God. You were headed overseas.'

'That's it,' he said, looking hunted. 'I only just got back.'

'It was a Teach Abroad-type thing, wasn't it? Somewhere in South America?'

His blush intensified. 'Mexico,' he said. 'Technically North. But yeah. Pretty great. Thought I'd never come home, actually.'

'I bet.'

He glanced at the house, still flushed. 'It's weird to be back. Everything's the same and everything's different, you know?'

'I bet,' Shelley said again.

'This looks amazing though.' He made a gesture that incorporated the compost heap, the polytunnels, and the potting bench. 'I heard it's all still going strong?'

'Yeah,' she said, looking around as well. 'Santa's workshop.'

'Exactly,' he said, and laughed. He looked relieved. 'You live with Mira?'

'Yeah,' Shelley said. 'I did back then, as well. We moved into the Hansons Lane flat just before you left. About a month before.'

There was a slight pause.

'I remember your leaving party was pretty wild,' she said.

'Hey,' he said. 'Look. I'm really sorry—'

'Nah,' she said, waving him away. 'I'm just making you feel bad.'

'Well, if I can't – I mean, clearly I was a massive dick back then.'

'Steady on,' she said. 'Bigger than average maybe. I wouldn't have said massive.'

'Oh, Jesus,' he said, putting his hands on his head. 'Okay. You're messing with me.'

She grinned at him. 'And didn't I lend you some money? Like, quite a bit of money? Yeah, you know, I think I did. And you never paid me back.'

Now he was smiling too. 'You're really enjoying this, aren't you?'

'It's a very powerful position,' Shelley said. 'I don't want to waste it.'

She almost didn't recognise herself. The adrenaline she had built up in rehearsing for her confrontation with Mira was allowing her to speak and act in ways that were utterly unlike her; she felt at once both dangerously reckless and dangerously calm. The normal Shelley would have been horrified on his behalf, would have apologised for being so thoroughly forgettable, would have reassured him that she had no expectation whatsoever of his remembering anything about her, since it was so long ago, and their friendship had been so fleeting, and those days were such a blur. The normal Shelley would have teased him, in a tone of sisterly indulgence, that back then he had been so patently in love with Mira – and everyone had known it – that it was only natural that his memory would be distorted; of course, it would make perfect sense if the only thing he could remember from that time was her. In the spirit of their shared affections, and to put him even further at ease, the normal Shelley might even have confided that although she shouldn't really be the one to tell him this, for Mira, he had always been the one who got away.

But she did not feel normal. A solution had occurred to her, an exit strategy so clean and absolute that it was almost bloodless. She would sleep with Tony. She would sleep with Tony, and she would confess what she had done to Mira, and Mira would not be able to forgive her. There would be no need for any confrontation, no need for apologies and tearful explanations and long arguments late into the night. There would be nothing to say. There would be only the fact of her betrayal, which Mira would not be able to forgive; and whether Shelley would then leave Birnam Wood of her own volition or because Mira demanded it would scarcely matter. She would sleep with Tony, and after that, leaving would not be something she was asking for, but something she had already done.

'Is she home?' Tony said. 'I didn't call ahead or anything.'

'She'll be out for another couple of hours,' Shelley said, the lie coming easily: she didn't break eye contact; she didn't blush. 'Hey,' she added, naturally, as if the thought had just occurred to her, 'do you want to go somewhere and get a drink?'

He hesitated, but it was clear that he owed it to her, and he could hardly say that he was otherwise engaged. In her new and preternatural confidence Shelley had no fear that he would turn her down. She was going to sleep with him, tonight.

'Sure,' he said, very reluctantly. 'Yeah, let's do it.'

'Great,' said Shelley. 'Just let me go and grab my phone.'

Tony Gallo had not been entirely truthful: he had actually been back in New Zealand for almost five weeks, and although he would never have confessed it, he had observed Shelley from a distance twice already, though without recalling that they had ever met. On both occasions, she had been with Mira; on the first, cycling together through the teacher-training college campus, Shelley grinning broadly while Mira, who was riding one-handed, gesticulated wildly to accompany a joke; and on the second, sorting through refuse behind the junk shop that adjoined the tip where, before Tony's departure, Mira had worked on Saturday mornings, and where he had gone the first Saturday after he had seen her cycling in the hope that her schedule hadn't altered in the years that he had been away. Evidently it had not; but as he turned into the car park and was preparing to cut the engine and get out of the car, he saw that Mira was again occupied in conversation, this time gravely, nodding along with solemn emphasis while Shelley spoke. None of Tony's rehearsals for the scene of their reunion had allowed for the presence of a third party, and to see her so engrossed in whatever it was that Shelley was saying made him abruptly lose his nerve – as if her complete absorption in the present moment proved, in itself, how little she now thought of him and how seldom she had recourse to the past. She was dressed, as Shelley was, in a boiler suit and regulation steel-capped boots, and as he sat in the idling car with his hand on the ignition, Tony felt suddenly acutely conscious of his own freshly laundered clothes, which smelled of the eucalyptus fabric softener used by his mother that, of all the scents of his childhood, held the strongest associations for him of being home. Seconds later, something Shelley said caused Mira to throw her head back and laugh, and almost as a reflex Tony reversed out of his parking spot, jammed the gearstick into first, and drove away, hunching unnaturally low over the steering wheel and praying that she would not look over and recognise the receding licence plate of his father's car.

His appearance at the flat that afternoon had been more carefully curated, from the clothes that he was wearing and the mode of his arrival right down to the contents of his backpack, which included his journal, his fountain pen, a vintage 35mm camera, and several books that he had already read. He had come by bus, intending to arrive a little after four – a respectable hour for a social visit, and still early enough in the day that if there was nobody at home, he could sit on the doorstep and read for a while without it seeming as if he meant to ambush her. True, he had not called ahead, but this was in keeping with a challenge he and Mira had once set themselves to communicate as much as possible off-grid – and anyway, the contract on his old New Zealand phone had lapsed, and in switching to a new provider he had lost everybody's numbers. All these mental preparations now felt rather foolish. As he waited in the yard for Shelley to collect her things and lock up the house, he looked around him at all the signs of industry and productivity and was again overpowered by a gloomy sense of his own redundancy in Mira's life. It was clear that Birnam Wood had flourished in his absence, which itself was bittersweet; and although he had prepared himself, resolutely, for the likelihood that Mira would be in a relationship, and possibly a very serious relationship, now it struck him that to learn that she was single might feel weirdly even worse.

Tony's homecoming had been unexpectedly dispiriting. He was sensitive to condescension, and had detected in his siblings a kind of provincial triumph that the terms of his visa had at last obliged him to return; he felt himself admonished, as he had just remarked to Shelley, both by the fact that everything was different, and by the fact that everything had stayed the same. His younger brother and his father had become very close in his absence, but in a way that seemed exaggerated for his benefit, as though to make a point of all the many intimacies he had missed. The pieties of his sisters he now found almost too much to bear, and his mother's complacency in the face of his father's patent scorn for her enraged him. He was hurt by their apparent lack of curiosity in his adventures overseas, and angered by his own regression back to sulky adolescence, which had been almost instantaneous, and which felt disturbingly out of his control. This, in fact, was the main reason that he had not called on Mira any sooner: he had spent much of the past five weeks in a cycle of fury and impotent resentment that he knew was deeply unattractive and that he did not feel that he could trust himself to hide.

Tony was the middle child of five, and the exception, as he saw it, to the family rule, which, unusually in New Zealand, was devoutly Catholic, conservative, and very strict. All of his siblings had followed the example set by his father, his sisters into medicine, his father's profession, and his younger brother into the seminary, his father's boyhood dream. This road not taken was of great significance to Dr Gallo's personal mythology, and by extension the family mythology, which he controlled: a failed celibate, he regarded the existence of his wife and children with disappointment and profound regret. His own father, Tony's Grandpa Gallo, had been an envoy to the Holy See, and was so large a figure in the family lore that as a child Tony had confused him with the Pope, boasting to the neighbours' children that *his* grandpa was the guardian of the Keys of Heaven, which a half-grasped Easter Sunday homily had convinced him were not metaphorical, but real. When Tony's father heard this, he responded by docking Tony's pocket money for a month. Dr Gallo's preferred mode of discipline was to impose arbitrary sanctions on his children for specified periods of time. He kept a calendar on the fridge devoted to the purpose of recording which child had been banned from what luxury, and for how long: pocket money, but also television, the computer, rainy-day school pickups, the trampoline, pudding, bedtime cocoa, playing in the common spaces, and snacking between meals. Of all the children, it was Tony who was most often sentenced. As the eldest son and the third child, he bore the brunt of both his father's expectations and his father's impatience, and as a result his moral conscience had been shaped, from as far back as he could remember, by a vivid sense of his own damnation, and a bitter yearning that punishment, for once, should be made to fit the crime.

Inevitably, the first great rebellion of Tony's adolescence had been to renounce his faith. He was a bright boy, prideful of his intellect, critical often to the point of indignation, and observant of hypocrisy, especially, he insisted, in himself; and while he could accept that there was more than a touch of petulance in his decision to stop attending Mass – he made an exception for funerals and weddings, but refused to take Communion, genuflect, or sing – he was careful to subject his atheism to the same doubts and provocations with which he had once challenged his belief. Intellectual rigour was the habit he most admired in others, especially when combined with an inclination to debate, and he found it not among his siblings or his schoolmates, but online, chatting with strangers on the badly formatted discussion boards that just predated Twitter and Facebook, where conversation was impermanent and anonymity was guaranteed. As his rhetoric and reading life matured, he grew intensely scornful of what passed at his high school for 'education' – the mania for testing; the intolerance of real dissent; and the conformist celebration of the honed and polished 'all-rounder' student destined for high income, who was deferent and well-spoken, invariably good-looking, and proficient in music as well as in one summer and one winter sport. He neglected his schoolwork as a form of protest, and surprised his parents, every year, when he earned top marks on his exams.

At university, he majored in political philosophy and gained a reputation for being adversarial in seminars, to the point that he was often asked, in the language of the day, to check his privilege – most often, it seemed to him, at the very moment that his opponents' other, better arguments ran out. Politics, as the adage goes, is first experienced at home, and the autocratic Dr Gallo had ruled his household in a manner that was so oppressive and so patently unjust that Tony had grown used to thinking of himself in insurrectionary terms. All his life he had been overlooked, subjugated, ridiculed, and deprived of opportunities for self-defence, and he would not be persuaded, now, that his sole emancipation from Dr Gallo's tyranny – his mind – was merely a symptom representing him as yet another tool of the oppressor class. It was a sentiment not of victimhood exactly, for he was too proud to indulge the term, but of an open licence to rebel; his intellect was his liberty, and he knew no greater provocation than to have his vocabulary or his style of rhetoric policed. He had followed his bachelor's degree with a master's critiquing the anti-humanism of post-structuralist political thought, by which point he felt that he had reached the limit of what a remote, sparsely populated, historically benign island nation could offer him. Two days before his graduation, Grandpa Gallo died, leaving an estate that was far larger and more lucrative than anybody in the family had imagined, and the first thing Tony bought, once everything had been settled and all the legacies disbursed, was a ticket overseas.

Shelley came out of the house, wearing a down jacket and carrying a small backpack of her own, and he arranged his face into an expression of polite expectancy as she locked the deadbolt and pocketed her keys. 'All good,' she said, smiling at him. He smiled back and indicated with his open hand that she should lead the way.

It troubled him that he could not remember who she was. Tony considered himself to have a healthy respect for women – healthy, that is, because it was not entirely unconditional. He in no way opposed the fundamental aims of feminism, and indeed would have welcomed, he felt sure, any well-argued point in its favour; but over the course of his twenties, he had found himself increasingly at odds with the prevailing orthodoxies of the contemporary feminist left, which seemed to him to have abandoned the worthy goal of equality between the sexes in pursuit of either naked self-interest or revenge. He could not accept a worldview whose terms he was not allowed to question, and he resented the caricature of power and entitlement that he was forever being told that he embodied, automatically and absolutely, no matter what his intentions were, and no matter what he felt or thought, or even did; but he could not deny, now, that in forgetting Shelley Noakes – and he really did not remember her *at all* – he conformed, or at least had once conformed, to this very picture; and the knowledge rattled him. He felt, obscurely, as though he had been led into a trap – not by Shelley, but by all the women who had accused him, without basis, of sexism in the past.

'Was it a good programme?' Shelley asked, as they set off down the driveway together. 'Where you were teaching? Would you recommend it? Was it a good deal?'

'Keen to go yourself?'

'Maybe,' Shelley said, sounding as if the answer surprised her. 'Maybe, yeah.'

'I could definitely help you out,' Tony said. 'I mean, if you're serious. There are heaps of people I could put you in touch with.'

'Bit dangerous, when you don't know who the hell I am.'

'Well, I doubt you're an axe murderer. I don't quite get that vibe.'

She considered his remark. 'Why do we always say axe murderer, but we never say gun murderer or knife murderer?'

'Or chainsaw murderer.'

'No, you would definitely say chainsaw murderer.'

'Would you?'

'Definitely,' she said. 'That's key information. Can't sit on that.'

'But wouldn't you say, like, "she was a murderer, and she used a chainsaw"?'

'Hey,' Shelley said. 'Why "she"?'

'Aren't you the example here?'

'Okay,' she said. 'Then it'd be "chainsaw murderess". That's what they'd call me: "the chainsaw murderess".'

'Sounds like a band.'

'That's what everybody says. Right before I cut their faces off.'

Tony laughed. 'Well,' he said. 'We are really getting to know each other.'

They walked on in silence for several paces.

'Tell me about it, though,' she said presently. 'You were teaching English? What level? What kind of students were they – how old? Was it through a charity? What was it like?'

These were the questions Tony's family had never asked – that he had longed for them to ask; and as he began to answer, describing his experience in Mexico City, his teaching life, his colleagues, the essays he had published, the protest marches he had attended, and the friends he had made, he felt for the first time since his return a genuine pleasure and contentment. It was almost a surprise to remember that he could be proud – that he *was* proud – of all that he had seen and done abroad, and to feel himself distinguished by the habituated worldliness that since his homecoming had seemed to mark him only as a deserter, a tiresome condescender, and an apostate – not just of his religion, but of his family, of his country, and even, in some impenetrable way, of himself. Shelley was not well-travelled, but she expressed no envy or impatience when he told her about backpacking through Guatemala, Honduras, and Nicaragua; Brazil and Venezuela; Ecuador, Chile, and Peru, instead asking him with unfeigned curiosity about the food, the local customs, what differences he had observed between the countries, whether his preconceptions had been challenged, and whether he felt changed. She was a good listener, inquisitive, empathetic, generous with her attention, and associative in her replies, and they had been talking for almost twenty minutes before the conversation turned to her – whereupon Tony was surprised again, and gratified again, to discover what a great deal they had in common.

It turned out that they had both tutored high-school English as undergraduates, had both found their schooling underwhelming, felt similar exasperations with the state of public discourse in New Zealand, and shared a love of John Wyndham and Ursula Le Guin. Politically, Shelley was the outlier in her family, as Tony was, and she confessed that this had been a source of some sadness during her years at Birnam Wood, since most of the members had inherited their politics from their parents, and could not understand the loneliness, even the sorrow, in having forged a path alone – an achievement that deserved some commendation, Shelley felt; she had read online somewhere that one's parents' voting preference was by far the most accurate predictor of one's own political alignment, way more than age, ethnicity, gender, educational attainment, or locale. Tony was very pleased by this statistic, which he had not heard before, and as they swapped tales of their mutual disenchantment, he felt more and more astonished that he could ever have forgotten someone so thoroughly simpatico as Shelley Noakes. It never crossed his mind that since *she* had not forgotten *him*, the personality that she revealed to him might very easily have been customised, the opinions tailored, the résumé adapted, to suit what she remembered of his interests and his taste; never dreaming that she might be flirting with him, he reflected only that there was something appealingly familiar in her candid warmth and air of frank and ready capability – qualities of a certain type of Kiwi woman that until that moment he had not realised he had missed.

'Whenever I did anything with Birnam Wood,' he said, 'like, even if I just mentioned it, even just said the name, my dad would say, without fail, "So who's Macbeth?" It was his one joke.'

'You should have said, "Actually, Dad, you are,"' Shelley said.

'Exactly,' Tony said. 'Only I think that's kind of what he wanted me to say.'

'My dad used to call it Birnam Woulda Coulda Shoulda,' Shelley said.

Tony burst out laughing. 'Oh my God,' he said. 'Brutal.'

'Just – if that makes you feel any better.'

'You know,' Tony said, still laughing, 'it kind of does.'

They had arrived at the bar. 'My shout,' Shelley said, as she opened the door. 'Only fair: I am about to kill you, after all.'

'Well, thanks,' he said. 'Beer would be great. Whatever ale they've got on tap. Monteith's.'

He went to find a table, now feeling quite cheerful, and thinking that perhaps it had been a stroke of luck that Mira hadn't been at home when he had called. The last time they had spoken had been at his leaving party almost four years ago, a night that hung in his memory as a dozen dimly lighted moments threaded on a string: Mira on the dance floor, turning her hands in the air above her head; Mira flushed on the fire escape, her eyes closed, pressing the globe of her wine glass hard against her cheek; Mira with an avid look; Mira with her hand around his wrist. The next morning, in the forlorn self-pity of a severe hangover, he had composed a long and tormented email to her that had sat on his desktop for six weeks before, drunk again, he had dragged it to the bin and deleted it forever – and that was that. They had had no contact since; in four years, no messages, no emails, no calls. He had no idea whether she had composed and deleted any comparable messages to him; no idea whether she had missed him; no idea how she would receive him, what she would think of him, what she would say – but now, he thought happily, as he unwound his scarf and unbuttoned his coat, now, thanks to Shelley, he had the means of finding out. Now, when he and Mira reunited, he would be forearmed.

Shelley set down a pitcher of honey-coloured ale and two glasses. 'Happy hour,' she said.

'Awesome,' Tony said. 'Thanks heaps.' He watched her pour, and then said, 'So you stuck with it, all this time.'

'You mean, with Birnam Wood?'

'Yeah. Just – that's a big commitment, is all. You must be pretty hardcore.'

She handed him his beer and began to pour her own. 'It's changed quite a bit since you left,' she said, seeming to be choosing her words with care. 'You might be disappointed.'

'How do you mean?'

'More mainstream, I guess,' she said. 'Not as many anarchists. Do you remember the crust punks? Dan Javins, and what's-his-name – Fink?'

'Oh my God, Fink!'

'Yeah,' said Shelley, 'they're long gone.'

'That's me out, then,' he said, feigning disappointment. 'I was all set to come back, but if the crust punks are gone – fuck that.'

She smiled at him. 'It's just become a bit more of a business, is what I mean. Still non-profit and direct-action and all of that, just more – above board. More bureaucratic.'

'You sound like you're over it.'

'I just feel older, you know?'

He waited for her to elaborate, but she glanced away, her attention caught by an advertisement on the television above the bar. He took a gulp of beer, watching her. After a moment he said, 'What does Mira think about all that?'

'Oh,' she said, 'you know. Still wants to take over the world.'

'No change there, then.'

'Oh,' Shelley said again, looking into her glass, 'I don't know. Maybe.' She sipped her beer, suddenly remote; but when she put her glass back down on the table, she seemed to rouse herself, and smiled at him again. 'So – obvious question. What are you going to do, now that you're back?'

'Freelance is the plan,' he said. 'Essays, articles, whatever I can think up. Maybe a podcast.'

'Like journalism?'

'Yeah – long-form investigative stuff. Social commentary. A bit of theory. Not that personal essay travelogue shit – stuff that actually takes a stand, you know, that actually demands a bit of time and attention. Not those fucking – what's the word? Hot takes.'

'Spit takes.'

'"Here's my spit take of your latest hot take."'

'Reckons,' Shelley said. 'That's the word here.'

'No – really?'

'Yeah. Like, "Here's my reckon on mass incarceration."'

'. . . Total endorsement?'

'See, you got it. *That's* a reckon.'

'"Mass incarceration: not nearly mass enough"?'

'Boom,' she said. 'It writes itself.'

'Nah,' he said, 'we shouldn't even joke about that, eh.'

They were both quiet.

'That's the plan, anyway,' said Tony, resuming the thread. 'Investigative journalism. I've got a website, and I've had a few things in journals and magazines and stuff. Nothing huge, but it's all about building up a profile in the beginning.'

'I feel bad,' said Shelley. 'I never even knew that you were published.'

'Only online,' he said. 'And it's all pretty niche. I've never been paid or anything.'

'Hey, man,' she said, lightly, 'look who you're talking to.'

She was grinning, but he had a guilty feeling, and ducked his face into his glass.

He was embarrassed to have mentioned money. The Gallos had always kept a frugal household, and it hadn't been until Tony went abroad that he realised that what he had always taken to be middle class was really, by any global standard, rich. The revelation had produced in him not relief or gratitude, but a new and deeply unpleasant sense of his own complicity, for Grandpa Gallo's legacy – a fortune he had never known existed, let alone expected to receive – had left him suddenly much wealthier than any of his friends. He had never mentioned the bequest to anyone; instead, he practised inconspicuous consumption, and began to cultivate a shabby hand-me-down appearance as a way of implying to everyone around him that, like them, he was only barely scraping by. It was partly to atone for this deception, and partly in continuation of it, that he had turned to journalism; having pretended for so long that the asceticism of his lifestyle was a sacrifice he had no other option but to make, he now felt an almost desperate desire to earn an income from his writing, and thereby prove in concrete terms that his life's project, the expansion of his mind, was more than what he feared it might be – merely a form of inauthentic tourism financed, hypocritically, by those very social and economic structures that he claimed so energetically to oppose.

Despite the depth of his ambition, however, a part of him was relieved that Shelley had not heard about his online publications, for his debut – an experiential travelogue of the very sort that he had just denounced to her – had provoked an outrage so comprehensively humiliating to him that he blushed to remember it. Nearly four years later, he still anxiously self-googled on an almost daily basis, knowing even as he did so that by his frequent searches he was helping Google's algorithm, in however small a way, to make the very connections he most wanted the search engine to forget. The offending piece had long since been taken down, but he could not erase the furious responses, the majority of which he could now quote by heart; the criticisms felt indelible, and he felt sure – he *knew*, with a hideous, sickening certainty – that it was only a matter of time before news of his disgrace would surface and make its way back home.

The essay, which was titled *In the Bronze*, had begun with what Tony had thought was an illuminating anecdote from his first day in Mexico City. A scheduling confusion at the airport had meant that he was assigned a driver at the airport who spoke no English and drove not a taxi but his own private car; his name was Eduardo, and he was the cousin, Tony found out later, of the administrator at the English language school where Tony was to teach. For reasons obscure to Tony, they had been obliged to make a detour through a slum. 'Bronze,' Eduardo kept saying, gesturing about, 'bronze, bronze,' which Tony had taken to be a local form of slang he didn't know. As he was looking around him to try and decipher the meaning of the word from the context, he witnessed, from the safety of the vehicle, a fight between two young men that, as he later wrote, was the most confronting display of violence he had ever seen first-hand. Later, with the help of a third-party translator, he learned that the word was actually *Bronx*: Eduardo had been trying to warn him that the neighbourhood was dangerous, using what he evidently assumed was a common reference to a place afflicted by poverty and crime. The essay had developed from there to meditate more generally on language barriers, class difference, Tony's philosophy of teaching, and his first impressions of living in a foreign place; but to his detractors, the damage had already been done. A doctoral student in cultural studies (San Diego) was the first to tweet a link to the essay, writing 'I can't even deal with how much is wrong here' and adding a trigger warning and the hashtags #whiteprivilege, #povertytourism, and #yuck.

The fury spread from there. Tony's name was trending in a matter of hours, and the more attention his essay attracted, the angrier his critics seemed to get. He was accused of colonialist condescension, of reinforcing harmful stereotypes, of sentimentalising violence, and of being yet another entitled white man presuming, in a way that somehow managed to be both predatory and insipid, that the most valuable aspect of a thing was always, and only ever, his experience of it. Disgusted tweeters demanded to know why, if Tony had travelled to Mexico in order to teach English, he had not learned Spanish before he arrived; they pointed out all the invidious ways in which his essay implied the inarticulacy of his native guide, as though it were Eduardo's failure that Tony could not understand him; they asked what right he had to appropriate the fight that he had witnessed, to instrumentalise it, and to seek to profit from it in the form of cultural cachet; they analysed the inherent problematics of his rather florid prose style; and they invited him, in less than cordial terms, to apologise to Mexicans, renounce all forms of white supremacy, and go home.

To Tony's great surprise, he found himself now narrating all of this to Shelley. He had never spoken of the episode before, to anyone – even at the time, he had experienced the fallout almost entirely alone – but he was warmed by the ale, and encouraged by Shelley's easy familiarity and natural good humour, and for once, he did not fear he would be judged. He knew, he confessed to her, that he had been absolutely in the wrong: he realised now that his essay had been hopelessly misguided, stupid, ignorant, and ill-conceived. But it had not escaped his notice that the most vocal of his critics were not Mexicans, but American graduate students, the vast majority of whom were white – people, in other words, who were a lot more like him than like Eduardo, and even less like the youths he'd seen fighting from the car ... And surely his remorse was worth *something?* He had accepted his error, withdrawn the piece, sworn that he would never write in such a way again – surely that meant *something?* And even if it didn't – even if the offence he'd caused was irredeemable by anything that he could do, or say, or even swear, in reparation – surely the whole point of mercy was that it did not have to be deserved?

The pitcher was now empty.

'My round,' Tony said. 'And we're talking about me too much.'

'It's fine,' Shelley said, touching his arm. 'It's interesting.'

At the bar, he ordered another pitcher of ale and a bowl of fries, reflecting with appreciation that Shelley was not one of those tedious women who counted carbohydrates and made a show of regulating what they ate and drank. It was only just after six – still happy hour – but he was starting to feel quite pleasantly buzzed, and as he tapped his pin into the credit card machine, it occurred to him that Mira would be getting home quite soon; perhaps, he thought, in beery complacency, he might suggest that she join them for dinner.

'How's she doing, anyway?' he said, after he'd returned to the table and refilled their glasses. 'Mira.'

Shelley didn't answer at once. Then she said, carefully, 'I wouldn't want to answer for her.'

'No, I meant, from your point of view. Like, how's she getting on.'

'She's good,' Shelley said. 'She's doing good.'

'Yeah?'

'I mean, so much has happened, you know? It's like, where do you start?'

'Yeah,' Tony said. 'Completely.'

He took a long pull from his glass, wanting to ask if Mira was seeing someone, but lacking the courage. 'I don't know how much she told you,' he said instead, and then immediately regretted it.

Shelley glanced at him, but said nothing, waiting for him to go on. When he didn't, she said, '. . . You mean, about your leaving party?'

'Okay,' Tony said, making a comical wince. 'So you know.'

Another pause. Then Shelley said, 'Well, it was a long time ago.'

'Yeah.'

'And she was pretty drunk.'

'Yeah,' said Tony, too quickly, wincing again. Shelley seemed much stiffer and colder than she had before he had got up to go to the bar. Wondering where their affinity had gone, he remembered, suddenly and with a spike of guilt, that she had also been in attendance at his leaving party: he had probably hurt her feelings by reminding her that he had not remembered who she was. 'Well,' he said, to excuse himself, 'we were all pretty drunk that night.'

She was watching his expression closely. 'It was a different time, eh? Even just four years ago. But it was a different age.'

'Completely,' Tony said again, not quite sure what she meant, but relieved to have an opportunity to agree with her. He took another gulp of beer to cover his embarrassment and cast his gaze around the room, cursing his clumsiness, and wishing he had introduced the subject in a different way. She was still looking at him – he could see her in his peripheral vision – so he sucked his cheeks between his teeth and shook his head regretfully, as though to suggest that the issue was far too complex for ordinary conversation. He found he couldn't meet her gaze.

Even though he had been fishing for it, he was hurt to learn that Shelley knew. Of course, people talked – and they had been so young; sexual gossip was considered common property back then, especially at Birnam Wood, where their assemblies had a reckless, proselytising energy, and they all competed to perform their lack of inhibition and to prove their deviation from the status quo. No piece of information held a higher value, in those days, than the confession of a one-night stand; they had all been obsessed, Tony included, with each other's dalliances and conquests, endlessly comparing the grossest, the wildest, the most confounding, the most regrettable, the best. Had he really expected Mira to be any different?

But he had. He recalled that night again: her expression, solemn and determined, when without warning or pretext she put down her glass and cut him off mid-sentence by calmly taking hold of his wrist. Her look was open, avid, grave, even frightened – and she said nothing, just pulled on his wrist with a firm and level pressure that made her meaning absolutely clear. He hadn't said anything at all; hadn't asked her where they were going, hadn't made a joke, or made a sound, or said her name; he had simply allowed her to lead him out of the house and down

43

to the dewy slope at the bottom of the garden, where she had kissed him, kneeling, on the grass.

Shelley was still watching him. At last she said, 'It's just like your essay, I guess.'

He glanced at her, frowning. 'What do you mean?'

'Just that there was a time when publishing something like that would have been totally normal. Not that that was right,' she added quickly. 'I mean, in so many ways it's a good thing that we don't tolerate that stuff any more, that people are calling out injustice and holding power to account. But I also feel a certain . . . I mean, I look at my own life. Like on social media, when I first got a Facebook account. I was just posting all sorts of shit, you know, just *shit*, ignorant, self-serving – stuff that I would never dream of posting now. Some of the stuff I said, when I remember it . . . ugh! It makes me feel sick. Not because it was hateful, not at all, just because it was so . . . so blatantly . . . *out of touch*, you know, not with back then, but with right now. So yeah, I mean, while it's a good thing that people in power can't get away with stuff so easily any more – myself included, absolutely – still, it's like, the expectations were so different. Even four years ago. It was a different time.'

'Wait,' he said, still not quite following. 'I don't get the connection. What's just like my essay?'

She stared at him. 'I mean,' she said, 'she was pretty drunk.'

A group of businessmen in the far corner of the bar erupted into laughter at a joke. On instinct Tony turned his face towards the noise – but he hardly heard them. His face felt tight all of a sudden, as if his head had filled with blood. When he found his voice, he said, 'Is that what she said about it?'

'You really don't have to worry,' Shelley said quickly.

'I didn't,' Tony said. 'Until right now.'

She looked confused. 'But—'

'But what?'

'You never called her,' Shelley said. 'And you never wrote, or stayed in touch. I mean, it kind of seemed—'

'She never called me either!' Tony burst out, cutting over her. 'And I was on a plane the next day. I was gone. It was my fucking leaving party – she *knew* I was leaving. She could have called to say goodbye, but she didn't, and neither did I. And *she* came on to *me*, by the way. I don't know what she told you, but *she* came on to *me*.'

The evening was ruined, and the pitcher was still three-quarters full. He remembered suddenly, with a spike of fury, that he had ordered fries.

'Honestly, Tony,' Shelley said, his name sounding foreign in her mouth, 'she barely talked about it. Honestly.'

'Except to tell you she was really, really drunk.'

'She didn't have to *tell* me,' Shelley said, with a nervous giggle that sent a spear of anger into Tony's gut. 'She spent the whole next day throwing up. She threw up so much she gave herself two black eyes. Both eyes. It was horrific.'

In a voice that Tony hardly recognised, he said, 'So I gave her two black eyes?'

She looked horrified. 'No,' she said, drawing back, 'no way. I didn't say that.'

Tony was aware of a ringing in his ears, a sense of monstrous unreality. In his mind the memory of the kiss dissolved, and he saw them fucking on the grass, still quiet, the only sound the broken rhythm of their breath. He saw Mira's look of aching openness, searching his expression even as they moved; he felt her start to tremble, an uncontrolled vibration in her pelvis as she gripped him with her legs and held him there. He heard the sudden swell of music, as someone opened the door and called out Mira's name; and he saw her reaching up to press her forefinger against his lips, still staring at him, before she slipped out from underneath him, got up, and went quietly inside.

'Hey,' Shelley said, putting up both hands, 'what's happening?'

'I have no idea,' Tony said.

Shelley's phone was buzzing. She shifted her body to muffle the sound. 'Come on, we've all made mistakes,' she said. 'You were young. You hooked up. It's nothing.'

Her phone buzzed again.

'Are you going to get that?' Tony said coldly.

'No,' she said. 'Look – you honestly don't have to worry. It's not like she ever mentioned it again. It was just a stupid—'

'It might be important,' Tony said.

Miserably, Shelley fished out her phone and unlocked the screen. He watched as she scrolled through the messages.

'Everything okay?' he said, after a few seconds.

'Yeah,' Shelley said. 'It's Mira.'

He noticed she was blushing. 'What does she want?'

'Nothing,' she said. 'It's fine.'

'Well, what does she say?' Tony knew that he was being rude, but it was costing him considerable self-restraint not to reach over the table and rip the phone out of her hand.

'Just Birnam Wood stuff,' Shelley said, still not looking at him. 'She's heading out of town. New planting site, maybe.'

'Where?'

She didn't answer him at once: she seemed to be battling with something, perhaps deciding how, or whether, to respond to Mira's messages. Eventually, reluctantly, she shut off the screen and put the phone back in her pocket.

'Did you hear about that landslide?' she said. 'On the Korowai Pass?'

*

Mira's first thought, on coming home to the empty flat, had been that Shelley had finally done it: packed up all her things and left, without warning, and without a note. After calling Shelley's name and hearing no reply, she had stood in the open doorway for several seconds, reconciling herself to the new though long-expected reality of Shelley being gone – before her vision clarified and she saw that Shelley's bike was still in the laundry, and her shoes were still piled beneath the radiator, and her beloved bomber jacket was still hanging on its coat hook in the hall. Feeling foolish, Mira hastily revised her thought to wonder, instead, if some sudden emergency had taken Shelley from the house ... But if that were the case, then wouldn't she have called – or texted, at the very least?

She remembered suddenly the location tracker app that they had both installed some months ago, and never used. She got out her phone to check if the connection was still active, but in the brief time it took for the device to fetch Shelley's data from whatever configuration of satellites and local masts were coordinating her position, she grew ashamed of the intrusion, and exited the map before it fully loaded, reproaching herself that it was no wonder Shelley had been feeling smothered, and wondering, not for the first time, when exactly she had become so technologically dependent that her first instinct in every unpredicted circumstance was to outsource her imagination to her phone.

Two weeks had passed since she had first divined that Shelley wanted out of Birnam Wood, and for two weeks she had been paralysed by the same mute and stricken helplessness that she had felt when her parents first announced their separation – chiding herself, as she had then, that at her age and state of independence it was absurd that she should feel so childishly forsaken, and so sad. Mira was a remorseless critic of her own emotions. She frequently disparaged what she felt and thought, and she was quick to punish anything she judged to be a sign of moral weakness, no matter how privately or invisibly it was expressed. She hated how the divorce had come to quantify her relationships with both her parents, such that one weekend dinner with her mother now placed her one weekend dinner with her father in debt, and every conversation, every holiday, every shared interest, even every congenital resemblance now felt inscribed in a vast ledger of credit and debit that somehow it was her responsibility to balance. She felt cheapened by the effort, monetised, contractualised, demeaned – and so she did not allow the feeling; instead, she simply squashed it, telling herself, in a tone of matronly admonishment, that divorce was not uncommon, that other people were vastly more unfortunate, and that unless her health or her life had been threatened, then she had no business to complain. So it was with Shelley now. Mira was devastated by the thought of her departure, but her instinct for self-censure was so strong that she denied her devastation almost before she had even identified that that was what it was; this left her with the sense of being both entirely bereft and entirely blameworthy, having condemned herself for what she would not permit herself to feel.

The maxim of Mira's childhood had been that she was older than her years. Her parents had been fond of entertaining, and when she was young it had been a point of pride for them that she could hold her own among their adult friends, sitting up late at the dinner table in the bohemian detritus of empty bottles and dripping candles burning low, following the conversation, and even interjecting now and then with her own precocious point of view. When she was a child her father had worked as an urban planner for the city council, and her mother as an academic in the field of international relations; their circle of acquaintance was wide, and – as Mira would only really comprehend much later – almost universally left-wing, a fact that naturally came to shape Mira's own political expressions, for her contributions at the table were never more appreciated than when they reflected what was commonly agreed. She had grown up with a stout faith in the proven clarity of right and wrong, and had never doubted for a moment that to be treated as an adult was better than to be treated as a child; but she had feared, in lonely moments, that for her parents she existed merely as a kind of party trick, a dazzling proof of how well she had been parented, a living testament not to her own powers of conviction and discernment, but to theirs. Even as an adult she could not dispel, at times, a nagging sense of fraudulence, that she was most valued for what she most easily performed.

Her parents had been surprised by her vocation. Like many ardent followers of politics, they tended towards impatience when it came to the processes of natural change; they were indifferent gardeners, and had kept a compost heap more to reduce the volume of their household waste than out of any fascination for its uses. The backyard of Mira's childhood home had been mostly laid to lawn. There was a raised bed against the bottom fence that Mira's father had turned into a sandpit when she was very young, only to be abandoned when the neighbourhood cats began to use it as a litter box. It had stayed untouched for almost a decade, the plastic starfish and crenellated buckets fading to pastel against the darkening crust of sand, before anyone raised the prospect of restoring the bed to its proper function – which had happened, Mira could remember exactly, on the evening of her first day of high school. At her Year 9 induction she had been paired with a girl named Emily Alcorn whose lunch contained the unimaginable sophistication of cherry tomatoes, basil leaves, and baby mozzarella balls, each ingredient stored in a separate compartment and then combined, with great ritual and solemnity, on the back of her lunchbox lid. Mira had been entranced. She had rushed home to beg her mother to begin buying cherry tomatoes instead of regular, and her mother, who at the time was reading a self-help book on the power of initiative, had replied that maybe she should try to grow her own.

The challenge was accepted with far more seriousness than it had been made. By the following year, Mira had two dozen different crops in germination, and had extended the reconverted sandpit the full length of the fence. She planted marigolds as pesticides, planned crop rotations, built cold frames and hotbeds, saved the family's coffee grounds for mulch; and the more her parents wondered at her perseverance, the more she persevered. With her schoolmates, however, she was intensely secretive, and took to pushing soft soap beneath her fingernails before she gardened, to make it easier afterwards to wash away the dirt. She knew that horticulture was a strange passion for a teenage girl, and for all her inherent unconventionality she was not above the adolescent terror of exposure, the dread of never being normal and never fitting in. Emily Alcorn had long since moved on to other friends and no doubt other lunches, but she remained for Mira a kind of private benchmark of refinement and good taste – an image that was largely fantasy, since they had hardly spoken on the day of their induction, and after it, they never spoke again.

None of Mira's boyfriends had ever lasted more than a couple of months, and because she had never been the kind of girl to claim best-friendships, it had come almost as a shock to recognise, belatedly, that her relationship with Shelley had been the closest and most constant of her adult life. She was ashamed to realise how completely she had taken Shelley's friendship for granted, all the more because a source of private guilt for her was the fact – never openly acknowledged – that deep down, she preferred the company of men. Her favoured style of conversation was impassioned argument that bordered on seduction, and although it was distasteful, not to mention tactically unwise, to admit that one enjoyed flirtation, she never felt freer, or funnier, or more imaginatively potent than when she was the only woman in the room. If ever this preference were to be pointed out to her, Mira knew that she would stridently deny it. She felt that it exposed a defect in her character – disloyalty to her own sex, first of all, but deeper than that, a vanity, an appetite, a capacity for manipulation that she would rather other people did not see; she knew, and was ashamed to know, that one of the reasons she had never taken Shelley's friendship all that seriously was that it lacked any sense of sexual possibility or contest. There was no danger between them, nothing fearsome or uncertain, no provocation, no romance; with Shelley, she always knew that she was safe.

Except she wasn't, because she had treated Shelley badly, and now Shelley wanted out – and Mira found herself, as she had with her parents' separation, in a situation where her most cherished and most practised social skills were simply of no use. Debate was worthless, the exercise of charm beside the point; and having committed, long ago, to the performance of a mature and self-sufficient rationality, she now found herself without either the language or the power to express how deeply she was grieving. She wished more than anything that she could reverse her course, convey more gratitude and sympathy, show more interest in Shelley's inner life, confess, as she could still barely confess to herself, that the air of fearless self-assurance she projected was merely an imposture, a front designed to ward off intimacy and to banish her immense uncertainty and moral guilt. She wished that she could tell her friend the honest truth, which was not that she loved her because she needed her, but that she needed her because she loved her, and in her monumental stupidity and self-absorption, she had only just figured that out.

Mira disliked to feel that she was wallowing; she tended to follow moments of severe self-criticism with rapid and decisive action. She had come home intending to suggest to Shelley that they drive down to Thorndike on the weekend, a five-hour trip that would take them well outside their usual sphere of operation and afford them both a healthy change of scene. Cycling back to the flat that afternoon, she had imagined describing to Shelley what a single season at the Darvish farm could do for Birnam Wood, had envisaged Shelley's excitement at the prospect of the trip, had conjured, in her mind's eye, the conversation that in recent weeks had become a persistent and increasingly alluring fantasy: Shelley confiding, with none of the fatigued apprehension or forced politeness that had dogged her manner lately, that she *had* been on the verge of leaving, but this – Mira had auditioned many schemes for 'this' – had changed her mind. Now, standing in the kitchen with her phone loose in her hand, Mira rebuked herself again for having indulged in such craven wishful thinking. She told herself, sternly, that Shelley needed space – and then resolved, immediately, to be the one to give it to her. Even before she had fully voiced the thought, she was decided. She would go to Thorndike alone, at once, tonight; she would scope out the farm; she would give Shelley a few days to relax and hopefully to reconsider; and she would come back having killed two birds, as it were, with one stone. She kicked off her shoes and went into her bedroom to pack.

One of the reasons that horticulture held such strong appeal for Mira was that it offered her a respite from this habit of relentless interior critique. When she made things grow, she experienced a kind of manifest forgiveness, an abiding moving-on and making-new that she found impossible in almost every other sphere of life. Even in her failures and mistakes – as when she learned that onion seeds don't tend to keep, or that low soil temperatures result in carrots that are pale, or that fennel inhibits growth in other plants and should be propagated only on its own – she never felt chastised, for truth, in a garden, did not take the form of rectitude, and right was not the opposite of wrong. To learn even something as simple as to water the roots of a plant rather than its leaves was not to be dealt the harsh reality of cold hard fact, but rather to be let into a secret. In a garden, expertise was personal and anecdotal – it was allegorical – it was ancient – it had been handed down; one felt that gardeners across the generations were united in a kind of guild, and that every counsel had the quality of wisdom, gentle, patient, and holistic – and yet unwavering, for there was no quarrelling with the laws and tendencies of nature, no room for judgment, no dispute: the proof lay only in the plants themselves, and in the soil, and in the air, and in the harvest.

As she saw it, the opportunity presented by the Darvish farm was twofold. First was the fact of the land itself: one hundred and fifty-three good hectares in a town that was likely to remain deserted until at least the spring. None of Birnam's planting sites in the city offered anywhere near that kind of scope – Mira was constantly frustrated by their inability to produce at scale – and if they could just manage to get a season's worth of crops into the ground without getting caught, she thought, then the income they could generate might be enough, in and of itself, to give Birnam Wood a shot at solvency. Maybe Shelley could finally launch the subscription service that she had always talked about; or maybe they could put the funds towards their own expansion, reaching out to like-minded organisations perhaps, or registering as a charity, or maybe even paying for a spot of advertising to grow their client base, little though Mira liked that idea.

And if they *did* get caught – well, that also presented an interesting opportunity. Between the press coverage of the knighthood and the reporting on the landslide on the pass, Thorndike had been much in the public consciousness in recent months, and if Birnam Wood could stage a demonstration on the Darvish property, Mira thought – if they could arrange to be caught in the act of trespassing – if they could invite prosecution, even, for the alleged crime of planting a sustainable organic garden on an empty tract of land – and if they could then present to the media exactly what they'd planted, and explain their mission, and enumerate their goals, and prove themselves to be serious and good-hearted professionals whose work was tidy, and efficient, and fruitful, and thoughtful, and respectful of the land – would that not be a form of breaking good? They would risk criminal charges, of course, but at least they'd get their message out. And since Owen Darvish was to be knighted for services to conservation, at the very least they might provoke an interesting debate.

As she hunted through her chest of drawers for woollen socks and polypropylenes, she rehearsed in her mind the message she would send to Shelley. 'Hey,' she imagined writing, 'I've been getting the sense that you could do with a bit of space' – but that was too accusing. 'Hey,' she tried again, 'I figured you might appreciate a bit of time to yourself.' Too passive-aggressive? 'Hey, I thought we could both do with a bit of a break.' Inaccurate – and too cloying. 'Hey, I've been a bit worried lately that...' 'Hey, I hope I haven't misread this, but...' 'Hey, just to let you know...' At last, zipping up her duffel bag, she settled on, 'Hey Shel. I'm going to get out of your hair for a few days. Reckon you deserve a break. Interesting possible site in Thorndike down south – looks like the town's emptied out post Korowai Pass closure which could be good for us. Breaking good?! I'll let you know … anyway take care and see you in a bit x'. She typed it out, but hesitated over pressing send: better perhaps to wait until she was on her way out of town, in case Shelley texted back and asked to come along – for Mira had convinced herself that the only practicable course of action left to her was to go to Korowai alone. She saved the message as a draft and went outside to load the van.

Ordinarily, if she were planning a trip as far afield as Thorndike, she would ask around at Birnam Wood to see if anyone might be heading in the same general direction. She had inherited from Rufus a 1994 Nissan Vanette that routinely failed its warrant and was always breaking down; its fuel efficiency was poor, especially on the open road, and if she shared the journey even part of the way then she could ask for ten or twenty dollars towards the cost of petrol. But thinking about Shelley had left her in a nettled, agitated mood, and she couldn't bear the thought of explaining her intention for the journey, let alone of running the risk that someone might volunteer to join her all the way; and so, to foreclose the possibility completely, she packed the footwell of the passenger seat with her duffel bag and camping gear and buckled a stack of seed trays on to the seat. The Vanette comfortably slept two – she and Shelley raised occasional income by decamping to somebody's driveway and renting out their flat short-term – but whenever Mira was scoping out a site for Birnam Wood she preferred to park it somewhere inconspicuous and sleep outdoors, alternating between her two tents, one yellow and one navy blue, and never staying anywhere longer than a night. The van had the disadvantage of a licence plate – though it had never yet been reported; at least, not as far as she knew.

She loaded fast, dreading the thought of Shelley coming home and intercepting her: tools, tarpaulins, silicone buckets for conveying water, fertiliser, half a dozen empty water-cooler tanks, an irrigation backpack, salvaged panes of Perspex, stakes and shadecloth, seed trays, seeds, canvas bags, polytunnels, a garden hose and sundry different-shaped attachments, and her bicycle. But Shelley did not appear, and Mira's phone stayed dark, and twenty minutes later she had locked the house and was on her way.

At her mother's flat, she printed out aerial plans of Thorndike and the Darvish farm, first in map view and then in satellite, at different scales; she was taking a plastic wallet from her mother's desk to store them in when she heard the key in the door and her mother calling out her name.

'Sorry,' Mira said, coming out into the hall, 'I'm blocking the garage.'

'It's fine – I took the bus. Couldn't be stuffed with parking.'

'I'm stealing this,' Mira said, holding up the plastic wallet. 'And I used your printer, and I ate some of your food.'

'Did you see the leftovers?'

'Yeah, sorry, I finished off the dal. I was going to leave a note.'

'Not bad, was it?'

'Really good. Better than from the old place.'

'You should have texted,' said Harriet Bunting, hanging up her coat and nudging her shoes into alignment with her toe. 'I would have cooked you something.'

'I'm not stopping. I'm actually heading out of town,' Mira said, but her mother was already padding into the kitchen and opening the fridge.

'Stay for a glass of wine? How's Shelley?'

'She's fine,' Mira said. 'I can't drink, I'm driving.'

'Small one?'

'No, really.'

'Teensy-tiny?' Her mother waggled the bottle. 'Just a splash?'

'You know, Mum, there's a word for what you're doing.'

'"Relaxing",' her mother said. 'After a long bloody day.' She poured herself a large glass and sighed theatrically.

Mira didn't ask her what there was to sigh about. 'I'm heading down to Thorndike,' she said.

Harriet peered at her in pretended consternation. 'What – tonight? What for?'

'Just for a break. Thought I'd get amongst some green.'

'Thorndike?' Harriet repeated, perplexed.

'It's a long drive,' Mira said. 'I should really be going.'

'You can stay two minutes.'

'Mum, it's a five-hour drive.'

Her mother stuck out her bottom lip. 'I don't like you driving at night.'

'I like it better,' Mira said. 'Less traffic. But if I leave it too late, I'll catch all the drunk drivers coming home from the pub. I really should go.'

'Thorndike,' Harriet said again.

'It's just for a few days. And I've got my phone.'

'Is your friend still living there? Kevin Gaffney?'

'You're thinking of Rufus.'

'I thought he was your friend.'

'No,' Mira said.

'Kevin Gaffney,' her mother said again. 'His parents had a lifestyle block. They called it their life sentence.'

'I never knew him,' Mira said.

'It was in Thorndike,' her mother said. 'I'm sure it was. We stayed with them once when we were passing through, and after we went to bed, they had a lovers' quarrel and we heard it through the wall. It was absolutely riveting. Start to finish. *So* interesting to hear how other people argue, especially when you don't know them very well, so you haven't already picked a side. We were practically glued to the wall. Not just me. Roger too. He said it was like going to therapy, the whole thing.'

Not very effective therapy, Mira thought; you got divorced.

Harriet smiled at her. 'Kevin had a pet rat, do you remember?'

'No,' Mira said.

But her mother was laughing now at some private memory. 'God, Kevin Gaffney!' she said. 'I haven't thought about him in years.'

'Well, I've never thought about him,' Mira said tartly, 'because I've never met him. Or his parents. Or his rat.'

'Mira,' Harriet said, reproachfully. 'What's the matter?'

'Nothing's the matter,' she said. 'I just need to get going. Thanks for the curry.'

'Why don't you stay the night, and leave in the morning? Oh, *go* on, baby girl. Then you could have some wine.'

She arrived in Thorndike a little after midnight and parked in the deserted Department of Conservation campsite by the lake. Her phone had buzzed sometime after she turned inland from the coast, and after she had cut the ignition and set the parking brake, she checked it to find two messages from Shelley. The first was a bland response to hers – 'sounds good, have fun x' – but the second, sent an hour later, read: 'get in ok? hey thanks for giving me a bit of headspace, very kind and much appreciated. hope all goes well in korowai x'. Mira felt her mood lift at once. She texted back to say that she'd arrived safely, received a thumbs-up emoji in reply, and went to pitch her tent feeling great relief and optimism, buoyed by the clean sub-alpine air and by the deep mossy scent of the outdoors. She could see her breath in the pool of blue light cast by her head torch as she snapped the poles together and drove the pegs into the frosty ground, but the sky was cloudless, and above the black void of the Korowai ranges, the Milky Way was a liquid swash of white; it was the kind of night, she felt, that could only precede the very best kind of winter's day, cold, brilliant, and still. Feeling suddenly indulgent, she told herself, kindly, that perhaps she had been wrong; perhaps Shelley hadn't been on the verge of leaving after all; perhaps all she'd needed was a bit of space. Mira climbed into her sleeping bag and lay in the dark listening to the distant two-toned call of a ruru on the far side of the valley before the exhaustion of the drive overcame her, and she fell asleep.

The next morning dawned just as bright and clear as she had hoped, and after she had struck her tent and made coffee on her little butane stove, she took out her bicycle, loaded the panniers with a day's supply of food and water, and locked the van – first closing the calico curtains and leaving a tramper's guidebook on the dashboard in plain view. Half a dozen walking tracks led from the car park up into the ranges and around the lake, giving a ready explanation – in the unlikely event of an inspection – for where the van's driver might have gone. There was no charge for parking, though welded to the guide board was an honesty box for camp fees that Mira pretended not to see. She zipped into her jacket the plastic wallet she had taken from her mother's flat, clipped on her helmet, and adjusted her camera on its branded strap across her chest. The camera didn't work – she had found it at the tip, still in its carry case, defunct – but she had taken to heart a reminiscence of her father's, who in his youth had hitch-hiked all around the country, that no matter how dirty or unshaven he had been, or how far into the wilderness, or how late the hour, whenever he wore his long-lens camera round his neck, he always got a ride; it was an accessory that seemed to put strangers instinctively at ease.

Riding into Thorndike, she met with no traffic at all. Signs along the roadside warned her that the pass ahead was closed until further notice and advised her to seek an alternative route. It was still before nine, but even in the ordinary quiet of the morning, the town had an eerily abandoned feel. The main street was shuttered; the only sign of life she detected was behind the window of the petrol station, where the teller was counting the day's cash balance into the till. He didn't look up as Mira cycled past, and she continued on up the road without seeing anybody else.

Several details in the press coverage of Owen Darvish's impending knighthood had led Mira to believe that he and his wife would not be home when she arrived. It was probably not their only property, first of all. The farm had come to them five years ago, and it was clearly surplus to requirements, given that they had planned to subdivide it. The fact that they had taken down the listing following the landslide on the pass proved that they were not in any rush to sell, and Mira saw no reason why a fêted businessman at the high point of his career would spend a winter in deserted Thorndike if he had the option, and possibly several options, of being somewhere else. Second, she was reasonably certain that it was not a working farm. The realtor's listing had described it as a *former* sheep station, and as the satellite map had shown, the Darvishes were not in the habit of shutting their gates, which would have been unthinkable if they were keeping livestock. Rural authenticity was no mere detail that a journalist might have overlooked; if, in addition to managing a successful business, Darvish had kept even the smallest flock of sheep or herd of cattle, it would have surely been reported, in the national papers most of all. Last, there was the partnership between Darvish Pest Control and the American tech giant Autonomo, which Darvish had mentioned in every interview that she had read. The project was soon to launch in Northland, the northernmost province of the North Island, and his pride in the project had been so palpable, and his excitement in the new technology so boyish and eager, that Mira felt sure that he would want to manage it first-hand. It was possible, of course, that even in his absence, she would find the house tenanted, or the fields leased out to neighbours' flocks as winter feed; but Darvish had made such a point of his Korowai connection in the press that somehow Mira doubted he would dare.

She was almost at the barricade when she realised from the incline of the hills around her that she must have passed the Darvish driveway by mistake. She doubled back, and soon discovered why she'd missed it. Evidently, in the time since the map on her phone had last updated its street view, the Darvishes had renovated. The main approach to the property was no longer through a standard farm gate over a cattle stop, as she had been expecting, but through a pair of curving wrought-iron gates set into a rather ugly semicircular stone wall. The gates were closed, and appeared to be motorised, judging by the metal boxes that encased the lowest hinges on either side.

Coming closer, she saw a hooded keypad on a metal post, and above the keypad, an intercom that presumably communicated with the house. She could see no camera, and after a moment's hesitation she wheeled her bike up to the keypad, cocked her foot on the pedal, and firmly pressed the call button. If anybody answered on the other end, she told herself, she would just ride away; the house was far enough back from the road that it would surely take a couple of minutes for Darvish, or his wife, or any one of the friends or family members who might be minding the house in their absence, to appear – by which time she would be well on her way back to town.

She waited; but nobody answered, and the iron gates stayed closed.

Mira dismounted, took the printed maps out of her mother's plastic wallet, and sat down on the driveway to examine them. It was impossible that a farm of this size would have only one point of access from the road – and sure enough, when she pored over the satellite image, she could see a rutted vehicle track running straight across the hillside to the southern fence. The track was so direct in its course, and terminated at the fence line so abruptly, that it could only indicate an exit – in which case the stripe of bare ground beyond the boundary, which she had taken for a firebreak, must be an unsealed service road connecting the highway with the back end of Korowai National Park.

She got back on her bike and cycled up the hill again, going further this time than she had before. She had been right about the service road: it was unmarked, and so well concealed behind a curve in the highway that even on her bike she might have missed the turning had she not been looking for it. The gravel was too deep and too uneven to allow her to continue on at any speed, so she stashed her bicycle in a patch of scrub and proceeded up the road on foot, carrying one of her panniers as a backpack and reflecting what a rare pleasure it was to be able to hear only birdsong, her own footfall, and the distant sound of the wind.

By the time she reached the second gate – there was a second gate; she had been right about that as well – she was perspiring. She peeled off her jacket and tied its arms round her waist, welcoming the chill, and as she caught her breath, she shaded her eyes with her hand and looked out over the valley in appreciation of the view. She had gained enough elevation that the highway had shrunk to a silver band beneath her, and the clustered roofs and wires of Thorndike now seemed like a set for a model train. The hills on the far side of the lake were bathed in sunlight, their brown and purple slopes transformed to amber, steel, and sage, the sky behind them a perfect watercolour fade from azure down to baby blue. To the north, she could see the rumpled patch of lowland forest where the van was parked, and to the south, the high saddle of the pass – though not, from this angle, the raw channel down the mountainside, nor the colossal mound of rubble or the fractured viaduct, that she remembered from the footage on the news.

She turned her attention to the gate. It was chained and padlocked, and she could see no obvious tyre tracks in the mud that might suggest that anyone had lately driven through. Feeling encouraged, she climbed over it, taking care not to leave any footprints, and set off north, across the hill. The track seemed much more overgrown, to her eye, than it had in the image captured by the satellite; judging by the height of the grass, the field had not been grazed for at least a season. She looked around for fresh manure, but could see only rabbit droppings.

The track proceeded along a shelf of limestone and through a shelterbelt of pines, the ground more undulating than Mira's map had made it seem, and the incline of the hill a little steeper. Her view of Thorndike disappeared, returned, and then disappeared again as she traversed furrow, ridge, and furrow, keeping an eye out for creeks and ponds, but seeing no water at all. There were enough irregular outcroppings of stone around her to suggest caves and fissures in the ground beneath her feet; little likelihood, then, of a handy water source, at least not this far from the house. She would have to make do with collecting rainwater – acidic, but the limestone would help to counteract that – and, perhaps, with filling tanks of water at the lakeside and driving them up the service road at night. She was wondering how often it rained in Thorndike when she crested yet another ridge and found herself on the edge of a wide, level terrace – an airstrip, she realised, because at the far end, parked with its nose towards her, was an amphibious four-seater plane.

The sight of the aircraft was so unexpected that Mira leapt at once for the nearest patch of trees; but after crouching in the brush for several minutes, scanning the hillside furtively, she let herself relax. There was nobody around – and the morning had been so still and quiet that she would certainly have heard the engine noise if the plane had landed anytime in the last hour. It must have been parked there for at least a little while, possibly overnight, or even longer. Had Owen Darvish – or his wife – been learning to fly? But again, this seemed like the kind of humanising detail that would surely have made it to the press – all the more, she thought, shaking her head slightly, because they had given up their house to Search & Rescue following the landslide on the pass.

Mira considered her options. If the plane was in frequent use, then her activities on the farm would need to be invisible from the air as well as from the house or from the road. Collecting rainwater in tarpaulins would be risky, as would planting or cultivating anywhere without shelter readily to hand. Then again, the farm was large, with a great many possible sites for planting, and the plane was parked near the top of the property, at least a kilometre above the house, which itself was a good few hundred metres above the road; anybody wishing to take off would either have to enter at the front gates and drive up the main track, or enter by the service road, the way that Mira had come, and cut across the hill – and either way, she would have fair warning, and a chance to hide.

She decided to make her way down to the house to reassure herself beyond a doubt that nobody was home. Keeping as much as possible to the cover of the trees, she struck out for the more rutted track that led down the hill, scanning the fields around her, and listening out for the sound of voices or a four-wheel drive. But there was little need for subterfuge. Descending on the house, she saw that the light in the rear porch was on, and when she tried the tap by the garage, nothing happened: the mains water had been shut off. She cupped her hands around her eyes and peered in the garage window. The interior was too dark to make anything out, so she got out her phone, intending to shine its torch through the glass to get a better look – and discovered to her annoyance that it was dead. Stupidly, she had forgotten to switch it to a power-saving mode; it must have used up its battery searching for a signal. She put it back in her pocket.

The house was better lit, and through the kitchen window she could see that the interior was spotless, the fruit bowl empty, all the surfaces bare of clutter, nothing in the sink or on the stove. The place was a classic Kiwi bungalow, white weather-board with blue-grey trim, maybe eighty or ninety years old; it was in good condition, freshly painted and re-roofed, and when she walked round to the front, Mira saw that the lounge room had been extended, apparently quite recently, to create a double-height picture window with views over the lake. She kept walking, peering in through all the windows in turn. Every room was tidy, and all the beds were neatly made. The only sign of recent occupancy was an off-road vehicle parked askew beside the woodshed, but it was covered with a fine layer of dust, and when she touched the handle of the driver's door, her finger made a clean dark stripe in the grey. Nobody had driven it for at least a few days.

Satisfied, she left the house and continued down the hill. The part of the farm the Darvishes had been hoping to subdivide lay below the house, along the highway frontage, and as she neared the bottom of the driveway, she found herself looking down on a vast mound of gravel that had been dumped in the paddock nearest the main gate. This was presumably in preparation for the private road the Darvishes had planned to build, which would give drive-on access to each subdivided plot, terminating, she remembered from Mrs Crowther's correspondence, in a roundabout landscaped with tussock grass, flax, and local stone. The realtor had supplied Mrs Crowther with an artist's impression of what the little street might one day become, a fresh and vibrant sketch depicting elegant, sun-drenched homes, shining SUVs at the kerbsides, laughing children, and healthy people walking happy dogs – all set against a lush backdrop of mature trees that would have had to have been planted, Mira reckoned as she looked around her, maybe ten or fifteen years ago at the very least. There was nothing in the field except stubbly grass and the pile of gravel – no string lines; no mixers or excavators; not even any tyre tracks from the truck that must have brought the gravel there. It would seem the subdivision plans had well and truly stalled.

At the northern fence, she met with even more good fortune: the dilapidated shearing shed and livestock pens that on the map she had taken to be part of the neighbouring property were in fact situated on Darvish land, offering ample room for storage, and even a place to hide the van, if she ever figured out how to get around the code on the front gate. The slatted fences of the pens were bleached with age and falling down in places, but they offered some concealment, as well as shelter from the wind. She counted nine galvanised water troughs, and more than a dozen slimy bales of straw, years old, but perfect for mulching; surely nobody would miss a bale or two? As she knelt down to feel the texture of the soil, Mira was suffused with a restless, excitable energy, already mapping out in her imagination where every bed and every crop would go.

The open fields beside the road were too exposed to be of any interest, and so she headed back up the hill again to take a closer look at the plane. It was now well after noon. Driving south, she had gained a few degrees of latitude; sunset would be early, especially in the valley, where the light would fade rapidly once the sun had sunk behind the ranges in the west. After she had explored the upper paddocks, she told herself, she would return to the campsite and fill the water tanks at the lake; then, after nightfall, she would drive the van up the service road and unload the contents over the fence, ready to begin preparing the site in earnest the following day. She was just forming this resolution in her mind when she returned to the airstrip – and a man stepped out from behind the plane.

He was in his forties, lean, smooth-faced, and wearing a navy tracksuit and an unbranded baseball cap. His clothes looked new, and in the split second before either of them spoke, Mira found herself recalling, bizarrely, a comment by her cousin Eve, who was the mother of two small children, and who had once remarked despairingly to Mira that when it came to children's clothing, you had to spend a lot of money to look like you were hardly spending anything at all. This man's tracksuit was so ordinary and unassuming, and so simply cut, that Mira felt absolutely certain it was more expensive than any garment she had ever owned.

Her heart was thumping; but she knew that the best strategy, in these moments, was to pretend that she had every right to be exactly where she was, so she smiled and waved as he approached, striding forward confidently to meet him halfway. 'Another beautiful day,' she said warmly, spreading her arms wide.

He didn't return her smile. 'Who are you?' he said, when he was close enough to speak without raising his voice. He had an American accent.

'Sarah Foster,' Mira said, choosing one of her false identities. 'With the production. Is that your plane?'

He didn't answer. 'You're trespassing,' he said.

'Well, that's kind of my job,' Mira said, with a little laugh. 'I'm a location scout. "Any house with a view of a lake" is my brief. Been all around the country and haven't found it yet, but that's the nature of the beast. Is that your plane?'

'What do you think?' he said.

'I think it's a pretty nice plane,' Mira said, laughing again. 'Must be magic once you're up above it all. It'd make my job a little easier, one of those.'

He didn't smile. He was staring at her, unblinking, his expression cold. Then he said, very quietly, 'Who do you work for?'

She frowned, pretending consternation. 'My producer was in touch last month,' she said. 'Ben Sharp? He said he cleared it with the farmer. Someone called Darvish, I think it was?'

'Cleared what?' the man said.

'Well, we're just taking photos at this stage,' Mira said. 'No promises. But of course, with the landslide on the pass, no traffic, nobody around, what better time to make a movie?'

'A movie,' he repeated.

'That's right,' Mira said. 'I can't tell you what it is, unfortunately – non-disclosure, all of that – but it's an international production, quite big, and there are a few names attached already. *I'm* excited. And God knows the economy round here could use the boost. What about you? Are you visiting?'

He didn't answer.

'I thought I heard an American accent,' Mira said.

She was cursing her choice of cover story. Ordinarily she could trust that the allure of Hollywood would dazzle whomever she was speaking to, but he didn't seem dazzled in the slightest; he didn't even seem curious. She hoped he wasn't from the movie industry himself.

'Say your name again,' he said.

'Sarah,' Mira said. 'Foster. What's yours?'

He said nothing. He was studying her face.

Mira was starting to sweat. She kept her voice light. 'Well, anyway, the house I'm looking for is supposed to be English,' she said, turning away from him to gesture out over the hillside. 'Somewhere in the Lake District, but you know, it's Hollywood, so, close enough. We're hoping to start shooting in the summer.'

'How did you know I was here?' he said.

'I didn't,' Mira said. 'I have no idea who you are. I mean, no offence. I'm sure you're really important, if you've got your own plane.'

Again he said nothing. He raised his eyebrows a little, making it clear he didn't believe her, and waited.

She smiled bravely and lifted up her camera. 'Only taking photos,' she said. 'I swear.'

'You've been on this property four hours and you haven't taken out your camera once,' he said.

Mira's smile faltered in a way that was partly performed and partly real. 'Look,' she said, 'honestly, my producer cleared this with the farmer weeks ago. Feel free to ring him up if you don't believe me. Owen Darvish is the farmer's name.'

'You're lying,' he said.

Mira tried to laugh. 'I don't know what to tell you, then.'

'There is no production,' said the man. 'And your name's not Sarah Foster.'

She made a show of patting down her pockets. 'I don't think I have a card on me,' she said, 'but like I said, Ben cleared everything with Mr Darvish, so—'

'Give me the camera,' said the man. He put his hand out.

Mira took another step back. 'Hey,' she said, 'I think you've got the wrong idea. I honestly don't know who you are, or what you're doing here, or what's going on—'

He took another step forward. 'Give it to me,' he said.

'No,' she said.

'Mira,' he said, 'I am asking nicely.'

It chilled her to hear him use her name. Dumbly – she was starting to tremble – she slipped off the carry case and held it out. He took out the busted camera and turned it over, saw the cracked display screen, tried the power button, then opened the back and peered into the empty cavity where the batteries should be.

'How do you know my name?' she said.

He ignored the question. 'This is broken,' he said, holding it up.

'I know,' Mira said.

'What are you doing here?' he said. 'Don't lie.'

'I'm a gardener,' Mira said. 'I plant things on other people's properties without them knowing. And in public places. And I cultivate the plants and water them and then harvest the produce at the end, and I'm part of a collective, we're like an activist collective, only I'm here in Thorndike on my own. It's just me. But a lot of people know I'm here,' she added quickly. 'A lot of people would come looking for me if anything—'

She found that she couldn't go on.

He didn't flinch. 'Keep talking,' he said.

'I truly have no idea who you are,' Mira said, 'and I've never met this Darvish guy before in my life either, I just read about him in the news and I figured that since the pass is closed and he's just about to become a knight or whatever, there was a good chance he'd be away, and that's why I came here, because the town's cleared out and it seemed like a good opportunity, and I thought I could maybe get in a growing season before they open up the pass again and things go back to normal. All the stuff I said about the movie was a total lie, there's no Ben Sharp, he doesn't exist, and my name's not Sarah Foster, it's Mira, like you said, Mira Bunting. And that's the whole story. That's the truth.'

He listened to this in perfect stillness, his eyes fixed on hers, hardly even seeming to breathe. He didn't move or speak after she fell silent. They looked at each other for one second, two seconds, three – and then Mira turned and ran, not looking back, not slowing, not even when she reached the shelterbelt, the gate, the gravelled service road, the patch of scrub where she had stashed her bike, which she dragged to the highway, bashing her shin on the crossbar in her haste to get astride it, and pedalled furiously down the hill, past the renovated drive-way, along the lakeshore, into town, and past the solar-powered signs that warned the pass ahead was closed. By the time she reached the campsite and skidded to a halt beside the van, she was drenched in sweat, her windpipe ragged, her legs trembling so violently that she could hardly stand. Still coursing with adrenaline, she clambered off the bike and let it fall away from her, the front wheel spinning as it struck the ground. She had walked only a few weak steps away from it when her knees gave way beneath her, and she fell forward on to the grass.

It was over, she thought. She should leave. There was only one road out of Thorndike, which meant that he knew the direction she had taken; and even if he hadn't seen her bicycle, he had certainly seen her pannier. He knew her alias, her busi-ness, her intentions – and he had known more than what she'd told him. He had known she hadn't taken any pictures with her camera. He had known she'd been on the property four hours. And somehow, *somehow*, he had known her name.

And what did she know about him? That he was American.

That he wore expensive-seeming clothing. That he hadn't answered any of her questions. That he had seen through her, and had assumed at once that she had seen through him. That he had menaced her, not physically or violently, but quietly, implicitly, expecting his commands to be obeyed. Nothing else. She didn't know what he was doing on the Darvish farm, or how long he'd been there, or how long he planned to stay. She didn't even know if it was his plane. In other words, jack, Mira thought, in a spike of furious resentment against herself. She knew jack shit about him, and her cover was well and truly blown.

She had begun to shiver. She got up and unlocked the van, stripping off her sweat-drenched shirt and bra and slipping on a dry merino turtleneck that felt clean and soft against her clammy skin. The touch of the fabric was so restoring that she changed her socks and underwear as well, standing in the cubicle formed by the van's open door. Then she leaned over the passenger seat to plug her phone into the cassette converter and put the key in the ignition to charge it. She suddenly felt ravenous. There was a box of snack bars in the glove box, and by the time the phone's display winked back to life, she had eaten three, and was feeling steady in herself again. She climbed into the driver's seat, typed her pin into the phone, and waited for any messages or emails to download, but none appeared. Batting away the reflexive despondency that always struck whenever she checked her inbox and found it empty – ridiculous; she had no correspondents anyway – she opened her browser and typed 'Owen Darvish airstrip' into the search field.

It cost a fortune to use the Internet on data, but Mira's pride would not allow her to leave Thorndike without at least a partial understanding of what had happened up at the Darvish farm. In all her years at Birnam Wood she had never met anybody she had so completely failed to charm. There had to be a reason; and for the sake of the collective, she had to find it out. Everything about the site was perfect, and she hated the thought of letting it go simply on account of a single brief encounter with a stranger, who for all she knew might have been trespassing as well – for now that she was alone and the threat had passed, she had begun to feel embarrassed that she had ever felt afraid of him.

Her first search revealed nothing of interest, so she tried 'Owen Darvish plane', 'Owen Darvish pilot', 'Thorndike private plane', 'Thorndike private airstrip', all without success. 'Owen Darvish American' resulted in a deluge of news articles about the partnership between Darvish Pest Control and Autonomo, the American company that manufactured drones, and 'Autonomo New Zealand', 'Autonomo Thorndike', 'Autonomo national park drones', and 'Autonomo Korowai' all directed her back to the same dozen articles she'd already read. She switched her search mode to images and typed 'Autonomo' on its own – and found him. Her stomach lurched. The picture was a few years old at least – his face was a little fuller, his hair a little longer, his cheekbones a little less pronounced – but it was unmistakably him. He was pictured sitting on a leather chesterfield, legs thrust out, ankles crossed, both arms extended casually along the back. 'Pits to the wind' was what Mira's father always said whenever he saw a motorcyclist with ape-hanger handlebars, 'spread those pheromones' – and this was the phrase that now appeared in Mira's mind. His chin was slightly raised, and he was looking into the lens with the same expectant, disbelieving expression that he had worn with her. *Is that it?* he seemed to be saying to the camera. *Did you really think that I would fall for that?* She clicked on the image and learned that he was one of the co-founders of Autonomo. He had been the CEO of the company in its early years, and now served on its board of directors; he was a serial entrepreneur, a venture capitalist, and, apparently, a billionaire. His name was Robert Lemoine.

She heard engine noise behind her and glanced at the rear-view mirror to see a black SUV turning into the campsite. It had tinted windows and looked new; it looked, in fact, like just the sort of vehicle a serial entrepreneur venture capital-ist former CEO company director billionaire would choose to drive. Heart sinking, she willed it to be just a tourist in a flashy rental ... but then it pulled up right beside her, and Lemoine got out.

The key was already in the ignition; it would need only another quarter turn to start the engine. Moving discreetly, Mira released the handbrake and placed her feet on the foot-brake and the clutch. Her bike was in her blind spot, right behind the van – she would have to run it over if she reversed in a hurry – and the passenger door was still open: her duffel bag, which was on the passenger seat, would probably tumble out. Even as she was making these calculations, he appeared at the driver's window and held up the broken camera.

'Sorry,' he said. 'Here.'

She wound down the window and he passed it through to her. She took it with her left hand and held it on her lap, look-ing at him, waiting for him to speak. Her feet were still on the pedals, and her right hand was inches from the key in the igni-tion. Her heart was beating fast.

After a moment he said, 'I guess we got off on the wrong foot up there.'

'I guess we did,' Mira said.

'My name's Robert,' he said. 'I'm sorry to have frightened you. I thought you were someone else.'

'Someone else named Mira?'

He smiled. Instead of responding, he took his phone out of

his pocket, tapped the screen, then turned it around to show her. Under the list of detectable devices nearby was listed 'mira's iPhone'. 'Next time try leaving it at home,' he said.

Mira was embarrassed that she had been so easily unmasked. She put her left hand on the gear stick, ready to place it in reverse. 'Robert what?' she said, to cover her embarrassment.

He glanced down at her phone, still plugged into the cassette converter and balanced on her knee, and for an awful fraction of a second Mira wondered if her search results were visible – but mercifully, the screen was dark. Heart still pounding, she squared up to him again. 'Robert what?' she repeated.

He didn't answer. He was searching her expression, still with the trace of a smile. 'You seem like a smart young lady,' he said at last. 'I'm sure you'll figure it out.'

He went back to the SUV and opened the driver's door, but before he got in, he paused and looked at her across the bonnet. 'See you up there,' he said. 'Just stay away from the airstrip. I can take off all right, but I'm still learning how to land.'

He got into the driver's seat and shut the door.

'Wait,' Mira said, but he was already starting the engine and backing the SUV out of the campsite. 'Wait,' she said again, and scrambled out of the van. 'What do you mean?'

The driver's window lowered silently. 'I mean,' he said, one hand on the wheel, 'I'll stay out of your way if you stay out of mine.'

She was still confused. 'Why?'

He smiled. 'Why?'

'Yeah. Why would you do that?'

'Because you intrigue me, Mira Bunting, and I want to see your garden grow.'

She came closer. 'What about Darvish?'

'What about him?'

'You're not going to tell him?'

He was about to reply, and then seemed to change his mind. 'Now really,' he said, after a long pause, 'where would be the fun in that?'

He went to put the window up.

'Wait,' Mira said again. But she had detained him before she had a question ready. He was looking at her expectantly, and so she said the first thing that came into her head: 'What's the code for the front gate?'

He grinned – broadly, showing a perfect set of square white teeth. '6061,' he said. 'It's the house number backwards. Anything else you want to ask?'

'Yes,' Mira said. 'How do I know you're not setting me up?'

'You don't,' he said. He put the window up and drove away. About half an hour later Mira heard the distant buzz of a light aircraft, and she looked up to see his plane climbing up out of the valley, then banking west, over the lake, over the hills, and out of sight.

It had taken Robert Lemoine barely twenty minutes to execute the man-in-the-middle attack. He had first sighted Mira when she turned off the highway on to the gravel access road and stashed her bike in the patch of scrub, and had gone at once to his controls; by the time she reached the second gate, he had forced a connection with her phone, accessed her identifying information, obtained her stored encryption key, simulated her over-the-air transmissions, established a connection with the local mast, and then authenticated himself so that from that point forward, he could appear to Mira's service provider as Mira's phone, and to Mira's phone as her service provider. Not only did he now have complete access to her data, both present and historic, he also had the power to intercept and change her messages in both directions; now, if he wanted, he could both alter what communications she received, and send messages – to anyone – as her. It was a flawless capture. Had she ventured a little further up the gravel road, she would have come upon the trailer-mounted mobile cell site, fitted with an IMSI-catcher device, that he had used to carry out the operation; had she taken her phone out of her pocket, she might have noticed that it was hotter than usual, and less responsive, and that the battery was draining fast; and had she looked directly overhead at any time while she was exploring the farm, she might have seen, high above her, the dark blur of a surveillance drone, hovering in place. Of course, she'd done none of these things – but that wasn't surprising; no one ever did.

Lemoine adjusted his bearing. Beneath him, the glaciers and snowfields of the Korowai ranges were glowing peach and ochre in the late-afternoon light, the shadows mauve and violet, the seams and the crevasses midnight blue. He dipped his starboard wing to get a better look, passing over the high peak of Mount Korowai, with its distinctive triple step, like a serrated blade, and then straightened out and radioed for clearance to descend.

It wasn't true what he had told her – that he was still learning how to fly. He'd logged over thirteen hundred flight hours in the past two years alone; the running joke at Autonomo, trotted out at every tedious toast and ribbon-cutting function he could remember, was that he didn't trust his company's own product, and that somehow, in all his years designing unmanned aerial systems, he had failed to grasp the meaning of 'unmanned'. The jokes were tiresome, but he could admit the truth they gestured at. Lemoine loved nothing better than to fly. Nothing in the world compared to the liquid thrill of piloting a craft through three axes of movement, feeling the vertical, the lateral, and the longitudinal as divergent possibilities curving away from him through air that was tactile and elastic and textured with a warp and woof. When in flight, he experienced a double re-alignment, a shrinking of the universe inside the cockpit that matched the dilation of the universe outside it, so that as the aircraft climbed and the air thinned and the ground fell away and seemed to flatten far beneath him, he began to hear his own breath through his headset, and to feel his heartbeat magnify inside his chest; he achieved, at altitude, a profound sense of his own proportion, of the sheer scale of everything he could be, everything he had been, everything he was – and in descent, as now, he always had a holy sense of having pilgrimaged, of returning having seen behind a veil. He was an excellent pilot, and although the airstrip on the Darvish farm did suffer from a crosswind, he'd never had any difficulty coming in to land.

Lemoine touched down at the airfield in Kingston and brought the aircraft to a graceful halt. His driver was already waiting, together with his security detail, to convey him back to his hotel, but after he had called in the landing and shut off the engine, he remained seated in the cockpit, smiling to himself, and tapping out a syncopated rhythm on his knee. It was seldom that he got the chance to interact with perfect strangers, and he had forgotten how arousing it could be to gauge his own effect on a genuine blank canvas, someone who had no idea what he was worth. Even more arousing was the fact that she had lied to him – and not in the squirmy, tiresomely self-exculpating way that he was used to whenever one of his factotums let him down, but flagrantly, defiantly, and with the kind of individual flourishes that bespoke a genuine enjoyment of the practice of deception. The camera was an especially nice touch. He might even have fallen for it if he hadn't known already from her data that she was in the habit of assuming false identities. He smiled wider. *Mira Bunting*, he thought, tasting the syllables, *you little criminal.*

For Lemoine could recognise his own. He at least had not been trespassing – Jill and Owen Darvish had invited him to make full use of the place in their absence, to stay at the house if he wanted, to keep a car in their garage, to explore, to get a feel for the area, and by all means, please, to make himself at home – but like Mira, he was nursing ambitions for the Darvish farm that went far beyond the crime of trespass, and like Mira, he was highly practised in concealment; the Darvishes would have been very surprised to learn, for example, that in fact Lemoine had no need whatsoever to familiarise himself with Thorndike, since he had been conducting close surveillance of the region for the past seven years.

Not that they would ever find that out. As far as they knew – as far as they would ever know – Lemoine was just a billionaire looking for a bolthole, the kind of man who saw every crisis as an opportunity, and so had begun perusing real estate listings in Thorndike in the hours directly following the landslide on the pass. He was simply a far-sighted, short-selling, risk-embracing kleptocrat, an incarnation of unapologetic zero-sum self-interest, a radical misfit, a 'builder' in the Randian sense, a genius, a tyrant, an obsessive, a prophet, a status-symbol survivalist hedging his bets against any number of potential global catastrophes that he himself was doing absolutely nothing to prevent, and might even be taking active measures to encourage if there was a profit to be made, or an advantage to be gained, in the pursuit. This was the impression that Lemoine had taken pains to create, and it was in this guise that he had told the Darvishes that he was prepared to pay well above the asking price for their property, on the condition of absolute secrecy until the instant that the bunker – he watched their eyes widen – was safely in the ground.

He had already purchased a small fleet of diggers and earth movers to carry out the excavation, along with a few RVs and kitset mobile offices to accommodate the crew; these were waiting in a warehouse at the Lyttelton port, along with the bunker itself, which had arrived disassembled, the component parts flat-packed into a dozen shipping containers that were ready to be loaded on to trucks and driven south. But the interment of the thing was only pretext. The real work would happen in the clean-up, after the bunker was interred. When all these vehicles left Thorndike, they would not be empty, or filled with slurry, or stacked with broken pallets or packaging or other waste. They would return to the port carrying a cargo worth not just billions, but trillions – a dollar value so enormous that Lemoine liked to put it in perspective by reminding himself, periodically, that one million days had not yet passed since the birth of Jesus Christ. If he pulled this off – and he had never failed in any of his ventures yet – he would become, by several orders of magnitude, the richest person who had ever lived.

The plan was so audacious that a part of Lemoine almost wished that he had conceived it right from the start, inviolate; but the truth was that his presence in New Zealand was an emergency measure, adopted in haste after the landslide had very nearly exposed his entire operation. He had known, of course, that solution mining was extremely hazardous, and that leaching rare-earth elements in situ by pumping lixiviant through boreholes drilled directly into the ground risked causing fissures in the bedrock that might precipitate a slip. But he had judged the size of the deposit to be worth the risk, guessing – correctly, as it turned out – that Korowai was close enough to the alpine fault that any accidents his men might cause would

be taken for ordinary seismic activity. Little quakes and rum-
blings were a daily occurrence in that part of the world, though
most were too faint, or too deep, to be felt without equipment.
What was more, Thorndike was generally considered to be the
back end of Korowai National Park; the vast majority of visit-
ors entered the park from the south-west corner, nearer to Lake
Hāwea, where the terrain was more varied and the views more
sublime, and even on a good day the Korowai Basin rarely saw
more than a dozen or so hikers passing through, mostly in pairs
or in family groups of three or four. The site was so remote that
Lemoine had assumed – this time incorrectly – that if an accident of some kind were to happen, the fallout would be fairly
easily contained.

He had been in Miami when the landslide happened, and
as he'd logged in to the surveillance feed over the pass to see
the Search & Rescue helicopters sweeping overhead, and the
television vans arriving, and the gazebos going up to assist the
first responders and the engineers, he had come very close to
cashing in his chips entirely. But in all the news coverage of the
disaster, nobody had thought to ask, even rhetorically, if the
earthquakes might possibly have been man-made; and although
the landslide had wiped some of the value off his enterprise –
somewhere in the region of a hundred million dollars, give or
take – the actual damage had been minimal. None of his men
on the ground had been spotted, and the extraction site itself
remained secure.

The real difficulty had come with the closure of the road over
the pass. With Thorndike deserted and the barricade in place,
a procession of heavy-duty vehicles out of the national park
would be sure to attract attention, and the operation was far too
sensitive, and worth far too much money, for Lemoine to want
to wait until the road had been repaired and the viaduct rebuilt

before he gave the order to his soldiers to pack out. Playing the survivalist afforded him the perfect cover; the bunker was the perfect Trojan horse. It would have been far safer to have kept his distance, of course – to have used a proxy, and never to have personally entered the country at all – but Lemoine's risk appetite tended to be whetted by unforeseen disaster; he experienced the deaths of other people as a challenge, a chance for him to test his own mortality and win. There was also a way in which the landslide had played directly into his hands, for he had always intended, once the container ships had left the port with the processed rare-earth elements aboard, to detonate the site in Korowai remotely, to remove any evidence that anyone had ever been there – and now any explosion he might cause would be even more likely to be taken for an earthquake. No, not just an earthquake, Lemoine thought, still smiling, still tapping out a rhythm on his knee. Not just an aftershock. An act of God.

The soldiers on the ground in Korowai were all special forces mercenaries who believed they'd been contracted – through an intermediary organisation – by the CIA. They had travelled to New Zealand under a multitude of covers: as IT consultants, scientific researchers, entrepreneurs, and employees of an American military analytics company that was seeking to open a Queenstown office to create a round-the-clock workday, maximising productivity through all the hours of the American and European night. Their real mission was to capture the payload in the Korowai Basin, leaching the elements on site and then smuggling them out of the country when the separation process was complete, and their real objective, as they understood it, was to help an alliance of western nations work in secret to wrest rare-earth market dominance away from China, by securing a rare-earth supply chain, from mine to magnet, for the United States.

The mercenaries' understanding was, in other words, about seventy per cent correct. The rare-earth market was indeed almost entirely controlled by China, and this stranglehold was indeed of great concern to many western nations, given the vast number of critical technologies that depended on rare earths, from smartphones to precision-guided weapons to wind turbines, solar panels, and electric cars. New Zealand had indeed explored the possibility of mining its own national parks – Lemoine had first learned about the Korowai deposit from a report commissioned by the New Zealand government seven years ago – and the United States was indeed scrambling to establish its own rare-earth supply chain to challenge the market dominance of the Chinese: just that year, a US mining corporation had received Pentagon funding to build two separation facilities in Texas, one of which, if Lemoine played his cards right, would eventually serve as a laundromat for the Korowai lode. But what the mercenaries did not know was that their operation was being carried out without the knowledge of the New Zealand government, or the US government, or either of their militaries, or the government or the military of any country in the world. Only about a half a dozen people on the planet knew the full extent of what was happening in Korowai National Park – and every one of them answered to Lemoine.

'Yes,' he said aloud, as if answering a question from the floor. Yes, he had caused the earthquakes that had caused the landslide. Yes, five people had been killed already. Yes, their blood was on his hands. But how many died every day in Chinese rare-earth mines and processing facilities, many of which used forced labour, and child labour, and were controlled by criminal syndicates who were themselves murderers, and gunrunners, and human traffickers, and worse? How many died downriver from all the toxic and radioactive sludge that these facilities pumped out? How many had died to supply the rare-earth components of the plane that he was sitting in, and the phone in his pocket, and the phone in everybody's pocket, and all of everybody's electronics, with all their cameras, and their GPS capabilities, and their LCD displays, and all the navigation systems that had shipped their parts around the world, and all the robotics and computers at all the factories where they were manufactured, and assembled, and warehoused, and packaged, and sent out? Five dead was nothing, thought Lemoine. Five dead, in the scheme of things, was basically no dead at all.

Outside, his bodyguards were pacing. They didn't like him flying solo, didn't like his choice of destination, didn't like that he kept going back there, didn't like that he wouldn't tell them why. Partly, it just went against their programming – they were ex-Mossad, the top of their game, the best of the best – but the bigger reason, Lemoine thought, was that they were bored senseless; they'd been detailing him for almost a decade, all over the globe, and in their years working for him they'd never had so little to do. They'd begged him to let them charter a second plane to shadow him, and when he refused, they'd begged to drive the long way round, to meet him on the other side of the slip; they'd tried to frighten him with threat levels and danger signs and foiled kidnapping attempts, and they'd come as close as they dared to reminding him of his late wife. But Lemoine didn't take orders from his own security. He got out his phone and dicked around on Twitter for a few minutes more, just to remind them that their time was his to waste if he wanted to, and then at last he descended from the cockpit and crossed the runway to the waiting SUV.

'The Lodge or the Peak, sir?' said his driver, as he got in.

'The Lodge,' he said, and two of his bodyguards mounted their outriders and peeled off. Lemoine always checked in to at least two luxury hotels at once, and switched between them frequently, often in the middle of the night. All his clothes and luggage were in duplicate, and in each hotel suite he placed a decoy laptop, loaded with malicious code, in case anyone got nosy or light-fingered while the room was being cleaned. For the most part, it was just for show. People expected him to be entitled, and he enjoyed cultivating the persona of the paranoid eccentric. It meant that no one ever asked him to explain himself, for one thing; and it always paid to have some handy pretext for throwing his weight around. This was more a tactic than a strategy – he only truly lost his temper very rarely – but in a way, to remain in tactics *was* the strategy. No one got to where he was in life without some instinct for the madman theory of control.

He settled back against the leather headrest and thought again of Mira. It was pure serendipity that they'd encountered one another. Since the Darvishes had left, he'd used the airstrip only a handful of times, some days staying only the few minutes that it took to turn the plane around; he kept a car in their garage, as they'd invited him to do, but today was the first he'd ever driven it, and although he had access to the house in case he ever needed to stay over, to date he'd never even put the key in the front door. He had actually been planning to return to California for a week or two, and had messaged his PA that very morning to tell her to start working on his diary. The PA was new, and still needed to be broken in; perhaps he'd wait a few days, he thought, before informing her there'd been a change of plan.

At the Lodge, he accessed Mira's browsing history and saw that after he had left her, she had spent the better part of an hour reading up about Autonomo, which had led her, naturally, to the news articles about his wife. She had lingered over these even longer, switching her search to images, typing in 'Gizela Kazarian', and then clicking back and forth between pictures of the two of them together and pictures of each of them alone; the pictures of the crash itself she barely dwelt on. It was only when she received a warning message saying that she'd reached her monthly data limit that she exited the browser and powered off the device. Lemoine checked his watch: that was half an hour ago. He could turn her phone on remotely if he wanted, but he considered that an act of last resort; instead, he connected to the live feed of the drone that was tracking her from overhead, and saw that she'd reversed the van a short distance to the water's edge. The rear doors were standing open. She was stooping in the shallows of the lake, her forearms underwater, almost as if she were drowning something. Lemoine peered at the image, trying to decipher it. Presently she braced her legs and stood, and he realised that she had been filling a water-cooler bottle that she now lugged, with effort, back to the van. She exchanged it for an empty one and returned to the lake to repeat the process. As she submerged the snout of this second vessel, it seemed to occur to her that maybe she was being watched. She craned back her head and looked straight upwards, right into the lens, and for a thrilling moment Lemoine felt that they were seeing eye to eye. But the light was fading, and the drone must have been too high to make out, for in the next moment she dropped her gaze to scan the ranges, and then the treetops, and then around the pebbled lakeshore, seeming only thoughtful, and not in the least suspicious or afraid. The bottle was full. She set it on its end and screwed on the cap, then hoisted it bodily out of the water; minutes later, she was shutting the van's rear doors, climbing into the driver's seat, and turning back on to the highway.

Lemoine kept his laptop open while he shaved and show-ered, and when he returned from the bathroom, naked and towelling himself, the drone had switched to night vision. He could no longer see the van, but the camera was hanging steady over the roof of the shearing shed, suggesting that Mira had driven the vehicle inside. The image showed no further movement as he dressed, and so after he had brushed his teeth and spritzed his hair with texturiser, he disconnected from the feed, locked the laptop in the safe that contained all his live devices, and called his driver to take him to the restaurant, where his guests – an obnoxious right-wing talk show host and his brash producer wife – were already waiting.

One of the many things that a career in covert monitoring had taught Lemoine was that in most circumstances, nothing attracted more attention than somebody attempting to blend in. A far better form of camouflage was to choose a costume that conformed to some blatant stereotype and then to wear it openly, deliberately courting judgment and inviting bias, until general opinion had been fixed; after that, one could virtually do as one pleased, for while people were quick to form opinions, they were just as slow to change them, and – to rephrase the aphorism slightly – there were none so blind as those who had already decided what it was they saw. Mira had plainly understood this – at least, as far as her own deceptions were concerned; whether she would fall for *his* was another question – but she had crumbled under pressure; she had allowed herself to be frightened, and she had given everything away. That was something Lemoine would never do. He was smiling again as the car arrived at the restaurant and he stepped out, but he wiped his expression clean before he entered the building, for his own chosen costume that evening was to be Lemoine the libertarian, Lemoine the misanthrope, Lemoine the doomsday-prepping, New Zealand–citizenship-seeking, investment-opportunity-dangling billionaire. He was forty-five minutes late – a power play so standard in his circle that he had sometimes wondered if actually the more disconcerting move would be to arrive on time, or even early – and his guests were visibly relieved to see him. They exchanged pleasantries, agreed the weather was just marvellous, and sat down.

Lemoine had been a teetotaller all his life, and if there was one expression he could recognise in any circumstance, it was the look of panicked disappointment worn by a certain kind of social alcoholic when he declined a drink; he caught it now on the faces of his dinner companions as he waved away the wine list and ordered soda water with a twist, and knew at once that he was going to find a way to cut the dinner short – before the main course, if necessary. 'But don't let me stop you,' he said politely. 'Please.'

They looked even more panicked.

'No, no, no,' said the talk show host, very loudly, 'we'll join you. It's good to take a night off.' He inclined his head beseechingly towards Lemoine, as if expecting the billionaire to thank him. 'We'll have the same,' he said to the waiter, when Lemoine said nothing. 'Two more of those. Yeah, mate. Thanks.'

'Are you sober, Robert? Or just taking a break?' said the wife when the waiter had departed, and Lemoine covered his annoyance by giving his standard response to importunate questions: 'Yes,' he said, not specifying, 'ever since my wife died.' This was true, but misleading. He watched her blush.

'I'm so sorry,' she said. 'Of course.'

'Nah – but good on you, though,' said her husband, coming to her aid. 'So many benefits to it, aren't there? I always think I'd get so much more out of the day if I cut back.'

The wife was nodding. 'And I bet you sleep so well,' she said.

'Like a baby,' said Lemoine, flashing her his best, most roguish smile. She looked startled, but the talk show host laughed and sat back in his seat with a new confidence, as if the first hurdle of the evening had been cleared.

'Whereabouts are you staying, Robert?' he said.

'The Peak,' said Lemoine.

'Oh, very nice,' said the wife.

'I hope they're showing you a bit of Kiwi hospitality?'

Lemoine decided to fuck with him. 'What's that?' he said.

'I mean – I hope they're taking care of you?'

'But what would make it Kiwi? Specifically?'

The man looked a little flummoxed. 'Just – really friendly, I guess.' He appealed to his wife.

'And informal,' she said. 'Down to earth.'

'Good food,' he said. 'Good coffee. We're very snobby about our coffee here.'

'Flat whites,' said the wife.

'It's the one thing,' said the talk show host, holding up one finger. 'It's the one thing we're really snobby about.'

They were visiting from Auckland. It would be an understatement to say that Lemoine was not typically in the habit of fraternising with the locals, but political alignment was part of his disguise, and he had learned, within minutes of making their acquaintance at the golf club, that the talk show host had recently been suspended from the air following some violation of broadcast standards, and that the wife had resigned in solidarity as his producer. Following a very public row about offence and overreach – Lemoine hadn't cared enough to be able to recall the details – they had decided to turn the period of enforced time off into a holiday, and they had the defiant, mildly aggressive air of two people now determined to enjoy themselves at any cost. They had told him, standing on the seventh green, that they had begun incubating an idea to establish a right-wing media platform in New Zealand, of the kind that was enjoying such runaway success elsewhere, and before Lemoine had time to comment, they'd added, without even an attempt at subtlety, that, in actual fact, they were on the hunt for an investor. This was not at all Lemoine's usual mode of doing business, but he had his disguise to think about, and as a libertarian survivalist, he could hardly find anyone more sympathetic to his existence than a nihilistic shock jock with a fragile ego and an axe to grind. What the hell, he'd thought, and had suggested that they get to know each other better over dinner – causing such undisguised avarice and triumph that he'd almost retracted the invitation on the spot.

'Yes, I had a flat white,' he said now, lying. 'It was good.'

They looked pleased. 'So we're treating you okay, then,' said the man. 'Well, we must be, if you're looking to stay on.'

'You're certainly doing something right,' said Lemoine.

'Best little country in the world,' said the woman.

'Most of us,' said the man. 'Most of the time.'

'The Godzone,' said the woman. 'Have you come across that at all?'

'No,' said Lemoine.

'It's from "God's Own Country". God's Own. But it's like – the Godzone.'

'It's how you feel when you're down here,' the man explained. 'You're in the Godzone.'

'Not a bad brand,' said Lemoine.

'I think it's taken,' said the man. 'But you're not wrong, actually.'

'I see the way you think,' said the wife, teasingly. 'Always thinking!' – and this time, they both laughed.

Lemoine suppressed an urge to get up from the table and walk out. 'So, give me a sense of the media landscape here,' he said. 'Where do you see it all moving? What's changing?

What's not changing? What are the flashpoints, where are the gaps?'

But as they began to answer, his mind flitted back to Mira, and he saw, again, the fearful challenge in the way she'd looked at him. He saw her calculation in summoning her courage, and in making her escape; he saw her fascination; he saw her desire; he heard the reedy wobble in her voice that had betrayed her apprehension when she'd asked him how he'd known her name. As he conjured her deliciously inside himself, he realised, all at once, that *she* would be his acquisition. *She* would be his venture. *She* would be the final piece of camouflage. Not these dime-a-dozen, grasping, self-important outrage-mongers, these obsequious nonentities, these small-time pseudo-pundits who traded in stupidity and called themselves subversive for shitting where they ate. Everyone expected him to move into the media; well, he was going to do what nobody expected. He was going to put his money into Birnam Wood.

He heard his name and blinked. They were staring at him. 'What?' he said.

There was a little pause. Then the woman said, in a strange, frightened voice, 'You were laughing.'

Three weeks had passed since Shelley's evening with Tony at the bar, and she hadn't seen or heard from him again. They had exchanged numbers in the car park before they parted ways, but when later that night she texted him a link to the open-source folder that they used as a kind of internal database and message board – an innovation since his time at Birnam Wood – she had received no reply. Of course, she had reasoned, Tony's attraction to the cause had always been more theoretical than practical, and most of his closest friends in the group had long since moved on, and their more anarchistic activities – in which he might genuinely feel an interest – weren't recorded on the document anyway; most likely, he had never actually intended to return to Birnam Wood as a fully fledged member, and had only shown curiosity in her to be polite. Shelley tended to over-justify the actions of others whenever she knew she couldn't honestly justify her own, and since the night of Mira's departure she had been feeling both deeply ashamed of herself and deeply embarrassed: ashamed that she had set out to betray Mira's trust so awfully, and embarrassed that she hadn't even come close to succeeding. She was determined to give Tony every benefit of the doubt, and as the days passed without any further sign of him, she even began to feel oddly grateful, as though his silence were in fact a kind of mercy, sparing her, graciously, from any chance to mortify herself again.

She had resolved to tell Mira he'd returned just as soon as Mira got home from Thorndike; there was no reason, she'd decided, to break the news before then. After all, it wasn't as though Mira had been expecting him – and the news was hardly urgent, since he'd said himself that he was home for good – and while he evidently felt far more conflicted about what had happened at his leaving party than Mira had ever realised at the time, well, that was their own business, a matter to be discussed in person, not through a third party, or by text message, or over the phone. And anyway, Shelley thought, with dwindling conviction, nothing in Mira's intermittent texts from Thorndike suggested that Tony had been in touch with her directly, so clearly he too felt the news could keep.

She knew that she was in the wrong, but with Mira absent from the flat and no further word from Tony, it was not too difficult to put the matter out of her mind. Midwinter was a fallow time for Birnam Wood. There were succession plantings of spinach and silverbeet to go in at the start of every week, and empty beds to dig over and prepare for the first crops of spring, but by this point in the season the cabbages and cauliflowers were well enough established that they hardly needed cultivation, and the leeks and carrots had all been thinned; the work was light, the yield was steady, and the gardens mostly took care of themselves. The previous year they had planted Jerusalem artichokes in the abandoned earthworks of a stalled construction project out of town, and the crop had since run rampant. Digging up the tubers and bagging them for sale was Shelley's only major project in the first week of Mira's absence, and she completed it at leisure, relishing the solitude, and experiencing a kind of pre-emptive nostalgia for all the years she'd given Birnam Wood; she had already begun looking for a job, and every day she found herself cataloguing, fondly, all the things that she would miss when she was gone.

She spent her evenings updating the Birnam Wood Facebook page, putting out new calls for equipment and volunteers, posting 'before and after' photos of their official plots around the city, and inviting hosts to share upbeat testimonials and to post candid photos of their own. Mira had always regarded the page as a necessary evil, useful only in putting prospective hosts at ease, but it was Shelley who maintained it, and Shelley was too much her mother's daughter not to know that prospective employers would invariably cross-check the claims she made on her CV by turning to Facebook, where Birnam Wood was defined in carefully apolitical language as a grassroots community initiative that planted sustainable organic gardens in neglected spaces and fostered a commitment to helping those in need. As she posted that week's Top Tip for Gardeners – bigger isn't always better when choosing seedlings from a garden store! – she wondered if a part of her had always known, deep down, that she would one day want to leave the group. Maybe, on some level, she had curated the page specifically with her current circumstance in mind – namely, in order to provide future employers with a coherent explanation for what Mira, in a cartoonish imitation of Shelley's mother, had once called the lost years of her career.

Over a fortnight passed without Mira making any mention of when she was planning to return. Their messages were brief and breezy, Shelley not wanting to give Mira any reason to cut short her trip, and Mira still mindful, clearly, of Shelley's need for space: she'd barely described the site at Thorndike, except to say that the town was very quiet and conditions were ideal, and although the date of Birnam Wood's next full-caucus hui was fast approaching – the group met quarterly, on the first Monday night of every February, May, August, and November – they both steered well clear of the subject. Late on the first Sunday night of August, Shelley was getting ready for bed and reflecting on the fact that the impending hui might well be the first that Mira had ever missed, when she received a text: Mira had 'big news' and was heading home first thing in the morning in order to make an announcement to the group the following night. '???' Shelley messaged back, and a few seconds later the reply came through: 'crazy couple weeks . . . didn't want to get your hopes up earlier but I think we might have actually broken good! I'll explain properly in person- see you tomorrow xx.' 'Omg what???' Shelley wrote, and then waited – but the receipt function that marked the message as 'delivered' didn't update the tag to 'read': Mira must have already turned off her phone and gone to bed.

The next morning, Shelley woke to see that her text was now marked 'read', but Mira had replied only to say that she was hitting the road and expected to be home by the early afternoon. Shelley felt a returning apprehension, and as she made breakfast and sat down at the table to eat, she forced herself to count her blessings. She had no idea what Mira's news could be, but if Birnam Wood was truly within sight of solvency at last, then she could quit the group with a clear conscience; no one could accuse her of abandoning Mira when her chips were down. Mira would be returning in a good mood, which would make her well disposed towards the news that Tony had come home; and her announcement, whatever it was, might well provide the perfect chapter break for Shelley to announce her own intention to depart. The hui was at seven that evening, and Mira would be back by two; there would be ample time for conversation in the later part of the afternoon, and ample time for Shelley to tell her friend once and for all, without fear, and without embarrassment, that although she wouldn't change her years at Birnam Wood for anything, it was time – she practised saying it out loud – it was time for her, finally, to move on.

As she showered, she wondered if Tony would make an appearance. It seemed unlikely, since he hadn't touched the open-source folder or responded to any of her calls for volunteers, and she hadn't seen him at any of the planting sites, and nobody at Birnam Wood had so much as mentioned his name, even in passing, even just to remark that he'd come home; but to reassure herself, after she had dressed and dried her hair she opened her laptop and sent out a group email on the Birnam Wood mailing list, reminding everyone of the hui that evening and asking for a quick confirmation, for catering purposes, of who was planning to attend.

They held their assemblies in a café managed by one of the longer-serving members – Amber Callander, who would remember Tony, though in Shelley's recollection they had not been friends – and it had become a tradition to mark each quarter

95

with a ceremonial bowl of soup, the ingredients sourced from Birnam Wood planting sites and prepared in the café kitchen by Amber herself. Shelley had been so preoccupied with her own intentions for sending out the email that she had forgotten that hosting was a source of great pride and satisfaction for Amber – and that Amber, whom Mira had once described, unkindly, as a walking list of grievances, was notoriously quick to take offence. Almost immediately Amber fired back with a reply-all, asking in a tone of deep affront if Shelley was taking over the task of catering, because she had already laid on a dozen heads of broccoli, and she would have appreciated a bit more notice in the event of a change of plan, and Shelley's email had made it seem that there was reason to expect a greater crowd than usual, which might be a problem because they were already nearing capacity in terms of how many people could legally cram into the café at once, and fire hazard violation fines were quite expensive, and while she had the future of the café to think of, at the same time, she really didn't want to have to be the one to turn any members of the group away.

By the time Shelley had made amends – she was obliged in the end to send a second email, clarifying that Amber was of course cooking as usual, thanking her publicly for hosting once again, and adding, so as not to debase herself too thoroughly, that it might be worthwhile attending because Mira would be making a surprise announcement – she had received more than a dozen emails of confirmation. One of the names, Finn Koefoed-Nielsen, she didn't recognise, until she saw that he had signed off 'Finn (K)', and she realised that this must be the crust punk whom she'd only ever known as Fink. She hadn't even realised that his email address was still on the mailing list, as he hadn't attended any of their meetings in at least a year; curious as to what might have drawn him back, she looked him up on Facebook to discover that in the time since she'd last seen him, he had exchanged his glued Mohawk and eyebrow rings for a pair of stylish thick-rimmed glasses and a military fade. According to his profile, he was now respectably settled and working for his local district health board as a software engineer. If she hadn't been looking for it, she wouldn't even have recognised that he was the same person. Diverted, she began swiping through his profile pictures to see if she could pinpoint the exact moment his appearance had transformed, and nearly fifteen minutes went by before it occurred to her that if Fink's address had remained on the listserv all this time, then perhaps Tony's had as well. She called up the mailing list again and scrolled through the addresses, and sure enough, he was there: gallos.humour@gmail.com. Funny that in all the years he'd been away, he'd never asked to be unsubscribed, she thought – and then she felt embarrassed when she realised that everything she'd told him during their conversation at the bar about how much Birnam Wood had changed in his absence must not actually have been news to him at all.

She spent the morning tidying the flat, and after lunch she cycled to a nearby hardware store to ask about collecting sawdust from beneath their on-site cross-cut saw. The duty manager, a young man she hadn't met before, looked amused when she explained that she wanted the sawdust for her compost heap, but his amusement faded when she added that it was useful both to aerate the heap and to provide a carbon boost to complement the nitrogen, and that she had found the ideal compost was formed of plant matter, sawdust, and animal manure at a ratio of 1:1:3. Grudgingly, he allowed her to sweep up a small bag of sawdust at no charge, but his manner had become curt and disapproving, and as she cycled home Shelley reflected that in all her years at Birnam Wood she had never quite mastered the skill of knowing in every individual circumstance whether to overplay or underplay her expertise. It was something that Mira seemed to know instinctively – that a demonstrated competency reassured some people and aggravated others; she could pitch herself at exactly the right point between whimsical amateur and winsome entrepreneur, a performance that, when Shelley tried it, only seemed to make it much less likely that the person she was talking to would want to give her things for free.

It was past three o'clock by the time she had dug the sawdust through the heap, and she checked her phone to find a message waiting from Mira. The van had broken down a little south of Timaru. She'd had to call roadside rescue, and she was now waiting for a mechanic to determine whether the problem was fixable within the next few hours. If worse came to worst and she didn't make it back in time for the hui, she'd call and relay her announcement over the phone – but she'd much prefer to break the news to Birnam Wood in person if she could. She sounded harried, and Shelley hesitated for several minutes over what to reply. She typed out an experimental message: 'okay, crazy- tony gallo's back in town- he stopped by the flat a while back looking for you, not sure if he'll come tonight but just fyi i just realised he's still on the mailing list so it's conceivable he might show up . . . anyway fingers crossed the van gets fixed, let me know how you get on xx'. She stared at it, chewing her lip, for a long time before pressing delete. Tony hadn't RSVP'd, and among the thirty-odd members who now had, the only people who had any connection to him whatsoever were Amber, who had never much liked him, and Fink, whom he'd never much liked. In all probability, he wasn't coming, and there was no need to warn Mira in advance. 'bummer,' Shelley wrote instead, 'hope it's fixable . . . keep in touch xx'.

She passed the rest of the afternoon preparing sets of peas and lettuces – for the last few days she had been soaking pea seeds in saucers of water to hasten germination, and at last they had begun to sprout – and cleaning out the busted drinks fridge that she and Mira had brought home from the tip and were planning to convert into a greenhouse. A little after half-past five, Mira texted to say that the van had been fixed at last and she was on the road again. She would drive straight to the café, arriving only a little late: 'save me some soup,' she wrote, 'only . . . remind me who's cooking again??' Grinning, Shelley sent back a witch emoji, then washed up, locked the house, and strapped a box of seed trays on to the back of her bicycle, figuring she would just have time to deliver them to empty plots around the city before it was time to head to the café.

The wind was against her, and she misjudged the distance between two of their most recent planting sites; she arrived at the hui twenty minutes after seven to find the windows steamed and the scent of lemongrass and coriander wafting out into the open air. As she locked her bike to a parking meter, she had a sinking feeling that she could hear Tony's voice, and when she opened the door, her heart sank even further. She was one of the last to arrive. The tables had been stacked against the window and the chairs arranged in an ellipsis, and at the top of the ellipsis Tony was holding court. He was addressing Amber, who was still wearing her chef's apron, and whose body language made it clear that she was decidedly put out. They hardly looked up as Shelley slipped in.

'You're still inside the paradigm,' Tony was saying. 'Can't you see? You're still treating people as consumers, you're just saying that they should consume more responsibly and consume less. But as long as you keep talking in the language of the market, you're never going to address the root cause of the problem, which is *the market itself* – and how we've all become so fucking individualistic and consumeristic that we can't even conceive of anything any more except in market terms. If we want to mount any kind of serious challenge to neoliberalism at all, we have to go way deeper than just changing our spending habits. We have to change the way we actually *think*.'

'Well, that's easy to say,' Amber objected, but Tony was still going:

'Like, think about the fact that nobody's willing to use the language of morality any more. We can talk about power – *all* we talk about is power, who's got it and who wants it – and we can talk about privilege, which is basically the same thing, entrenched power, but to use words like good and evil, or not even *evil*, just good and *bad*, when it comes to people's behaviour, or their lifestyle choices, or their forms of self-expression – their *freedom* – that's, like, totally taboo. Especially on the left. Where do you think we got that from? It's the market. The idea that human choices can *ever* be without morality, without a moral dimension – that's pure capitalism, seeing the market as a value-neutral space, where morality doesn't exist and people are free to compete on equal terms, and there are, like, natural laws of supply and demand or whatever – and of course it's all bullshit, markets are *created*, they're *always* created, they're *always* policed and regulated and interfered with by the state. But we totally repeat that same logic. Don't you see? We treat power both as an absolute, as a natural law, *and* as something that's completely relativised in terms of moral value – so basically, exactly the same as how we think about so-called market forces. There's no difference. And the sad thing is that we can't even see that we're doing it. We think we're *above* this shit. We're inside it.'

Shelley looked around the room, suppressing an urge to turn, walk back out the door, and disappear from Birnam

Wood forever. Although everyone was quietly eating, she felt she could detect a note of glee in how closely Tony's words were being followed, and how disinclined they all seemed to interrupt. Amber was not well liked among the group – she was touchy and officious, proud of her seniority, and jealous of her rights – and there were many, Shelley included, who would be only too glad to see her schooled in public, and possibly even shamed. Even so, something about Tony's energy made Shelley uneasy. He was sitting forward on his chair and giving his opinions eagerly and quickly, like someone who had been prevented from speaking for a very long time. He kept glancing towards the door.

'Or, like, the term "free market",' he was saying now. 'It's totally a propaganda term, and yet we all use it, even on the left. It's insane. We should be asking ourselves, why are we using their words and their logic? Why are we doing their job for them?'

'But I didn't use that word,' Amber said. 'I never said "free market". All I said—'

'I know, I know, I know, but my point—'

Shelley went over to the kitchen hatch. 'What's going on?' she asked the person serving, a soft-spoken session drummer whose name was either Callum or Colin.

He shrugged. 'I guess his name is Tony? He showed up with Finn.'

'Who?' Shelley said stupidly, before she saw that Tony was sitting next to a well-groomed young man with glasses and a military fade. 'Oh, right,' she said. 'What are they talking about?'

'Capitalism, I think?' He ladled out a bowl of soup and passed it to her.

'Didn't we already solve that one?'

'Ooh,' said Callum or Colin, 'you should tell him that. I dare you.'

Shelley thanked him for the soup and went to find a seat. 'Smells fantastic,' she whispered to Amber as she passed her, holding up her bowl, but Amber didn't smile. Shelley noted with annoyance that Amber was the only one in the room who wasn't eating. 'Addicted to martyrdom,' Mira would have said, rolling her eyes. 'You know nothing would make her happier than if it was all gone by the time she went to serve herself. She'd be over the moon.'

Tony was still talking. 'As long as you keep treating the individual as the basis of political agency,' he was saying now, 'you're going to be stuck with different forms of capitalism. This is my whole idea. This is what I'm trying to write about. What if we stopped talking in terms of individuals at all, and instead we took the *relationship* as the base socio-economic unit? The relationships, the bonds, the connections – they're just as basic to any system as the actual individuals, the actual data. Right? And in relationships, we do all sorts of things that radically challenge the neoliberal status quo: we make sacrifices, we put the other person first, we learn to compromise, we care, we help, we listen, we give ourselves away – and fundamentally, those are different kinds of sacrifices to the kind that are all about self-discipline and following a regime. They're not individualistic; they're *mutual*. Like, all the stuff that you were saying before, stopping eating meat, flying less, shopping local, I mean, all power to you, for sure, but there's something so puritanical about it, like, it's a programme of asceticism, always being strict and consistent and never being lazy or whatever – and at the end of the day it's still about you as an individual. *Your* purity, *your* moral conscience, the sacrifices *you've* made.'

'But you can't force people—'

'There's something so *joyless* about the left these days,' Tony continued, 'so forbidding and self-denying. And *policing*. No one's having any fun, we're all just sitting around scolding each other for doing too much or not enough – and it's like, what kind of vision for the future is that? Where's the hope? Where's the humanity? We're all aspiring to be monks when we could be aspiring to be lovers.'

The door opened, and he glanced up again, but it was just a smoker returning from a cigarette break.

'But you can't force people into relationships,' Amber said, taking advantage of the momentary pause. 'And even when you're in a relationship, you're still an individual.'

Tony was following his own line of thought. 'Take the concept of equality,' he said, turning away from Amber slightly to address the rest of the group. 'You could argue that it's only really meaningful on a human scale. In large numbers, all it means is homogeneity, or conformity – huge numbers of people who are exactly the same – I mean, who would want that? It's oppressive, it's inhuman, it's boring. It's everything everyone says about communism and how deadening it is. But between two people, equality is a totally radical idea. I mean, how amazing, that two different people, with different values, and different experiences, and abilities, and needs, that they could see eye to eye, and live in such a way that brings out the best in both of them, right, and allows both of them to flourish! That's symbiosis, it's mutuality, it's *love* – that's just the kind of relation to the world that the left should be aiming for. Not where you *have* to help someone other than yourself, but where you *want* to. Romantic love, that could be our ideal. Our *political* ideal.'

Amber was frowning. 'But aren't you just doing exactly what you're accusing me of doing? How is this not you talking in the language of the market? I mean, we literally call it "the marriage market"—'

'That's within a capitalist structure though, you have to—'

103

'And we had to *fight* for equality. That was never a given. For most of history, marriage was about property. It was a transaction. You're making it sound—'

'Sure, sure, sure, but if it was the bond *itself* that was the economic unit—'

'You're making it sound all cuddly and everything, but equality isn't the *norm*, there are power imbalances in every relationship, people are always being coerced and—'

'But if we took an ideal of non-coercion—'

'Like being exclusive,' Amber said, cutting over him. 'That's just a kind of ownership, right? I could just throw all this back at you, and say you're being so capitalistic and individualistic for assuming that relationships have to be, like, monogamous, and traditional—'

'Oh, give me a break,' Tony said. 'Polyamory is *so* fucking capitalistic. Yet again, you're proving my point. You literally couldn't have picked a more individualistic example.'

Amber looked confused. 'What?'

'It's Consumerism 101!' Tony burst out. 'It's like going to a department store! The idea that *this* partner gives you a little bit of this and *this* partner gives you a little bit of that, and you don't want to risk missing out, so you buy them both – it's a hedge! You're like one of those people at restaurants who order something off the menu and then reserve the right to change every little part of it. No tomatoes, can I swap out the bread, sauce on the side. It's like, just *eat* it, you're not fucking "*allergic*", your life's not in *danger*, you're just *picky*. You're just *rude*. It's so fucking self-obsessed and *boring*. It drives me nuts the way we talk about polyamory as if it's the new frontier, as if it's an act of *protest*, like you've transcended ownership and bravely liberated yourself from patriarchal structures or whatever, when it's literally the complete opposite, it's that you don't want to take moral responsibility for the fact that you want to fuck other people, or the fact that you can't commit, or the fact that you're unhappy and unfulfilled, so you just redefine morality so that you don't have to face your own selfishness and actually call it out for what it is. Polyamory doesn't lead to fucking *socialism*, it leads to hyper-egoistic, Mormon, hyper-capitalist—'

'Jesus,' Amber said. 'I guess I hit a nerve or something.'

Tony had flushed. 'Here's the test,' he said. 'Here's what you should be asking yourself. What if it was *me* saying, "Hey, but what about polyamory, though, that's a great idea, guys, isn't it?" Me, Tony? You'd be all up in my face telling me it was the most patriarchal thing you'd ever heard of, but when it's *you*, all of a sudden it's supposed to be this amazing liberation. Shouldn't that tell you something? Shouldn't that ring any bells, that maybe you aren't as progressive as you think you are, that maybe there's some other power structure at work? This is just what I've been saying the whole time! I mean – intersectionality, neoliberalism, what's the difference? It's the same old bullshit.'

Amber drew back. '*Excuse me?*' she said.

'Just hear me out,' Tony said. 'Hear me out, all right? Just listen. Any conversation on the left these days, it's always so competitive, it's always each person trying to outperform the person before them in terms of their oppression or their lack of privilege or their personal trauma or, like, the fact that *actually* they're Jewish or *actually* they're bisexual, or guess what, they're a quarter this or that ethnicity, which gives them the right to speak or the right to take offence or whatever. It's a marketplace! Yet again! You can dress it up in the language of sensitivity and social justice and blah blah blah, but the point of intersectionality isn't to learn how to *transcend* our differences, or *eliminate* them, the point isn't *solidarity*, it's about shoring up your brand, cornering the market, everyone out for themselves, maximising profit and minimising risk—'

'I can't believe I'm hearing this,' Amber said.

'It *locks us into* our differences,' Tony said, 'it's segregationist. And it's also just *advertising*. It's brand management. That's my point. *We're still inside the fucking paradigm!*'

He looked around, seeking agreement, but the mood had turned decisively against him; Shelley could sense it, and she could tell that Tony could, too. They made eye contact for the first time that evening, and she felt, to her surprise, a surge of pity for him. His face was very flushed, and he had a wild, almost forsaken look, as though he were on the verge of breaking something that he knew he didn't have the means to fix.

'Um, just so I'm clear,' Amber said, 'you're saying that *intersectionality* is *bullshit*?'

'Oh, come on,' Tony said, disgustedly. 'Don't do that.'

'Don't do what?'

'Don't make out like I've stabbed you in the fucking heart, just because—'

'Oh my God,' Amber said. 'This is not about *me*, Tony—'

'Yes, it is,' Tony interrupted. 'Of course it is. You're getting offended. You're making a big performance out of how unbelievably offended you are. It's not a debate. It's not an argument. It's just another way for you to pull the identity card. It's the same old shit.'

Next to him, Finn was shifting in his seat uncomfortably. 'Hey, man,' he said quietly to Tony, 'read the room, maybe?'

'I *am* reading the room,' Tony said. 'Everybody here is white. Am I wrong? Everybody here at this "hui"' – he put exaggerated quotes around the word – 'is white and middle class, just like Amber, and just like me.'

'This is so fucked up,' Amber said.

'If I'm wrong, please tell me,' Tony said. 'Please. Somebody put me straight. Because I honestly would love to be corrected.'

Shelley looked around her in dismay – for although the present company didn't show it, the membership of Birnam Wood had broadened in the years that Tony had been overseas. She did a mental head count to assuage her ugly feeling of complicity. There was Winnie, and Jinan, and Amara, and Sameer, all regular faces at Birnam assemblies. There were the Tamanis, the Fijian Indian family who sold Birnam produce at their corner store; Agnes Vaai, a Samoan art student who'd signed up to help with household junk collections; Nancy Chen, a dentist who'd donated the strip of earth beside her parking space at work, and who grew seedlings on her windowsill at home; Mr Sichantha, who hosted a plot in his garden; his daughter Vanida, who hosted another on the other side of town; kindly Mrs Li, who always bought more than she needed when they came knocking on her doorstep with produce for sale . . . And that was to say nothing of all the dozens of volunteers who were Asian and Pasifika – and Māori, too – surely there was someone present who was Māori? Wincing, Shelley looked around the room again, scanning all the faces, and caught the eye of someone on the far side of the ellipsis who was doing the exact same thing. They both flushed and quickly turned away.

'You're being so fucking disrespectful,' Amber said.

'To *what?*' Tony said. 'Your *brand?*'

'Like, is somebody filming this?' Amber said, looking round. 'For the record?'

'Oh sure,' Tony said, throwing up his hands. 'Sure. Commodify this moment. Go ahead. Please. Prove my point.'

'This is *so* fucked up,' Amber said again.

Shelley raised her hand. 'I feel like this has maybe gone far enough?' she said. 'What does everybody think? Should we call it, maybe?'

There was a stirring of agreement around the room; but Tony wasn't about to back down. 'Just hear what I'm actually saying,' he said, still addressing Amber. 'Okay? Just actually think about the connection that I'm making. A marketing algorithm doesn't see you as a human being. Right? It sees you purely as a matrix of categories: a person who's female, and heterosexual – or whatever-sexual – and white, and university-educated, and employed, who has *these* kinds of friends and shares *these* kinds of articles and posts *these* kinds of pictures and makes *these* kinds of searches, and on and on – and the more sophisticated the algorithm, the more subcategories it's able to diagnose, and the better it's able to market whatever it is it's selling. Identity politics, intersectionality, whatever you call it – it's the exact same thing. It's the same logic. The smaller the category, the better you're able to sell yourself. The safer you are, economically.'

'That's so fucking cynical—'

'Yes, it is, and that's exactly what I'm saying: as long as we keep thinking like this, we're stuck with cynicism. There's nothing else. We'll never be able to agree to work towards a common goal, and that means the whole project of a genuine left-wing politics is fucked. How can we even get started on the project of creating and protecting public goods when within every interest group there's always a subgroup, and each one has their own particular agenda, and they're all in competition with each other for airtime and market share—'

'You talk about *airtime*,' Amber said. 'Literally, look who's talking! *Literally!*'

This got a laugh.

'Sorry,' Tony said. His flush had deepened. 'Okay, you go.'

'Well,' Amber said, tossing her head, '*I* don't think it's an accident that whenever anyone seems to have a problem with intersectionality, they always happen to look exactly like you.'

Tony's expression hardened at once. 'Oh, come on,' he said, 'this is exactly—'

'And "identity politics", that's *also* a propaganda term, by the way,' Amber went on. 'People who are *actually* marginalised, people who are *actually* systematically oppressed, whose lives are *actually* in danger, they don't say, "Oh, have you heard about this great new thing, it's called identity politics?"! They're talking about *justice*, and *representation*—'

'And survival,' someone said.

'And *survival*,' Amber said. There was a flurry of nodding.

'But I'm not against any of those things,' Tony said. 'Not at all. That's not my point.'

'Maybe it's *you* who's still inside the paradigm,' Amber said, with growing confidence. 'Maybe you'd always taken it for granted that you were going to come out on top in the quote-unquote *marketplace of ideas* or whatever, but now these spaces that *you've* always monopolised have been opened up—'

'No, that's not what this is about—'

'And all sorts of people who have traditionally been excluded are now being let in and given a voice, and they're pushing *you* out and reducing *your* airtime, and threatening *your* privilege, and you're like, hey, guys, the world is so capitalist, everything's a marketplace, that's so terrible, and we're all like, yeah, we *know*, it's a system that *you* created, so why should we listen to you any more? About *anything*? Because guess what, Tony, *times have changed!*'

Around the room, people were snapping their fingers and voicing their assent.

'Hey, I'm not arguing for the status quo here,' Tony said, putting up his hands. 'Fuck the patriarchy. Fuck capitalism, fuck white supremacy, one hundred per cent, bring it all down. I don't want things to stay the *same*—'

'Oh right,' Amber said, 'because it's such a *novelty* to be lectured at for literally half an hour by a straight white—'

'I just don't think that intersectionality is the answer to the problem!'

'Well, you know who else thinks that? Fucking white supremacists, Tony!'

'Look, clearly this is a touchy subject—'

'*That's* fucking patronising—'

'But I'm not just being a dick, all right? I'm not just name-dropping and being a cliché. I've actually got ideas. I'm actually proposing an alternative.'

'Yeah, well, maybe you don't get to do that any more!'

'But that's so crazy,' Tony said. 'What kind of a solution is that? You can't just tell me to shut up—'

'I'm not telling you to *shut up*, I'm telling you to *listen*. There's a difference.'

Several people broke into applause.

'But listen to *what?*' Tony said, starting to laugh. 'Can't you see what you're doing? That's not an argument!'

'Yes, it is!'

'It's not! It's just your fallback position. You say *listen*, yeah, sounds great, awesome, but listen to *what?* You haven't got any actual *ideas*. All you have is your identity. All you have is your brand. You're just trying to promote yourself. Do you honestly not see that?'

'Let's look at what *you're* doing,' Amber said. '*You*, Tony. You come back after how many years, you completely dominate the conversation, you're rude and dismissive, you're eating food that *we* grew and *we* cooked for you—'

'The food was delicious,' Tony said. 'I should have said that.'

'And it's like, *this* is why intersectionality's important! You, right here, talking like you've been talking all night, *laughing* at me! *This* is the argument!'

The door opened, and Mira walked in.

'So sorry I'm late,' she said to Amber. 'It smells amazing.' Then she saw Tony. 'Oh my God, fuck!'

'My sentiments exactly,' Amber said, clearly hoping for a laugh that didn't come.

'What?' Mira said, half-smiling. She looked from Amber to Tony, but he wouldn't meet her gaze. He got up to take his empty bowl to the kitchen.

'It doesn't matter,' Amber said. 'Everyone's here now. Let's get on with it.'

Mira was still trying to smile. 'Guys,' she said, looking around, 'what did I just walk into?'

But a collective shame had taken hold. 'It's nothing,' someone said. 'Don't worry.'

Amber looked nettled. 'It wasn't *nothing*,' she said, in a prim voice. She went over to the serving hatch and began straightening the spoons.

'What wasn't?' Mira said, appealing to Shelley. 'What's going on?'

This is all my fault, Shelley thought. *This is absolutely and entirely all my fault.* She glanced at Tony, who was rinsing his bowl at the sink, his back turned. 'Maybe we should take five or something,' she said. 'Cool off a bit?'

'*I* don't need to cool off,' Amber said. 'I'm fine. I just want to get on with it. You can leave that,' she said to Tony, raising her voice louder than she needed to. 'We have a dishwasher, you know.'

He pretended not to hear her.

'Can someone just tell me what's going on, please?' Mira

said, but people were starting to sigh and murmur their annoyance, and when someone said, 'Actually, could we do that later? I have a babysitter and I can't stay past nine,' others began making the same petition, saying that they had work in the morning, or that they had to catch a certain bus, or that it was late enough already, and within seconds the group had come to life: they began stacking their empty bowls, getting out notebooks, asking whose turn it was to facilitate, and reminding each other loudly of the schedule of topics for discussion. Mira hesitated, seeming unsure whether she should follow Tony into the kitchen or stay where she was. Shelley got up to go and speak to her, but Amber got there first, handing Mira a bowl of soup and a spoon and saying, underneath the hubbub, but loud enough for Shelley to hear, 'Just so you know, Tony's turned into a real asshole.' Mira caught Shelley's eye and made a quizzical face, which Shelley met with a miserable shrug that was half head shake, half nod. There was no time to say anything else. The facilitator called the meeting to order, and Tony crossed the room again and resumed his seat, not responding to Finn's look of pained commiseration as he sat down. Pointedly ignoring everybody's gaze, he folded his hands in his lap and looked at his shoes, ready to listen. Shelley sat back down again, Amber retreated to the hatch to serve herself, and Mira took her own place in the last available chair.

Meetings at Birnam Wood were broadly horizontalist. The role of facilitator was allocated on a roster – this time, to a sweet-tempered paediatric nurse named Katie Vander – and discussions proceeded through five set phases: putting forth proposals for action; asking for clarifying questions; raising objections and concerns; making amendments; and finally, testing for consensus, which was demonstrated by wiggling one's fingers upright to signal agreement, downward for disagreement, or sideways

to indicate a stand-aside. Katie began, as was always the custom, by reminding everyone of the format and then reading out
the group's three Principles of Unity: 'to develop and protect a
classless, environmentally sustainable, direct-democratic economy that is both regenerative and responsive to human need;
to operate as much as possible outside a capitalist framework;
and to practise solidarity and mutual aid'. The principles had
been devised so long ago that ordinarily Shelley hardly paid
attention, but now, with the substance of Amber and Tony's
argument ringing in her ears, she felt a flush of guilt, first at
the word 'capitalist', and then again at 'solidarity'. She glanced
at Tony, but his expression was impassive. He was still staring
at his shoes.

Mira's was the first proposal to be tabled, and after setting a
time frame for the discussion, Katie gave her the floor.

'Okay, well, hi, kia ora tātou,' Mira said, looking around. 'So,
as some of you know, I've just come back from Thorndike, down
by the Korowai Pass where there was that landslide recently?'

Shelley felt another flush of guilt to observe that Mira
seemed, unusually, a little nervous. Tony hadn't moved.

'While I was down there,' Mira went on, 'I met this guy, kind
of by accident, this American guy, and as we got to talking, he
sort of expressed an interest in who we are and what we do, and
– this sounds a bit strange, but – he's offered to give us some
funding. Like, to help us to become a proper not-for-profit type
of organisation. I mean, if that's what we want. And I guess like
a kind of test, he wants to commission us to come and plant a
garden on this farm, to see what we're made of, and to see if we
can handle a budget and a schedule and parameters and stuff.'

She was usually more fluent than this, Shelley thought uncomfortably, and more authoritative.

'So, his offer is a hundred thousand dollars,' Mira went on, 'just cash, no strings attached, not as a contract or anything – this is just, like, a donation. He said that by Christmas, if he's happy with the work, and we've proved that we're for real and that we know what we're doing and everything, at that point, we'd have another conversation about actual proper long-term funding and how to grow and what steps to take and all of that. But whatever happens, the hundred grand would be ours to keep.

'I know it sounds mad,' she went on, now addressing Shelley, 'I mean, honestly, it kind of does to me as well, but he's, like, really, really rich, like, *really* rich – and I think he's, like, one of those people whose self-mythology is all about spotting enter-prising young people and making their careers – like, he sees himself as this rebel, and when he found out about us, it was like, hey, one rebel to another. And I know,' she added, talking faster, and looking apologetically round the room, 'rich Ameri-can buying a bolthole in New Zealand, I mean, it's not exactly the kind of bedfellow any of us would choose, and he's totally one of those apocalypse preppers or survivalists or whatever you call them, you know, like, he got his pilot's licence, he has a plane, he's bought this farm, like, totally off the radar, and he's even putting in a bunker, so, full cliché – but for what it's worth, he's invested in this conservation project up north, so his heart's at least kind of in the right place, and I've talked to him a bunch over the past couple of weeks and I don't think he's an entirely bad guy.'

'Who is he?' someone asked, but Katie put out her hand to shush them: asking clarifying questions was a part of the second stage. 'Sorry,' she said to Mira. 'Go on.'

'Well, I guess the only other thing to say is that he's already given me ten grand,' Mira said, blushing slightly. 'I didn't ask him to – we didn't make any kind of agreement or anything, and I was super clear that I wanted to run the offer past all of you before making anything official. But then he told me to check my bank balance, out of the blue, and I did, and he'd already made the deposit. I think it's part of the self-mythology I was talking about, like, being all theatrical about it. I have no idea how he got my bank details . . . and none of this is in writing either, by the way, that's the other thing. It's actually because we're so off-grid that he was attracted to us in the first place. So this is definitely not like a legally binding kind of deal. It's very informal. It's more like a bet. Or like a dare, like, he's daring us – or maybe, like we're daring him? But anyway, that's the whole pitch. His name is Robert Lemoine.'

Tony looked up for the first time since Mira had started to speak. '*Robert Lemoine?*' he repeated.

'Yeah,' Mira said.

'Hang on,' Katie said, 'are we ready to move on to questions? Mira?'

'Yeah, ready, thanks,' Mira said to Katie. To Tony she said, 'You've heard of him?'

They were looking at each other for the first time. 'He's the Autonomo guy,' Tony said. 'He's not just *rich*. He's a billionaire.'

Mira blushed again. 'Well, like I said, not exactly the bed-fellow we'd choose, but—'

'You *think*? He's literally the opposite of everything we stand for.'

'Just making sure we're *only* asking questions,' Katie said.

'What's Autonomo?' someone asked.

'It's a tech company,' Tony said. 'They make drones.'

'Surveillance drones,' Mira said quickly, 'not the military kind.'

Tony made a scoffing noise. 'Sure,' he said. 'Because there's absolutely no overlap.'

'Let's keep it to questions, guys.'

'You must remember his wife,' Tony said, addressing the others. 'It was this huge deal – she was in a helicopter and it crashed for like totally no reason, when he just *happened* not to be on board.'

'Tony—'

'I'm just saying,' Tony said. 'This is the kind of guy we're talking about.'

'So not like an accident?' someone said.

'Well, it was a bit weird. I mean, a helicopter – that's like, his actual field of expertise.'

Shelley could see that Mira was trying to control her temper. 'No one knows what happened,' she said, tightly. 'No one. Including you.'

Tony shut his mouth. They held each other's gaze for a little beat, but before Shelley could decipher the look that passed between them, Mira had turned back to the group.

'Look, I mean, full disclosure here,' she said, 'he's on one of those investor visas and he needs to sponsor Kiwi enterprise if he's going to qualify for a passport, so this isn't just a straight-up philanthropic type of deal. He's getting something out of this too. And yeah, he's a billionaire, and if anybody had a problem with him just on principle, then I would totally understand, absolutely. There are, like, twenty-five red flags. I get it. But again, for what it's worth, I've done a bit of reading about Autonomo online, and it honestly doesn't seem like they—'

'They buy up the Google searches,' Tony burst out, 'they buy up all the search results so that you can only see the favourable stuff, these are, like, *professional surveillance operatives*, of course you're not going to find anything—'

'Let's stick to asking questions, please,' Katie said.

'This is nothing to do with his company anyway,' Mira said. 'It's just him.'

'So essentially,' Tony said, 'you're proposing to help a billion-aire drone manufacturer buy a passport to our country so that he can fulfil his grand plan to outlive everyone else on Earth?'

'We're only doing questions,' Katie said.

'That was a question. I genuinely want to know the answer.'

'He's going to get a passport anyway,' Mira said, defensively. 'It's not like we're the only business that he—'

'Since when was Birnam Wood a *business*?'

Amber spoke up from the kitchen. 'You can have a not-for-profit business, you know,' she said. 'Guess what, you can even have a socialist business. Like an independent co-op. That's not a contradiction. *Tony.*'

Tony shut his mouth again, crossed his arms, and resumed staring at his shoes.

'So, in terms of time frame,' Mira said, answering a question that hadn't been asked, 'it would be, like, a few months' commitment at least, starting as soon as possible in time for spring, and obviously it's not like the Korowai Pass is just down the road, so even if people can only commit for weekends and stuff, that's still a lot of driving and a lot of expense. And we'd have to have a big conversation about how to allocate the money – I mean, how much of that should go on transport and on sustaining the crew that goes down there, for example.' She was addressing Shelley again. 'But a hundred thousand bucks,' she said, 'I mean, and that's just the *tip* of it, that's not even the money he might actually commit. And when we're up and running, I mean, we could give ourselves proper salaries potentially, we could go nationwide, this could be really, really big. If we wanted it to be.'

Her look was pleading, and when someone else piped up with a question – would there be accommodation at the farm? – she didn't immediately turn to face the questioner: she was searching Shelley's expression, hopefully, beseechingly . . . and Shelley realised with a lurch that Mira was desperate for her approval. It struck her, with a kind of wonderment, that maybe Mira had been nervous not because of Tony, but because of her.

Mira turned away to answer the question. 'I assumed that we'd be camping,' she said. 'When I was down there, I just lived out of the van.'

'So we might have to sort out a composting toilet or something?'

'Yeah, something like that.'

'How do you know he's good for the money – I mean, the rest of it?'

'What's the conservation project he's involved in?'

'There's no chance you'd be taxed on the money, is there? Down the line?'

'How did you actually meet him?'

'Yeah – how did this even come up?'

Shelley hardly followed the discussion. She kept her eyes on Mira, the feeling of wonderment huge in her chest and in her lungs. Tony asked no more questions and made no further movement at all. When the conversation turned to objections and concerns, there was a loaded pause, everybody clearly expecting that he would be the first to speak. He must have sensed it, for without looking up, he said, very quietly, 'It's blood money.'

This time Mira didn't try to argue with him. 'How?' she said, with barely repressed impatience.

'Drones are weapons of terror,' Tony said, counting on his fingers. 'Mass surveillance is totalitarian and oppressive. The billionaire class undermines solidarity by its very existence; it's fundamentally unsustainable, it's regressive, and it's unjust. Citizenship should not be able to be bought and sold. Protest action should not be able to be *commissioned*. Jesus, do I have to go on? You're literally getting into bed with the enemy, you're violating every principle this group was founded on – am I really the only one who sees that?'

'You've been away for a really long time, Tony.'

'Clearly!'

'I mean, maybe you don't understand how hard it's been for all of us, just trying to keep this going all these years. Trying to break even, every day.' Mira glanced at Shelley, who nodded, automatically at first, and then with conviction.

'I do understand that,' Tony began, but Mira was still going.

'Sure, in an ideal world, would people like Robert Lemoine exist? No. But in an ideal world, we wouldn't need this opportunity. We wouldn't be massively in debt. We wouldn't be struggling every day to get our message out. We wouldn't be in fucking existential crisis mode every single minute of our lives.'

Everybody in the room was nodding now, apart from Tony.

'You talk about violating our principles,' Mira said, 'Tony, we're *living* our principles. The work we all do, the time and labour and effort we put into this, every day – not to mention our own money – *those* are our principles.'

'So the blood-money aspect doesn't bother you at all,' Tony said, raising his voice over all the sounds of sympathy and affirmation.

'I really don't see how it's blood money.'

'Yeah, I guess you wouldn't,' Tony said, disgustedly, 'since you *also* don't see how this is totally fucking selling out.'

Mira was now looking visibly angry. 'Can you calm down just a little bit, please?' she said. 'Look, this isn't him saying, "Hey guys, here's a hundred grand, now forget about Birnam Wood, go off and start a hedge fund." The reason he made this offer in the first place is because he's *interested* in us. He wants to see what's going to happen. He's *curious*. He's *impressed*. Forget who he is for a moment and just think, someone wants to give us money to keep on doing *exactly what we're already doing* – but just at a bigger scale, and with a bigger impact.'

'What *we're* already doing,' Amber said to Tony, indicating the group. '*Us*.'

Mira expelled a breath. 'And by the way,' she said to Tony, 'this is literally the first real shot at solvency that we have ever had. Like, in *all* the years you've been away.'

'I'm confused,' Tony said. 'Am I supposed to be remembering that this guy is so curious and so impressed and so interested, or am I supposed to be forgetting who he is? Don't you see? You're cherry-picking. You clearly know that this totally goes against our principles in every way, so just admit that you're not being *rational* here, this isn't *reason*—'

'Why are you even saying *our principles*,' Amber began, but Mira interrupted her:

'Yes, it's a compromise,' she said, 'yes, there are things about this situation that we're going to have to think about really, really carefully. But there comes a point where refusing to compromise basically means choosing to be ineffectual, and how is *that* not a violation of our principles? Isn't that worse – to throw away everything we've done, all our hard work, just for the sake of being able to tell ourselves that we were *right*? "Oh yeah, Birnam Wood, they don't exist any more, but they sure had good principles!"'

'But where does it stop, though?' Tony said. 'I mean, don't you see, by that logic, there's really nothing—'

'*No*,' Mira said, cutting over him, 'no, sorry, Tony, this isn't about *logic*. This isn't a thought experiment where you can just take my position to its logical extreme, and that's the point of the tutorial. This isn't a philosophy class. This is a real, practical choice that we face as a group, about the problem of how to sustain ourselves moving forward—'

'Hey,' Tony said, 'what happened to direct democracy? I'm raising my objections and concerns—'

'And she's answering them!' Amber said.

'So what do you propose?' Mira said to Tony. 'I give the money back? I take it out of my bank account and physically hand it back to him—'

'Yes,' Tony said.

'—and tell him, actually, sorry, Mr Lemoine, this is *blood money*, in case you didn't know, so whatever we could have spent this on, however much good we might have done with this money – none of that matters?'

'Yes,' Tony said again. He crossed his arms across his chest. 'One hundred per cent. Yes.'

'Fine,' Mira said. 'Duly noted. Any other objections, or shall we vote?'

'The fucking *vote*!' Tony burst out, uncrossing his arms again. 'We should fucking kill him is what we should do, and call it collateral damage, like every civilian killed by fucking drone strikes in Iraq, and Yemen, and Syria—'

'Robert Lemoine is not *personally responsible* for—'

'Absolutely he is. Absolutely he's responsible.'

'Fucking go and kill him then,' Mira said, losing her temper at last. 'I'll give you the address. Go and kill him, since things are so fucking black and white, and you're so pure, and so ideologically consistent all the time, and everyone else is such a hypocrite, and you're so ashamed to even be here. Go.'

'All right,' said Katie. 'I think we—'

'You know you don't have to stay,' Amber put in. 'You're free to leave, you know that. Any time.'

'I think we should move on,' said Katie, firmly.

Tony's expression was cold. 'I move to make this a consensus vote,' he said. 'Not just a majority.'

'Majority *is* consensus,' said Mira. 'If everyone agrees to go along with a majority decision, then you've got consensus. That's how democracy works. If you have ninety-per-cent agreement on an issue, that isn't inherently more democratic than sixty-per-cent agreement. Democracy isn't about everyone voting the exact same way, it's about whether you agree to go along with the outcome of the vote *even if* it turns out you're in the minority. That's consensus.'

'Mira,' Katie said, 'I think he gets it.'

'I'm in,' Shelley said.

'*Really?*' Mira said, turning to her with a look of such naked relief and gratitude that Shelley felt her heart swerve in her chest – but whether from endearment or from shame, she wasn't sure.

'Yeah,' Shelley said, smiling at her. 'A hundred grand, man. Bring it on.'

They took the vote. Tony left the café shortly afterwards, and the following day Mira and Shelley boxed up their belongings, cleaned the flat, placed an advertisement for a sublet, gave their house keys to a friend, and loaded up the van a second time; and as they backed out of the driveway, selected a playlist, and left the city for the open road, five hundred kilometres away, under a vast unsmiling portrait of Queen Elizabeth II, Mr Darvish knelt, and Sir Owen arose.

II

'IS THAT A MEDAL?' SAID MARK MULLOY, TILTING THE photo frame towards the light. 'I thought it was a pacemaker.'

'Let me see,' said Cathy. 'I want to see.'

'They've got different names,' said Lady Darvish from the kitchen. 'The one on his chest is called a breast star, and the one on the sash is called a badge.' She reappeared with a fresh bottle of champagne and handed it to her husband to uncork.

'A breast star?' said Mark. 'Like in blue magazines? To cover up the naughty bits?' He stuck out his chest mincingly and covered his nipples with his fingertips.

'Oh, Mark,' said Cathy, in pretend despair.

But Sir Owen Darvish was grinning. 'Mate,' he said as he peeled the foil from around the mouth of the bottle, 'you need to find a better class of magazine.'

'No one says "blue" anymore,' said Cathy, making a face. 'Do they?'

'Sure they do. Blue movie?'

'No, they say porno. Or just porn.'

Lady Darvish hadn't been following this exchange. 'He wears it on the left pocket,' she went on, 'but if he dies and I survive him, then I get to wear it, only on the right.'

'Excuse me,' said Sir Owen. 'Still alive. Hello.'

She smiled at him across the candle flames. 'I said if.'

'I love knowing little rules like that,' said Cathy.

Mark had thought of another joke. He pointed to the neck-tie Sir Owen was wearing in the photograph. 'And what's that noose around your neck? What's that called?'

Sir Owen popped the cork. They had known the Mulloys forever – their children had grown up together – but it was the wives who had the friendship, and sometimes it fatigued him that he and Mark had no mode of dialogue except to break each other's balls. The women steered the conversation, volunteering information, rescuing the silences, fetching props, as Jill had done, rather embarrassingly, with the framed photograph of his investiture, and making plans to get together down the line; if the men interjected, it was either to grouse about expenses, or to boast about some cunning savings they had made. He was sure it hadn't always been like this – though perhaps it had; perhaps he only noticed it now that they were empty-nesters – but it seemed to him that every dinner party now followed the same pattern: in the early part of the evening, they were all competi-tively thrifty; then, when they were drunk enough, they became competitively lewd.

'Be honest though,' Mark was saying to Jill. 'Tell the truth. Does he think he's better than us now? Has it gone to his head?'

'God knows it's gone to mine,' she replied with a laugh. 'I booked a flight the other day, and in the drop-down menu, you know, where it says your title, I was all, Lady, Lady, Lady – and then it wasn't even an option! I was so ripped off!'

'I heard her say "fuck" from the living room,' Sir Owen said. 'She really shouted. I came running. I thought something ter-rible had happened.'

'Is that how you let him know you're in the mood?' said Mark. He cupped his hands around his mouth. '"Fuck!"'

'Mark, stop it,' said Cathy, flapping both her hands at him.

'No, he's right,' said Lady Darvish, 'it is what I do,' and they all laughed.

When their laughter had subsided Cathy said, 'It's not very equal though. You get to be Lady Darvish, just on the back of—'

'Too right,' said Sir Owen loudly, grinning at his wife as he topped up her champagne flute. 'Make your own bloody lunch.'

'No, but what I mean is, if it's a damehood – like, if I became Dame Cathy, Mark wouldn't be Lord Mulloy.'

'He wouldn't be Sir Mark?'

'No, I don't think he'd be anything.'

'Consort?'

'Escort!'

'Ooh – Escort!'

'Or Gentleman?' said Lady Darvish. 'Gentleman Mulloy?'

'Maybe just Man,' said Mark. He flexed his biceps. 'Man Mulloy.'

'I don't think he'd be anything,' Cathy said again.

There was a pause. Mark's expression had tightened; Cathy either hadn't noticed, or she didn't care. She sipped her champagne, and Mark looked down at his plate and began picking up crumbs with the pad of his finger. The Darvishes exchanged a glance.

Mark was a contractor; he'd had a residential renovation business way back when, and had made good money doing it until he had fallen from a scaffold and broken his back. He'd been in physio for months, and when he was finally well enough to return to work, he discovered that in his absence his business partners had restructured the company – as he described it – to cut him out. After months of bitter disagreements and legal back-and-forth, he had finally given up and struck out on his own, but he'd met with a string of bad luck – a client who refused to pay, a flood, a false insurance claim – and he'd had to shut up shop; now he was working for a big construction firm as a gun for hire and telling anybody who would listen what a rotten hand he had been dealt. Mark was a catastrophiser, but even so, you had to feel a little sorry for the guy. Cathy had confessed to Jill that he was taking medication for depression, and it was clear the pills were making him gain weight. Maybe, thought Sir Owen, they were going through something.

Lady Darvish had already changed the subject. She'd meant to tell them, she said, that she'd driven past their old house in Masterton the other day, and the new owners had knocked out the front fence and built a garage, right smack in front of the lounge window. Had they seen it? Talk about lose a room to gain a room – it was such a shame; it didn't suit the property one bit. Mark muttered something about useless amateurs, and Cathy said, 'Here we go,' because nothing got Mark going like people who thought that they could learn a trade by watching videos on YouTube, and in seconds Mark had perked up again and was telling a story that he'd told the Darvishes before. Jill was good like that: she could always find a way, with perfect plausible deniability, of nursing someone's ego back to health, and as Sir Owen chose another truffle from the chocolate box, he reflected that if there was one thing these dinner parties really did have going for them, it was to remind him that he didn't envy other people's marriages one bit.

His mind wandered over the chores he'd set himself to do that weekend. The Audi needed to be taken in for servicing; the LPG tank on the barbecue was dry; the kitchen knives could do with being sharpened; and he wanted to get up into the eaves and find out why the gutter guard kept popping out. Nothing particularly pressing, but he liked to be kept busy. They had bought the flat in Wellington, where they were now, purely as a pied-à-terre, and the place seemed much smaller now they were living there full-time. Jill had teased him that he'd started breaking things on purpose, just to give himself a reason to get out his tools; it wasn't true, of course, but he had begun to feel a little crazy, having stayed in town so long. He missed the sense of scale at Thorndike, the far shape of the ranges, the open views across the lake; he missed the ancient thrill of being dwarfed by nature, while at the same time feeling his dominion over it.

He hadn't lied when he'd told the local rag that Thorndike was the best place he'd ever lived. When Jill's dad died and they inherited the property, they'd sold their sprawling family home in the Wairarapa and given most of the proceeds to the kids to help with their down payments and, in Rachel's case, to blow on a 1920s-themed vineyard wedding that he still couldn't hear mentioned without rolling his eyes at the expense. The plan had been to subdivide, carving up the fields beside the road, but keeping the original farmhouse, which Jill couldn't bear to part with, for themselves. He'd dragged his heels at first – who didn't feel exhausted by the thought of moving house? – but he reckoned now that he loved the place as much as she did. Before the landslide, he used to fly to Wellington several times a month for work, and to Auckland too, when he couldn't avoid it. Descending into Queenstown Airport and thinking ahead to the long drive home over the ranges had become one of the great joys of his late middle age, suffusing him with a deep sense of presence and arrival; perhaps because of this, the closure of the pass had felt strangely personal to him, and strangely debilitating, as if a crucial pathway in his mind had been peremptorily shut off.

His train of thought must have been following the conversation unconsciously, for he came out of his reverie to hear Cathy say, 'So I guess you'll wait until the pass has opened up again?'

Lady Darvish hesitated, meeting his eye, and in the brief pause before either of them spoke, Mark said, 'That's not going to happen any time soon.' He shook his head, exhaling heavily. 'Look at Kaikōura. Look at the recovery there. And Christchurch, where are we at – what, six years on? Nah.'

'The land will hold its value, though,' Cathy said. 'Those gorgeous views – and so close to the lake. You won't have any trouble selling it.'

'Down the line, maybe,' Mark said. 'But try and get construction crews in there right now. Where are they going to stay? And the supply routes? Where's the nearest town – Omarama? Nah. It's a cul-de-sac. No one's going to touch that job until the pass has opened up again, and that'll be years. Three years, I bet you. Maybe four.'

'At least you're not in any rush,' said Cathy, consolingly.

'Well, you don't have a choice now,' said Mark. 'Do you. Few months later and you'd have been sweet. They'd have sold like hotcakes, and then it'd be someone else's problem. Wouldn't it. Nah, it's just bad luck. Bad bloody luck, mate.'

Sir Owen was growing irritated, and he could tell from the way that his wife was turning her rings around her fingers that she was trying to restrain herself from saying something she'd regret. It had been clear from the moment the Mulloys had got there that Mark begrudged him his good news. Cathy had been all right – a bit insincere maybe, but she'd gone through the motions at least. Mark hadn't said congratulations, hadn't asked any questions, hadn't mentioned that he'd seen the headlines, which of course he had; and he'd put the framed photograph aside, not propped upright, respectfully, back on the shelf, tidy, out of the way, but in the middle of the table, on its back. Sir Owen didn't give a shit, didn't care about the photograph, didn't need congratulations, didn't need anything at all, from anyone, but it pissed him off that Mark was calling him unlucky. There's busting balls, he thought, and there's savouring another man's misfortune.

'I guess it just goes to show,' said Cathy inanely, and Lady Darvish smiled down at her rings.

Because it *wasn't* a misfortune. The farm *had* sold – or was about to, just as soon as the conveyancing was done. They had taken down the listing not because of the landslide, not because of any stroke of bad luck, but because the buyer had made absolute secrecy a condition of the sale. Lemoine had offered double what they'd hoped for – maybe more than double, when you factored in the side project with Autonomo, which Sir Owen had negotiated, rather cleverly, he thought, as part of the sale and purchase agreement, and which had already paid dividends in the form of exposure and PR. The deposit had been paid, so even if the sale fell through – and there was no reason to think it would – even then, they would still be sitting pretty. They were high on the hog, richer than they'd ever been, millionaires a few times over – but they were bound by a non-disclosure agreement not to say so; not, at least, until Lemoine had put the bunker in.

'So you're going to wait, then?' said Mark. 'Park the sub-division, stay up here, just wait it out?'

He was addressing Sir Owen, but it was Lady Darvish who replied. 'Actually,' she said, in a breezy voice, 'we sold it.'

Sir Owen gaped at her in shock. 'Jill!'

'Oh, come on,' she said. 'Who are they going to tell?'

'Jill,' he said again, and shook his head, 'don't.'

'Owen, these are our friends,' she said. 'Our oldest friends. It's not like we're going to the media. This isn't a press release. Relax.'

He recognised that breezy, almost sing-song voice from

when they argued. It sounded innocent, but it meant that she was out for blood.

He put up his hands. 'Well, this wasn't me,' he said. 'Let the record show: I kept my mouth shut. I was a good boy.' But suddenly he felt like laughing, for the truth was, he'd been on the verge of telling them himself. Another crack from Mark was all it would have taken – he knew it. Maybe she did, too.

'They can keep a secret,' said Lady Darvish, still in the same voice. 'I mean, for heaven's sake.'

'Well, this is awfully mysterious,' said Cathy.

Mark was frowning. 'So what's the secret?' he said. 'You sold the farm?'

'All this melodrama,' said Lady Darvish. 'It's ridiculous, really. Yes, we've had an offer. From someone who's seen a few too many James Bond movies in his life, let's put it that way.'

'You can't say who it is?'

Lady Darvish hesitated. 'Maybe we shouldn't.' She looked queryingly at Sir Owen, who just shrugged, masking a smile.

'Developer?' said Mark.

'No, it's for a private dwelling. But he wants the whole tract, all of it, the whole subdivision. He offered on the house as well, didn't he, Owen? But we said absolutely not.'

'Kiwi?' said Mark.

'He's American,' said Lady Darvish. 'A billionaire.'

Cathy gasped.

'I know,' said Lady Darvish. 'A billionaire next door.'

'I hope you absolutely rinsed him then,' said Mark to Sir Owen.

'Oh yes,' he said, enjoying himself, 'we got a very good price.'

'He didn't want a discount because of the landslide?'

'The opposite, actually. It was a drawcard, wasn't it, Jill?'

'That's just what I mean,' she said. 'The James Bond thing.

He wanted somewhere that was easily defended. He actually used those words: "easily defended".'

'Oh go on,' said Cathy. 'Just say his name. We won't know him anyway.'

'Well, you didn't hear it from us,' said Lady Darvish.

'You didn't hear anything from us,' said Sir Owen.

'His name is Robert Lemoine,' said Lady Darvish.

'Robert Lemoine?' said Cathy.

'Remember that helicopter crash in Florida?' said Sir Owen. 'Big story – everyone on board was killed – few years ago? That was his wife.'

'Kazarian,' said Lady Darvish.

'Yeah. Gizela Kazarian. A model. She was only young.'

'Have you heard of him?' said Lady Darvish.

'No,' said Cathy. She looked at Mark, who shook his head very slightly. 'So why is it a secret?' she said. 'I don't understand.'

'Well,' said Lady Darvish, 'I guess when you've got that kind of money—'

'Kidnapping,' said Sir Owen, cutting her off. 'That's what they're all afraid of. And extortion. They're all paranoid as hell. Security is through the roof. Everything they do, everywhere they go, plans, flights, holidays, the most innocent thing, it's all top secret.'

'It's also just ego,' said Lady Darvish. 'I mean, that's what it comes down to. Swearing us to secrecy – that's just to feed his ego. That's the real reason, Owen, you know it is.'

'Yeah,' Sir Owen said, 'all right, Jill, but his wife did *die*.'

'But how can it be a secret?' Cathy said. 'Property – that's public record.'

'Shell company,' Sir Owen said, 'owned by a trust, owned by another company, and back and back and back. You'd have to do a lot of digging if you wanted any names.'

'So he could just be blowing smoke,' Mark said.

Sir Owen smiled. 'No,' he said, 'it's a genuine offer.'

'And he's paid the deposit,' said Lady Darvish. 'He's not going to walk. I mean, he *could*. He wouldn't miss the money.'

'But defended from what?' said Cathy. 'Easily defended from what?'

'It's just a fantasy,' Sir Owen said. 'It's what they all crave, isn't it? These billionaires. They all want it to be just like *Game of Thrones*, or just like, bloody—'

He couldn't think of a second example.

'Well, it's also because of what he wants to build,' said Lady Darvish. 'That's the other reason. Right? He doesn't want anybody to see what he's—'

'They're all doing it,' Sir Owen said, turning to their guests. 'They're all putting them in, these—'

'Have you seen them?' said Lady Darvish, now addressing the Mulloys as well. 'These mega – and they can withstand anything, absolutely anything – they call it submarine function.'

'Any kind of bomb,' Sir Owen said, nodding. 'Flood, fire. Extreme weather. Anything.'

'But inside, they're like hotels, they have everything, all underground, and it's crazy what they – I mean, some of them even have a garage with a car lift, a swimming pool—'

'Gun range—'

'Bowling alley, movie theatre—'

'Crops,' said Sir Owen. 'Under heat lamps. Underground.'

'Yes, and they have their own power and water and air and everything. Totally self-contained. They're kind of incredible actually.'

'Doomsteading,' said Sir Owen. 'That's what they call it. Bunking down for the end of the world. They're doomsteaders, that's the word.'

'And this is just what you can find on Google,' Lady Darvish said. 'I mean, it's not like we've actually – this is just your standard off-the-shelf type of—'

'Bloody high shelf,' said Sir Owen, laughing. 'The cheapest one is three and a half million!'

'Really,' said Lady Darvish, 'you should google them. Google "luxury bunker".'

'"—for the ultra-rich",' Sir Owen added. They were both nodding. 'Look at the floor plans. Even just the floor plans. They'll blow your mind.'

Now it was the Mulloys who exchanged a glance. The look that passed between them lasted barely a second before Mark dropped his eyes back to his plate, but Sir Owen had caught it, and he felt stung; it was the kind of glance that confirmed a shared opinion and promised to revive it on the car ride home. What was it that they had noticed? Something they had seen before, something they'd discussed in private, some pet theory they'd formed and developed over time – or something that surprised them, something new and disappointing, some proof that he and Jill had changed? Embarrassed, he looked across at his wife, but she was draining the last of her champagne.

'I don't know,' said Cathy, 'I guess it just makes me kind of sad.'

There was a little pause.

'It's not like our view is going to change,' said Lady Darvish. 'Best of all worlds really. And it's not like he's going to be living there full-time.'

'How'd he make his money?' said Mark.

'Aviation technology,' said Sir Owen. 'Drones.'

'Wow,' said Cathy.

Sir Owen waited for them to make the connection to Autonomo and his conservation project, but neither of them did. Maybe they hadn't read the news reports about him after all. He felt a little spike of indignation, which he was damned if he was going to let them see; to cover it, he picked up the bottle to make another round of refills, suddenly wishing very much that they would both drink the hell up and go home.

'Anyway,' said Lady Darvish, sitting back, 'it's been a crazy last few months. The whole thing is just ... I mean, with him making this incredible offer, way above, and how it's all played out, and keeping everything a secret, it's all just, he's very ... how would you describe him, Owen?'

'He thinks he's God's gift to all mankind,' said Sir Owen, shortly. 'He's American,' and before Lady Darvish could agree with him, he turned to Cathy and asked about her job.

Sir Owen Darvish had never felt more acutely conscious of his nationality than he did when he was with Lemoine, and in the brief time that he had known the billionaire he had experienced two quite different forms of patriotic feeling. He was intensely proud of their association, and felt he had fulfilled a lofty duty to his country, not just in having courted foreign wealth, but in proving – in being proof – that New Zealanders could hold their own among the world's elite; to have secured not just Lemoine's business, but also his approval and his respect was, in Sir Owen's mind, a matter of high national service, and in fond moments, when he was in the shower, or on the verge of sleep, he expressed deep gratitude towards himself from an imagined common point of view. At the same time, however, he wanted desperately to see the man cut down to size – and in this, he felt even more acutely Kiwi. He was long accustomed to regarding his country as an automatic underdog, as a righteous, plucky, decent, and fundamentally good-natured contender, unfairly disadvantaged, in any instance of unflattering international comparison, by its small population, its short history, and its geographical remoteness from the great power centres of the world. A habit of defensive self-exception masked a deep fear of his nation's insignificance, and a deep anxiety that at the end of the day, poetic justice might not in fact be served, and although this was largely a subconscious attitude, he did register in himself a genuine discomfort whenever New Zealand was held to any international standard that afforded no handicap for scale. All of this lent itself quite naturally to an anti-American sentiment; and as he could not help but view Lemoine's colossal wealth and confidence in metonymic terms, he'd felt, ever since he'd met the man, an almost moral longing to defeat him. When he and Jill were alone, they often spoke about the billionaire in tones that bordered on contempt – a contempt made all the more bitter by the knowledge that Lemoine probably never spoke of *them* to anyone at all.

The Mulloys didn't stay much longer, and later, as he was stacking the dishwasher and Lady Darvish was boxing up the leftovers for lunch, he said, 'So our big news fell a bit flat.'

'Well,' she said, not looking at him, 'it's money, isn't it? People are always weird about other people's money.'

'Yeah,' he said.

She still wasn't looking at him. 'Mark's looking very heavy,' she said. 'He gets such a red face. I wonder if he takes Viagra.'

'What? Why?'

'It's a side effect. The red face. And slightly blurry eyes.'

'Excuse me,' Sir Owen said. 'What do you know about the side effects of Viagra?'

'It's common knowledge.'

'Not to me.'

'Well, now it is,' said Lady Darvish crisply. She swept the crumbs from the breadboard into the bin, and it occurred to Sir Owen that they might be having an argument.

'What's wrong?' he said.

'I'm just so pissed off that I told them,' she said. 'I can't *believe* that I told them.'

'Oh,' he said, relieved. 'I'm sure it's fine.'

'But why would they keep the secret – right? I mean, they don't owe him anything. They haven't signed anything. They're not waiting on conveyancing. What do they care?'

'It's like you said. Who are they going to tell?'

'It's all so silly anyway,' said Lady Darvish, clicking the Tupperware lid shut with unnecessary force. '"Keep the secret." It's so juvenile.'

'They don't know anyone, Jill. Who are their friends? There's us. Who else? No one. It's fine.'

'Usually it's you who has no self-control,' she said.

'I know,' he said. 'Who do you know who takes Viagra?'

'Well, nobody for sure,' she said. 'I just have my suspicions.'

'Oh – your suspicions!'

'Yes. Based on the side effects.'

'Oh – the side effects! I see. Because the *actual* effect – you wouldn't know anything about that.'

'No, big man,' she said, smiling at last, and allowing him to pull her close against him, 'I wouldn't know anything about that.'

They went to bed, and in the morning he took the Audi in for servicing, swapped the LPG tank, cleared out the gutters, and sharpened all their kitchen knives. A former neighbour from their Wairarapa days dropped by in the late afternoon, and in the evening he and Jill went for a swim and a sauna and ordered takeaway Chinese. By Monday morning he had for-gotten all about their dinner party, and he arrived at the head office of Darvish Pest Control in good spirits, eager to begin the week. He found a gift from his secretary on his desk: she had updated his business cards to read 'Sir Owen Darvish, KNZM', and he had just sat down and was turning the card admiringly so that the blue ink turned silver in the light when his computer pinged, and he looked up to see an email in his inbox with the subject heading 'Request for interview re Robert Lemoine.'

He reached out and tapped it open.

'Dear Mr Darvish,' it began, incorrectly, 'I am a freelance journalist currently working on a long-form investigative piece about the practice of "doomsteading" among the super-rich. I would like to ask you a few questions about your association with Robert Lemoine, specifically in relation to your property in Thorndike. Could we arrange a time to speak? This could be off the record if you prefer. Yours sincerely' – and then a name Sir Owen didn't recognise, and a phone number.

Heart sinking, he forwarded it to Lady Darvish with the message, 'What do you make of this?' and then sat rereading the email and anxiously tapping the edge of his business card against the desk. Barely twenty seconds passed before his phone rang. He picked up.

'Shit,' said Lady Darvish.

'What do you think?' he said. 'Was it Mark?'

'No idea,' she said. 'Shit.'

'Pretty damn quick if it was.'

'Shit,' she said again.

'It could have been someone else,' he said. 'One of the lawyers, or a neighbour who saw something . . . or someone we don't even know.'

She made a doubtful noise. 'Could you just ask him?'

'Who – Mark?'

'No, this journalist. Ask him how he found out.'

'You mean actually talk to him?'

'Well, he does say it could be off the record.'

'Yeah, but that doesn't mean anything. That's just something they say. Right? I mean, who is this guy?'

He could hear her tapping keys in the background. 'Hang on,' she said, 'I'm just looking him up. Okay, he's not with a major paper or TV—'

'He said that. He said he was freelance.'

'What's the address – "gallo's humour"? Is that like the name of a magazine?'

'I think it's just a joke.'

'All right, so maybe he's nobody,' Lady Darvish said, still tapping. 'Anthony Gallo . . . Yeah, I'm on his website . . . He looks pretty small-time. I mean, there are some blogs and things, but nothing—'

Sir Owen opened his browser on his own computer. 'Do a search for him and Mark,' he said. 'And him and Cathy, and him and the kids.'

They were quiet for a moment as they both searched.

'No,' said Lady Darvish presently. 'No connection.'

'Try Facebook.'

'I did. He's not on.'

'What if I just forward it to Robert?' said Sir Owen. 'I could forward it right now and say that I have no idea who this guy is or how he found out – which is true.'

'No,' she said. 'Don't. Just in case.'

'What, then? Should I just ignore it? Pretend—?'

'Call him,' said Lady Darvish. 'Just remember the first rule of PR.'

'What's that? Smile?'

'It's also the last rule of PR.'

He made a noise of impatience. 'What is it, Jill?'

'Say nothing.'

*

The morning after the disastrous vote at Birnam Wood, Tony had awoken in his childhood bedroom with an idea for an article so fully formed in his mind that it was almost as though he'd written it already, in his sleep. The piece would be a searing indictment of the super-rich. He would expose, remorselessly, those hypocrites and cynics who publicly denied the catastrophe of climate change while secretly short-selling that very same position and hedging all their bets; the millionaires and billionaires who preached self-reliance while accepting vast handouts in the form of subsidies and easy credit, and who bemoaned red tape while building contractual fortresses to shield their capital from their ex-wives; the tax-dodging economic parasites who treated state treasuries like casinos and dismantled welfare programmes out of spite, who secured immensely lucrative state contracts through illegitimate back channels and grubby, endlessly revolving doors, who eroded civil standards, who demolished social norms, and whose obscene fortunes had been made, *in every case*, on the back of institutions built with public funding, enriched by public patronage, and rightfully belonging to the public, most notably, the fucking *Internet*; the confirmed sociopaths who were literally vampiric with their regular transfusions of younger, healthier blood; the cancerous polluters who consumed more, and burned more, and wasted more than half the world's population put together; the crypto-fascist dirty tricksters who pretended to be populists while defrauding and despising the people, who lied with impunity, who stole with impunity, who murdered with impunity, who invented scapegoats, who incited suicides, who encouraged violence and provoked unrest, and who then retreated into a private sphere of luxury so well insulated from the lives of ordinary people, and so well defended against them, that it basically amounted to a form of secession. Robert Lemoine was one of dozens, maybe

141

hundreds, of super-rich survivalists buying boltholes in New Zealand for the end of days. Tony would investigate them all.

So he told himself as, feeling more energetic than he had in months, he opened up his laptop and began to type; it wasn't until his animosity ran dry several thousand words later that he was able to admit the real spur to his ambition for the essay, which was that he was sitting on a scoop. The offer that Lemoine had made to Mira was a proper story, the stuff of feature articles and documentary podcasts and international attention. It presented Tony with the opportunity of a lifetime, a chance to affirm his principles while also bagging the exclusive that would make his name – for who was better placed to write the thing, after all, than one of the founding members of Birnam Wood; the very member, in fact, who'd composed the Principles of Unity that Lemoine's proposal so egregiously and shamelessly profaned? Tony sat back, feeling his guts clench with excitement. He could go undercover. He could drive down to Thorndike and tell them that he'd changed his mind, that he was sorry, that he wanted in; he could report on the project from the inside; he could keep a journal, take photographs, conduct clandestine interviews perhaps, then stage a dawning disaffection, to give the piece an arc ... He shook his head. It would be too much of a betrayal. It would mean the end of his relationship with Mira, and maybe the end of Birnam Wood. But did he even *have* a relationship with Mira? And hadn't they betrayed themselves already? Hadn't they made their beds already? Hadn't they sold their souls already, by joining forces with Lemoine?

No, Tony thought sternly, in a tone of remonstrance towards himself: he would draw the line at going undercover. These were his friends – at least, they used to be – and he wouldn't openly deceive them. But it was a free country, and there was nothing to stop him from planning a little road trip down to Thorndike, if the mood struck him – just for a bit of camping, maybe; and if he saw something while he was down there, if he stumbled on something, or heard something, or discovered something, well, there would be nothing to stop him from investigating it in the public interest, and reporting – purely in the public interest – what he found.

To have talked himself down from a more drastic course of action gave Tony a pleasing sense of his own judiciousness and clemency, and when he finally traipsed downstairs a little after one o'clock, ravenous, and not yet showered, it was with the calm conviction of a man who had faced a moral test and chosen right.

'You were late in last night,' his mother said, as he opened the refrigerator and peered in. 'Was it a good meeting?'

Tony's equanimity dissolved at once. 'No,' he said curtly. 'It was shit.'

'Oh – but you were so looking forward to it,' said Brenda Gallo, clapping her hand to her heart. 'What happened?'

'I wasn't looking forward to it *that* much,' Tony said. He unscrewed the cap on the milk bottle and sniffed.

His sister Veronica was on her way into the kitchen. 'Do you really have to sniff like that?' she said, making a disgusted face.

'I want to make sure that it's fresh.'

'Just look at the expiry date.'

'It's not always accurate.'

'It is when it's, like, a week away.'

'What's the big deal?' said Tony. 'I'm not breathing *out*. I'm not *blowing my nose* on it.'

Brenda handed him a cereal bowl, anticipating his need for one. 'Well, I'm sorry you had a bad time,' she said.

'Where?' said Veronica.

143

'At Birnam Wood,' said Brenda, and Tony felt the odd twinge of dislocation he always got whenever he heard one of his parents speak the name of the group aloud. 'He had a meeting.'

'When?' said Veronica, frowning.

'Last night. At that nice café – that's owned by that nice girl – what's her name?'

'Can we stop talking about this, please?' said Tony, taking his breakfast to the table.

'Callander,' said his mother. 'Chelsea Callander?'

'Amber,' Tony said, through gritted teeth.

'Yes, Amber. With the chin.'

'I'm really done talking about it,' Tony said. 'Thanks.'

Veronica had started to laugh. 'You are so full of shit,' she said to Tony. 'You are so unbelievably full of shit!'

'Veronica,' said her mother reprovingly.

Tony was scowling at her. 'Why?'

'You weren't at Birnam Wood last night,' she said. 'You were at the Fox and Ferret making out with Rosie Demarney.'

'What?' cried Brenda, clapping her hand to her heart again.

'You are so busted,' said Veronica.

'How the hell do you know that?' said Tony.

'Hamish Loaker saw you. He texted me, and he was like, I'll give you three guesses who your brother is making out with at literally this exact moment.'

'Do you even know how much of a creep you are?' said Tony.

'You went to the Fox and Ferret?' said his mother.

'Want to know who I guessed?' said Veronica.

'No,' said Tony. 'Please don't talk.'

'You told me you had a meeting,' said Brenda.

'I *did* have a meeting,' said Tony. 'And it was shit, and I basic- ally got expelled, so I went to the pub to have a drink, and I saw Rosie Demarney, and I guess I forgot I was living in Stasi fucking East Germany in fucking 1984—'

'Language,' said Brenda. 'What do you mean, expelled?'

'Just forget about it.'

'Fiona Keen,' said Veronica. 'Number one.'

'Veronica, shut up,' said Tony.

'Daisy Willetts.'

'Oh, no,' said Brenda, 'I never liked that girl.'

'Please shut up,' said Tony to Veronica.

She was grinning. 'And Mira Bunting.'

'Will you shut the fuck up?' Tony exploded, pushing his chair back from the table. 'You don't know what the fuck you're talking about, Veronica!'

'Language!' said his mother. 'Tony!'

'I *know*,' said Veronica, holding up both hands. 'I *know*. That's what I'm *saying*. *I couldn't guess*.'

'Why were you even trying to guess?' Tony said. 'What's wrong with you? Are you that sad and desperate? Texting fucking Hamish Loaker? Jesus Christ!'

'Tony!'

'Why are you embarrassed?' said Veronica. 'Rosie's great.'

'I'm not embarrassed,' said Tony. 'I'm creeped out.'

'What do you mean, expelled?' said Brenda again.

'I said I didn't want to talk about it,' Tony said. He picked up his cereal bowl. 'And Mira hates my guts, by the way, so, thanks.'

'Why?' said Veronica.

'What happened?' said his mother. 'Tony?' But he had already slammed the door.

As he ate cross-legged on his unmade bed, he recalled a conversation that he'd had with Mira in the early days of Birnam Wood. They'd been debating the ethics of wealth redistribution, and Mira had told him about an old custom in her father's family, where, if ever there was a piece of cake or a biscuit to be shared between two children, the rule was that one child would get to cut it, and the other child would get to choose. The child with the knife always tried to cut as evenly as possible, to avoid getting stuck with a much smaller portion, and Mira had suggested that this might be a rather good method for ensuring fairness in other contexts too – in designing a national budget, say: what if those who determined where a country's tax revenues came from were from an entirely different political party from those who decided how to spend them? A small-government conservative might feel differently about lowering taxes, and a big-society liberal might feel differently about raising them, if the pot was then handed to the other side to divvy up; and a display of moderation from one party might go a long way to fostering goodwill and compromise in the other. The parties could even switch back and forth, Mira had said, her eyes sparking, to prevent either side from becoming complacent or from calcifying in their respective roles. It could work.

Tony had rebuffed her. What she was describing, he'd told her, was essentially just a variation on Rawls, the arch-liberal arch-enemy of the *actually* authentic left. Didn't she call herself a radical? Because he was surprised, and frankly a little disappointed, that she saw any attraction at all in such a moderate and – let's face it – out-of-date position. But to his astonishment, Mira hadn't been at all chastised. She'd shot back that anyone could drop a name, but this idea was *hers*; she'd come up with it on her own, having never heard of Rawls, and having never felt she needed to. How could an original idea be out of date? That was a contradiction in terms, a category error. And as for being moderate – sure, he meant it as an insult, but didn't the entire project of left-wing politics depend on people being willing, at some level, to share, and wasn't sharing basically just moderation by another name – and anyway, between the two of them, wasn't *he* the one who was more guilty of propping up the status quo by shooting her ideas down and dropping names of dead philosophers as if that was in any way a legitimate response to *anything* any more – and why was it that people on the left were always talking about who was *actually* on the left – wasn't *that* kind of out of date? And if it wasn't, then maybe it should be, because it was pretty bloody off-putting to be treated like a double-dealer all the time. Tony had been slightly dazed by the force of these counterarguments, and had taken refuge in a lengthy explanation. He could still see in his mind's eye the way she'd listened, scowling slightly, looking at each of his eyes, and then at his mouth, and then at his eyes again, as he'd described the concept of the veil of ignorance to her – and then, when he was done, he could still see her grinning at him, and shaking her head, and saying no, that he was wrong, that there was no comparison with Rawls at all, because her idea was so much better.

Tony wondered why he hadn't kissed her right then, sitting in the box window of the library stairwell, he cross-legged, as he was now, she with her knees drawn up to her chest. He could still see her forearms resting on her knees, hands cupping elbows, close enough to touch, her brown leather lace-ups, her bobby socks, the rolled-up hem of her jeans. Why hadn't he kissed her? Why hadn't he slipped his hand round her ankle, or reached out to stroke her forearm, or – most daringly – tucked a strand of her hair behind her ear? Why hadn't he just leaned in and kissed her, as he'd so desperately wanted to, as he'd imagined doing ever since? He'd kissed Rosie Demarney. It was easy. It was almost unnerving how easy it had been. 'I really want to kiss you,' he'd said, and she'd smiled and said, 'Do it, then,' and so he had. Tony imagined Mira saying, 'Do it, then.' He imagined leaning in across the window seat, imagined spreading his hand on the small of her back and pulling her towards him. 'Do it, then,' said Mira in his mind, and Tony drank the last of the milk out of the bowl, set it down on his bedside table, and stood up.

In all the days and weeks that had passed since Tony's evening with Shelley at the bar, it had never occurred to him to wonder if she had relayed to Mira the news that he'd come home. He was certain that they told each other everything – he had first-hand proof on that point, after all – and as he'd waited every day for Mira's call, becoming more and more depressed, and more and more despairing, he'd told himself firmly, and repeatedly, that the ball was in her court, for if she felt any unease at all about the circumstances under which they'd slept together – and he'd racked his memory; he was positive that *she'd* been the instigator, that he'd done *nothing* dishonourable, that it had been *her* decision, that *she'd* come on to *him* – he was determined not to make the situation any worse by hounding her. When three weeks passed and Mira hadn't called, he'd had to conclude that she was sending him a message, and while he'd known he ought to let the matter drop, he'd also known that he couldn't rest until he'd seen her. He'd been debating showing up at the hui alone and unannounced when he'd seen that Finn Koefoed-Nielsen had RSVP'd on Shelley's email chain, and on a sudden impulse, he'd called him up to invite him for a beer beforehand. He'd intended – it seemed so stupid now – to make it seem as though one thing had simply led to another: since he'd been out with Fink already, he'd imagined telling Mira with a shrug, he'd figured what the hell – for old time's sake – he'd tag along.

It had been a bad idea. Finn had been plainly baffled by the invitation, since he and Tony had never been that close, and Tony had been too nervous and distracted to care about trying to make the conversation flow; they had passed a stilted hour together, and he'd arrived at the hui already irritated and defensive, his stomach sour from two pints of beer, only to find that Mira wasn't even there. He had taken her lateness, irrationally, as a further sign of her cold feelings towards him; and although it hadn't escaped his notice that she had been patently astonished to see him when she'd finally arrived, he had been so worked up by that point that he'd interpreted her shock as mere amazement that he'd had the temerity to show his face at Birnam Wood at all. Even now, he had no doubt that she and Shelley were united. Shelley could have hardly acted faster to cast her vote in Mira's favour, and he'd caught the look of sympathy and gratitude that had passed between them afterwards, which he'd experienced almost as a personal rebuke. He'd left the hui feeling comprehensively humiliated, and when Rosie Demarney tapped him on the shoulder in the queue to the bar at the Fox and Ferret an hour later, he'd actually groaned: he was really sorry, he'd told her, but seriously, all he wanted was to have a drink alone. It was a bit depressing, Tony thought now, to realise that he'd never had more luck, romantically speaking, than when he'd felt that he had hit rock bottom; he was never more attractive, apparently, than when he knew that he had nothing whatsoever left to lose.

There was a knock on his bedroom door as he was crossing to it, and he opened it to find Veronica holding out a mug of coffee.

'Sorry,' she said. 'I was just giving you shit.'

Tony was touched. 'Thanks,' he said, taking the mug.

'Mum said you were really looking forward to the meeting.'

'You can't say "meeting" any more,' Tony said darkly. 'You have to say "hui".'

'Is that why you got thrown out?'

He exhaled and shook his head. 'Nah. Just people being dicks.'

'People meaning Mira?'

'Aagh,' said Tony, lifting his shoulders to his ears. 'Doesn't matter. It was dumb.'

'How can they throw you out, anyway?' said Veronica. 'Isn't that, like, against the whole—'

'Exactly,' said Tony.

'I mean, did nobody point that out?'

'Clearly you should have been there.'

'Clearly.' She shook her head in mock dismay and turned to go.

'Hey Ronica,' he said suddenly.

'Yeah,' she said, her hand on the banister.

'Can I borrow your car to drive to Thorndike?'

'Thorndike?' she said. 'Why?'

Some instinct told him not to mention the connection between Lemoine and Birnam Wood. Instead, he told her that he was working on a piece of long-form investigative journalism and wanted to pursue a lead: the piece was about super-rich survivalists, he said, and he'd recently learned about somebody in Thorndike who might be of value to him as a source. Veronica was much more impressed by this than he'd expected, and said immediately that of course he could borrow her car – for as long as he wanted it; she hardly ever drove it anyway. They arranged that he would leave that coming Friday, and after he had drunk the coffee, done his daily push-ups, showered, and dressed, Tony sat down again at his laptop with restored confidence and energy. He began bookmarking articles and laying out parameters for his research, and when Rosie Demarney texted him a few hours later, saying how much fun she'd had last night, he texted back to say, sincerely, that it was the best thing that had happened to him since coming home. He added that he'd love to see her again before he left for Thorndike, and she replied with three emojis, a party hat, a jazz hands, and a blush.

They went out to dinner on Thursday night. Like Veronica, Rosie seemed impressed when he described his general intentions for his essay, but Tony detected a little pause, a touch of incredulity, or pity maybe, when he admitted that the piece hadn't been commissioned, and that in all likelihood he wasn't getting paid; and even though she smiled and said warmly that she couldn't wait to read it as soon as it was done, he couldn't quite shake the sense that she had formed an opinion about him that she doubted she was going to have to change. The evening passed pleasantly enough – she was a solicitor in family law, played indoor netball, liked Marvel movies, loved *Battlestar Galactica*, and had recently holidayed in Vietnam – but when she expressed remorse that he was heading down to Thorndike the next morning – it was such bad timing, she said; how long did he think that he'd be gone? – he realised, with total, guilty clarity, that it was simply never going to work between them. He pushed down the feeling, promising to keep in touch, and, of course, to let her know the moment he returned. They kissed again outside the restaurant, and he declined her offer of a lift by saying that he'd parked two streets away. He waved her off, his smile fading as her scarlet Ford Fiesta rounded the corner and disappeared from sight, and on the bus home he put his forehead against the seat in front of him and stared down at the pebbled linoleum between his knees until he could tell from the ambient noise around him that the bus was drawing close to the set of traffic lights that marked his last chance before his stop to ring the bell. Walking home past familiar high fences, and familiar gated driveways, and familiar large suburban houses set well back from the road, he felt his phone buzz in his pocket; thinking it was probably Rosie, he didn't check it until after he'd got back to his parents' house and gone to bed. But it wasn't Rosie: it was a notification that a new document had been added to the shared folder 'Birnam Wood' by the user Shelley Noakes. Tony turned his bedside light back on. He sat up in bed, opened the file, and began to read.

The file was headed 'Schedule – 1606 Korowai Pass Rd', and it comprised a roster of tasks to be completed, a planting programme and crop inventory, a rolling budget, a wish list of supplies, and a hand-drawn map of the farm. Tony scrutinised it carefully. He could see an airstrip near the top of the property which was marked 'keep clear', but there was no reference to a bunker, and no indication of a potential building site, and so, after downloading a copy of the file for his records, he opened his browser and called up the local council's database. Lemoine would need resource consent to build, and if Tony was in luck, then the plans for the bunker might be accessible online.

He wasted over an hour in fruitless navigation before he found any planning permission associated with 1606 Korowai Pass Road, but it was only a subdivision permit, and it had been granted to Owen and Jill Darvish in November of the previous year. They must be the people who had sold Lemoine the farm. Searching their names, Tony was directed to the glut of news articles about the recent knighthood – establishment incarnate, he thought, cynically – and from there, to the news of the partnership between Autonomo and Darvish Pest Control, which aroused his cynicism even further. He could not see how a tech giant like Autonomo could possibly benefit from such a small-time connection, and he severely doubted the conservationist credentials of any company whose brand name ended on the word 'control'; he was certain that all signs pointed to a quid pro quo, and he scowled, as Mira had, to learn that the orange-fronted parakeet was – allegedly – Owen Darvish's favourite native bird. In fact, Tony discovered, the Autonomo project was unlikely to affect the fate of this critically endangered species in the slightest, since the project was set to launch in the North Island, and the orange-fronted parakeet (like Mira, he'd had to google it) was found only in a few remaining valleys in the South – including, he read, the Korowai Basin, which lay just behind the Darvishes' – and now Lemoine's – back fence.

He opened another tab on his browser to try to find out when exactly the sale of the farm had taken place, and how much, exactly, Lemoine had paid; but to his surprise his search returned no results. The real estate listing for 1606 Korowai Pass Road had been taken down, and he could find nothing that connected Robert Lemoine with Thorndike – or, for that matter, with Owen or Jill Darvish – in any way. Combing back through the news articles about the knighthood, he noticed that although Owen Darvish had mentioned Autonomo several times in the interviews he'd given to the press, he had never actually named Lemoine. Tony was starting to feel excited. Mira had said that Lemoine had bought the farm off-radar, but if the sale wasn't public knowledge yet, then he was looking at yet another scoop – a particularly damning one, he thought, for the decorated Owen Darvish, Knight Companion of the New Zealand Order of Merit, who played the part of Mr Fully Kiwi, Mr 100% Pure, Mr Yeah Nah She'll Be Right with such aplomb. Tony called up the land records database and submitted a request to view the title certificate to the property, paying a five-dollar fee for the privilege, and when he finally turned off his light again a little after 2 a.m., the last thing that crossed his mind before he drifted off to sleep was a quotation that he'd heard someplace, whose attribution he'd forgotten – that only something that a person didn't want to see in print was news, and everything else was advertising.

He arrived in Thorndike late the next day and parked in the long-term car park next to the visitor's centre, which was empty save for one other car. He had brought with him his reporter's notebook and a Dictaphone, but before he made his presence known among the locals, he wanted to conduct a few days' observation of Birnam Wood, to learn their daily patterns and – if possible – to try to get a sense of Lemoine's. Shelley's document hadn't mentioned the billionaire at all, and although Mira had said at the hui that Lemoine used the airstrip frequently, she'd seemed to suggest that the farm was his destination, not his point of departure, which would imply that he was living somewhere else. Despite exhaustive online searching, Tony hadn't managed to discover even the most basic details about Lemoine's present circumstances; clearly, the man was adept at shielding his information from public view, and the first task that Tony had set himself – having taken inspiration from Shelley's impressively well-ordered schedule – was to find out the tail number of his plane. With this, he could reconstruct Lemoine's past movements using open sources, and possibly anticipate his future movements, too.

He opened the hatchback of Veronica's car and sat down on the rear bumper to change his sneakers for his tramping boots. He was stiff from the long drive, and he had the kind of dull headache where he could feel the backs of his eyeballs in their sockets and the sides of his brain against his temples; he needed to get moving, and as he laced his boots, he squinted up at the lowering cloud and reckoned that he just had time to make camp before nightfall. 'Camp' was just his backpack and a bivvy bag, but there were few things Tony enjoyed more than sleeping out alone under the stars, especially in winter, and even – he felt the first few drops on his shoulders – when it rained.

He had done a bit of tramping in the Korowai ranges as an undergraduate, and he knew the area around Thorndike moderately well. His plan was to head into the national park on the track that led up to the Madrigal Hut, below the Madrigal Glacier, where he'd spent a night on a climbing expedition once before. The hut was a good six-hour tramp south of the pass, but he remembered that for the first hour or so, the track traversed the ridge above the township, and he figured that if he left the trail before it reached the edge of the Korowai Basin and cut west, then he could bush-bash down the hill and approach the Darvish property from the rear. Although the national park land there was mostly forested, above the tree line he could recollect wide, open views over the township and across the lake; he was sure that he could gain a good vantage point over the farm from somewhere higher up the mountainside, and to that end, he'd stopped at an outdoor store on his drive south and purchased a pair of binoculars, amusing himself with the imagined cover story, should he need one, that he was a birder looking for the famous orange-fronted parakeet that he'd heard spoken of so glowingly in recent news.

He shouldered his backpack and set off into the national park, feeling his headache dissipate as the track climbed sharply up out of the valley to meet the ridge. Sheets of grey cloud were gusting down from the pass, cutting off the view beneath him, and seeming to arrest the twilight as the colours leached from green and blue to shades of grey. It was now raining steadily, and by the time he came down off the ridge and began looking for a sheltered place among the trees to spread his bivvy bag, he was soaked to the skin, and the light was almost gone. He could only guess at his precise location; before he'd left the car park, he had measured the distance on the map between the visitor centre and the farm's front gate, divided this by his average walking speed, and added an extra twenty minutes to ascend the hill, and if his calculations were more or less correct, then he was somewhere on the slope above the airstrip, north and a little east of where the road began to climb towards the pass.

He continued down the mountain and presently came upon a slab of granite protruding from a mossy bank that offered some protection from the weather. As campsites went, he thought, he'd seen worse. He shucked off his backpack, shook out his bivvy bag, and strapped his head torch over his balaclava. The last of the daylight faded into dark as he screwed his stove together and set a pan of water over the flame, and all at once he realised, blinking, that the rain had stopped: the noise that he could hear was the endless patter of water dripping off leaves and branches, and behind it, a distant roar that must be the wind in the valley behind him – it couldn't be a river or a waterfall, because he knew that there was nothing of the kind nearby.

At Birnam Wood they would have welcomed the rain. He imagined them spreading tarpaulins in the fields, weighting the middles and staking down the corners so the canvas wouldn't fly away, perhaps setting out rainwater butts under drainpipes, and fashioning catchments in run-off ditches beside the road, and then piling back into Mira's van, drenched and laughing, to drive back to the shearing shed where they'd set up their base of operations; he imagined them stringing a clothesline among the ancient wooden chutes to hang their wet jackets up to dry, and he conjured in his mind a lofted space beyond the chutes where, in a happy hubbub of cross-pollinating chatter, they would all gather round to help prepare the evening meal, chopping vegetables for curry, and washing rice, and rolling out chapatis with an empty wine bottle dusted with flour, and someone would be strumming a guitar, or reading out *Listener* crossword clues, or narrating the gist of some recent article that had done the rounds online, and someone would be making an inventory of their progress to date, or delegating tasks for the coming day, or labelling seed sets for planting, and someone would be knitting, and someone would be poking irrigation holes in the bottoms of empty yogurt pots with a heated needle, and from time to time a snatch of melody from the guitar would cut through their conversation and they would all sing along in unison for a phrase or two – and then dissolve into embarrassed laughter, for at Birnam Wood such instances of unprompted and un-affected concord were always followed, Tony remembered, by a discomfiting self-consciousness, for a moment everybody feel-ing, squeamishly, just a tiny bit like members of a cult.

The water was boiling. He cut the flame and poured half the saucepan into a pouch of dehydrated rice and beans, which he sealed and set aside to stew. With the rest he made tea, squeez-ing a ribbon of sweetened condensed milk over the tea bag and stirring it with the spoon end of his all-purpose silicone utensil until the milk had dissolved and the liquid was slick and faintly iridescent in the smoky blue light of his torch. The tea bag split open when he pressed it against the side of the pot to wring out the last of the flavour, and he was obliged to spend the next few minutes fishing out tea leaves – a task he found so enjoy-ably absorbing that he consciously stilled his body and slowed his breath in order to focus on it, willing himself to move only his wrist, and then only his fingertips, as he chased the little specks of darkness around the toffee-coloured surface of the liquid with the tip of his spoon.

He ate his dinner out of the pouch, drank the tea, then peeled off his sodden clothes and exchanged them for a fleece and a pair of woollen leggings, rubbing his arms and legs vigorously to warm up. His phone was in a ziplock bag at the bottom of his backpack, powered off; he doubted that he'd get a signal, but when he turned it on to check, he was surprised to see four bars of service. A text message was waiting from Rosie, asking if he had arrived okay, and if he was having a good time. He typed out a bland reply, sent it off, and then turned off the phone again before she had a chance to respond, feeling oddly a little disappointed that despite his intrepid circumstances he still had ready access to the Web. After brushing his teeth and spitting the foam into the undergrowth, he climbed into his bivvy bag, turned off his head torch, and fussed for a minute with a spare jersey, which he folded and refolded and then tucked beneath his head as a pillow. It couldn't be later than nine, and after a couple of months living with his parents, he'd become practically nocturnal; but the dark was so total, and the woodsy smell of the rain so cosy and confidential seeming, that as soon as he'd stretched out in his sleeping bag and scootched to find a comfortable position on the forest floor, he fell asleep.

The bush was alive with birdsong when he woke the next morning: he could hear bellbirds, fantails, grey warblers, and others whose calls he didn't know, chiming and trilling and cheeping and fluting and crying in a shifting, enveloping cloak of sound – magnified, he thought, by the heavy skies, which hung low and overcast over the treetops, filling the valley and shearing off the peaks on either side. He lay in his sleeping bag for almost twenty minutes, smiling up at the canopy and savouring the sounds, before he got up and boiled another pot of water for his breakfast – an instant porridge mix, which again he ate directly from the pouch, and a cup of instant coffee with the rest of the hot water. He relieved himself behind the granite slab, brushed his teeth again, and then packed up his things, tying the arms of his jacket around his backpack to dry. The cloud was starting to lift as he set off down the hill to find a place where he could get his bearings.

Soon he reached the base of a stony outcrop that seemed as if it might afford a view. He climbed up, and when he looked out across the valley, he saw at once that he'd overshot the farm. His heart sank. He was now well to the south of the barricade, almost at the site of the landslide, in fact, judging from the height and shape of the ranges around him; the valley had narrowed as it began to climb towards the pass. He must have walked faster than he'd thought the previous night, perhaps because of his headache and the encroaching twilight – or maybe he'd overestimated the distance from the visitor centre, which he'd measured by eye, using the scale at the bottom of the map and the side of his finger. Tony felt chilled by his mistake, and suddenly very much alone. He was foolish not to have shared his plans with anyone. Even his family didn't know exactly where he was; he'd told them Thorndike, but he hadn't mentioned that he was heading to the backcountry, and he hadn't specified how long he'd be away; it might be weeks before they'd miss him. At the very least, he should have filled out an intentions form at the visitor centre, so that Search & Rescue would know where to start looking for him in the event that he didn't return to the car. He thought about getting out his phone again to send a message to his mother, but the idea embarrassed him even more. Instead, chastened, he set off to the north again, now paying close attention to his surroundings, and stepping with exaggerated care.

He knew that it hadn't been exactly necessary to bivouac – he'd passed a perfectly serviceable Department of Conservation campsite on his way into town – and he could admit that his plan to bush-bash down the hill had been possibly a touch extreme; perhaps, he reflected now, he'd been trying to atone somehow for what had happened at the hui, to prove to himself that he was not just yet another Marxist intellectual cliché, not just yet another armchair critic with soft hands and smug opinions, who theorised about the working class while never having done a day of drudge work in his life. Tony was very proud to be well read, and had often railed against the defensive anti-intellectualism that defined his country's culture, but he had nevertheless recognised in himself, at times, a deep desire to perform a kind of excessive rugged practicality in compensation for his bookishness, submitting himself to physical privations, testing his strength and his endurance well beyond what was called for, and devising circuitous home-made solutions to problems that could be solved much more easily, and often more cheaply, by paying someone else to fix them. It hadn't been until he'd gone abroad that he'd been able to identify this trait as itself peculiarly Kiwi, reflecting a broader attitude held among his countrymen that to do a thing with effort was always more respectable than to have it done with ease; inconvenience, in New Zealand, tended to be treated as a test of character, such that it was a point of national pride to be able to withstand discomfort or poor service without giving in to the temptation to complain. Tony had never considered himself to be particularly patriotic – he did not accept, in fact, that there was any material difference between the patriot and the nationalist – and so he had been surprised, and even a little ashamed, to realise just how strongly his nationality had shaped him, not just in his actions and his expectations, but in his political convictions, which he would have liked to think had been formed through his powers of reason and his intellect alone. His loathing of the super-rich, for example, was on some level not a political stance at all, but merely a very Kiwi expression of disdain – disdain for those who lived in childish comfort, and who delegated labour, and – to put it plainly – who simply weren't hardcore enough to do without; their luxuries had not been earned or exerted for, but had been merely purchased, and *that* was something any fool could do.

Stepping over a fallen tree trunk, he saw, in the ferny under-growth in front of him, an unsupported chain-link fence, the temporary kind used at music festivals, but here plainly long untouched. It ran up and down the mountain, the wired sections curving away from him, encircling what seemed like several acres up ahead. Affixed to one of the sections was a lichen-spotted plastic sign that read 'RESEARCH IN PROGRESS – PLEASE KEEP OUT'. Tony peered through the fence with mild curios-ity, but he could see no clues as to what kind of research was being carried out beyond it. Maybe it was something seismo-logical, he thought; the landslide had been triggered by a spate of earthquakes, after all.

He diverted his course uphill, keeping the fence on his left, and presently came over a little rise to find what he recognised as a trailer-mounted phone mast, still attached to the truck that had evidently hauled it there; a faint vehicle track led away through the bush and out of sight. A second trailer, a mobile home, was parked behind it. The door of the mobile home was open, and sitting on the step, smoking a cigarette, was a burly man in his forties, wearing a woollen beanie and a green zipped-up fleece. He saw Tony and stood up at once.

'Kia ora,' said Tony.

'Hi there,' said the man with trepidation. He flicked his cigarette away.

There was a little pause, each evidently waiting for the other to speak first. Then Tony nodded at the truck. 'Bit of a job driving that up here.'

'Yeah,' said the man.

'No four-wheel drive, I'm guessing?'

'Yeah, not so much.' His accent was either American or Canadian; Tony could never tell the difference, and never asked, in case he got it wrong.

'You must really need the signal,' he said.

The man glanced towards the fence. 'I guess somebody does.'

'The research there,' Tony said, after another little pause, 'is it – ?'

'Yeah, geophysics,' said the man. 'Radiometric survey.'

'Oh right,' Tony said. 'What does that involve?'

'Don't ask me,' said the man. 'I'm just security.'

'But like – radiation? Like radioactive?'

Tony knew that granite contained radioactive elements – he recalled a chemistry class in high school where he'd set off a Geiger counter by waving it over a chunk of granite, a banana, and a vintage watch with hands that glowed in the dark – and there was plenty of granite around the Korowai Pass; he'd spent the night beside a giant slab of it. He looked at the fence with new interest.

But the man only shrugged. 'Like I said.'

'Huh,' said Tony. 'You'd think they would have told you.'

'Yeah, well,' said the man, and shrugged again.

'How long have you been over here?' Tony asked, and then added, to be friendly, 'For your sins?'

'Long enough,' said the man. 'What about you?'

'Yeah, just a bit of tramping,' Tony said. 'Trying to shake out the cobwebs.'

'Right.'

'At least it's not raining, right?'

'Yeah,' said the man. 'Right.'

Tony couldn't think of anything else to say. 'Well, have a good one.'

'You too,' said the man.

They exchanged a nod. Tony turned, and had just set off again when something caught his eye: on the roof of the mobile phone site, clinging to the base of the latticed signal tower, was a small, slender parakeet, almost sea green in colour, with a yellow crown and a distinctive orange band above its beak. Tony stopped in his tracks. 'Holy shit,' he said, turning back to point the creature out – and then he froze, for in the few seconds that his back had been turned, the man had silently unzipped his fleece, and he was now putting his right hand into his left armpit, as if reaching for a gun.

They stared at each other.

'Yeah?' the man said, without moving.

Tony's mind had gone blank. His heart was pounding.

'What?' said the man, still not moving.

'Parakeet,' Tony said. He pointed at the bird. 'Super endangered. There's only, like, sixty of them left.'

The man said nothing. His eyes moved to the bird. It cocked its head, hopped off the signal tower, and ducked out of sight. When it was gone, he looked again at Tony. His hand was still in his armpit. His eyes were narrowed.

'Pretty lucky,' Tony said. 'I mean – jeez. What are the chances?'

The man nodded very slightly, his eyes still narrowed.

'Well . . . see ya,' Tony said, and turned away. After a few steps he looked back and saw that the man had taken out a pack of cigarettes. He shook one out and put it in the corner of his mouth, and then returned the pack to his breast pocket and zipped up his fleece again. He was dipping his face into his lighter as Tony disappeared into the trees.

Had he just imagined it? A flash of brown leather inside

the guy's fleece, a suggestion of a holster, a certain stiffness to his posture, shoulder blades drawn together, elbows held apart, chest thrust forward, the weight of something solid knocking at his ribs? The harder Tony tried to picture it, the more ludicrous it seemed. After all, he told himself, the biggest predator in Korowai was probably a ferret. There might be a few deer in the park, or pigs, but there was no rabies in New Zealand, nothing that might make those animals in any way a threat, and Tony had never heard of anybody going hunting with a handgun – let alone one that was concealed. And anyway, what kind of research, in the middle of a national park, could possibly merit *armed security* – in a country where even the police only carried guns in special circumstances?

Of course he'd only imagined it. He must have done. This was New Zealand, for heaven's sake; people didn't carry guns. He'd just spooked himself. Feeling foolish, Tony quickened his pace and made a studied effort to think of something else, forcing his mind back to the orange-fronted parakeet, and then to one of his school friends growing up, Nick Wiley, who'd had a budgie named Luigi, and then to a summer party at the Wileys' house, playing sardines by torchlight in the garden, and then to the generator torch with a pump handle that he'd loved to play with as a boy, squeezing the beam of light to whirring brightness and then watching it fade as the mechanism wound down under the heel of his hand. He came over a bank of ferns and looked up to see that he'd arrived at a stock-wire fence that he guessed must mark the upper boundary of the Darvish property. He proceeded along it, stepping as quietly as possible and peering down through the trees below him, and soon he spied a forlorn-looking windsock at the end of a wide, level terrace that could only be the airstrip. He came to a halt, disappointed: the plane wasn't there.

It was Saturday, and Tony knew from Shelley's document that a carload of Birnam Wood members had driven down the previous night to spend the weekend working at the farm. The principal planting sites were all near the bottom of the property, in the livestock pens that adjoined the shearing sheds, along the northern fence line, and in some patches of scrub in the paddocks just above the house. They would probably confine themselves to those areas, and the farm was large enough, and forested enough, to offer plenty of cover if he wanted to explore . . . But it would be foolish to venture out on a day when their numbers were expanded, Tony thought, and he didn't want to risk being spotted before his investigation had even properly begun.

He spent the rest of the day in reconnaissance, traversing the hillside above the fence, scouting on bluffs and boulders, and tramping back up above the treeline to triangulate his position between the ranges and the lake. He found an elevated spot that offered a decent view over the shearing shed, but although he could just make out the faces of the crew using his binoculars, it was hard to tell what exactly they were doing as they moved among the livestock pens, bending and straightening and hauling things in and out of view, and Tony found he got a headache if he stared through the binoculars too long. He camped near the airstrip that night, and on Sunday morning he returned to the track along the ridgeline and built a cairn to mark the turn-off, in case he ever approached from there in heavy cloud again.

When the cairn was built, he ate a cold lunch of apples and cheese in a sheltered spot below the ridge, and washed it down with the last of the water he'd brought with him from the car. He was just considering where the nearest place to refill his water bottles might be when a light aircraft whined directly overhead. The plane was flying low, clearly coming in to land;

it banked over the Darvish farm and then dropped out of sight behind the trees. Tony stuffed his water bottle back in his bag and hurried after it. He arrived at the fence about fifteen minutes later, panting slightly, to see that the plane had landed – its propellers were still – and the pilot was nowhere to be seen; but Tony was elated, for the registration mark on the tail was clearly legible from where he stood. He took his fountain pen out of his pocket and wrote the letters on the back of his hand. 'Zulu Kilo Charlie Uniform Oscar,' he murmured aloud with some relish, for he had learned the phonetic alphabet at school, and he always enjoyed having a reason to recall it.

He watched the plane for almost an hour without seeing any movement, and briefly considered climbing over the fence to get a closer look; but he was rewarded for his patience when a man in a dark tracksuit finally strolled up the hill and into view. It could only be Lemoine; at his side was Mira, and they appeared to be deep in conversation. Lemoine was gesturing around him at the hillside, and Mira was nodding, and gesturing as well; after ten minutes or so, they seemed to reach an agreement, for they shook hands and said goodbye. Mira headed back downhill and Lemoine returned to the plane and climbed back into the cockpit, and Tony made a gun out of his index finger and his thumb, aimed it at the billionaire, and pulled the trigger. 'Pow,' he whispered. The propellers juddered to life. Lemoine reversed the aircraft in a neat half-circle until it was facing south, and then he opened the throttle, roared down the airstrip, and took off.

Tony hadn't stayed to see him go. By the time the plane had vanished over the peaks of the Korowai ranges, he was on his way back to Thorndike to refill his water bottles, retrieve his laptop from the boot of Veronica's car, and pursue the first proper lead – he whispered it – of his career.

Back in the visitor centre car park, he plugged a USB WiFi adapter into his laptop and sat in the passenger seat of Veronica's car exploring the website of New Zealand's Civil Aviation Authority for almost two hours. He had just discovered that the plane Lemoine was flying, registration mark ZK-CUO, was owned by an aero club near Queenstown when a notification popped up to say that his battery was about to die. The visitor centre had now closed, but he could see a chip shop on the highway frontage that appeared to be still open, and he went in to ask if the proprietor would allow him to recharge his laptop behind the counter if he ordered a meal. A fee of two dollars was agreed for the use of the power, and Tony had handed over his device and was counting out cash for a burger and a battered hot dog when the guy said, abruptly, 'Plane spotter?'

It took Tony a moment to realise that the guy had seen the registration mark written on the back of his hand. 'Oh,' he said. 'No, actually, I'm more interested in the pilot than the plane. Robert Lemoine?'

The guy made a blank face.

'Billionaire?' said Tony. 'American? I'm working on a story about him.'

'Oh yeah?'

'Yeah,' Tony said, handing over the money. 'Actually, I was going to ask if you'd seen him.'

The guy shrugged. 'I wouldn't know.'

'Small seaplane, in and out of the airstrip, up by the pass?'

'You mean the Taranow place?'

'Darvish, I think?'

But the guy was nodding. 'Yeah,' he said. 'Jill Taranow. Back in the day. Her dad.'

'Oh right,' said Tony, remembering the Darvishes had inherited the property. 'Yeah.'

'They were going to subdivide.'

'That's the one.'

'Couldn't do it,' the guy said. 'Took it off the market. No takers.'

'No, I thought they sold it,' said Tony. 'Didn't they?'

'No, mate. Not after the road closed. Couldn't get a price.'

'Huh,' said Tony, with interest. 'My mistake.' He watched as the guy peeled waxed paper from a pre-made burger patty and slapped it on the grill. 'So you haven't noticed a plane?'

'There's always planes,' said the guy. 'They're up there all the time, the aero club. Well – used to be.'

'Right,' said Tony, not quite following. 'Are you a plane spotter yourself, then?'

'No, mate,' the guy said again. He put Tony's hot dog into the fry basket and dunked it into the vat, and then added, 'He was, though. Jill's old man.'

'You mean Taranow?'

'Yeah. The airstrip, Search & Rescue, that was all him. That's not Darvish. *He* couldn't care less.'

Tony detected a note of bitterness. 'He just got a knighthood, didn't he – Darvish?'

The guy snorted. 'Such bullshit.'

Tony nodded sympathetically. 'Reckon he didn't deserve it?'

'It's just who you know,' said the guy. 'Isn't it. They just hand them out to their mates. Doesn't mean anything. It's all just a load of shit.'

'You mean he's got mates in government?'

'Probably.'

Tony waited, but the guy didn't elaborate. 'You know the wife better, then?'

'Jill,' he said. 'Yeah. She's good people.'

'But he's not?'

'He's not even *from* here,' said the guy, darkly. Suddenly it seemed to occur to him that Tony wasn't, either. 'So, what,' he said, eyeing Tony up and down, 'you're some kind of reporter?'

'Not yet,' said Tony. 'Next time you see me, ask me again.'

The guy seemed satisfied with this answer, for he didn't say anything more, and when Tony's food was ready, he handed it over the counter with a respectful nod. Tony ate while paging through a stack of peeling *Woman's Day* and *Woman's Weekly* magazines, and then ordered a chocolate milkshake for dessert; by the time he'd finished the shake and thrown all of his wrappers in the bin, he had gained expert knowledge of all the celebrity marriages, divorces, and diet fads of 2014, and his laptop was recharged. The guy unplugged it and handed it back across the counter, and Tony was slipping it back into its padded sleeve when another question occurred to him.

'By the way,' he said, 'do you know anything about a research site up near the pass, above the landslide? A radiometric survey?'

'Don't think so,' said the guy. 'What's that?'

'Doesn't matter,' Tony said. 'Thanks for the food.'

Searching the name 'Taranow' along with 'airstrip' and 'Thorndike' yielded a small cluster of results, all several years old. They confirmed what the chip shop guy had told him: Nigel Taranow, Jill's father, had created the airstrip on his property for the benefit of the local aero club, and on occasion Search & Rescue had used it as a training ground. Taranow himself had been a Search & Rescue volunteer; he had died from a stroke at the age of 79, a little over five years ago, and it seemed that after his daughter and her husband had inherited the farm, the relationship with the aero club had mostly ceased. As far as Tony could discover, the aircraft ZK-CUO was the only plane to have used the strip since Taranow's death. Open-source flight

169

logs showed that it had landed there more than a dozen times over the past few months alone.

It was getting late, and his battery was running low again. He put away his laptop and drove the short distance to the Department of Conservation campsite by the lake, wondering as he shook out his bivvy bag whether it would be worth investing in a solar-powered portable generator, if he could find such a thing available for sale. Mira would have laughed at the idea, he thought. She would have immediately gone scouting around the garages and back patios of Thorndike, and would have come back triumphant, armed with a list of addresses with unattended outdoor charge points meant for fairy lights and lawn mowers and power washers, or a list of names of all the soft-hearted locals she'd won over, who were willing to exchange the use of a power strip for an hour or so of light domestic chores. 'Keep your money,' she would have said, affecting a lordly magnanimity, 'put away your little coins; I give you electricity for free.' But that was the old Mira, Tony thought with bitterness as he climbed into his sleeping bag. God only knew what the new Mira – the fully funded, value-maximising, if-you-can't-beat-'em-join-'em Mira – would do.

He woke on Monday morning to find an email waiting in his inbox; it was the title certificate for 1606 Korowai Pass Road that he'd requested, and he opened the attachment to discover that the title was held by Jill and Owen Darvish, as it had been since May 2012, and that although permission had been sought to subdivide, no material changes to the property had yet been carried out.

Tony sat up in his sleeping bag, frowning. At the hui Mira had said explicitly that Lemoine had bought the farm. He must have done – he'd paid her ten thousand dollars already. Why would he pay her to come and cultivate a patch of land he didn't own? And what about the bunker? Mira had definitely said that he was putting in a bunker. What kind of survivalist would build a bunker on property that belonged to someone else? That would defeat the whole purpose, surely. Tony reread the title certificate a second time, feeling a rising annoyance, for if the land hadn't legally changed hands, then he had no story – or rather, he *did* have a story, only it was one where a foreign billionaire had donated ten thousand dollars to an activistic, not-for-profit, avowedly left-wing enterprise at no obvious benefit to himself, and Tony would rather drink his own urine than write *that*.

He decided to email Owen Darvish directly. Perhaps there was a perfectly logical explanation he was missing – and in any case, it was good journalistic practice to give all parties a chance to explain themselves up front. Eyeing the seven-per-cent battery level remaining on his laptop, he found an email address on the Darvish Pest Control website and tapped out a brief enquiry. He sent it off, and then went for a freezing dip in the lake before getting dressed and making breakfast on his butane stove. He ate slowly, enjoying the view, and had just turned on his phone to begin searching for the nearest hardware store that might sell solar-powered portable generators when it started ringing, making him jump. He picked up.

'Hello?'

'Anthony? Owen Darvish,' said a loud, thickly accented voice in his ear.

'Oh wow, hello,' Tony said, scrambling to his feet and fishing in his pocket for the car keys. 'Thanks for getting back to me so quickly.'

'Just responding to your email,' Sir Owen said. 'Just a quick courtesy call back. You said you were writing an article?'

'Yeah. Hang on, just let me get my—' He slid into the car and scrabbled around to find his Dictaphone. 'Yeah, I'm writing a piece about Robert Lemoine.' He put his phone on speaker and clicked 'Record'.

'And what is it that you want from me exactly?'

'Well,' said Tony, deciding to go all in, 'I guess I wanted to ask you if you sold him your property in Thorndike.'

There was a little silence. Then Sir Owen said, 'Anthony, I'm sure you know already that my company's in business with Autonomo; it's an ongoing relationship, and I'm not going to compromise it by talking to the press.'

'He paid you a sum of . . . ten million dollars for the land, is that right?'

Tony had no idea if this was a plausible figure; he was hoping that Darvish would correct him. But Sir Owen only said, 'I'm not sure what you're trying to achieve here, mate.'

'I'm just trying to get my head around it,' Tony said, feeling a spike of excitement, for if he'd been on the wrong track altogether then Sir Owen would surely have denied it out of hand. 'So you do confirm the sale has taken place?'

'No, I don't confirm it. I'm not confirming anything.'

'Could you tell me why not?'

'Look, before we go any further, Anthony, I want to know who you've been talking to, if that's all right. Where have you got this from?'

'I can't reveal my sources, I'm afraid,' Tony said.

'Then I'm not interested in giving any interviews. Sorry.'

'You gave some interviews quite recently,' Tony said quickly, before Sir Owen could hang up, 'and I noticed that you never mentioned Robert Lemoine by name in any of them. Could you tell me why that was? Sorry if that's a silly question – it's just that in my line of work, it's easy sometimes to mistake an innocent omission for a cover-up.'

Another little silence. Tony realised he was holding his breath, hardly daring to believe his own audacity. Then Sir Owen said, more carefully, 'Whereabouts are you based, Anthony?'

'Actually, right now I'm in Thorndike,' Tony said.

'Is that right,' Sir Owen said.

'Nice place,' Tony said. 'I got a good view over your farm from up on the ridge there. Amazing position. Worth what he paid you, for sure.'

Sir Owen expelled a breath. 'You've got it wrong, mate.'

'So help me get it right,' Tony said. 'What's your arrangement with Robert Lemoine?'

'Anthony, you're talking about a business relationship; I'm not prepared to—'

'So there is a relationship? You know each other personally?'

'I'm not prepared to comment on that.'

'When did you first meet? Can you tell me that much?'

'I'm afraid not,' Sir Owen said.

'Well, maybe I can jog your memory a bit,' Tony said. 'I've been looking at the flight log of a plane that's made quite a few trips to Thorndike recently. Registration mark Zulu Kilo Charlie Uniform Oscar. Does that ring any bells?'

'Look, Anthony,' Sir Owen said firmly, 'you emailed me, and I'm doing you the courtesy of giving you a call back like you asked, but I'm not interested in talking to the press, all right? Good luck with your—'

'Just one more question,' Tony said quickly, before he could hang up. 'Mr Darvish?'

Sir Owen made an irritated noise. 'I've got nothing to tell you, Anthony. You're wasting your time.'

'It's about something else, actually,' Tony said, choosing a subject almost at random: all he wanted was to keep Owen Darvish on the line. 'It's about … um … a radiometric survey project? As I said, I was up in the—'

'We're not involved with radiometrics,' Sir Owen interrupted, impatiently. 'We're just pest control. That's a whole separate technology. Different kind of drone.'

'What?' said Tony. 'Did you say drone?'

Sir Owen made the irritated noise again. 'Sorry, Anthony,' he said. 'You'll have to talk to someone at Autonomo. That's nothing to do with us.'

'Autonomo?' said Tony. 'Wait. What do you mean, a different kind of drone?'

There was a certain kind of man who couldn't resist giving a scientific explanation when asked; Owen Darvish, it seemed, was one. 'It's called an airborne magnetic and radiometric survey,' he said, still terse, 'and they do it from way, way up. Thousands of metres up. High-flying aircraft. Geophysical mapping. Totally different to our project. Different technology, different drone, different everything.'

'I'm sorry,' Tony said, 'I'm not quite following.'

'Radiometric survey,' Sir Owen repeated. 'That's what you said.'

'No,' Tony said. 'I meant the research site in Korowai National Park. Above the landslide.'

The line went quiet. Then Sir Owen said, 'What?'

'The radiometric survey site. Up near the pass, above the landslide.'

'I think we've got our wires crossed somewhere here,' Sir Owen said.

'I spoke to a security guard,' Tony said. 'He said it was something involving radiometric—'

'Security guard where?'

'In the national park,' Tony said. 'Right behind your back fence.'

'Sorry, mate, you're not making any sense.'

'There was a mobile phone tower and a security guard and a fence around—'

'Sorry, mate. Sorry.'

'You mentioned Autonomo,' Tony began, but Sir Owen said, loudly, 'Thanks anyway,' and before Tony could say anything else, he'd hung up.

Tony clicked off his Dictaphone and sat in the front seat frowning and staring out through the windscreen at the cloudy surface of the lake. His phone buzzed in his hand, startling him, and he looked down to see that he'd received a text message: it was from Rosie, and she wanted to know if he was winning.

'Well, I just had my first "no comment",' he texted back, 'so I guess that means I'm onto something.'

'Definitely,' she replied, and Tony was plunged instantly into doubt. Was it really that suspicious? Yes, Darvish had refused to talk to him. So what? He had no obligation to the media. He hadn't taken any oaths of office. He hadn't been deposed. He was a private citizen. His affairs were none of Tony's business. He had refused to confirm that he had sold Lemoine his property – because he *hadn't* sold Lemoine his property. Tony knew that for a fact; he had the title deed right here. Fine, Lemoine had told Mira something different – but maybe he was putting in the bunker on a lease. Or maybe he and Darvish had a gentleman's agreement. Or maybe a sale *was* in the offing, but they were still negotiating terms – in which case Darvish would have no reason whatsoever to want to answer any questions – least of all from a nobody like Tony, a wannabe investigative journalist, a let's-pretend reporter, a trust-fund dilettante who was basically unpublished, and so inexperienced he could hardly even call himself a hack!

'Jesus Christ, Tony,' he said aloud. 'Pull your head in.'

His phone lit up again: Rosie had sent two emojis, a gun

175

followed by a cigarette. Then she wrote, 'oh wait,' and sent them again the other way, first the cigarette, and then the gun. 'Smoking gun,' she wrote, in explanation. 'Because I really hope you find one!!!!!!'

Tony didn't smile. 'Funny you should say that,' he typed, his expression grim, thinking back to his encounter with the guard on Saturday morning; but then he felt stupid and deleted it. 'I might be out of range for a few days just fyi,' he wrote instead. 'Following a hunch . . .' He looked at the message for a few seconds, making up his mind, before hitting send. 'Amazing,' she wrote again, and then, 'mysterious,' and then, 'be careful'. Tony's thumb hovered over the keypad. Rosie didn't know about the offer that Lemoine had made to Birnam Wood. He'd told her only that he was investigating super-rich survivalists, having been unwilling – little though it mattered – to mention Mira's name; but he didn't want to think about Mira right now, and so it was partly out of guilt and bitterness, and partly out of wishful thinking, and partly just to end the conversation, that he responded, 'xxx'.

'Do you think,' said Mira, leaning on her spade, 'that the kind of person who can never say sorry is *also* the kind of person who can never say thank you, or do you think that those are two different categories of people?'

'Ooh, that's a good one,' Shelley said. She considered it.

'Because I saw this blog a while back,' Mira went on, 'where this woman had just decided to stop saying sorry, like, ever, and every time she would have said it, she found a way of saying thank you instead. So, like, instead of saying "sorry for being late", she'd say, "thanks for waiting", and instead of saying "sorry for being such a mess" she'd say, "thanks for being so understanding", and on and on like that. And she wrote in this blog how this one little change like totally transformed her life and all her relationships, like all of a sudden, her friendships got so much healthier and more mature and more honest, and because she was appreciating everyone in her life way more, they started appreciating her back, and it was this whole thing.'

'Wow,' Shelley said. 'Thank you for telling me that story.'

'Thank you for listening.'

'Thank you for assuming that I was listening.'

'Thank you for not making it obvious if you weren't.'

They dug the ground in silence for a moment, both grinning. Then Shelley said, 'It's like they point in different directions. Thank you is, like, giving someone credit, whereas sorry is, like, taking the blame.'

'Yeah,' Mira said. 'That's what this blog was about – saying that they're like two sides of the same coin.'

'But not in *every* situation,' Shelley said. 'Right?'

'Well,' Mira said, 'I guess it got me thinking about privilege, and the guilt of that, and how there's this need to apologise for it all the time now, if you're in a position of privilege I mean, and maybe – I don't know – maybe we're like, totally missing something as a society or something – like, maybe we could just as easily be saying thank you, in, like, the exact same situations, and maybe we'd all be healthier and happier that way.'

Shelley was frowning. 'But how do you say thank you to someone who's been systemically oppressed?'

'I don't mean, like, "thank you for being oppressed", I mean, like, finding ways to appreciate other people's existence instead of just apologising for your own. You know? And not like, as the *only* thing that you're doing, obviously, not like, "okay, I've said thank you, yep, job done, social justice achieved" – I mean, just as a first step, just to see what effect it has, and then go from there.

'And anyway,' she added, 'how do you say *sorry* to someone who's been systemically oppressed? I mean – like, really? It's the same problem.'

'Yeah,' Shelley said, but with a doubtful note in her voice.

'I just think this might be kind of a radical idea,' Mira said, feeling herself warming to her subject. 'Because like, when somebody shows appreciation for something good that you've done, or notices something true about you as a person, that's an amazing feeling, right? And it gives you, like, this sense of pride in yourself, and this sense of honour and dignity, and maybe the knock-on effect from that would, like, totally transform society. I mean, who knows? It's worth a shot, right?'

Shelley still looked doubtful. 'Sometimes people really do need to say sorry though,' she said.

'Yeah, totally, for things they've done wrong, but not in a way that, like, apologises for existing, right? I mean, how actually meaningful is that?'

'Maybe,' Shelley said, and lapsed into silence.

They were preparing a bed for carrots, having mixed the fine carrot seed with radish, which was faster-growing and would come up first and mark the rows; over the coming weeks, they'd thin the bed down to the strongest plants, eating the radishes along with the thinnings of the beets and leeks and lettuces that they'd sown already, the seedlings transplanted from their potting sheds back home. Kale was next, and peas, and onions, and potatoes in growing bags – with all the limestone around, Mira had reckoned that the tubers wouldn't thrive if planted directly in the ground – and then broccoli, and cabbages, and herbs along the borders, and cucumbers on climbing frames . . . and that would take them to September, and the spring. Already the livestock pens beside the shearing shed had been transformed into a kind of patchwork hothouse, assorted panes of glass and

Perspex laid across the rails, and lengths of plastic sheeting stapled to the posts against the wind. The weekend crew had brought down a trailer load of compost from the city, and they'd spent all of Saturday and Sunday digging it in; the earth was no longer grey and compacted underfoot, but dark and rich and damp and airy – 'Friable tilth,' they always said, putting on an accent, laughing at the sounds, 'Yessir, you've got your-self a fine patch of friable tilth right there'; 'Hoo-ee! I do love me some friable tilth!' Ordinarily Mira would have scoured the neighbours' fields for cowpats, but practically every farm along the highway sold bagged manure for cash at the front gate, and with the money that Lemoine had deposited in her account, there was no real need to scavenge for anything any more, least of all, actual shit. They had bought two dozen bags of it so far (from four different farms, so as not to be conspicuous) and Mira had spent that morning putting in a germination hotbed on the sunny side of the shed – mulching heavily against the frost, for the conditions at Thorndike were more subalpine than any of the crew were used to, and she was expecting that some of what they sowed would not survive.

'But you didn't answer my question,' she said after a moment. 'Do you think there are two different types of people, or just one?'

'Well, obviously there's overlap,' Shelley said, 'like, assholes don't say thank you for anything, and they don't say sorry for anything either . . . But I think about myself, like, would I rather be forced to say sorry for something that's not actually my fault, or be forced to say thank you when I don't actually mean it?'

'That one, surely.'

'No, actually,' Shelley said. 'I mean, saying sorry isn't my favourite thing in the world, but if it makes someone else feel better, then, you know, I don't really care. It's like, I can take it, whatever, I know that it's more about them than about me anyway. But I *hate* being forced to say thank you.'

'Really?' Mira said. 'That's so weird.'

'Yeah, I mean, when I was little, I used to hate my birthday and Christmas so much, like, I dreaded getting presents that I really didn't like and then having to seem like I was so happy and so grateful. I just couldn't imagine anything worse than that. I don't know why. And so I'd pretend to be into things that I didn't even care about, just so I'd know in advance what people were going to give me and I wouldn't have to be surprised. Like the dollar-mixture thing. I told you about this, right?'

'No,' Mira said.

'Oh man, I thought I did,' Shelley said. 'Well, anyway, for years I told everyone that I had this insane sweet tooth, and I made it this whole thing that I was always looking for the perfect dollar mixture, and it was the only present that I ever wanted, just that little white bag of lollies with the twisted top, that was it, that was everything to me, I was the dollar-mixture girl, I was like a connoisseur, but really, it was all just this huge lie that I'd invented because I so hated the idea of having to say thank you for a present that I didn't actually like.'

'That is so funny,' Mira said. 'Especially because you picked something so cheap.'

'I know,' Shelley said. 'Like, you literally can't spend more than a dollar on a dollar mixture.'

'It's so modest. I feel so sad for little Shelley.'

'And I never ate the lollies either,' Shelley said. 'I just kept them until they went hard and then I threw them away.'

'That's even sadder!'

'I can't believe I've never told you that before,' Shelley said.

'Now I'm trying to think of all the birthday presents I've ever bought for you,' Mira said.

'Nah, you never stress me out,' Shelley said. 'It was only, like, aunts and uncles and stuff. And Mum and Dad's friends. People who didn't actually know me.' She unearthed a piece of concrete and hefted it aside.

'I bet you're weird, though,' Mira said. 'I bet most people find it harder to say sorry.'

'Yeah,' Shelley said. 'Like Amber.'

'Totally,' Mira said. 'Oh my God. When has she ever apologised for anything?'

'At least she can say thank you.'

'Well, yeah, as long as she can put the boot in. Like, "Thanks for doing such a shitty job."'

'"Thanks for ruining my life."'

'"Thanks for ruining my entire fucking life with your stupid email, Shelley."'

'Her *entire fucking life*,' repeated Shelley, laughing. '*Ruined.*'

'We're so mean,' Mira said, but she was pleased.

'So mean,' Shelley said. After a moment she said, more soberly, 'Poor Tony.'

Mira glanced at her. 'Why do you say that?'

Shelley wasn't meeting her gaze. 'I don't know,' she said. 'Just thinking about Amber, and that whole thing.'

'I thought you said it was all his fault,' Mira said.

'Yeah,' Shelley said, again with a note of doubt. Then, more decisively, she said, 'No – yeah. It was. It totally was.'

Mira felt a stab of impatience. 'But?'

Few things were more tantalising to Mira than when she missed out on an interesting argument only to hear it summarised badly – or too briefly – after the fact. She hated having to rely on someone else's version of events, for she was much too proud of her own powers of discernment ever to accept another person's judgment over whose ideas had been valid, whose logic convincing, and whose rhetoric fair; still more infuriating was the thought that an interesting argument could have even taken place without her, for she was long accustomed to being thought the liveliest and most original thinker of any company in which she found herself, and she had met few people in her life whom she honestly admired and envied when it came to the art – the many arts – of conversation. Tony Gallo was one; she had felt his absence acutely when he'd moved away, and over the past four years she had so often fantasised about his homecoming that to have missed it altogether was aggravating in the extreme – all the more so, since, from the little she'd been able to gather about the disagreement between him and Amber, it seemed that he had come off much the worse in the debate. Mira had grilled Shelley repeatedly over what exactly had been said that night, and in what tone, and to what effect, but Shelley's account of the scene had been strangely unforthcoming: Tony had 'come looking for a fight', he had been 'a total swinging dick' and had spoken in a way that was 'seriously offensive'; but she had also admitted that 'nobody really took Amber's side until the very end', and that 'Tony did say some pretty confronting things actually', and that 'Amber was a dick as well', and when Mira had asked more about the substance of Tony's argument, Shelley had blushed and mumbled that it had been something to do with the market logic of relationships, but to be honest, she couldn't really remember the actual thrust.

'Hey, you know when we incorporate,' Shelley said now, 'like after Christmas, with the hundred grand?'

'You're totally changing the subject!'

'No, it's related. You know when we incorporate?'

'Yeah – if.'

'What do you think about the idea of changing our name?'

Mira looked up. 'What's wrong with Birnam Wood?'

'I was just thinking it might make more sense if it was something Māori,' Shelley said.

'What?' Mira said. 'Why?'

'Well, like you said, this could be really big, right? And like, if this spreads outside New Zealand—'

'But don't you think it's a bit . . . I mean, we're not Māori.'

'Well, yeah, but we're Kiwi, and it's a Kiwi—'

'So isn't it kind of like appropriation?'

'How?' Shelley said. 'It's just using the language.'

'But Māori horticulture is, like, a whole thing,' Mira said. 'And like, the relationship with the land, it's super important and sacred, there are all sorts of things that we don't—'

'But if we become a proper business, then we'll have to think about the Treaty and biculturalism and all of that anyway,' Shelley said, now sounding a little defensive. 'I mean, we'll have a board and everything, right? And we'll have to think properly about diversity hiring, and messaging, and making sure—'

'I guess I hadn't thought that far ahead,' Mira said.

'Because didn't Tony come up with the name Birnam Wood? And if he's not a part of it any more—'

'It wasn't Tony's idea,' Mira said. 'It was mine.'

'Oh,' Shelley said. 'Sorry.'

'The Principles of Unity was him. Because of Occupy Wall Street. That was their thing.'

'Oh, right,' Shelley said. 'Okay, yeah, that makes more sense, I guess.'

'I mean, it was ages ago. It doesn't matter.'

'No, no,' Shelley said, 'it totally matters. I should have—'

'No, it's fine,' Mira said. 'You should table the suggestion, for sure.' She staked her spade and went to fill a bucket at the water trough, lingering longer than she needed to, and then detouring on the way back past the polytunnel to reattach the corner of a piece of plastic sheeting that had come unfastened in the wind.

It bothered her to hear Shelley say so casually that Tony was no longer part of Birnam Wood – though, of course, he'd said as much himself the night of the hui, when they took the vote, and 'those in favour' turned out to mean everyone but him: 'I'm out of here,' he'd said, standing up and reaching for his jacket, looking only at Mira, his face very red. 'And I just want to say that this is so disappointing. I'm so fucking disappointed, Mira.' And then to Amber: 'Thanks for cooking, the soup was really good.' As the door slammed shut behind him, someone had said, 'Who the hell was *he*?' and everyone had laughed. Mira had felt sick; she'd stood up to follow Tony out into the street, but Shelley had grabbed her hand, detaining her – 'He got home three weeks ago,' she'd whispered, intensely, with a strange beseeching look, 'he came by the flat – I don't know why he didn't call you,' and Mira had frowned and nodded and disengaged her hand and slipped out into the street, only to see that Tony was sprinting – *sprinting* – down the block away from the café. She'd called his name, twice, but he hadn't turned, and then Shelley had come into the doorway behind her, seeming oddly nervous. 'I don't know what happened tonight,' she'd said. 'He was like a different person.'

It hadn't seemed that way to Mira. His beard had been per-haps a little thicker, his eyes a little sharper, and his features a little more mature, but he had the same pugnacious energy, the same righteous indignation, the same revolutionary zeal; the moment she'd first laid eyes on him, in fact, her heart had plunged, for she'd known that he, of all people, was the worst possible audience for what she had driven there that night to say; she'd been absolutely certain, without the smallest shred of doubt, that he was going to be appalled by her announcement, appalled by the prospect of Lemoine's involvement, appalled by the very notion of Lemoine – and so he had been. No, he was still the same old Tony, Mira thought now, in bitter remonstrance. He wasn't a different person. She was the one who had changed.

Of all the mistakes and indiscretions that Mira had committed in her life, of all the social blunders that she relived when she was tired but couldn't sleep, the petty grudges that she'd held, the acts of selfishness and cowardice, the awful moments when her vanity had been exposed, the shameful times she'd failed to come to someone's rescue, or failed to turn the other cheek, or failed to let an insult go, of all these memories, the night of Tony's leaving party rankled worst. There had been a period, in the weeks directly after he had left the country, when she had thought about their last encounter almost constantly, replaying it – what she remembered of it, anyway – with an almost unendurable self-loathing. What had she been expecting – that if she slept with him, he'd stay? That he'd change his mind, tear up his ticket, renounce his dream to see the world, because of her? She blushed to admit it, blushed to remember how stunned he'd been when she took his arm and led him down the grassy slope into the dark, how vulnerable he'd seemed, bewildered almost, how his breath kept catching in his throat – and then, afterwards, how she'd walked away and left him there – no; how she'd *wanted* to leave him, how she'd slept with him precisely so that she could give herself the *chance* to leave him, precisely so that *he* could be the one *she* left behind. She'd gone inside and poured another drink, and then another, and another, and another, and another, and another, dancing so she didn't have to talk to anybody, nodding so she didn't have to listen, avoiding Tony, smiling, turning, swaying, keeping time, and knowing that if she said anything, to anyone, if she even opened her

185

mouth to speak, her voice would crack, and she would start to cry. She'd woken the next day trembling uncontrollably, head throbbing, heart racing, so hungover she could hardly move, and of course it had been Shelley who had taken care of her, Shelley who'd cleaned where she'd been sick beside the bed, and made her milky tea with sugar, and run her bath, and Mira had felt so ashamed, and so feeble, and so desperately miserable that Tony's flight had left, that he hadn't called, that he was gone, that she'd consoled herself by telling Shelley a contorted version of the story, playing up her drunkenness, and claiming hardly to remember, and feigning bewilderment that he'd chosen *that* night, the final night before he left the country, to make his feelings known; of course, it had been a long time coming, as everybody knew, but didn't that make the timing even more cowardly on Tony's part – and, when she actually thought about it, even more cruel? – but then shaking her head, and shrugging it off, and chalking it up as a youthful misadventure, a stupid but ultimately harmless incident, and pushing down the knowledge that what really scared her more than anything was that when Tony came home, if he ever did, he would finally see her for what she feared she was, an ordinary fish in a small and rather stagnant pond.

'I actually had a couple of ideas,' Shelley said when she came back. 'For the name.'

'Oh yeah?' Mira brought the handles of the silicone bucket together so that the edge formed a spout and the water slopped out over the soil.

'Yeah. So at first I thought, okay, just a straight translation of Birnam Wood, like, "the wood that moves". Which is "Te Ngahere Neke", or "Te Ngahere e Neke Ana" – I mean, it's good, but it's a bit of a mouthful if you don't speak te reo. So then I thought, well, actually, that doesn't really capture what we really do anyway – like, the gardening element – so I came up with "Te Māra Neke" – the moving garden.'

'Te Māra Neke,' Mira repeated. She tipped the bucket over and watched the last of the water seep away.

'Yeah. Te Māra Neke,' Shelley said. 'What do you think?'

'I don't know,' Mira said. 'I guess I'll have to sit with it for a bit.'

'Cool,' Shelley said. 'Hey, but way more importantly, though: do you reckon this tilth is friable enough?'

'So fucking friable,' Mira said. 'Yeah, I think we're sweet.' She left Shelley to sow the carrot seed and went to update the planting schedule, feeling so guilty suddenly that she feared she might be on the verge of tears.

Mira had not been entirely honest in her pitch to Birnam Wood. She wished that she could say that this had been because of Tony, that his presence at the hui had so blindsided her, and his manner had been so hostile, and his opinions so combatively expressed, that she had found herself forced on to the defensive; but the truth was that well before she had arrived at the café that night, she had already decided to leave certain details out. The Darvishes, for example, who as far as she knew had no idea what was going on at the farm behind their backs; Lemoine had told her that he did not yet own the land outright, but so far had only put down a deposit. She had reasoned to herself that since many of the members had no idea that Birnam Wood ever engaged in any trespassing at all, to have told the truth would have only sparked a long and tedious debate over when, and how, it was appropriate to break the law – and she'd been so anxious that Shelley had been on the verge of leaving – and she'd never even dreamed of an opportunity like this one – and after all, it was only a partial deception, since the Darvishes had given Lemoine full use of the farm in their absence, including the farmhouse, and had encouraged him to make himself at home. Whether this hospitality would extend to Birnam Wood, of course, was doubtful, but when she'd raised the issue with Lemoine, he had only shrugged and smiled and said he thought she called herself an anarchist; surely the danger was part of the appeal?

Mira knew that a large proportion of the world's billionaires were psychopaths, and she also knew that one defining feature of psychopathy was a tendency to lie. It was possible that Lemoine had never even met the Darvishes. Maybe he was trespassing as well. Maybe he wanted to acquire Birnam Wood in order to destroy it – or maybe he was looking for a loss to write off against his taxes; maybe his whole intention was to run them into the ground. Or maybe he'd never intended to invest in them at all. He might have dangled his offer only as a lure – or he might be grooming her for something else entirely – or he might be trying to frame her – or he might be simply toying with her as a joke. He might be sick in the head. He might be planning to kill her. He might be planning to kill the whole group. Mira tried her best to scold herself, but even at her sternest, she could never quite repress the knowledge that the only person who she knew for sure had lied to Birnam Wood about the Darvish farm was her.

She had told the others that the house was strictly out of bounds, explaining that Birnam Wood was being auditioned as a fully nomadic and self-sufficient enterprise, and that Lemoine wanted them to do as much as possible off-grid; he'd also asked them to keep a low profile when in town, she added, so as not to spoil their chances when trying to make a first impression as a business. 'It's about keeping control of the narrative,' she told them; 'he doesn't want us going live before everything is ready and we're all properly set up' – and somewhat to her surprise, this was met with no objections. She had been worried that somebody might wonder why the house was still fully furnished, and why there were still boots in the porch, in several sizes, not to mention an enormous photo of the Darvish family above the mantel in the living room; but evidently no one had got close enough to peer in the windows, for the question hadn't come up. They pitched their tents inside the shearing shed, cooked with bottled gas beneath the eaves, and, after several days of roughing it, politely voted in favour of hiring an eco-toilet and a cold-water camp shower, to save the hassle of bathing in the lake; even with a monthly discount, this would constitute the biggest single expenditure in the history of Birnam Wood, and Mira felt a pang to think of the Darvish bathroom, empty and unused, just up the hill . . . But she cast her vote along with the majority and held her tongue. Shelley had arranged the rental. She'd asked if they ought to put Lemoine's name on the invoice, seeing as the facilities would be used at his address; Mira had pretended to consider it, and then replied casually that perhaps they'd better not, since it wasn't public knowledge yet that Lemoine had bought the farm, and it would be a shame if somebody at the hire company recognised his name and word got out. Shelley accepted this quite naturally; she was so unsuspicious, in fact, that she booked the delivery using Mira's credit card and contact details – causing Mira some anxiety, until the two cubicles arrived at the front gate several days later and Mira asked the driver quietly if she could just forget about the invoice and pay in cash instead, whereupon his mood improved so visibly that she knew that he was planning to erase the transaction from his records and pocket what he would have had to pay in tax.

Only three thousand dollars now remained of the ten thousand that the billionaire had given her. A thousand had gone on petrol vouchers for the weekend crew, and another two thousand on food – mostly non-perishables, though in addition to the bags and bags of store-brand rice and pasta, the cans of chick-peas and kidney beans, the bulk sacks of oatmeal and powdered milk, the jumbo jars of peanut butter, and the restaurant-sized drums of vinegar and olive oil, Shelley had also bought stuffed olives, and kimchi, and anchovies, and semi-dried tomatoes, and exotic chutneys, and fancy biscuits, and chocolates, and pancake mix, and salsas, and potato chips, and marshmallows for roasting, and cured meats, and hard cheeses, and decent coffee, and kombucha cultures, and candied fruit; years of co-ordinating Birnam volunteers had left her with the stout belief that there was nothing more beneficial to group harmony than to ensure the food was plentiful and good, and with that prin-ciple in mind, she had put in a thousand-dollar order at the liquor store as well. It was clear that she was greatly enjoying having money to burn, but Mira had never spent anywhere near that amount of money in a week before, and privately she was aghast at how quickly and easily the funds had drained away. In Birnam Wood tradition, they held a horizontal catch-up meet-ing every evening and made sure that all significant decisions were subject to a vote, but the debates were much less involving now that they had ready cash to hand, and so far, every motion considered by the group had passed. To date, they had bought a camping fridge, and a six-burner gas barbecue, and a port-able router equipped with a pop-up Internet subscription, and a solar-powered generator to charge their phones, and a trailer load of firewood for the impromptu firepit they'd dug on the lee side of the shed – and with each purchase, their camp had become a little more established, and a little more conspicuous, and a little more incriminating, in the event – Mira prayed it wouldn't happen – that the Darvishes came home.

There were seven of them living at the farm for now, though as yet nobody apart from Mira and Shelley had committed to staying in Thorndike past the end of the month. Work and family obligations had prevented most of Birnam Wood from making the trip at all; those who had been able to afford the time away were either freelancers, or temporarily out of work, or from a wealthy family, or – as was often the case – all three. Hayden Michie and Katrina Hunt, both actors, had been touring the country's prisons teaching drama to inmates, and would shortly be heading home to start rehearsals for a summer production of *Cabaret*; Aaron Chang was a playwright and Hayden's friend from school; Natalie Ormison had just finished a PhD in anthropology and was applying for post-doctoral fellowships overseas; and Jessica Barratt, a visual artist, would be moving to Wellington in October to take up a maternity leave cover position at the national museum; in the meantime, she was writing advertising copy, which she could do remotely from the farm. Mira didn't know any of them all that well, and the collective ice might have remained unbroken, so to speak, if it hadn't been for a budding attraction between Aaron and Jessica, who had been smiling foolishly at one another almost from the moment of first sight. They had begun inventing increasingly flimsy reasons to seek out each other's company alone, and their long absences had soon become a common joke, giving the rest a shared parental feeling, and a tender recollection of their own past romances, and an unfolding drama to invest in, semi-ironically, as a group.

That afternoon – it was a Monday – the two of them had just left in Aaron's car to buy some eggs. Hayden and Katrina were in the shed, catching up on emails, and Natalie was taking a nap. Mira went to fetch her irrigation backpack and her long-handled hoe, intending to take a walk up the northern fence line to check the crop she'd sown about a month ago, when she'd been camping on her own – though this was mostly a pretext: her conversation with Shelley had left her in a squirmy, self-searching mood, and she wanted to be alone with her thoughts for a while.

When she reached the terrace, she discovered that only a few of her broadcast-seeded lettuces had taken root – she counted six plump chalices, a week away from harvest, crinkled leaves of pastel marbling to brown – but the baby beets and spinach were thriving, bordering the yellow grass of the paddock with a stripe of intermittent burgundy and green. She proceeded up along the row, wielding the irrigation wand in one hand and hoeing with the other, and as she worked, her mind drifted back to the day she'd dug the furrow – the day after her first encounter with Lemoine, in fact, when, late in the morning, she'd heard engine noise and looked up to see his aircraft cresting the Korowai ranges and then dipping a wing to cut a wide circle overhead. The plane had passed out of sight over the treetops, and a short while later he'd appeared in person over the brow of the hill, making his way down the field towards her on foot. He was dressed, as before, in a plain tracksuit and unbranded baseball cap, and she'd had a fleeting vision of a panelled closet with dozens and dozens of identical outfits on carved wooden hangers spaced uniformly along the rail, everything hushed and immaculate, and all the shelves backlit like vitrines in a museum. She'd bowed her head and kept digging, willing herself not to react, not to speak first, not to give herself away this time, but he'd walked right up to her and sat down in the dirt, crossing his legs and placing his hands comfortably on his knees, and as he'd moved, she'd caught a faint current of his aftershave, with notes of fennel and pepper that lingered on the air between them, and she hadn't been able to hold her nerve: she'd turned and looked at him.

'So – Birnam Wood,' he'd said when their eyes met. 'Tell me everything there is to tell. Start at the beginning, and don't leave anything out.'

She hadn't replied at once. 'That's funny,' she said, carefully, pulling her gaze away from his, and looking down at the earth between her knees, 'I know I told you I was part of a collective. But I could have sworn I never said the name.'

'No?'

She glanced at him again. 'No,' she said. 'Actually, I'm positive. I never said what we were called. I would have remembered that.'

'So what does that suggest to you?'

'I guess . . . that we've been googling each other.'

He smiled at the tacit admission. 'Well,' he said, 'it sure beats googling ourselves.'

She felt embarrassed; to cover it, she set her jaw and squinted at him with distaste. 'Why do you want to know about Birnam Wood?'

'I take it that you've found out who I am?'

'I've found out *what* you are,' Mira said, with a touch of scorn. 'Not who.'

'That's an interesting distinction. Maybe I can help you bridge the gap.' He was still smiling. 'I have a lot of money.'

'Yeah,' she said. 'I gathered that.'

'And I'd like to give some of it to you.'

She stared at him.

'Tell me about Birnam Wood,' he said. 'Pitch it to me. The whole concept. What it is, what it could be. What you want from it. Everything you've ever wanted. Lay it on me.'

But she was frowning. 'I don't understand.'

'I think I'm being pretty clear. I've been researching your collective, like you said; I've found out a little bit; I'm intrigued; and I'm asking you to walk me through it as a concept.'

'You realise that our charter is, like, explicitly anti-capitalist,' Mira said.

'Is it?'

'And you're a *venture capitalist*. It's literally right there in your name.'

'Strange bedfellows,' he said. 'Keeps it interesting. Don't you think?'

'No,' she said. 'Not really. Nope.'

He smiled. 'So you have a charter,' he said pleasantly.

Mira drew back from him. 'What are you trying to do here?' she said. 'What is this?'

'It's an invitation,' said Lemoine.

'But, like, is this some kind of reputation management or something? Like, some focus group told you to go and slum it with the socialists, to distract from some other shitty, totally illegal thing you did?'

He laughed. 'No focus group has ever told me what to do,' he said, 'and if one ever did, I promise you, I'd do the opposite.'

Mira said nothing. She was searching his expression, trying to catch him out.

'So you don't need money,' he said after a moment.

'Not from you.'

'Oh, I know the world is going to hell,' he said, making a dismissive gesture with his hand. 'I know it's burning up. And all because we're all so incredibly selfish and greedy and polluting. I know that.' He gazed across the field for a moment, smiling thoughtfully, and then said, 'Actually, this farm is where I plan to see it out. Come the apocalypse, this is where I'm going to be. I'm putting in a bunker. Right there.'

She didn't look where he was pointing. 'Congratulations,' she said.

'Thank you,' he said. 'Tell me about Birnam Wood.'

She glared at him. 'Why?'

'Well,' he said, 'because I take a long position on the sharing economy, and I've never seen an organisation quite like yours before, and from what I've been able to gather from my googling' – he paused, grinning at her – 'I think it has potential. And, on a personal level, because I like your gumption. I find it appealing.'

'And?'

'And what?'

'And what's the real reason?'

He studied her with amusement. 'What makes you think there's a real reason?'

'I don't know,' Mira said. 'I guess you seem like the kind of person who'd have a secret agenda.'

'Because of what I am? Or are you taking a stab at who I am now?'

'I'm starting to form a picture.'

'God help me.'

'You're a billionaire,' Mira said. 'I'm pretty sure he already has.'

Lemoine burst out laughing. 'Okay – you're right,' he said, very cheerfully now. 'I *do* have a real reason. Here it is. I think Owen Darvish is a little prick, and that makes me well disposed towards anyone who's stealing from him. There.'

'Why are you in business with him if you think that he's a prick?'

He laughed again. 'Now *that*,' he said, 'is a most refreshing question.'

Mira looked away. She was determined not to let him see how reassured she felt that he was laughing – because didn't that mean that he couldn't be a psychopath? Her father had given her a copy of *The Psychopath Test* one Christmas (having read it already; they'd had great fun diagnosing all their relatives in turn), and she had a hazy memory that one of the items on the checklist was an inability to laugh – was that right? Or had she misremembered it? Well, in any case, she thought, more sternly, being charming was definitely a sign – a very bad one – and Lemoine was nothing if not charming. She could feel herself becoming very seriously charmed.

He was still watching her. 'All right,' he said after a moment, 'here is the absolute truth. A few months ago, I made Owen Darvish an offer on this farm. It was a handsome enough sum of money that he decided he could probably squeeze me for a little more, and he told me that he'd only sell the place to me if I agreed to sponsor some sideline project he had going on. Some conservation thing. I didn't really care about the project, but I wanted the land, so I said fine, let's work something out, and we started to negotiate. While we were going back and forth, I asked him and his wife to sign a non-disclosure agreement. Privacy is a critical issue for me, for a number of reasons, and I made it very clear that I didn't want either of them talking about our arrangement with anyone until well after the deal was done. Owen Darvish chose to interpret that request selectively, because that's the kind of puffed-up little prick he is. He figured out that as long as he didn't mention me by name, he could talk about his pet project all he liked without violating the terms of the NDA. He had his cake, and he ate it right in front of me. That pissed me off, and I've been looking for a way to get him back. A large part of why I want to fund your enterprise is because I know how much it would kill him if Birnam Wood becomes the next big whatever, which it *will*, and you, Mira Bunting, become a household name in this country, which you *will*, and then the story comes out that it all started here, under his nose, and it was nothing to do with him, and he didn't even know about it. Nothing would irritate a guy like this more than being left in the dust by some twenty-something anarchist planting vegetables behind his back, and I find that prospect incredibly amusing.'

Mira had stopped pretending to be aloof and unimpressed; she was now staring at him with fascination. 'So I'm, like, your revenge,' she said.

He smiled again. 'Sure,' he said. 'If you'd like to be.'

'Are you a psychopath?' she said.

He pretended to consider it. 'Now,' he said, musing, tapping his chin with his finger, 'how would a psychopath respond?'

Their conversations never lasted long. As Mira got to know him better, she came to be able to anticipate the precise moment when his intense absorption in whatever it was that she was saying would suddenly evaporate, and he would become fidgety and curt, often interrupting her mid-sentence to say that he was going to leave now, and then abruptly getting up and walking off. 'Those are some pretty shitty manners, by the way,' she'd shouted after him the first time he'd done it, but he'd made no sign that he had heard her, and she'd felt too embarrassed to bring the subject up again next time they met; like all proud and accomplished debaters – or, perhaps, like all proud and accomplished flirts – Mira had a deep instinctive horror of ever being thought to be a nag, and despite what she pretended, she was still more than a little afraid of him. She compensated by putting on a tough and scornful attitude, by refusing to laugh when he said anything remotely funny, and by adapting her conversational style to be much more like his, firing a pointed question at him in lieu of a greeting, and answering elliptically whenever he countered with a question of his own. She was so determined to prove to him that he had met his match in her (for that was how she phrased it to herself – never that *she* had met *her* match in *him*) that although she still had a sense, somehow, that he was hiding something from her, she had an even stronger sense that she would be the one – that she *had* to be the one – to find it out.

'So what is it about billionaires and survivalism?' she'd asked him, the third or fourth time they met. 'Is it just an arms race? Like, just a pissing contest? Or do you all know something that we don't?'

'Both,' he said, quite calmly. 'I mean, of course it's a pissing contest. What isn't?'

She tried to think of something that wasn't, then decided that that was too predictable. 'So what do you know that the rest of us don't?' she said instead.

'I know how easy it was,' said Lemoine.

Mira didn't follow. 'How easy what was?'

'All of it,' he said, shrugging. 'Getting rich. Staying rich. Winning. It was all so easy. I just took what I wanted, and it was mine. I said what I wanted, and people got it for me. I did what I wanted, and nobody stopped me. So simple. And if it was easy for me, then it could be easy for anybody, and that's a very frightening thought. Apart from anything else, it would be untenable. Everyone can't be on top, or it wouldn't be the top any more, would it? That's just a fact.

'And I've been in the citadels of power,' he added. 'I've eaten at the high tables; I've seen behind the doors that never open. Everyone's the same. You reach a certain level and it's all exactly the same: it's all just luck and loopholes and being in the right place at the right time, and compound growth taking care of the rest. That's why we're all building barricades. It's in case the rest of you ever figure out how incredibly easy it was for us to get to where we are.'

'Jesus,' Mira said. 'That's fucking dark.'

'Well, if you get too depressed, remember that it's also just a pissing contest.'

'The whole thing is so fucked up to me,' Mira said. 'And so *childish*. Like, it basically just comes down to you just wanting to make a mess of the planet, and then not wanting to take responsibility for the clean-up, so instead you, like, build this little fortress for yourself so that when the shit really hits the fan, you can just run and hide, and nobody can hold you accountable for anything you did. Right? I mean, people talk so much shit about the "nanny state", but what kind of person makes a huge mess and then has to get someone else to clean it up? A baby. Someone with a fucking nanny.'

'I don't like the term "nanny state",' said Lemoine. 'I find it misogynistic.'

She glared at him. 'Are you trolling me right now?'

'Just trying to find some common ground.'

'Do you actually believe the apocalypse is going to happen?' Mira said. 'Like, in your lifetime?'

He smiled. 'Well – I'm hoping to live a very long life.'

'But you're actively planning for it. You're actively making a plan.'

'I make a lot of plans,' he said.

'Here's what I don't understand,' Mira said. 'You've clearly devoted a lot of time and energy to the idea of a future global catastrophe. But when you spend all this time preparing for this one highly particular scenario, at some level you must be kind of willing it to happen. Right? I mean, like, you're putting in all this effort, you're building your bunker and you're stockpiling all your guns and astronaut food and medicine and whatever else, and when you've done all that, there's got to be a part of you that doesn't actually *want* everything to turn out fine. You want the apocalypse to happen, because that will prove that you were right never to have trusted anybody. Whereas if things actually get *better*, not worse, if people actually start working *together*, and putting *aside* their differences for the sake of the common good and so on, if *that* happens, then you're just going to look like a stupid paranoid dick. Right?'

Lemoine shrugged. 'I've never thought about it,' he said.

'And what's even *more* fucked up is that you totally have it in your power to *make* things better. Like, in all of history, there has literally never been a group of people better equipped to avert catastrophe than the billionaires alive today. The technology you have access to, and the resources, and the money, and the influence, and the connections – literally, no one in history has *ever* been more powerful. *Ever.*'

'Yes, we're like gods,' he said, matter-of-factly. 'But gods can be capricious, Mira. They don't always do what you want them to. They move in mysterious ways.'

She was so astounded that she laughed. 'You're seriously telling me that you think that you're a *god*? Like, not ironically at all?'

He stared at her without blinking. 'I get it,' he said. 'You want me to apologise for my existence. You want me to kneel down before you, and bow and scrape, and ask for your forgiveness for all the bad and greedy things I've done, and you want me to say that I repent, and then you want me to give away all my money, because at long last, after all these years, *finally*, I met you, and I saw the light. Is that it?'

'Sounds pretty good,' Mira said. 'For a start.'

'So in other words,' he said, '*you* want to be a god as well.'

Mira scowled. 'Hey, I'm not the one trying to live forever here,' she said. 'I'm not a survivalist. I'm not a fucking techno-futurist. I know I'm going to die. I'm fine with that.'

'You're fine with it because you think you have no other choice,' said Lemoine.

'I *don't* have any other choice. It's called being human.'

'And if you found out you *did* have another choice, then you'd feel very differently about it. That's human too.'

The next time she'd seen him, she had greeted him by saying, 'You do realise that on paper we're, like, mortal enemies.'

'Whose paper?' he'd replied.

He had flown in only once since she'd returned to Thorndike, to introduce himself to the rest of the group and give his un-official blessing to the project, and although he had made a generally good impression, repeating everybody's names, show-ing a professional interest in their operations, asking brief but intelligent questions, and wishing them all good luck, by the time Mira saw him off an hour later, her clothes were drenched in sweat – and not ordinary sweat, from ordinary exertion, but a strange, sharp, animal sweat that smelled of terror and arous-al; she'd been so jangled and exhausted afterwards that she had crawled into her sleeping bag and fallen fast asleep. It had been profoundly odd, after so many one-on-one encounters, to see him in a social context; perhaps he had felt the same, for when they'd said goodbye, he'd told her frankly that he wasn't planning on dropping in so often now that she was no longer on her own. She had awoken two hours later in the cabbagey-plasticky fug of her tent feeling deadly certain that she had failed somehow, that he had been expecting something to hap-pen between them, and now it wouldn't happen – or couldn't happen – because she was no longer on her own.

In the weeks since she had met Lemoine, Mira had enter-tained a recurring fantasy in which he begged to be allowed to sleep with her, and she rejected him with scorn. She knew that it was a highly conceited thing to imagine. It was shamefully conceited. It was juvenile. It wasn't even sexy. Their bodies were barely even involved. But even though the fantasy embarrassed her, whenever her imagination circled back to it, she never stopped the scene from playing out. She had imagined count- less permutations: sometimes Lemoine tried to kiss her, sometimes he said he loved her, sometimes he tried to bargain with her, sometimes he ejaculated prematurely, sometimes he offered money, sometimes he cried. Her reaction was the only thing that stayed the same. She was always withering, always lofty, always cold. She knew that it probably meant that she was hopelessly sexually repressed, or worse – it definitely said some- thing bad about her, that her go-to sexual fantasy was hardly sexual at all – and so she had already made the decision that if he ever *were* to proposition her, she would *not* refuse him, just so she could prove to her subconscious that she *wasn't* a narcissist, she *wasn't* an ingénue, and she *wasn't* a prude.

Mira severed the weeds at the root and flicked them neatly away, sever-and-flick, sever-and-flick, sever-and-flick. She was almost at the end of the row when she heard engine noise and eagerly looked up – but the sky was empty; in the next second, the sound clarified behind her, and she turned to see that it was just Aaron and Jessica returning from the dairy, the city car revving painfully as it bumped along the vehicle track towards the shearing shed and out of sight. She watched it go with regret, and then, feeling self-conscious, she looked up at the ridge again, scanning it carefully this time, as though to make it seem, for the benefit of anyone who might be watching – which was ridiculous; nobody was – that she had been alerted by the sound of something else entirely. Then she started, for silhouetted against the sky was a lone man in a red jacket; he was wearing a large backpack and making his way rapidly south along the ridge, and although he was much too far away for her to be able to make him out, there was something in his gait and in his proportions that seemed weirdly familiar to her. Mira shaded her eyes to get a better look. The distance between them was so great that it would be absurd to say she recognised him – really, he could have been anybody – but for a strange, fleeting, inexplicable moment, she would have bet every dollar she had ever touched that it was Tony.

'Ten million?' said Lady Darvish. 'It was a bit more than *that*, thank you very much.' She set two plates of fettuccine down on the table and returned to the kitchen to fetch the pepper mill.

'He was all over the place,' Sir Owen said. 'First, he gets the price wrong. Then he starts on about this top-secret research site up in Korowai—'

'You don't know that it's top secret.'

'I do,' Sir Owen said, leaning back while she ground black pepper over his plate. 'Right after I got off the phone to you, I rang Jenny Scobee at DOC and asked her straight up. Just to be absolutely sure.'

Lady Darvish sat down and shook out her napkin. 'Asked her how?'

'You mean, what did I say?'

'Yeah.'

Sir Owen looked down at his meal without seeming to see it. 'I said: "Sorry, Jenny, I realise this is a bit out of the blue, but you wouldn't be able to tell me if there's any geological survey-ing of any kind going on in Korowai right now? Up above the landslide?"'

'And she said no?'

'She laughed,' Sir Owen said. 'She said, "Yeah, right." Like there's any money for anything like that anywhere. She told me she was waiting for the punchline.'

'There's parm in that bowl there,' Lady Darvish said.

He picked up the bowl automatically and spooned some out. 'It doesn't make any sense,' he said.

'Well, maybe she doesn't know,' Lady Darvish said. 'I mean, she's just a – what? A policy analyst? It's not like she's going to know every little thing that—'

'No,' Sir Owen interrupted, 'that's not what I meant. It's that Anthony specifically said the word "radiometric". That's what doesn't make sense. There wouldn't *be* an on-the-ground testing site for that, because nowadays they do it all from the air. They use high-flying drones. That's what I'm telling you.'

'Owen, this isn't your field,' Lady Darvish said. 'You might not actually understand—'

'I *do* understand, because that's the Autonomo connection. They did a survey of the whole country back in 2010 – I even asked Robert about it, the first time we met. It was a huge government contract. A comprehensive airborne geophysical survey. Magnetic and radiometric, both. The report's now on-line; anyone can look it up. No reason to do another one. It's free. It's available. And it's *geology*. The data's not exactly going to go out of date.'

'Can I have the Parmesan, please?'

He passed it to her. 'I looked up the report,' he said. 'This afternoon. I thought maybe they might have found something, like a uranium deposit, or lithium, or even gold, or – I don't know, *something* that meant they wanted to go back for a closer look.'

'You're not eating,' she said.

'Big, thick report,' he said, picking up his fork and waving it. 'Really dense, a proper scientific journal type of thing, with maps of every part of the country showing the geological make-up, right down to the acre. So I looked up Korowai, and guess what we're sitting on down there.'

'Diamonds,' said Lady Darvish.

He didn't smile. 'Just rocks,' he said. 'Three kinds of rock. That's it. The most ordinary—'

'Limestone,' she said.

'That's one.'

'Granite.'

'Right again. And—'

'Don't tell me.' She thought about it. 'My dad would have known this. Slate?'

'Schist,' Sir Owen said. 'Limestone, granite, and schist.'

'All right – so?'

'So, nothing. That's my point. It's so *ordinary*. There's nothing there.' He put down his fork again.

'How is it?' said Lady Darvish, pointing at his plate with her own fork.

'It's lovely,' said Sir Owen. 'Really good, Jill, thanks.'

'Owen, you haven't even tasted it.'

'Sorry,' Sir Owen said, pushing his plate away with a sigh. 'I'm just so bloody wound up. Ever since this call.'

'You're winding yourself up. He probably just made a mistake.'

'He knew we'd had an offer on the farm. *That's* not a mistake. Who the hell told him that?'

Lady Darvish put down her utensils and placed her hands palm-down on the table between them. 'Owen, just think about this calmly for a second. Whoever this guy is – and we have no reason to think that he's *anyone* – he's a pretty shabby journalist. Yes? He's got three things wrong already. The price was wrong; he said there's a research site in the park, that's wrong; and the radiometric part, like you said, the science of it, that's wrong.'

Sir Owen was shaking his head. 'But he called me *from Thorndike*. He said he'd been up on the ridge, and in the parkland,

and he explicitly said that he'd talked to a security guard *at* the research site. *In* the national park.'

'Above the landslide,' Lady Darvish said.

'Yeah.'

'All right, so maybe there *is* something there, but it's just something to do with the slip,' she said. 'Earthquake strengthening. Right? Maybe? Or some kind of testing, so that something like that doesn't happen again. Some structural engineering type of thing. Or civil. What's the difference between structural and civil engineering, by the way? I don't actually think I know.'

He ignored the question. 'But then why would he say radiometric?'

'Well, he's writing a piece about Robert,' Lady Darvish said. 'He could have read up about that big survey – online, just like you did – and then remembered it wrong. Right? That's plausible. He just got confused. Remember that this guy has no credentials, Owen. He could be thick as a boot.'

'He seemed quite quick to me,' Sir Owen said.

'And if this research site in the park *is* a civil engineering thing,' she went on, more confidently, 'or structural, or whatever – something to do with the landslide – then that would explain why they didn't know about it at DOC. See? Problem solved.'

'But it's conservation land. They'd need—'

'But maybe different rules apply in an emergency. They're going to have to rebuild the viaduct, aren't they? And the road over the pass?'

'I think so,' Sir Owen said.

'Well, there you go,' Lady Darvish said. 'Different department. I bet you that it's all totally plausible and totally legitimate, and Anthony just made a mistake.'

Sir Owen seemed to waver. 'But how did he know we sold the farm?'

'I can't tell you that,' she said firmly, 'but here is what I do know. If he publishes anything that's not completely, absolutely one hundred per cent factually correct, no matter where he publishes it, on the most incidental nobody-reads-it blog you've never heard of in your life, if we don't like it, then we sue. We come down on him like a ton of bricks for defamation, and we drag his reputation through the muck, and we make damn sure that nobody ever believes a word he writes about anything ever again. All right? Now eat.'

He took a bite. 'Tasty,' he said.

'Nothing wrong with my salmon carbonara.'

'No, ma'am,' Sir Owen said.

It was a long-standing joke between Jill and Owen Darvish that she knew her husband better than he knew himself. In restaurants, she could always say what he was going to order before he'd even seen the menu, and when they went on holiday, she always knew in advance what he'd forget to pack. She knew all his stories, all his pet theories, all his favoured puns, and often, when they were in company, she found that she could so easily predict what he was just about to say that to amuse herself she would beat him to it by a fraction of a second, launching into the exact same anecdote, with the exact same phrasing, the same vocabulary, the same emphasis even. He was never offended; he'd just start nodding along and chuckling and saying, 'This is a good one,' and, 'Yeah, guys – listen to this.' He seemed to accept as a matter of course that she had a greater understanding of his inner life than he did, and superior powers of recall to his own, and a better sense of his own best interests – both what they were and how they might be served. He submitted to her eagerly, and was never more content, it seemed, than when she was telling him, often in a slightly scolding manner, what he remembered, what he imagined, and what he believed.

'Bath?' she said, when his plate was clean.

'Bath and a whisky, I think.'

'I'll do the dishes,' she said. 'Go on. Scoot.'

'Are you sure?' he said, but he was already pushing his chair back from the table.

It had occurred to Lady Darvish, especially in recent years, that Sir Owen took a certain pride in being so predictable to her – that he played it up, in fact, deliberately caricaturing himself as a kind of dumb brute who was helpless to his instincts and to the force of his habits, which had become more and more circumscribed with age – for the simple reason that he loved to see her demonstrate how well she understood him, loved to see her take that caricature and refine it, improving the likeness, adding depth and subtlety, shading it in. For a while, when their children had been teenagers, they had worked it into a kind of cutesy double act: 'We've got to that stage of being married,' he would say, 'where we know each other so well that she can actually finish my—' 'Beer!' she would cut in, or 'Cigar!' or 'Pudding!' and he would pretend to be exasperated ('Sentences, woman, *sentences*!') and everyone would laugh – for of course, that was the whole point: she was always one step out in front of him, and that was just where he wanted her to be.

She was proud, as she knew he was too, that they were the kind of couple whom people spoke of only as a set. In vain moments, she saw their marriage as a kind of service to the public good, a relationship that others looked to as a standard, such that if they ever separated, she felt sure there would be widespread terror and despair among their friends and family, because if *they* couldn't make it, then nobody else had a hope. They had celebrated their silver wedding anniversary that February past. All their children were upstanding and gainfully employed. Their eldest was married, and the younger two might

as well have been; all three had been in the same stable and loving relationships for years. Money-wise, they were sitting pretty
– and had been long before the knighthood, and long before
they'd met Lemoine. They owned a decent portfolio of assets,
alongside two ample KiwiSaver pension funds, large enough
that they could both retire at sixty if they wanted to, which they
didn't, because they loved their jobs, and loved to see each other
challenged and fulfilled. They still had their health, touch wood.
They had their looks – 'the use of them, anyway,' Sir Owen
said; he liked to disgust his children by running his hand over
his silver stubble and telling them that each time a man truly,
passionately made love in his life, one of his hairs would turn
grey. And *that*, Lady Darvish thought, was almost certainly
an undercount. They loved each other. They made each other
laugh. They showed each other kindness. They were happy.

And yet – Lady Darvish sometimes felt that she had reached
a stage of life where behind every statement there lurked an
obstinate 'and yet' – middle age had wrought in them divergent
changes; over the past ten years she had felt herself becoming
more permissive and open-minded as her husband had become
steadily more conventional and risk-averse. Unquestionably,
they were growing apart – though not in the way the phrase
was often used, as a prelude to a separation, signalling a mutual
estrangement, a growing blindness and deafness to each other's
needs and wishes, an increasing independence and indifference,
a mounting sense of historical grievance perhaps, an early taste
of liberation, a fixation on coming out ahead and keeping score
– for Lady Darvish had experienced none of these things; if
anything, she felt she understood Sir Owen more intimately,
and more tenderly, than she ever had. She could simply see,
quite clearly, the ever-widening space between them. She felt as
she did when they watched a movie or a television drama that

they hadn't seen before and found herself forming two parallel impressions of it in her mind: her own, and what she was certain would be his, that she then compared with one another privately, internally, examining their differences, and even making them converse, so that what she shared aloud with him after the movie or the episode was over was often just a potted version of a much more probing and speculative conversation that had already happened in her head. Though it was rare that they found time to watch anything new; Sir Owen preferred revisiting his favourites, and he would not be tempted to the cinema for anything other than a Liam Neeson action movie or James Bond.

The bathroom door closed and the fan went on. A second later she heard running water, and then the clink of the toilet seat being put down, and then a sigh; now Sir Owen would be seated, unbuttoning his shirt slowly from the bottom up, and staring into the tub as it filled. She kept this image of him in her mind as she cleared away the dishes, reflecting as she loaded up the dishwasher that it was only natural, after all, that of the two of them, he should be the more conservative and even staid. He'd been in the same job since he was a teenager; her career had been much more varied, and it had tested her in different ways. She had trained as a paramedic when she was first out of school – she'd met Sir Owen on a call-out – but she'd quit when they'd had Rachel, and then along came Liam, and then Jesse, rambunctious boys just eleven months apart. Returning to work a decade later, she hadn't been able to face the thought of endless nights on call and back-to-back shifts at the weekend, so she'd put aside her early training and found a job in logistics and operations, of all things, for a haulage company, which in turn had opened the door to a sequence of sales rep, HR, and finally even management positions over the following fifteen-odd years. She'd been nudging six figures by the time she reached her early fifties, but with a nagging sense of having turned her back on her vocation early on, so she'd packed it all in to start her own business, blowing the dust off her old medical textbooks, circling back to where she started, and taking out a loan against the house – which she'd since repaid, thank you very much; her enterprise might not have reached the heights of Darvish Pest Control, which had only gone from strength to strength, but she was proud that she'd managed to turn a profit, without anybody's help, within two years. Her business was a one-woman outfit that offered accredited first-aid training courses for teachers, carers, sports coaches, antenatal classes, workplace groups, and the police; the classes ranged from basic defibrillator training to what was now called psychological first aid. It was flexible work that she could put down and pick up as she pleased, and so when her dad died and they moved into her old family house in Thorndike, she'd been able to find a new client base down south and carry on without too much trouble at all – though Sir Owen, predictably, had taken some convincing. They'd gone back and forth about the move, and back and forth about the prospect of commuting, and back and forth about the subdivision plans for months, until one night he'd told her, with sudden and disarming honesty, that he supposed that he was only putting up a fight about it because at some level he just hadn't quite accepted yet that her dad was really gone.

Yes, she thought, agreeing with herself as she returned the whisky bottle to its place on the shelf beside the microwave and picked up the sponge to wipe the kitchen counter down, yes, it made perfect sense that Sir Owen was more dyed-in-the-wool than she. He had always been his own boss, and always with the same company, and always in the same line of work, whereas she knew what it was like to have to work alongside and underneath people, and to have to work for companies whose products she didn't really care about, and to have to work as one of a team – and she now had the experience of being self-employed, to boot. She'd also spent a decade as a full-time mother, which had sharpened her perspective on herself, made her more efficient, and more appreciative of novelty and stimulation, and more determined to stick her elbows out and take her chances where she could. And on top of *that*, she thought, with an air of putting all other considerations firmly in the shade, on top of *that*, there was the simple fact that her husband was a man and she was a woman. Lady Darvish nodded sagely to herself. She believed, quite frankly and unapologetically, that women were superior to men; it seemed merely obvious to her that women's minds were subtler than men's, more flexible, more capacious, more resilient, and more socially and circumstantially astute, and to those who might doubt that a disparity between the sexes existed in the first place, or indeed, that one could speak of two such categories at all, she would only shake her head and laugh, and say emphatically that raising her daughter could *not* have been more different from raising her two sons: 'They were like two different *species*,' she would say, 'I mean – I'm telling you. Talk about "Men are from Mars"!' But it was as a consequence of her belief in the supremacy of her own sex that she held men to far lower standards than she did women, and so tended to be rather softer on them; with Sir Owen – as with her sons, and with her father before he'd died – her attitude of condescension could take the form of a cosseting, and even an obsequious, indulgence.

She heard a splosh and a plunk as Sir Owen stepped into the bath, and then a squeak as he slid down to partially submerge himself, first reaching back up to the basin for his whisky, which he would now balance on his breastbone, draping his arms over the sides of the tub, and resting the lip of the glass against his chin. Then quiet: only the hum of the fan, and the occasional creak as he shifted his weight to lift the glass and sip.

'Nice?' she called out to him.

'Really nice,' came the muffled reply.

Lady Darvish turned out the light in the kitchen and padded through into the study nook to check a Trade Me auction that was ending soon. She was one of three bidders in contest for a wall-mounted fish sculpture made of beaten aluminium, and although it didn't really go with their décor exactly, and she wasn't entirely sure where she would put it, and the auction had already blown well past the upper limit of what she felt the thing was worth, nevertheless she had recognised in herself a roving, disaffected feeling that meant that she was in the mood to buy something, especially something overpriced that she knew she didn't really need. Logging into her account, she saw that she had been outbid, and raised the highest bid by five dollars.

'Jill,' called Sir Owen from the bathroom.

'Yeah,' she said.

'Will you bring me the good scrub? It's in the other shower.'

By the time she came back to the computer, she had been outbid again. She increased her bid a second time, wondering, as the auction entered the final ten minutes and the countdown clock began to pulse, if perhaps her love for her husband was becoming more maternal as they approached old age. Though it was a maternal feeling of a kind she hadn't really known with her own children; perhaps, in fact, a grandmaternal feeling, wise, affectionate, forbearing, soft-hearted, but also a little weary, a little retrospective, a little removed ... But it was sisterly as well. She knew Sir Owen in and out. She was proud of him; she wanted the best for him. She had no desire to leave him, she felt no fear or worry that he wished to leave her – or that he ever had, or that he ever would, or even could. He had confessed to her, rather sweetly, on the eve of his investiture, that he felt his knighthood was in effect a tribute to them both, a just reward for having stayed together through it all; for having had a sunny outlook and an honest disposition all those years; for having loved each other decently and well. 'We deserve this, Jill,' he'd said to her, in the dark, in bed. 'Both of us. We really do.'

And yet.

For that was the peculiar thing, Lady Darvish thought, clicking through to browse the seller's other listings while she waited for the auction to elapse: ever since the knighthood – no, further back; ever since they'd met Lemoine – Sir Owen had talked incessantly about 'deserving', and it seemed to her that the more he'd dwelled upon the subject, the more his sense of satisfaction in his life had ebbed away. Now he was almost like a different person. Gone was the creature of habit, the man of confident complacency and firm, well-trodden ground; in his place was someone oddly younger, someone who was eager, and reckless, and unsettled, and unsure. The knighthood, which ought to have tickled him, ought to have made him shrug and laugh and throw away some joke about a bauble, instead had seemed to vex him; he brought it up almost every day to wonder who had been responsible for putting his name forward, and how the nominations really worked, and whether he had ever been in contention previously – only to doubt himself at once, reflecting darkly that the honour had probably only been bestowed on him because of the landslide – or because of some political reason that had nothing to do with him – or (and this was the suspicion that rankled most bitterly) because of his association with Lemoine.

His behaviour towards the billionaire had been strangely contradictory. One moment he was driving the negotiations, talking tough, and haggling over nothing just to throw his weight around; the next, he was giving Lemoine the run of their house and encouraging him to use the airstrip as he pleased, and inviting him for dinner, and proposing that they go hunting together, and asking – utterly bizarrely, Lady Darvish had thought – if maybe Robert would enjoy the experience of killing and butchering a lamb? (Robert would not.) In the billionaire's presence he was both fawning and strutting, both unnaturally macho and unnaturally sycophantic, and although it was rare that Lady Darvish felt embarrassed for her husband, there had been times over the past few months when she had even pitied him. This business about the radiometric survey, for instance: Sir Owen should have been relieved to learn that this so-called journalist – a blogger and a nobody, for goodness' sake – had plainly begun his investigations well before they'd hosted the Mulloys, which meant that they couldn't possibly bear any responsibility for whatever it was that he might or might not have found out about their agreement with Lemoine. Safe in that knowledge, Sir Owen should have then felt free to keep him on the line, to turn the questioning around, to ask him more about this alleged research site in the national park, and to find out what *he* thought was going on there; and *then*, if Sir Owen *still* had misgivings, he should have just called Lemoine directly, told him that a journalist was sniffing round his private business, and put the radiometric question – if there even *was* a question – to the billionaire himself. But Sir Owen's mind had gone straight to conspiracy. The call had unravelled him, flustered him, wounded him; it had convinced him that he'd missed something, that he'd been bested somehow, upstaged, embarrassed, even hoodwinked – and not by Anthony; he didn't give a shit about Anthony! By Lemoine. If she hadn't known her husband better, Lady Darvish thought sardonically, returning

215

to the listing for the final thirty seconds' countdown, she might have suspected that Sir Owen Patrick Darvish had a crush.

The auction ended: she had won. Lady Darvish logged into her Internet banking platform to put the payment through, wrote an email to the seller to confirm delivery details, and scrolled through the photos of the sculpture one last time, reckoning that it was worth perhaps fifty dollars less than what she'd paid for it, but feeling satisfaction in the purchase, nonetheless. Presently the bathroom door opened, releasing an aromatic gust of apricot and coconut, and Sir Owen came out, bringing with him the peaty, woodsy smell of his whisky that mingled pleasantly with the fruity aromas of the soap. He'd left the water for her. Lady Darvish went in, lit a candle, and turned off the overhead – she would never understand why he chose to bathe in glaring light – and then turned the hot tap on full to freshen up the water. As she unbuttoned her shirt and trousers and unhooked her bra, she appraised her reflection in the full-length mirror on the back of the door with the kind of cool, satirical look that passes between two old friends whose tastes and expectations are perfectly aligned, communicating a judgment of mingled amusement, resignation, and dismay. She reached down to stir the water, and then got in, lay back, and made a conscious effort to put all her ruminations out of her mind.

When she re-emerged from the bathroom half an hour later, she was expecting that Sir Owen would be in bed; she knew that he was heading up to Northland early in the morning to oversee the launch of his conservation project, which was to be filmed for a puff segment on the six o'clock news. But to her surprise, he was in the living room, hunched over his laptop and tilting his credit card to verify the number against something on the screen.

'What are you doing?' she said, cinching her dressing gown tighter round her waist.

He glanced at her guiltily over his reading glasses. 'I'm booking a flight down to Christchurch,' he said.

This was unprecedented: he never made plans of any kind without consulting with her first. 'Christchurch?' she said, in the same tone as she might have said, 'Antarctica?'

He was still confirming the number and didn't answer.

'What for?' she said after a moment.

'I want to see this research site for myself,' he said.

She gaped at him. 'What – down in *Korowai?*'

'Yeah,' he said. 'I'll rent a car at the airport and drive down.'

'Owen!' she exclaimed reproachfully. 'At least let's talk about this!'

He turned the credit card over to find the authentication code. 'You've got a course on Saturday,' he said, tapping it in. 'You're busy.'

'What – you mean *this* Saturday? No. Owen, stop. Talk to me.'

'It's just Friday night to Sunday night,' he said. 'In and out. Be good to check on the house, anyway.' He clicked the trackpad, and his computer made a whooshing noise.

'But all that driving,' she said. 'You'll spend the whole time in the car.'

'Well, it's booked now,' he said. He pointed at his laptop. 'I just booked it.'

She glared at him with helpless annoyance. 'What about Robert?' she said.

'What about him?'

'We said we'd let him know if we were coming back,' she said. 'He might be there.'

Sir Owen scoffed. 'He's not going to *be* there,' he said. 'Jill, please.'

'"Jill, please"?' she said, offended. 'Jill, please, what?'

'Just – come on. He was never going to *stay* at our *house*.'

'You told him that he could.'

'Yes, I realise that, thanks. I just think he's probably got better places to be.'

She detected bitterness. 'What is it that you think you're going to find down there, exactly?'

But as she sat down on the arm of the sofa, ready to talk, he got up, closing his laptop and folding his glasses away. 'If I knew that, I wouldn't be going down,' he said. 'Would I.'

'Owen, is this about the launch tomorrow?'

'Why would it be about that?'

'I don't know, just – it's a big day. Lots riding on it. You might be nervous.'

'Well, I'm not.'

'I know that you were disappointed—'

'It's not about the launch, Jill. I've said what it's about.'

'Owen, I told you, Anthony probably just made a mistake.'

'Yes, I heard you.' He wasn't looking at her. 'I'm going to bed. Will you turn the lights off?'

'*Owen*,' she said, baffled – but he was already gone.

Ever since the Queen's Birthday Honours List had been announced, and the citations published, and all those honoured fêted by the press, the Autonomo publicity office had been receiving repeated calls from New Zealand media outlets seeking a comment on the alleged partnership with Darvish Pest Control. While none of them had singled out Lemoine specifically, or made any mention of Thorndike, or the landslide, or the farm – it would seem the Darvishes had abided by the letter, if not the spirit, of the non-disclosure agreement that they both had signed – with each importunate contact, Lemoine had felt his irritation grow. It was one of his precepts that anyone who tried to get one over on him should always be made to regret it, and when he'd learned that Darvish was planning to launch his conservation project with some fanfare – invitations; speeches; a spot on the six o'clock news – he'd briefly considered getting his revenge by showing up. He could arrive by helicopter, steal the spotlight, cause a stir; he could then regally refuse to be interviewed ('No, no, this is Sir Owen's day,' he imagined saying airily, 'this was his brainchild; I'm just here for the birds') – whereupon the assembled journalists would inevitably turn to Darvish and ask him, mics hot, cameras rolling, how on earth the pair of them had come to meet. And why had Darvish failed to mention the billionaire's personal involvement in the project? *Was* it a personal involvement? What did their relationship comprise exactly? Or more bluntly: what was in this for Lemoine? Was he angling for citizenship, perhaps? Had he ever spoken with Darvish about that? About buying property in New Zealand? Settling here? Investing here? Was there more to this apparent partnership than Darvish had hitherto disclosed? However Darvish answered, he would be sure to breach the NDA in one way or another, at which point Lemoine would then step in, terminate the whole arrangement, and sue the little fuck for everything that he was worth. It was an appealing fantasy – and one that Lemoine would never carry out; for although he would have liked nothing more than to see Owen Darvish hoisted with his own petard, the fact remained that, for the next few months at least, he needed him.

When Darvish had first proposed the sideline partnership between Autonomo and Darvish Pest Control as a condition of the sale of the acreage at Thorndike, Lemoine had been convinced for a good few minutes that the other man must have found out about his operation in the national park somehow, and was now proceeding to lay out the terms of a blackmail. In retrospect, Lemoine could see that he'd probably come on a little strong in talking up the farm's defensible position, crediting the landslide with having gifted him with such an opportunity, describing the features of the bunker that he wished to build, and enjoying the role of the maniacal survivalist perhaps a little much; he'd overplayed his cover, to the extent that it had become, in a way, a kind of tell. 'So, you really want to buy this place,' Darvish had observed, correctly; 'well, in that case, mate, there's something that *I* really want, as well.'

It was not a blackmail, merely a rather dull business proposition for a conservation project that aimed to monitor endangered native birds by drone; what Darvish wanted, essentially, was the use of Autonomo technology for free. Lemoine could have supplied this with his eyes closed, but he did not like to be manoeuvred, and he liked environmental sanctimony even less; when would conservationists finally figure out, he'd thought, that you could not simultaneously beg for someone's help and berate them? He'd interrupted Darvish to reject the proposition out of hand, instead raising his offer on the farm by another half million, calling it final, and threatening to walk. 'I don't have any sway at Autonomo these days,' he'd told Darvish flatly, 'so I couldn't make that happen even if I wanted to. This is a private purchase. It has nothing to do with Autonomo at all.' He'd been astonished when Darvish had turned around and called his bluff – for he *had* been bluffing. Not only was Autonomo entirely at his disposal, in every shape and form, but the value of his operation in the national park was such that he could have paid the Darvishes a hundred times what he'd offered them and still come out very comfortably ahead. Darvish could not have known it, but as negotiations went, Lemoine's position could hardly have been weaker. The extraction site in the park was still hot; his men were still deployed; the leaching process had still a few months to run; and he had no back-up plan – in fact, this *was* his back-up plan.

Lemoine had covered by dialling up the billionaire psychology, acting spoiled and bloody-minded, telling Darvish that he wasn't used to being fucked with, and declaring, with exaggerated self-importance, that he always found a way to possess what he desired. He'd insisted on the NDA before negotiating any further, and only after it was signed and sealed had he agreed, very grudgingly, to furnish Darvish Pest Control with a small number of drones and operating systems, subject to a number of restrictions that Autonomo would retain the right to change. A contract was duly drawn up between them, and Darvish had gone crowing to the press; but then had come the matter of the orange-fronted parakeet. To Lemoine's intense irritation, it turned out that the world's last remaining populations of this critically endangered species could be found almost exclusively in Korowai National Park, which was the last place on earth that he wanted to invite surveillance. He had come up with a perfectly plausible objection ('That's going to be my back fence; I don't want drones over my back fence'), but Darvish had put up such a fight about it that Lemoine had begun to wonder, for a second time, if the man might know something. He had been considering drastically changing course when, in the weeks after the Queen's Birthday announcement, the Darvishes had invited him for dinner at their house, and late in the evening, after Darvish had excused himself to use the bathroom, the wife had leaned tipsily across the table and confided that actually there really wasn't any decent reason for the sticking point: her husband had come to see himself as a Korowai local, she'd explained, and he didn't want to seem disloyal to the region. That was all. New Zealanders could be very hard on their own, she said, and the knighthood meant the poor man's head was now above the parapet; he had to show that he was giving back, that he wasn't just in it for himself, that he hadn't forgotten who he was and where he came from. It was a Kiwi thing. Actually, she went on, he had never even seen an orange-fronted parakeet. Her dad had – there was a photograph somewhere – and that was just it, really, because the truth was, Owen had loved her dad more than he'd loved his own father, which was incredibly sweet, but it made him soft in the head sometimes, such that he couldn't see the wood for the trees, and this sentimental streak in him had become so much more pronounced after the landslide – terrible, what that had done to the economy – that she guessed that maybe he was feeling that Korowai could simply use the break? They heard the toilet flush, and she touched Lemoine's arm and whispered not to worry, she'd speak to Owen, bring him round – and all Lemoine could think was if he had ever caught *his* wife talking in this way behind his back, he'd have killed her.

Jill Darvish had been as good as her word; several days later Lemoine had received an updated version of the contract with several clauses tactfully amended and all mention of the orange-fronted parakeet removed. The New Zealand fairy tern was suggested, and accepted, as a substitute endangered species with which to launch the project; it was a frail sand-nesting seabird whose survival Lemoine found it virtually impossible to care about, but it had a solitary virtue – namely, that it could be found only in the province of Northland, a safe six hundred miles away. At long last, the deal was done – but somehow, over the course of the negotiations, it seemed that Darvish had convinced himself that he and Lemoine were really business partners, or even – and this truly was incomprehensible – friends.

He began to keep Lemoine abreast of the conservation project by email, and more than once, scrolling down past the badly formatted bullet points, the out-of-focus photographs, and the fluctuating font sizes, Lemoine had fantasised about replying, simply, 'unsubscribe' – pretending he hadn't noticed that each weekly update had been written specifically, and painstakingly, to him.

The night before the project was to launch, Lemoine boarded a commercial flight to San Francisco and flew home. He often acted out of impulse just so that he could then devote his leisure hours to mulling why; he relished self-analysis, though he had never undergone any form of therapy in his life, and never would. What thrilled him was the sense that he alone could understand himself. He loved to wonder at his own motivations, to marvel at his own eccentric mind, to evaluate himself in the second person, and then, even more deliciously, in the third. In a way, it was a form of playing chess against himself, which as a boy he had always preferred to playing against the computer. Sitting alone over the board, barefoot, cross-legged, his chin upon his fists, he had never tried to simulate ordinary playing conditions by forcing himself, every time he turned the board around, into an artificial state of ignorance about his opponent's – his – next move. Instead, he trained himself to do the opposite: to move in full certainty of where the other side was moving next; to plan ahead while knowing exactly what the other side was planning. His goal had been to become so ambidextrous when it came to action and reaction, move and countermove, that he would reach the point where half the games he played were won by white, and half by black: only then, he'd told himself, could he really call himself a master. This objective had so consumed him that in time he'd lost all appetite for playing with a living partner, and if ever somebody did challenge him, he would lie and say he'd never learned the rules. Even better if that person had already seen him playing by himself; better still if the invitation came *while* he was playing! Lemoine loved to present as an enigma. It made his self-dissections all the sweeter to know that he was outwardly inscrutable, a puzzle to which only he would ever hold the key.

For there was a key. There was a secret to his nature, a clue that explained everything about him, a single eight-week period in his very early adolescence that had forged, in every way, the man that he'd become; and it was one of his deepest satisfactions that, despite two unauthorised biographies, countless profiles, constant media speculation, and at least a dozen attempted investigative scoops, no one had ever discovered what it was. Lemoine leaned back in the upholstered airline seat, laced his hands behind his neck, and closed his eyes.

He had been raised by his grandparents in California. His father had worked as a computer technician servicing US embassies and diplomatic missions around the world; this was how he had met Lemoine's mother, an interpreter who at the time of their first meeting had been stationed at the US consulate in Shenyang. They had never married, and Lemoine had known his father only in his early infancy; soon after they separated, his mother accepted a higher-level State Department job in Cambodia and took the decision to send Lemoine back to the United States. Her family – the Ropers – had long ties to the US Army, and so Lemoine grew up near the base at Fort Irwin, where his grandfather, Captain Roper, was a JAG Corps attorney in medical and contract law. He lost all contact with his father, and saw his mother only rarely, sometimes as seldom as once or twice a year; after Phnom Penh came postings to Dhaka, Islamabad, Colombo, and Ulaanbaatar, places that barely existed for Lemoine except as syllables and colours on a map. As a boy he was far more interested in the idea of his father than in the idea of his mother, who was tense and unforthcoming whenever she returned. He began to play chess, his father's game; he formed an interest in cryptography, his father's passion; and with an ambition one day to follow in his father's footsteps, he started teaching himself programming in BASIC on Captain Roper's Commodore 64.

When Lemoine was nine, Captain Roper died, and almost overnight, his grandmother packed up the house and relocated with Lemoine to the border city of Calexico, where she'd grown up. He later understood that she had suffered a nervous break-down, brought on by the intensity of her grief; this took some time to dawn on him, however, for shortly after the move, Lemoine became aware that he was being followed.

A man with a thick neck and a sunken face began haunting the neighbourhood where they now lived. Lemoine first saw him on a city bus, and then again at the diner where he and his grandmother ate on Friday nights, and then again at the movie theatre downtown, sitting in the far corner by the exit, though the theatre was half-empty and much better seats were free. He saw the man leaning on the bleachers in the outfield, and browsing at the dime store, and reading a newspaper behind the wheel of a wood-panelled Chevrolet Celebrity that suddenly was everywhere Lemoine looked – at the bottom of his street, by the school gates, outside the hospital during his grandmoth-er's appointments, and then right behind them in the drive-thru afterwards, the driver's window open, one meaty elbow resting on the sill. Lemoine told no one, but he loaded Captain Roper's gun and began to keep it in his schoolbag, just in case.

Lemoine's grandmother was experiencing paranoid delu-sions; his mother was unreachable, halfway across the world; and he had no way of contacting his father. He was nine years old, in an unfamiliar city, without family, without friends, and he was being followed by a man he was utterly convinced was an assassin. Lemoine had no doubt that this man had come to kill him. He had possessed ever since he could remember a sense that he was special, that he was better than other children, that he was set apart, and it seemed merely obvious to him that if he was valuable – which he was – then he must be dangerous as well. For eight weeks, Lemoine waited for the man with the sunken face to find him; for eight weeks, he lay in bed at night with his hand on Captain Roper's gun.

And then, one day, the Chevrolet Celebrity was gone. The man was gone. Lemoine peered at faces everywhere he went, counted cars in parking lots, checked behind him constantly, twitched the curtains in his bedroom, doubled back on himself, behaved erratically, behaved predictably, lied about his where-abouts, advertised his whereabouts, set little traps, scanned every room he entered and both sides of every street he walked – but nothing. He never saw the man with the sunken face again.

His grandmother's health continued to deteriorate, but it wasn't until three years later, when Lemoine was twelve, that his mother moved back home. She had three things to tell him. The first was that she had never worked for the State Department, as she'd pretended; since before Lemoine was born, she'd been an active agent for the CIA. The second thing she told him was that Lemoine's father had also been a spy; in fact, their work together had been so sensitive and so perilous that once or twice they had placed Lemoine under protection from afar – not that Lemoine would ever have noticed – and of course nothing bad had ever happened to him – but there had been times when he'd actually had a secret bodyguard to keep him safe. She said this so confidingly, so cosily, with such little knowledge of the terror that Lemoine had felt, or the certainty that the man with the sunken face had been sent to kill him, and that he, Lemoine, was going to die, that he had hardly heard her third and final piece of news, which was that she had been diagnosed with stage 4 breast cancer and had only several months left to live.

At her funeral, Lemoine sat in perfect silence as her false co-workers delivered false eulogies about her false achievements in her false career, and when a grey-faced man with pouched eyes and a drinker's nose touched his shoulder afterwards and said, 'Rob? Robbie? I'm David Lemoine – I'm your father,' he showed no emotion at all; he only put out his hand and said politely, 'I go by Robert actually, but it's very good to meet you.' He was determined never to reveal what his mother had told him; seeing that his father appeared to want to broach the subject, he pretended to be stupid and self-absorbed, and affected such a studied lack of interest in his father's life and work that any relationship that might have formed between them had no chance. David fell out of touch again, and years later, when Autonomo reached a private valuation of 900 million dollars and began to drum up public interest for an IPO, Lemoine had the satisfaction of rejecting his call.

His sovereignty was his revenge, thought Lemoine, as the plane reached cruising altitude and he was presented with a soda water and a glass of ice. His wealth was his revenge. His mystique, his opacity, his protean curiosity and impenetrable charm – these were not intrinsic aspects of his character, but cultivated acts of vengeance against everyone who had deceived him, his parents, his grandparents, the army, the government, the CIA. He had risen to power to spite them. He had risen to brilliance to spite them. He had survived to spite them. For they were all dead now: his father, from a stroke, his grandmother, from pneumonia followed by the flu – and then, of course, Gizela. Lemoine tried to picture her, but for some reason he couldn't, and so he thought instead of Mira. He thought about the way she glared at him. He thought about the dirt beneath her nails.

Fourteen hours later he was back in his Palo Alto office, undergoing intravenous rehydration while he scrolled through a tiresome backlog of unanswered correspondence with his one free hand. It was almost nine in the evening local time. All of his assistants were still at their desks, working so silently and with such scrupulous self-consciousness that he could have no doubt it was a performance for his benefit, and they would have all gone home hours ago if he had not unexpectedly returned. There were few things Lemoine liked less than being humoured, so when he'd first arrived, he'd placed an order for a double-shot cortado, not to drink – he hadn't touched a cup of coffee since he'd started microdosing acid on a weekly basis – but just to see their faces fall when they realised that he must be planning on staying in the office till the early hours of the morning, if not through the night. The cortado was now cold, the foam pocked and sunken, and he had just moved the glass from his desk on to the sideboard, out of sight, when he heard an unfamiliar buzzing noise coming from his briefcase. Both his phones were on his desk in front of him, and for a crazy, still-jetlagged moment he wondered if someone could have planted something in his luggage . . . before he came to his senses and realised what it was. He detached the IV drip, opened the briefcase, took out a third, vibrating phone, and answered it.

'Yes,' he said, reaching out with his other hand to snap shut the venetian blinds.

'Hello?' said a distant-sounding voice on the other end. 'Mr Weschler?'

'This is Weschler,' said Lemoine. 'What is it?'

'Sir, we've just had our second security breach in a week. This isn't theoretical any more. We need more men.'

Lemoine had already jammed the phone between his ear and his shoulder; moving both hands over his keyboard, he disconnected from the local server and entered the Korowai operating system as a remote user. 'What kind of breach?'

'It appears to be the same individual. White male, travelling alone. We don't believe that he's a threat, but the issue is that thermal didn't pick him up till he was right on top of us, both times. This just proves what we've been saying, sir: we need backup. If one guy can get past us, that's one too many.'

'Where is he now?' Lemoine was accessing all cameras: the screen in front of him split into four, and then eight, and then twelve.

'Sir, I say again, we don't believe that he's a threat in and of himself. The issue—'

'Where is he now, soldier?'

There was a pause, and then the voice said, 'We don't know, sir.'

'You lost him.'

'Sir, with respect—'

'Don't give me fucking respect,' snapped Lemoine. 'Respect is doing your job. Respect is this never fucking happened in the first place.'

The voice held firm. 'Sir, we've said it before: the technology is not adequate to the conditions here. It's as simple as that. The drones can't penetrate the canopy, and they're next to useless in the rain. Thermal's all over the place. I agree, this should never have happened—'

'Oh great,' said Lemoine. 'So we agree.'

'This was not a failure of command or execution, sir. It was a matter of not enough men on the ground, and an over-reliance on technology that simply isn't up—'

'Shut up,' said Lemoine. 'Shut the fuck up.' He was hunched

forward, scanning each pane. 'Who am I looking for here? Give me a description.'

There was a brief pause, and then the voice said, 'Target is a white male, brown hair, beard, blue eyes, medium height. Maybe thirty years of age. Red jacket, black shorts, boots with gaiters, all very worn.'

Possibly somebody from Birnam Wood, thought Lemoine. He selected the feed over the shearing shed and enlarged it, swiftly counting heads. 'What else?'

'He was first sighted on Saturday morning at 1000 hours,' said the voice. 'He presented as a local. He was carrying a back-pack. He'd spent the night in the outdoors. He engaged in small talk; he moved on. Nothing to arouse suspicion.'

Lemoine had counted seven people: everyone accounted for. 'But then he came back,' he said.

'Yes, sir, he was sighted again today at 1440 hours near extraction point NE4. He was carrying—'

'So there *was* reason for suspicion,' said Lemoine. 'You just missed it.'

'Sir, he was carrying binoculars, and from his conversation on Saturday morning, we have reason to believe that he's a bird watcher. We're confident—'

'You missed it,' repeated Lemoine.

There was a little pause, and then the voice said, 'Yes sir, that's correct, we did.'

'Who's "we"?' said Lemoine. 'You *all* spoke to him? Every one of you?'

The voice became mechanical. 'We all take full responsibility for any individual action, sir. We act as one, we think as one, we move as one.'

'Good, then you'll move as fucking one to find him,' said Lemoine, and he hung up.

The trouble with private military contractors was they were too used to deep pockets, he thought, as he sat watching the feeds and tapping his index finger compulsively against his lip. It made them lazy. It meant they lost agility, lost the capacity to work creatively with what they had. They'd been asking for backup every week since they'd arrived in Korowai – and would have received it, of course, if Lemoine really had been Lt Col James Weschler, paramilitary commanding officer at the CIA's Special Operations Group, and if the operation in the national park really had been financed by an alliance of governments working in secret to curb the creeping market dominance of China, and if the rare-earth elements they were extracting really had been destined, as the PMCs believed, for top-secret applications in defence. But none of that was true. The truth was that there was no backup. There were no more men. No one could assist a mission that no one knew was being undertaken in the first place.

And the drones weren't useless. The soldier had only said that to try to leverage more men; he'd have shit his pants if he'd known that he'd been speaking to the founder of the company that made them. Yes, they had their limitations – as every technology did – but to hear the guy talk, you'd have thought he'd been given a pair of coffee cans and a piece of string, not a fleet of cutting-edge devices with an interface that was the envy of every company in Silicon Valley, bar absolutely none. Lemoine could feel himself becoming angry. It was pretty fucking irritating, he thought, that he was yet to go a single day of his existence without being reminded, at some point, that the only way of getting a job done to satisfaction was if he did every little part of it himself.

He minimised the live feed and called up the data on the mobile cell mast to see if he could access the interloper's phone.

He keyed in a command, and a spreadsheet unfurled down the screen in front of him; but either the guy was travelling without a phone or it was powered off, for the mast hadn't made any new connections that day, or on the day before, or over the weekend. Lemoine kept scrolling down, and then he saw that on Friday evening, an unfamiliar number in close range of the mast had come online, received a text message, sent a reply, and had then gone promptly offline again. The guy had spent the night in the outdoors; if he'd been sighted on Saturday morning, then it was plausible he could have used his phone on Friday night. Lemoine had no way of reading either message – at least not without involving others, which he definitely didn't want to do – but he extracted both numbers, and just to be sure, he checked them against the contact list in Mira's phone. There was no match. Definitely not a Birnam Wood connection, then. He fed the numbers one by one into his search engine. The first returned no hits, but the second was listed on the website of a Christchurch law firm in the contact details for a solicitor named Rosie Demarney. A solicitor was bad news; but perhaps she was just a girlfriend or a wife.

Her Facebook account was private, and her profile picture was of a balding teddy bear with one eye missing; nothing to indicate whether she was in a relationship or not. Lemoine opened a Burner application, keyed in the guy's number, and pressed dial. After several seconds of hissing silence – the app was routing the call through proxy servers in different countries around the world, making its origin impossible to trace – he heard a click, and then a recorded voice in his ear said, 'Hi, you've reached Tony, you know what to do. Cheers.'

Lemoine hung up before the beep. He checked the law firm's contact page to make sure there was no Tony listed – there wasn't – and then he dialled Rosie's number. This time, the call went through. She answered on the second ring.

'Hello, Rosie speaking.'

'Yes, hi, I'm trying to get in touch with Tony,' said Lemoine.

'What?' she said. 'Tony?'

'Yeah, I've been trying to call him. I wondered if you might know where he is.'

'Who is this?'

'Oh, sorry,' said Lemoine. 'It's John. From work.'

This was a gamble, as he had no idea where Tony actually worked – he had no idea who Tony was – but he figured that if she asked a question that he couldn't answer, he'd just hang up.

She was quiet. 'How did you get this number?' she said after a moment.

'It was on his desk,' said Lemoine. 'Look, I'm really sorry to disturb you – I've just been trying his cell and I'm not getting through. Is he on holiday or something?'

There was another little pause, and then she said, 'Yeah, he's on holiday.'

Lemoine decided to push his luck. 'Do you know when he's due back?'

'He's—' But she hesitated. 'Sorry, I'm just not quite—'

'Never mind,' said Lemoine. 'I'll keep trying his cell. Thanks anyway.' He was about to hang up, but she said, 'Wait.'

'Yes?' said Lemoine.

'He's just out in the bush,' she said. 'He's tramping.'

'Oh right,' said Lemoine. 'Birdwatching?'

'Um, yeah,' she said. 'That sounds right.'

'When do you expect him back?' said Lemoine.

'I think in the next few days,' she said. 'Um, what was your name, sorry?'

'It's fine, look, I'll keep trying his cell.'

'What did you want him for?' she said. 'I could pass on a message, if you—'

'No need,' said Lemoine. 'I'll reach him. Bye now,' and he hung up.

He was wasting his time, he thought, wiping his search history, changing his password, and then putting the clean phone back in his bag. The guy wasn't a threat. The PMCs would find him. They'd stick to the script, they'd encourage him to leave the area, and that would be that. Maybe in the coming days the girl would get in touch to tell him that she'd had a call from a blocked number – somebody named John, from work? They'd wonder together who it could have been, they'd agree that it was kind of weird, and then they'd shrug and never mention it again. Lemoine disconnected from the remote server and logged back into the local network as himself. He opened the venetian blinds again, making eye contact with several startled assistants on the other side of the glass, who quickly ducked behind their screens in a pantomime of conscientious productivity. Smiling now, he sat back down at his own computer, and saw that an email had just come in from Owen Darvish. 'FAIRY TERN TAKES FLIGHT!!' read the subject line. Beneath a long account of the conservation project launch, which Lemoine didn't read, there was a video attachment, which Lemoine didn't open. He was still smiling as he clicked the icon to send the email to the trash.

Tony heard the drone before he saw it: a distant rushing noise, somewhere between a hum and a hiss, rather like the sound inside a seashell. It was the same sound he'd heard on his first night out in the wilderness, that he'd taken for a waterfall, and it seemed to be growing louder and more distinct as he picked his way down the mountainside, now seeming more like a buzz, now seeming almost particulate, a kind of clatter curving up into a whine. He had returned to the national park intending to retrace the route he'd taken over the weekend, but more than three hours had passed since he'd left the track along the ridge, and he was yet to see any landmark that he recognised; the rushing sound was the only sign that he was anywhere near the place he'd bivouacked on Friday night, and he began, not quite consciously, to direct his steps towards it, fully expecting to step over a fallen tree trunk or push aside a curtain of vines and come upon a sudden spring, white rapids over mossy stones perhaps, a chasm cut and shaped by decades of cascading water, a torrent gushing noisily into a pool. The bush around him was too dense to be able to see more than fifty or so metres in any direction, and he was just wondering if he ought to get out his phone and try for a signal when he emerged on to a little bluff with views out over the Korowai Basin, and he saw, sweeping back and forth over the treetops, a sleek-looking quadcopter drone.

He stood watching it fly for almost a minute, hearing Owen Darvish in his head: 'It's called an airborne magnetic and radiometric survey,' Darvish had told him, 'and they do it from way, way up. Thousands of metres up.' This drone was barely fifty metres up, but for all Tony knew, it was carrying out some sort of task that could only be achieved close to the ground. Its movement was too methodical for him to think that it was being used for recreation; it looked to him like it was combing the area for something. Tony glanced around him at the view, discovering, to his relief, that he could orientate himself by the shape of the ranges on the far side of the basin. He wasn't lost. He'd just overshot again. The research site lay off to his right, not out in front of him, as he'd supposed, but a little to the north and west of where the drone was currently patrolling.

235

Before heading into the national park that morning, Tony had driven into Thorndike to charge his devices and replenish his supplies. The chip shop didn't open till the afternoon, but when he'd bought a basket's worth of groceries at the petrol station, the attendant had agreed to let him use a power point in the far corner of the store. Sitting on the dusty linoleum beside the drinks cabinet, his phone plugged into his laptop, his laptop plugged into the wall, Tony had searched the terms 'radiometric survey', 'Autonomo', and 'drone', typing with one hand, the other holding his Dictaphone to his ear and replaying at low volume his conversation with Darvish, who, it would seem, had been correct: geophysical surveys were indeed conducted from the air, and they were indeed one of the services Autonomo provided to clients around the world. What was more, Tony read, Autonomo had carried out a comprehensive survey of New Zealand back in 2010, as part of a dubious exploratory 'stocktake' of the country's mineral resources on conservation land; the survey had been commissioned by the government, and its brief, Tony read, had been to identify 'mineral deposits of economic interest', and to put a likely cost on their extraction.

At the time, the government had been considering a law change to allow mining in New Zealand's national parks. Tony remembered this proposition very well, not only because he had been one of the thousands who had marched against it – he had dressed as a coal-blackened chimney sweep, carrying a placard that bore the word 'MINE' with a line through it, and below it, the word 'OURS' – but also because its defeat ranked among the very few decisive victories for protest action in his lifetime: in the face of public outcry, the proposal had eventually been scrapped. He was smiling as he downloaded the report in order to skim the introduction, pleased that Lemoine's connection to New Zealand had such an unsavoury pedigree, and pleased that his essay would now have reason to mention and celebrate a recent triumph for democracy and for the left. For once in Tony's life, the privatising maniacs in power had been impeded; for once in his life, the greed and degradation of their placating free-market dogma had been exposed for what it was! The victory was so delicious to remember that Tony had been almost disappointed, when he reached the part of the report that dealt with Korowai, to learn that no deposits of economic interest had been discovered anywhere near Thorndike or the Korowai Pass.

Frowning, he had gone back to Google to ask what scientific research was currently being undertaken in the national park, trying to join the dots somehow between the fact of the Autonomo commission and what the guard had said to him on Saturday morning; but despite trying every search term in every combination he could think of, he had come up empty-handed. He could find nothing to suggest that any research of any kind was taking place in Korowai at all. That was odd. Korowai was public land. *Something* should have been out in the public domain; *something* should have been searchable online. Because something was definitely going on in Korowai. He'd seen it for himself.

He took a breath and held it.

Could the report that he was reading have been faked?

Tony had no difficulty whatsoever in believing the New Zealand government capable of rank conspiracy. What was the Cabinet anyway, he thought, his indignation rising, but a cabal of millionaire property tycoons who had spent their time in office beefing up their personal stock portfolios and actively discouraging the populace from turning out to vote? Most of them could hardly even breathe without lying. Certainly none of them had any respect whatsoever for the principle of public ownership. Had they not flagrantly ignored the result of a referendum on basically this very issue just a few years prior, selling off a tranche of publicly owned assets in spite of the fact that the New Zealand public – *to whom the assets rightfully belonged* – had voted to retain them? Exposing a billionaire would have been sweet, Tony thought, his imagination running ahead of himself somewhat; but exposing his own government, the *New Zealand government*, supposedly so green, so clean, and so famously inoffensive! That would be so much sweeter.

He was grinning again as he disconnected his devices and packed his cords away. Forget Birnam Wood, he thought, nodding goodbye to the station attendant and going outside to unlock Veronica's car. Forget the bunker, forget everything he'd planned to write about survivalism, and growth hacking, and techno-futurism, and imperial-stage-capitalist decline, and New Zealand's pathetically obsequious courting of the super-rich. Forget all of that. *This* was his story. He couldn't quite see the whole picture yet – but a picture was undoubtedly forming. Whatever was going on in Korowai was going on in secret, and he, Tony Gallo, *Anthony* Gallo, was going to be the one to flush it out.

He kept watching the drone, enjoying its motion as it coasted back and forth, sailing towards him, then away, towards him, then away. Presently he blinked and saw another, flying lower and faster than the first, and then he blinked again and realised, all at once, that the basin was absolutely swarming with them: all moving independently of one another, as though each had a mind of its own, some dipping down into the trees and up again, others circling, still others hovering in place. Tony felt a mounting curiosity. He set down his backpack and took out his binoculars for a closer look, remembering the trailer-mounted mobile phone mast that he'd come across on Saturday morning, and wondering if the purpose of the mast could be to furnish the drones with a wireless charge.

His attention snagged on something right in the middle of his field of view, and he raised the lenses to his eyes to see a drone hanging in the air right in front of him, startlingly magnified, shimmering with heat, propellers thrumming; and although the black dome of the camera housing that hung between the skids was opaque, the glass so polished it seemed almost wet, Tony had no doubt whatsoever that the machine had seen him – that it was *seeing* him, assessing him, in real time. His heart was thumping, but he kept the binoculars to his eyes and calmly panned away from it, moving slowly, acting as though he hadn't noticed anything unusual. He focused on a clump of trees in the middle distance instead, panned across those for a moment or two, and then yawned, stood up, and put the binoculars back in his bag. He did a couple of languid stretches, shouldered his backpack, and ambled off into the bush the way he'd come.

He was soon swallowed up by the trees, but he kept walking at what he hoped would seem like a contented pace until the noise of the drones behind him began to fall away. Then, still not daring to look back, he broke into a run, moving as fast as he could through the ferny undergrowth, scrambling over roots and fallen trees, pushing through vines and branches, and avoiding as much as possible the ribs of sunlight that came slanting down through the canopy in rays of olive and sea green. After half a kilometre or so, he turned sharply to his left and diverted his course downhill, doubling back on himself until he reached the bottom of the bluff where he'd been standing, and then altered his course again, heading to his right, into the heart of the Korowai Basin.

He was scanning for shelter as he went, and presently he came upon a giant totara tree that had fallen against the crook of its neighbour, pulling up a massive clump of roots and soil to form a kind of earthy amphitheatre in the forest floor. He ducked into the cavity, rolled on to his stomach, and then peered out at ground level, breathing hard, his heartbeat thudding in his ears. He could see the fence: it was about fifty paces from where he was hiding, close enough for him to read the plastic signs that warned, at regular intervals, 'RESEARCH IN PROGRESS – PLEASE KEEP OUT'.

He lay motionless until his breathing returned to normal and he was satisfied he hadn't been pursued. Then, moving as quietly and efficiently as he could, he opened his backpack and took out his balaclava and a pair of overtrousers. He put these on, checking that the cuffs were tight around his gaiters, and then pulled on a pair of woollen gloves as well. He had once attended a digital obfuscation workshop hosted by a civil liberties awareness group, and he knew that the drones' thermal imaging technology would have a harder time detecting him through insulated clothing. And the trees would help to disperse his heat signature. And it was daytime, which would help even more; thermal imaging worked much better at night, when the air was cooler and the contrast with the human body was more pronounced. He remembered that it had been raining the first time he had entered the national park; perhaps that was why the guard had seemed so surprised to see him the following morning. He looked down the length of his body, thinking he was probably as safe as he could make himself – but then, having second thoughts, he took off his red jacket and exchanged it for a darker-coloured fleece, tucking the hem of the fleece into the waistband of his trousers. Every inch of his body was now covered, except for the slot over his eyes.

He was just wondering whether he dared to climb out of the hollow and go to investigate the fence when he heard heavy footsteps clumping through the undergrowth nearby, and saw two men approaching, both wearing black puffer jackets, one fiddling with a flat handheld device – a control pad of some sort – and the other scanning the trees around them in a practised sweeping motion, keeping a lookout as they walked. Tony shrank back into the shadow, but the guard was glancing around at eye level, not scanning the forest floor; his gaze passed smoothly over the hollow where Tony was hiding. 'Anything?' he said to the man with the control pad, who shook his head and said, 'Waste of time. He was going the other way.' The first man nodded, and several seconds later they were gone.

They were looking for him. In his head, Tony saw his byline, imagined himself interviewed, heard the intro music for a podcast, a plucky glockenspiel, a shimmering undertow of strings. They were looking for him. They were on the alert. He'd seen three guys so far; there could be more. It would be senseless to try for the fence now, for getting over it was one thing; he also had to think about getting out again. Better to wait a day or two, he thought, let them think he'd left the area, undertake a spot of surveillance of his own. This hollow was as good a camp as any; a little spidery, maybe, but safe. He'd stay put, monitor the fence line, get a sense of their rhythms and routines, start keeping a diary, start making a plan. Tony was grinning underneath his balaclava. Everything that he was doing, running from the drones, hiding out in the hollow, layering up, employing obfuscation tactics – *these* were the kind of details that were going to make his story great. He was moving on instinct, following his hunches, living in the moment, using everything at his disposal in his pursuit of truth. He was risking his life for his investigation. He was a part of the story; he *was* the story! Still grinning, Tony allowed himself one last fantasy: he saw himself on stage, at a podium, collecting an award.

He probably shouldn't use his phone for a while either. That was a pity. It would have been nice to have got in touch with Rosie, just to let her know that he was really on to something, and to fill her in . . . but he was already shaking his head. Rosie was nice, but – well, but that was just it, really. She was *nice*. She was the kind of girl who trusted in her government, a good upstanding citizen who played by the rules and took people at face value and made it a point of pride to give everyone she met the benefit of the doubt. She wasn't a *radical*. If he told her what he suspected might be going on here, Tony thought, she'd only humour him. She'd agree that it sounded super crazy, and super dodgy, and super weird, but she wouldn't really mean it. She wouldn't believe that a government conspiracy was even possible – not in *New Zealand*, not in *2017*! She wouldn't understand the danger he was in, wouldn't appreciate the risks, wouldn't really comprehend the scale of it. And Tony wasn't in the mood to be patronised.

Anyway, he thought, as he took out his notebook and uncapped his fountain pen, he'd already told her that he was going to be out of range for a few days. She wouldn't be expecting him to get in touch. And it wasn't like she was even his girlfriend.

He opened his notebook to a clean page.

I heard the drones before I saw them, he wrote, and then he sat back, held up his notebook like a hymnal, and, in a whisper, said the words aloud.

'You know the bit in Harry Potter,' Shelley said, 'when Dumbledore goes something like, there comes a point where we all have to make a choice between what is right and what is easy?'

'I guess,' Mira said. She lifted up the tendrils of a strawberry plant to pour a dilution of tomato food into the soil.

'I reckon he's got it back to front,' Shelley said. 'I was just thinking about it. Like, no one ever actually knows what the right thing to do is. I mean, you can *think* that you know what's right, and you can *tell* yourself that you know, but at the point that you make your choice, like, in the moment, you're never really certain. You just hope. You just act and you hope for the best, and maybe it turns out that you did the right thing, or maybe it turns out that you didn't – in which case, all you can say is that at least you tried. But, like, the *wrong* thing to do, that's often much clearer. Wrong is, like, easier to see than right, a lot of the time. It's more definite – like, this is the line I *know* I will not cross, this is what I *absolutely* will not do.'

'Yeah,' said Mira. 'I see that.'

'So anyway,' Shelley went on, 'this is what I was thinking: that, like, the real choices that you make in your life, the really difficult, defining choices, are never between what's right and what's easy. They're between what's wrong and what's hard.'

'Ha,' Mira said. 'Yeah. That's a really good point.'

Shelley waited, but she didn't say anything else.

'I mean, come on, Dumbledore,' Shelley added after a moment, trying to make a joke out of it, but Mira had already picked up her watering can and was walking off to another part of the field. Disappointed, Shelley turned back to the straw bale that she had been pulling apart with her hands and gave it an exaggerated grimace – and then immediately felt disloyal. She wiped her expression clean, grabbed the bale firmly with both hands, and carried on.

In Shelley's time at university, she had contributed a regular book review to the English department's student magazine, and whenever she had run out of time before the deadline, or whenever the book in question had been too difficult or too politically contentious for her to know how to describe her own response to it not only truthfully, but responsibly as well, she had always taken refuge in excessive praise. People were always quick to criticise an act of criticism, and anybody could dismiss as lazy what professed to be lukewarm, but nobody tended to ask any questions of a gush. Even people who'd despised whatever book she happened to be praising never quarrelled with her if she really, truly rhapsodised about it; they simply wrote her off as a person with poor taste and stopped engaging with her critically, and that was that. The stakes had never been particularly high, of course; but even so, she still felt pained sometimes when she leafed through the back issues of the magazine and saw that all her most lavishly complimentary reviews had been of books whose authors frightened her, books she never finished, or books she'd been too cowardly to admit she didn't understand. With typical self-deprecation, she had been sure that she was quite alone in giving rein to this particular form of intellectual dishonesty, and so she had been surprised, several years into her time at Birnam Wood, to realise that one of the clearest signs that Mira was practising deception of some kind was when she began agreeing with everything that Shelley said.

The observation about Dumbledore, for example, was just the kind of rhetorical nicety that in normal circumstances Mira would have loved to take apart and puzzle over. Shelley had first thought of it two days ago, and she had been rehearsing and refining it in her mind ever since as she waited for an opportunity to come out with it to Mira offhand. She had hoped that it might prompt a philosophical debate about hard choices, that might then flow quite naturally into a discussion about the future management of Birnam Wood – 'Te Māra Neke,' she whispered defiantly, though neither she nor Mira had brought that subject up again, and she had decided not to table it, as Mira had suggested, for the consideration of the wider group – not, at least, until the next full-caucus hui, which was still two and a half months away. Shelley knew already that there would be no point in trying to revive the subject before then, for ever since that conversation, Mira had been nothing but agreeable towards her, going out of her way to voice her appreciation and her sympathy, backing down at once from any point of difference, and steering clear of any issues on which she and Shelley didn't see entirely eye to eye. At the nightly gatherings she had been uncharacteristically withdrawn, never impolite, but incurious, and distant to the point of disapproval, and several times Shelley had caught her gazing round at the assembled faces with genuine bemusement, almost as though she were seeing Birnam Wood in action for the very first time – seeing them not as herself, perhaps, but as Lemoine.

The dust from the straw bale made Shelley sneeze, once, twice, three times, and she heard Mira say, 'Bless you,' absently, from the other end of the field. Shelley didn't thank her. She rubbed her face bad-temperedly across her sleeve.

One of the cautionary tales that Shelley's mother liked to tell at her recruitment seminars concerned a watercolour hobbyist who had once been discovered while painting on a hillside on the Akaroa Harbour by a prominent figure in the art world – Mrs Noakes never named him – who had been honeymooning in the country from New York. This important man, Mrs Noakes narrated, had been so arrested by the modest sketch displayed on the easel of the hobbyist that he had vowed to one day mount an exhibition of her work; he had pressed his business card into her hand and made her promise that she would call him at her earliest convenience. An exhibition was everything the hobbyist had ever dreamed of, and yet for some reason she was filled with abject terror at the thought, and although she kept his card safe in her wallet, and took it out every now and then to look at it, somehow she could never bring herself to make the call. Months passed, and then years, and then one day she'd happened to come across a mention of the man in an article that she was reading, and she learned that he was dead, and that he had been dead for some time, several years in fact, and this was the final proof that she had missed her chance, that she had undermined her own ambition, and that, perversely, contrarily, against her own best interests, against the deepest and most secret wishes of her heart, she had run away from what she most desired – and here Mrs Noakes would pause and then say, in a solemn tone of voice, that the watercolour hobbyist was her. 'Total bullshit,' Mira had said when she'd first heard the story; 'that never happened; I bet you a thousand bucks' – but it was only now, years later, as Shelley knelt to disperse the loose straw over the ground, that it occurred to her that Mira had rather missed the point, for if the story *was* made up, then in a way that only made it all the more poignant – for how much more desiring must Mrs Noakes have been, and how much more perverse and more contrary, to have invented it entirely?

Shelley Noakes understood self-sabotage. Nothing could have made more sense to her than if Mira had confessed to her that, like Mrs Noakes, like Shelley, like human beings everywhere, what she had been hiding from Shelley was something she had also been hiding from herself: that she was afraid of Birnam Wood becoming famous, afraid of the money that Lemoine had offered them, afraid of exposure, afraid of opportunity, afraid of the future, afraid of success . . . Except that wasn't it, Shelley thought, with bitterness. That wasn't what was really going on. The reason that Mira had been lying to her was even more basic than self-sabotage, and Shelley knew exactly what it was.

Shelley had met Robert Lemoine only once, and the impression she had formed of him was one of smooth and impenetrable courtesy; 'a man under his own control' had been the phrase that had occurred to her, slightly unexpectedly, for she had never thought to describe a person in such a way before. He had studied Shelley's features very closely when they'd shaken hands, just as he'd gone on to scrutinise each member of the group in turn, peering into each of their faces one by one, and as he'd completed his introductions and they'd stood exchanging pleasantries in the livestock pens beside the shearing shed, Shelley had remembered something that Mira had said about him at the hui: 'it's like he's daring us,' she'd said, 'or maybe, like we're daring him?' Yes, Shelley had thought, assessing him, there was an unrepentant challenge in his manner, a tacit provocation in the way he held himself aloof, and in the way he seemed perpetually, but only ever so slightly, amused. She could not honestly say that she disliked him – he was confident, well spoken, dryly funny, wicked even – but what had unsettled her was how utterly and obviously Mira was in thrall to him, and how unaware she seemed that her infatuation was something that everyone, he most of all, could see. Shelley had been just starting to wonder, with rising trepidation, what this troubling development might mean for the rest of them at Birnam Wood when suddenly he'd turned and looked directly at her, raising his eyebrows in taunting expectation and flashing her a grin. Shelley had been so startled that she'd found herself unable to return the smile; she'd simply stared at him, and the thought that had filled her consciousness was not *it's like he knew what I was thinking*, but *it's like he wanted me to think that he knew what*

I was thinking, which had felt both much more sinister and, strangely, much more impressive.

'You guys haven't slept together, have you?' she'd asked Mira after he had gone.

'What?' Mira had said in a play of bafflement. 'No! No way!'

'It just kind of seems like it might be in the air.'

'Really?' Mira had turned prim. 'I've never got that impression.'

'Oh, come on. That's not true.'

'Honestly. It's never come up.'

'Yeah, but if it did, though – you'd be keen?'

'I'd be *terrified*,' Mira had replied, starting to laugh. 'Shelley! You didn't find him *terrifying*? Like, you didn't think, that man is the *scariest fucking human* that I have *ever* met in my *entire life*, and how is it even *possible* that we are *anywhere* within a *million miles* of him, and who the fuck *are* we, and what does *anything* mean?'

By then Shelley had begun to laugh as well, and then one of the others had asked what was so funny, which had somehow made it even funnier, and soon everyone was laughing at the sheer absurdity of their extraordinary situation, and it hadn't been until several hours later, as Shelley was settling down in her sleeping bag and making her usual mental review of all the conversations she had had that day, that she'd realised that Mira had rather neatly dodged the question.

But it wasn't just a question. It wasn't just rhetorical, Shelley thought, raking the ground with her fork, scoring it, pounding it, turning up stones. It was a serious existential problem for the whole of Birnam Wood, and the more she thought about it, the less inclined she felt to laugh. Lemoine had the power to withdraw his offer on a whim. There was no formal contract in place. If he tired of the arrangement, he could turn around at any point and order Birnam Wood to leave – and then what could they do? Who could they appeal to? The land was his, the power was his; the law would be entirely on his side. Shelley was striking at the ground. Couldn't Mira see that if she slept with him, she would be putting everyone at risk? She would be jeopardising all their hard work, all the sacrifices they had made to get there, everything that they believed in – and for what? She couldn't seriously believe she had a future with this guy! She knew what he was. She knew that he was toying with her, just like she knew that *she* was toying with him back. She was just fucking around. She was just doing whatever the hell she wanted, like she had always done, taking everyone else for granted, like she had always done, rebelling for the sake of it, like she had always done, acting as though the rules that bound the little people were just too tiresome and too ordinary to apply to her.

And it wasn't like this was anything new, Shelley thought, now with real bitterness. There had always been aspects of the daily management of Birnam Wood that Mira had seen as beneath her; she had always acted as though the administration and the democratic protocols were unworthy of her attention and her time. It was one of the ways in which the two friends perfectly complemented each other, for as Mira had often pointed out to her, Shelley really rather liked bureaucracy; she found genuine fulfilment in ticking items off a list, and organising, and making blueprints for the future, and establishing processes of feedback and methods of appeal. Mira had no patience for any of that. She loved to speculate, loved to feel the scope and flex of her own imaginative audacity, loved to test and contradict herself, to keep enlarging, constantly, her own sense of what it was possible to hypothesise and conjure up and entertain, and although this roving speculative energy was something Shelley honestly admired and envied about her, she could also see that it amounted, at times, to a kind of capriciousness, even a callousness, when it came to those aspects of mundane existence that could not be posited or wished away. There was a kind of safety in abstraction, Shelley felt, in visions that remained visions, in ideas that remained ideas; and it had occurred to her, in recent days, that maybe it had been the very formlessness of Birnam Wood, as an undeclared, unregulated, sometimes-criminal, sometimes-philanthropic gathering of friends, that had held Mira's interest in it for so long. She was expecting that her friend was going to find it very difficult, at the point the group officially incorporated, to leave this realm of abstracted possibility behind.

If they ever got to that point. They weren't out of the woods yet, Shelley thought, grimly registering the pun. They weren't anywhere close to solvent. It was still a matter of *if* – and in the meantime, Mira's attitude was starting to become a problem. For even though Birnam Wood was horizontal by design, and even though their meetings were always facilitated on a roster, and even though all the tasks of leadership were scrupulously divvied up and shared, no one could ever quite forget – no one ever *did* forget – that Mira was the founder. For one thing, she was not a natural follower; but for another, she possessed an authority that could not easily be yielded or rotated to another member of the group, and that was the authority of expertise. When she declined to register an opinion, submitting without comment to the will of the majority and then silently withdrawing as soon as the meeting was done, Shelley could see that it made the others nervous; they began to second-guess themselves, and to pull away from one another, and their work began to suffer – and somehow it always fell to Shelley, as the second-longest-serving member of the group, to muster an energy she did not feel, and step into the breach, and fill the gap, and pick up the slack, and make excuses for a friend who wasn't even showing her the simple courtesy of admitting what was glaringly obvious to literally everyone around her, Shelley most of all. Glancing over at her now, Shelley saw that she was scanning the sky above the ridge for what must have been the hundredth time that afternoon, and she felt a surge of anger. *I went all in with Birnam Wood*, she thought, *and all you wanted was to fuck around.*

Shelley had long grown accustomed to the expectation that she was fated to be always on the losing side. New Zealand had been governed by the centre-right since before she had been eligible to vote, and she could find little to excite her in any of the parties supposedly in opposition. A defeated, airless, ugly feeling rose in her whenever she heard a person of her parents' generation talking brightly about home ownership, or foreign holidays, or financial serendipity, or education for its own sake, or second chances in a crowded field; she felt this way some-times simply if someone spoke about the future – even the very near future – in optimistic terms. But she was not unaware that there was a certain satisfaction to be found in hopelessness, a certain piety, a touch of martyrdom, in feeling oneself and one's entire generation to have been wronged by those in power, and deceived, and discouraged from civic participation, and robbed, and made fun of, and maligned; and when the sound of an aircraft engine split the air and she looked over to see that Mira had downed her tools and was already striding up the hill towards the airstrip, smiling, Shelley felt disgusted sud-denly by her own complacency. She watched the aircraft bank and circle back around to land. And then she heard her mother say, 'Lean in.'

'Wait for me,' she called out, pulling off her gloves and jog-ging up the hill as well. She pretended not to see how Mira hesitated in confusion, her smile faltering and then becoming false as Shelley closed the gap between them; she seemed, Shel-ley thought, almost ashamed, almost cowed, as if Shelley had exposed her in a lie. But she said nothing. She just nodded, still smiling, and the two friends fell into step without another word.

The plane had landed and taxied to a halt by the time they reached the airstrip, and Lemoine was getting out. He didn't seem surprised to see the pair of them approaching – but then, Shelley thought, perhaps he never seemed surprised; it was an emotion that she couldn't picture on his face, somehow.

'I've been in California,' he said by way of a greeting. 'I brought you something.' He took a ziplock bag out of his pocket and held it up so they could see what it contained: a tiny piece of watercolour paper, barely bigger than a bus ticket, divided into squares like a miniature loyalty card. Each square was the size of a fingernail and had been stamped with a tur-quoise five-pointed star.

Shelley didn't know what it was. She glanced at Mira for assistance.

Mira was already shaking her head and holding up both hands. 'No thanks,' she said. 'Not for me.'

He held it out to her. 'It's a house-warming present.'

'Shed-warming,' Mira corrected him. She crossed her arms.

Lemoine grinned at her. 'Shed and house,' he said, passing the bag to Shelley instead. 'I'm going to stay over. I thought we could all sample some of this together.'

Mira scowled at him. 'What – you don't drink, but you do *acid*?'

So that was what it was. Shelley examined the bag with new interest.

'Ever tried it?' said Lemoine. He was addressing Shelley, but Mira answered, 'No.'

Lemoine was still waiting for Shelley's answer.

'I read an article about it,' Shelley said.

He burst out laughing. 'What was that like?' he said. 'Lots of colourful language? Lots of made-up words and new kinds of grammar?'

'I don't remember any specific words,' Shelley said, and he laughed again and said, 'Superb.' She felt a flush of pleasure. 'It did make me want to try it, though,' she said.

'Everyone should try it once,' he said, reaching back into the cockpit for a duffel bag. 'We use it all the time with start-ups, as a way of building trust among a group. A kind of bonding exercise.'

'Cool,' Shelley said, still flushed.

'It's amazing what it does to the imagination,' said Lemoine. 'Even just a taste. Doesn't have to be a full trip. It just brings you into the moment, you know, sharpens you up, makes you more present, more connected, more creative. You're going to love it.'

Mira was scowling again. 'Sounds like someone's paying you to say that.'

'No,' he said. 'That's the beauty of illicit substances: no advertising. You can make a pure decision for once in your life. No packaging, no algorithm, no big pharma shoving it down your throat.'

'Just some guy in a tracksuit telling us how much we're going to love it,' Mira said.

It seemed to Shelley that Lemoine's expression tightened slightly. Mira must have sensed that she had overstepped a mark, for she quickly turned away, narrowing her eyes and looking out over the valley, as if she'd heard a sound in the distance and she couldn't quite place what it might be. Shelley recognised the habit: this was something Mira did when she had been embarrassed. She was trying to hide her face.

'Well,' said Lemoine to Shelley, 'you can't please everybody.'

Mira was still turned away.

'People did it who were colour-blind,' Shelley said. 'In the article I read. And they saw colours for the first time. It was kind of beautiful actually.' She tried to give the ziplock bag back to him, but he shook his head.

'It's for you,' he said, gazing at her. 'Shelley, right?'

'Yeah,' Shelley said, astonished.

'It's for everyone,' he said. 'Socialism. See? I get it.' He dropped the duffel bag on the ground and went back into the cockpit to retrieve an aluminium cooler that he had stored behind the pilot's seat. Shelley glanced at Mira, but she was examining a cut on the side of one of her fingers. 'I brought dinner,' Lemoine said when he re-emerged. 'I thought we'd make a night of it. Relax, get to know each other.'

He set the cooler down, slung the duffel bag on top of it, and then picked it up again.

'Do you need help carrying that?' Shelley said, at the same time as Mira said, 'So what's for dinner?'

She was trying too hard to be caustic, Shelley thought, and it was coming off only as rude.

Lemoine answered Shelley. 'That's very good of you,' he said, slipping the duffel bag over his shoulder and handing her the cooler. 'Why don't you take that down to the camp and round up the others? Tell them we'll be down in just a moment.'

He was giving her the brush-off, but he touched her arm as he spoke, and smiled, and Shelley knew that she had won. With a final glance at Mira, who was looking at the ground, she set off down the hill towards the shearing shed, and once she was out of sight of the plane, she set the cooler down on the ground and opened it to see what it contained. Inside were stacked plastic tubs, each containing a preparation of a different ingredient: fat silky noodles, chopped peanuts, lime wedges, mung beans, sliced onions tossed in oil, diced chilli peppers, batons of tofu. There were two flasks, one filled with a thick golden-brown sauce, the other with what looked like beaten egg. It was a pad thai, Shelley realised, feeling oddly touched: a good choice for a group. A crowd-pleaser. Vegetarian, too. Of course, there was no earthly chance that he had prepared the ingredients himself – undoubtedly, he'd have a private chef – but Shelley felt a tenderness towards him, all the same. She put everything back in the cooler and replaced the lid.

She found the others in the livestock pens, building a frame for bird netting.

'How's our money man?' Hayden said as she approached.

'He's going to join us for dinner,' Shelley said, hoisting up the cooler. 'Pad thai.'

'Aww, he cooked for us?' said Natalie. 'He didn't have to do that.'

'He also brought us a house-warming present,' Shelley said, reaching into her pocket for the ziplock bag.

'A present?'

'Yeah,' said Shelley, holding it up. 'It's an absolute shitload of Class A drugs.'

They all started laughing – and after a moment, Shelley did too.

'Awesome,' Hayden said.

Mira was already regretting having taken such a hard line on the LSD, but she had given her opinion so scornfully that she didn't feel that she could change it now without losing face.

She was embarrassed that by acting aloof and disagreeable, as she always did around Lemoine, she had come off, instead, only like a killjoy and a prude; and she was disappointed, for she'd done mushrooms several times and enjoyed the experience enormously, and she knew that she would have accepted the ziplock bag with genuine curiosity and interest if the offer had come from almost anybody else. As Shelley passed out of sight below the shelterbelt of pines, she scowled and crossed her arms, preparing, with a grim kind of resignation, to double down on a position she had never really held in the first place.

Lemoine was grinning at her. 'I must say, I never picked you for a puritan,' he said. 'I'm surprised.'

'Well, I guess not everybody is a total fucking cliché,' Mira snapped.

He grinned wider. 'You don't like to be out of control,' he said. 'Is that it?'

'Hey, fuck you, I don't have to explain myself to you,' she said. 'We're in the middle of nowhere. We're like, hours and hours from the nearest hospital. Excuse me if I don't want to go on a fucking acid trip with a guy who has yet to put his money where his mouth is, by the way, which means we're basically trespassing already – and I'm sure that the law, like, doesn't exist for you or whatever, but it sure as hell does for all of us, and if anything went wrong, we'd be totally screwed. So yeah: no thanks.'

'That's a pretty good explanation, for someone who doesn't have to explain herself.'

'And I'm not a puritan,' Mira said. 'I'm just not a total fucking idiot.'

'Or a cliché,' said Lemoine.

She glared at him. 'So now you're going to tell me how actually I *am* a cliché, I just don't realise it. Right?'

'Not at all,' he said. 'I was just going to remark that being a cliché can be very useful. You ought to consider it sometime.'

'Oh yeah?'

'Yeah,' he said. 'It means people underestimate you. They think they've seen all there is to see. They drop their guard. They get lazy. They reveal themselves.'

'Thanks for the tip,' she said, 'but I'm a woman; I'm underestimated, like, every day of my life.'

He laughed. 'Good answer,' he said, 'but I don't believe it for a second.'

'You know, we've actually been working pretty hard here,' Mira said. 'We've been taking this pretty seriously. This isn't like a holiday for us. We've been working our butts off.'

'I'm sure you have.'

'So maybe before you drop your tab of acid tonight, we could actually put some stuff down in writing. Like, draw up a contract or something. Just so we can be sure you're not stringing us along.'

He said nothing, gazing at her thoughtfully.

'See, this is what I'm worried about,' Mira said. 'I'm worried this is just a bit of fun for you, like, it doesn't really mean anything, whereas for us, this is, like, our livelihood. Like, I realise that you've probably made a hundred thousand bucks in capital gains just while we've been standing here, but—'

'You're right,' he said, cutting over her. 'I have been stringing you along.'

She faltered, not understanding.

'This is a rare experience for me,' said Lemoine. 'This . . .' He gestured at the space between them. 'I've been wanting to enjoy it. Draw it out.'

'Right,' Mira said uncertainly. 'For sure.'

'But yes,' he said. 'Let's get something down in writing. Good idea.'

Mira was starting to feel embarrassed again. 'Just for our peace of mind,' she said. 'I mean, I don't think you'll be disappointed when you see what we've been doing.'

'Oh no,' he said briskly. 'I don't think I'll be disappointed.'

But she was blushing now. She felt that she had misjudged him, that she had failed to trust him, that she was in the wrong; he had been keeping a window of possibility open between them, and she hadn't seen it, and she had slammed it shut.

Abruptly, he said, 'I changed the code on the front gate.'

'What?' she said. 'When?'

'This morning,' he said. 'It's now 7172. I added one to every digit.'

She drew back. 'Hey,' she said in a tone of offence. 'It's lucky we didn't need the van today. We'd have been locked out.'

'7172,' he said again. 'It should be easy to remember.'

Mira could feel her embarrassment becoming scorn again. 'It's kind of weird you changed it before telling us,' she said. 'When we're the ones living here. That's kind of fucked up, actually.'

He stared at her for a moment without blinking. Then he said, 'When my wife died, Mira, I had paparazzi at my front gate for a year. If I came out of my house, if I even opened a window, they'd yell at me, "You knew about that helicopter, didn't you? That's why you stayed behind that day. You let her go on purpose because you wanted to be rid of her." They'd say, "Was it murder?" or "Was it sabotage?" or, I don't know, "Is it true you used to beat her up?" Of course not. Every allegation was utterly false and utterly obscene. But that was the point, you see. They were trying to make me angry. Because if I react, that's their story. And they're not breaking any laws. They're only asking questions. That's their job. They even used to say, "Is it true she's still alive?" How cruel is that? To a man whose wife is dead? And there was no basis for it. No justification. Nothing. It was just a question. And you can't stop someone asking questions. Can you.'

Mira was appalled. 'God,' she said. 'I'm so sorry. That's horrendous.'

'So, I don't think much of journalists,' he said. 'Needless to say.'

'I can't even imagine. Jesus.'

'I have to take certain precautions.'

She was blushing again. 'Yeah,' she said, 'of course.'

'And when Birnam Wood goes live—' He shrugged. 'Well, anyway. I've already said it. I *have* been stringing you along. I *have* been enjoying this – our little back-and-forth. And the privacy. The calm before the storm. But you're right. It's got to be about the work.' He smiled at her a little sadly, and gestured down the hill. 'Shall we head down?'

He had never spoken of his wife to her before. He had never spoken about any of his relatives, in fact, or any of his associates, or any of his friends. Perhaps he was starting to trust her, Mira thought, with a kind of fearful gratitude, as they set off down the slope, and he changed the subject back to Birnam Wood, asking about the health of the crops, and the planting schedule, and the weather. She noticed how he scanned the fields in front of them very closely as they walked, and she felt a surge of pity for him – and then shame, that she had endured nothing in her own life that could possibly compare with what he'd gone through.

The sun was setting by the time they reached the shearing shed, where they found Aaron and Jessica lighting hurricane lanterns and Hayden chopping kindling for a fire. The ingredients that Lemoine had brought for dinner had been lined up in their containers next to the barbecue, ready to be thrown together and fried, and inside the shed Shelley and Katrina and Natalie were setting the table for dinner – though it was not really a table; it was an old door they'd found propped inside the shearing shed and had placed on a pair of oil drums that they'd part-filled with gravel so it wouldn't move. The setting looked charming in the candlelight – mismatched crockery and camping cookware laid around an extravagant homemade centrepiece of toetoe and harakeke flowers – and when Mira glanced at Lemoine to gauge his impression, she saw with relief that he was smiling.

'I like what you've done with the place,' he said.

'Probably a bit posher than you're used to,' Shelley said, 'but hey.'

'I only hope I'm not underdressed,' said Lemoine.

'You are a bit,' Shelley said, 'but we won't hold it against you.'

It occurred to Mira that she was flirting with him. She looked around for the open bottle of wine that would explain the high colour in Shelley's cheeks. It was on the table, already half empty. She looked again at Shelley – and saw with a little jolt that her friend was looking back at *her*; clearly, she had caught Mira looking at the bottle. Mira tried to smile at her, but Shelley turned away.

'We were just talking about your costume parties,' Natalie said.

'Oh yes,' said Lemoine. 'Very famous.'

'We saw a picture of you as a clown,' said Katrina. 'With a graduation cap?'

'What was the idea – like, clown college?' Natalie said.

'We couldn't figure it out.'

Mira wasn't following. 'What are you talking about?'

'It's a tradition at Autonomo,' explained Lemoine. 'We have a costume party every year at Halloween. Silly really, but it's become a thing now. Every year it's bigger and bigger.' He turned back to the others. 'That was a good theme that year, actually,' he said. 'It was "Stations on the London Underground". I was Oxford Circus.'

'Oh!' the others all chorused, laughing.

'That's such a good theme for a party,' Shelley said.

'King's Cross,' said Natalie. 'Paddington. Hammersmith. There's so many good ones.'

'Elephant and Castle,' said Lemoine. 'That was the winner, I recall.'

'And the winner gets, like, a five-star holiday or something, right?' Shelley said. 'It's, like, a huge deal.'

'It's excessive,' said Lemoine. 'In fact, to be perfectly honest with you, the whole thing is a little out of control.'

'No! Don't say that!' Shelley said. 'It's great!'

She *was* flirting with him. And now she was avoiding Mira's gaze.

'Several Victorias that year, of course,' said Lemoine. 'And a very good Napoleon – for Waterloo.'

'What were some of the other themes?' said Katrina.

'Oh, let me see,' said Lemoine. 'Last year was – oh yes: it was "Bob Dylan Lyrics". I went as the world's biggest necklace. Except a couple of other people had the same idea, and it turns out I *wasn't* the world's biggest, theirs were bigger than mine. That was all a bit embarrassing.'

'I bet there were lots of leopard-skin pill-box hats,' said Katrina.

'There were indeed,' said Lemoine.

'I would have gone as – what's the line? Fog, and amphetamines, and pearls?'

'Fog is a good costume. It's just – fog.'

'Yeah, like, "What are you supposed to be?" "Oh, me? Just fog."'

'Rubik's cube,' said Lemoine. 'That was another year. You come wearing six items, in all the colours of the sides of the Rubik's cube. And the rule is that by the end of the night, you have to be dressed in all one colour.'

'Oh my God,' said Shelley, as she refilled the plastic camping mug she was using as a wine glass. 'That's *also* so good! I am totally going to steal these!'

Lemoine was watching Mira. 'You're seeing me differently now,' he observed.

She was surprised to hear it said so plainly. 'I guess I am,' she said. 'A wee bit.'

'I don't seem like a costume-party kind of guy? Don't worry: it has been said before.'

But it was more than that: it was how *normal* he seemed, how relaxed, how comfortable, how ordinary. She was almost ashamed to admit that he seemed fully human to her for the first time – like a man with preferences, and habits, someone whose experiences had shaped him, who had been both lucky and unlucky, who had a family, and memories, and a past. Someone who was flirted with, she thought, who existed for other people, who was thought about by other people, who was conjured, privately, in other people's minds.

He was waiting for her reply.

'I'm having that weird experience,' Mira said at last, 'where you realise that your search engine has, like, led you to this very specific tailored place based on what it's decided about you, and there are things that are fully searchable to other people that are totally invisible to you. Because I have definitely never seen this Oxford Circus photo of you – and I have googled you a *lot*.'

He grinned at her and winked. Mira could see in her peripheral vision that Shelley had caught the wink, and she looked at her, meaning to smile and try to share the joke, but again Shelley turned away.

'I wish Halloween was a bigger deal here,' Katrina was saying. 'It doesn't make any sense. It's the wrong season. It doesn't get dark till like nine p.m., and there are no pumpkins or falling leaves or anything.'

'Yeah, it's not scary,' Natalie said. 'It's springtime.'

'People don't get it either,' said Jessica, who had just come in. 'I went trick-or-treating once in primary school and nobody knew how it worked. It was so embarrassing, saying to your neighbours, "Well, here's the deal, you're supposed to give me lollies just because I decided to dress up, and if you don't, I'm going to trash your house . . ."'

'. . . like, basically a hostage situation,' Aaron put in.

'And nobody had any lollies in the cupboard either. They'd go and look, and they'd come back with, like, a piece of fruit or a biscuit. It was a total disaster.'

'Hey, man,' said Aaron to Lemoine, 'thanks for the acid, by the way. Tu meke.'

'Tu meke?' said Lemoine.

'Yeah, like – hard out.'

'Hard out?' said Lemoine.

Jessica was laughing. 'You totally just used one Kiwi-ism to describe another one,' she said to Aaron.

'Tu meke is, like, thanks. In the sense of, you didn't have to do that. Above and beyond.'

'And hard out is, like, impressive,' Jessica said. 'Like, awesome, I'm impressed.'

'It's a real cultural exchange,' Lemoine said, and they all laughed.

'Mira's going to sit it out,' Shelley said suddenly, her voice loud and brittle, 'but is everybody else keen?'

It seemed that everybody was.

'I wouldn't say no to some wine, though,' Mira said, trying to catch Shelley's eye for the third time, but it was Katrina who picked up the bottle and handed it to her.

'So, tonight we party,' said Lemoine, 'and tomorrow we talk business. Yeah?'

'But didn't you say the acid is kind of like business too?' Shelley said. 'You said it's like a bonding exercise.'

'Yes – I'm afraid that's a bit of a Silicon Valley cliché,' Lemoine said, with another wink at Mira. 'But it can be an amazing tool. I think of it a bit like how fifty years ago the cigarettes were on the shelves and the condoms were behind the counter, and now it's the other way around. It'll be that way with psychedelics and alcohol, I'm sure. It'll flip.'

As if to register her dissent, Mira drank deeply from her jar of wine. She could feel that Shelley was watching her, but this time she was the one who avoided Shelley's gaze. The conversation turned to the benefits of microdosing, and she excused herself to go and light the barbecue.

The voice that she was hearing in her head was Tony's. 'All this self-optimising, self-actualising bullshit,' she imagined him saying as she crouched down to open the valve on the gas tank, and then pressed the ignition switch until it clicked, 'you can't fucking get away from it. Every little thing now has to be about maximising your potential, and perfecting yourself, and honing yourself, and getting the best deal out of your life, and out of your body, and out of your precious fucking time. Everything's a corporate retreat now. Everything has *utility*. You want to get fucked up and just escape your own existence for once, just check out of your life for a while, like every other human being who has ever lived? No. Even a fucking acid trip has to be a means to an end. It has to be about team-building. It has to be about trust and wellness and creativity. It has to be about your authentic journey towards physical and psychological perfection. It has to be about you asserting the integrity of your choice to do it in the first place. It can't be a lapse of judgment. There are no lapses of judgment. It can't be *wrong*. There are no wrongs. There's just choice, and choice is neutral, and *we're* neutral, and everything is neutral, and everything's a game, and if you want to win the game then you're going to have to optimise yourself, and actualise yourself, and utilise yourself, and get the edge, and God forbid that you should have an actual human experience of frailty, or mortality, or limitation, or humanity, or of the fucking onward march of time – those are just distractions, those are obstacles, they're defects, they're *inconveniences* in the face of our curated, bespoke, freely fucking chosen authentic existence, and sure, we can never quite decide if we're the consumers of our lives or the products of them, but there's one thing we *are* damn sure of, which is that nobody on earth has *any* right to pass *any* judgment on us, either way. Freedom in the marketplace! It's the only thing that matters! It's the only thing that *exists*!'

They were talking about social media when she returned.

'I reckon there's a huge rejection coming,' Jessica was saying to Lemoine. 'Like what you said before, about condoms and cigarettes. It'll be, like, smoking while pregnant or something, like, there's going to come a time when we won't even be able to believe that we spent so much time online and we didn't know how terrible for us it was.'

'No way,' said Natalie. 'The opposite. *This* is what nobody's going to believe.' She gestured around. 'Meeting up in person. Actually having conversations face to face.'

'So – we're just getting started, in other words,' said Aaron.

'More social media,' said Natalie, nodding, 'more Internet, more virtual, more digital. Just – more. It's a part of the culture now. It's the way people think. I mean—'

She pointed at Hayden, who was turning his wireless speaker on with one hand and selecting a playlist on his phone with the other.

'Oi, Hayden,' said Katrina. 'You're being used as an example.'

'Biohacking,' said Hayden, looking up from his devices. 'That's the next thing. Like, where people microchip their hands so they can unlock their cars or whatever just by waving. That's already happening.'

'And we'll be, like, uploading our memories to the cloud.'

'Not just uploading them. Changing them.'

'Putting filters on.'

'Yeah, we'll basically merge with our phones.'

'Like a *Black Mirror* episode.'

'Let's face it,' Natalie said, 'that show is essentially a documentary.'

Shelley was watching Lemoine. 'What do you think?' she said.

There was a lull as they all turned to look at him. 'Well,' he said, rubbing his chin, 'the first Reformation followed the invention of the printing press. One would expect something similar to follow the invention of the smartphone.'

Shelley frowned. 'Like a revolution?'

Lemoine shrugged. 'You're the activists. You tell me.'

'Boo,' said Hayden. 'Come on. Make a prediction.'

'That's all anybody ever wants from me,' said Lemoine. 'Predictions.' He smiled across the centrepiece at Mira.

'But, like, a second Reformation? What would that even look like? I mean—'

'It's all beside the point anyway,' Jessica cut in. 'We talk about the future like we're going to be here to see it. We'll all be dead. We'll be so fucking dead. We'll be on fire.'

'Or underwater. Sea levels—'

'Or dead in a plague.'

'This conversation is bumming me out,' Hayden said. 'Can we do drugs now, please?'

Shelley produced the ziplock bag, and they began to discuss dosages and timing and what kinds of effects they could expect. Mira went outside again to check the barbecue. She took her time fussing over the wok, trying to find a level place on the grill to balance it – and then she sensed movement behind her, and glanced up to see that Lemoine had come out of the shed and was standing, hands in his pockets, in the shadow of the wall.

'I'm going to pass,' he said. 'Keep you company.'

'You don't have to do that,' said Mira.

'It's fine,' he said. 'Trust me, I know what it's like being the only sober person at a party.'

She couldn't resist. 'So it is a party?'

He smiled and put his hand over his heart. 'Darling, it wouldn't be, without you.'

She felt angry with him suddenly. 'You really don't have to sit it out,' she said. 'I can take care of myself. Like, really. Go and have your corporate team-building experience. I honestly don't care.'

'I'd rather be with you,' he said.

They were both quiet for a second, and then Mira said, 'Can I ask you something? If it's too personal, just tell me to . . .' She glanced at him, trying to read his expression in the dim light. 'I guess I was just kind of curious why you decided to learn how to fly.'

He didn't move. 'Because of how Gizela died, you mean.'

'Yeah,' Mira said. It was strange to hear him speak her name.

'I wondered if it was your way of dealing with . . .' She lost confidence. 'I mean, it's totally none of my business.'

Lemoine was quiet again. Inside, someone shrieked, and someone else gave a shout of laughter, and there was a sudden blast of 'Bad and Boujee' as someone cranked the volume way up. The containers of food beside the barbecue were vibrating with the beat.

At last, Lemoine said, 'My grandmother – the woman who raised me – was not a well person, mentally. She was an alcoholic, very changeable, very deceptive. A shapeshifter. You never knew where you stood with her, whether she was going to be up or down. She was institutionalised from time to time, later on, and one of the activities they encouraged at the mental hospital was building miniature dioramas. Because everything's so small, you see. It's manageable. You hold the figures in your hand. You can see the whole scene. You have perspective. It's a kind of therapy.'

'Right,' Mira said. 'That makes sense.'

'Well,' he said, 'when you're flying, that's another way of making everything seem small.'

Mira nodded down at the container of tofu. With her finger she flipped the plastic latch open and shut in time with the music. She had an odd premonition that he was just about to cross the space between them and come and kiss her – but when several seconds passed and he said nothing, she looked up and saw to her disappointment that he had already gone back in.

She felt foolish, and started opening the containers, ready to cook. Inside, she could hear that they were dividing up the tabs of acid, and someone must have offered one to Lemoine, because she heard him say, 'Not for me. I'm going to keep Mira company,' and then Shelley said, again in that loud, brittle voice, 'Oh, is that what people are calling it these days?'

There was a lull underneath the music; Mira imagined that they all must have turned to look at Shelley, for after a second she laughed in a way that was unnatural to her, and said, 'Sorry – were we pretending we didn't realise what was going on here?'

'Okay,' Jessica said, firmly, 'I think we should probably have dinner now.'

Then Lemoine said, in a cool, clear voice, 'Do you have something that you want to say?'

He could only be addressing Shelley. There was another lull. Mira stood in the dark astonished, mouth open, waiting for Shelley's reply.

'I guess I'm just a little worried that we might be doing this for different reasons,' Shelley said at last.

'But that's life, isn't it?' said Lemoine, speaking lightly. 'Everybody always has their own reasons for doing what they do. You can't police motivation.'

'No, I know,' Shelley said quickly. 'I know that.'

'Are you sure?' said Lemoine.

'Shelley,' somebody put in, 'this is kind of none of your business.'

Shelley laughed in that unnatural way again. Her face would have reddened, as it always did when she was drinking; there would be a dangerous light in her eyes. 'It kind of *is*, though,' she said. 'I mean, it's pretty clear you guys want to bone each other—'

Several people spoke at once: 'Shelley!' 'Hey, stop.' 'Come on, leave him alone.'

'And I guess I'm just a little worried,' Shelley said, cutting over them. 'Like – where does that leave the rest of us?'

Mira was straining to hear Lemoine's answer, but evidently he hadn't felt the need to make one; hearing nothing, she pictured him shrugging, pictured his expression, taunting, unruffled, lazily amused. Shelley would be appealing to the others, still half-smiling, holding out her palms perhaps, to suggest an open question – but Mira could hear that they were already changing the subject, trying to apologise, trying to laugh it off, and soon Natalie said, 'Where is Mira, anyway?' and Jessica said, 'She's cooking – we should probably go help,' and seconds later they had come out of the shed with bright, smiling faces and anxious eyes, and Mira was smiling back at them, pretending that she hadn't overheard, that she'd been in her own little world, that she was none the wiser, though she knew that they could tell she was pretending, and it was clear to her that they could tell she knew.

Over dinner, Shelley said nothing at all. She and Mira were seated at opposite ends of the table, but on the same side, so Mira only saw her profile whenever she leaned forward over her plate to take a bite. The others seemed to be conscious of needing to preserve the space between them, for nobody made any effort to draw either of them into the discussion, which centred, as far as Mira was aware, on the differences between the generations. As they ate, she heard Natalie teasing Lemoine that Gen Xers named their pets like they were children, and named their children like they were pets, and she heard Katrina saying that she'd never felt that the definition of 'Millennial' applied to her, and Jessica replying that that was *the* most Millennial thing Katrina could possibly have said, and when the conversation turned, as it so often did, to all the many ways in which the Millennials had been short-changed, she heard Lemoine remarking that he didn't understand why people their age were so nostalgic for the welfare state, since their parents, the baby boomers, were themselves such a good argument against it – look what happened when you gave people too much help: they just took it all for granted, and then they took it away from everybody else! She could hear herself laughing and protesting and begging to differ and taking a stand, but it was as though she was sitting outside her own experience somehow, participating only through a gauze, and it was only when someone said, 'Oh *shit*,' and they all began to laugh, one by one, around the table, that she remembered they had taken acid and realised that it must be starting to take effect; and then Lemoine caught her eye across the harakeke flowers, and made a movement with his head that meant, *Let's get out of here*, and Mira felt her stomach drop. Dumbly she got up from the table to see that Shelley was looking over at her with a weirdly teenage expression, a mixture of injury, defensiveness, and scorn. Lemoine was making their goodbyes; Mira held Shelley's gaze a moment longer, her expression cold, then turned her back on her and left. Lemoine followed her out into the darkness and around the Vanette, which was parked at an angle to provide a kind of windbreak for the barbecue, and neither of them spoke as he fell into step beside her, so afterwards she could not remember if she had taken his hand, or if he had taken hers.

It took them almost twenty minutes to walk back up the hill to the house, which was dark and cold, and had the soapy, indefinably foreign smell of someone else's family.

'Goddammit,' said Lemoine, as he let them in with a key. 'I forgot nobody has central heating in this fucking country.'

He went ahead to find the controls for the heat pump. Mira unzipped her jacket in a show of patriotism, then changed her mind and zipped it up again. She came into the doorway of the living room just as the louvres on the heat pump opened and it began to blast hot air into the room.

'Jeez,' she said. 'I reckon it's colder in here than it is outside.'

'Yeah,' he said. 'I should have turned this on before we went down for dinner.'

271

Mira said nothing, wondering if that meant he had always expected the evening to turn out this way. Then she wondered if *she* had always expected the evening to turn out this way – and she blushed to realise that she had. Her heart was beating fast. She felt as though she had become suddenly bodily, suddenly animal, suddenly incarnate; she could feel her pulse in every part of her, in her groin, in her stomach, in her mouth.

'There's got to be another heat pump,' said Lemoine. 'This is ridiculous.'

He left in search of it, and Mira looked around the Darvishes' darkened living room and sighed. She turned on a lamp, but the curtains were all open, and as the moon had not yet risen, the picture window reflected her image back to her in perfect clarity. She winced and turned it off again; instead, she moved to the window and looked out past her reflection into the dark. Then she froze.

There was a car at the gate. Its lights were off, and she couldn't tell if anyone was inside, but from the way it was parked, with the driver's door close to the keypad, it appeared as if the driver had pulled in meaning to input the code and enter.

'Robert,' she said.

He didn't answer.

'Robert,' Mira said again, louder.

He reappeared in the doorway. 'What?' he said.

She pointed through the glass. 'There's someone at the gate.'

In an instant, he was at her side and peering down through the glass. 'I don't recognise the car,' he said. 'Do you?'

'You changed the code,' she said.

He got his phone out. 'Shit,' he said. 'Someone tried the intercom. Twenty minutes ago.'

'Maybe it's a neighbour,' Mira said. 'Maybe someone heard the music.'

He was tapping at his phone. 'But where are they now?' he said, almost to himself. 'Did they come over the gate?'

He was keeping his phone angled away from her, but Mira could see it in the dark reflection of the glass, and she realised that he had opened an app that gave him a bird's-eye perspective on the farm – a live feed, it seemed like. Somehow, it had never occurred to her that he might be keeping the farm under surveillance; she opened her mouth to say something, but she was distracted when he scrolled past something that was moving . . . and then in the next instant she heard the roar of an engine revving painfully in a low gear. Stupidly, she looked down at the SUV at the gate, but it was still stationary, its windows still dark – and then, before she had time to speak, the Vanette came careening past the house and down the hill.

'What the fuck?' Mira said, as it disappeared from sight. 'Who was driving that?'

Lemoine was already running out of the room. Mira heard a thud and a screech of tyres and then a crack. She turned and followed Lemoine out of the house and ran to the crest of the hill to see that the Vanette had swerved off the gravel drive and crashed into a tree. She skidded down the slope, feet slipping on the dewy grass, and even from a distance she could see that the bonnet was steaming, and she could hear the bing-bing-bing of the indicator, and the swish of the windscreen wipers, though it wasn't raining, and it hadn't rained all week, and then she saw Shelley stepping down out of the driver's seat, looking utterly bewildered, and in the red wash of the tail lights she saw a body lying in the drive – a man, unmoving, pelvis twisted, one arm flung out, the other bent across his chest – and she broke into a run; but before she was close enough to recognise him, before she saw the colour of his hair and the shape of his skull and the mouth that was hanging blackly open and the eyes that were staring dull and white, before Lemoine caught the back of her jacket and pulled her sharply back, folding her tight against his chest, the closest she had ever been to him, the first time he'd ever put his arms around her, before Shelley sank to her knees and made a strangled sound, before she was even sure the man was really dead, she knew, with sick, guilty, hideous conviction, that it was Owen Darvish; that Owen Darvish had surprised them; that Owen Darvish had unexpectedly come home.

III

JILL DARVISH HAD LAST SPOKEN WITH HER HUSBAND when he'd landed at Christchurch Airport and picked up a rental car to make the journey south. He'd assured her that he'd ring again when he arrived, to say goodnight, but she had texted him a little after eight to say that actually she was turning in; a week of leading back-to-back mental health and wellbeing workshops had left her too exhausted even for trash telly and a takeaway, which was how she usually spent the rare nights they were apart. She had asked him please not to ring her after all, had said she hoped that he was driving safely and drinking lots of water and stopping every hour to stretch his legs and letting other people pass him in the passing bays, and had signed off by saying that she missed him, which wasn't strictly true, but was something that she knew he loved to hear. She no longer felt annoyed that he had booked the trip without consulting her. He'd been so nervous about the conservation project launch, she told herself, as she cleansed and toned and moisturised and then dabbed three tiny dots of serum underneath each eye; and then he'd been so disappointed when Lemoine hadn't showed up at the launch, though he'd done his best to hide it. The long drive down to Thorndike might be just the thing to set him right; he always said he did his best thinking behind the wheel. She turned out the light and slept soundly for almost thirteen hours. When she woke the next morning, she was a little miffed to see that he hadn't sent a text to say that he'd got in safe – but then again, she reasoned, belting on her robe, she had asked him not to wake her, and he would have been worn out from all that driving; he'd probably gone straight to bed when he arrived.

After she had showered and dressed, she walked down the hill to buy a cappuccino from their favourite Wellington café and drank it looking at the stationery display in the window of the post office, enjoying the sensation of allowing her mind to wander as it pleased, forming impressions and following associations that for once she was not obliged to share in conversation. She had one last mental health workshop to lead that afternoon, and she was just wondering if she had time to pop downtown before the class and do a little clothes shopping – something for her own mental health – when her phone buzzed in her pocket, and she took it out to see that her dad was calling. That meant the landline at the Thorndike house; she knew she really ought to update the contact details, but even after all this time, she still couldn't quite bring herself to delete his name. She binned her empty coffee cup and answered the call.

'Hello, love,' she said. 'How was the drive?'

But it wasn't Sir Owen; it was Lemoine. 'Jill?' he said. 'It's Robert. Sorry to trouble you – I'm trying to reach your husband.'

Lady Darvish felt her heart clutch in her chest. 'He's there,' she said, stupidly. 'He's at the house.'

'Yeah, I was waiting for him,' Lemoine said. 'He emailed a few days ago to tell me he was coming down, and I sent back a message to say great, see you then – but then I guess the reply got stuck in my drafts somehow, and I didn't notice till this morning. Sorry to bother you – I just thought he might have changed his plans because I didn't reply to his email. I tried calling his cell just now, but it's off.'

Lady Darvish was hardly following. 'But he's at the house,' she said again. 'He's in Thorndike. He drove down last night.'

There was a pause, then Lemoine said, 'No, Jill – he's not here.'

'He flew down to Christchurch,' she said, feeling a rising panic. 'Yesterday. After work. He rented a car at the airport. He was going to drive straight there.'

'That's what he told me too,' said Lemoine, sounding puzzled. 'You sure he didn't change his plans?'

'We spoke on the phone when he landed. Maybe three, three thirty.'

'Huh,' said Lemoine. 'Well, I flew in about five. I waited up for him till about—'

'He didn't think you were going to be there,' she said.

'Yeah,' he said. 'So stupid of me – this email thing. Got caught in my drafts.'

'But I don't understand,' she said. 'Where could he be?'

'Look, I'm sure everything's fine,' said Lemoine. 'Maybe he was tired and pulled over somewhere.'

'No, he would have told me,' she said. Her voice was getting high and tight. 'He would have texted me. Something's happened.'

'Let's not jump to conclusions,' said Lemoine. 'I mean, his phone might have died. He might have—'

'He charges his phone in the car,' she said.

'But didn't you say it was a rental?'

'Oh yeah,' she said, allowing herself to feel hope. 'Yeah. Okay.'

'It could be a million different things,' said Lemoine.

'Yeah,' she said again. 'Okay.'

'Let's figure this out,' he said. 'Is there anywhere he might have stopped? Any friends along the way he might have wanted to visit?'

'No,' she said. 'No, I told you. He was going to go straight home.'

'Okay,' said Lemoine. 'Okay.'

'And someone would have called me,' she said. 'If anything—'

There was a pause, and then Lemoine said, 'Sorry to ask, but did he ever pick up hitch-hikers?'

'Oh, God,' she said, horrified. 'No. I mean, maybe once or twice, if they ... But no. Not for years. Not at night. No.'

'Sorry to alarm you,' said Lemoine. 'The thought just occurred to me.'

They were both quiet.

'You said you just tried to call him?' she said.

'Yeah. I couldn't get through.'

They were quiet again.

'We could try to locate his phone,' Lemoine said. 'Oh – but no, I guess we'd need his Gmail password.'

'I know it,' she said.

'You do?' Lemoine said, sounding surprised. 'Well, fantastic. Then we can find him. Easy.'

'Really?' she said. 'We can do that?'

'Sure, if he's with his phone,' said Lemoine. 'You haven't used Find My Device before?'

'No,' she said. 'This has never happened before. This isn't like him at all.'

'Are you at your computer?' he said. 'Go to your computer and google "Find My Device".'

She had already started to run back up the hill. 'Wait,' she said. 'I'm going home.'

'Jill,' he said, firmly, 'let's keep our heads, okay? It's probably nothing, all right?'

She promised she'd call him back in a minute, then hung up and tried Sir Owen's number, just in case – but as Lemoine had told her, it was off. 'This is Owen Darvish, leave a message,' said the voice in her ear, more familiar to her than any other voice, dearer to her than any other voice, and she tried to keep her own voice steady, saying, 'Hi, love, it's Jill, just wondering where you are, give me a ring back as soon as you get this.' She hesitated, and then said, more huskily, 'I love you.' She was blinking back tears as she pressed the button to hang up, feeling the enormity of her love for him, and how utterly crucial he was to her, in every way, and how precarious and colourless and insubstantial her life would be without him – for it wasn't even her life; it was *their* life, it was a single life that they had shared between them, an existence they had forged and built together, that they inhabited together, and she was inextricable from him, and he from her – and if they could have their time again, she thought, wildly now, running up the hill, she wouldn't do any of it any differently, not even for a second, not even the hard times, not even the arguments and the mistakes; if she could do it over, she'd keep everything exactly as it was.

Back at the flat, she turned on the computer and called the landline at the farm. Lemoine waited while she googled 'Find My Device', typed in Sir Owen's email login details, and then pressed search. It took only seven seconds to return a result: a map popped up on the screen, and then a little grey icon of a phone appeared bearing the tag 'Owen's Phone' and, beneath it, 'Last Seen 18/08/17 23:32'.

'Oh!' she said, leaning close to the screen.

'What is it?' said Lemoine.

'He's in Thorndike.'

'Really?' said Lemoine. 'Well, that's good. What's the timestamp?'

'23:32,' she said. 'Last night. No – this can't be right.'

'What?'

281

'It says he was up at the lookout,' she said.

'What's the lookout?'

'On the road up to the pass. There's a lookout over the lake.'

'Isn't it closed?'

'Yeah,' she said. 'But the barricade is further on. You can still get to the lookout.'

'The location might be approximate,' said Lemoine.

'Could it be a mistake? Like a glitch? Could it be showing me past data or something?'

'Why do you say that?'

'Well – why would he go up there at night? There'd be nothing to see.'

Lemoine seemed to hesitate. Then he said, 'Dial back the clock a bit. Do you see the timeline function?'

'Yeah,' she said.

'What time did you say he left the airport?'

'About three thirty,' she said.

'Input that,' said Lemoine, and she did, and several seconds later the icon appeared again, showing Owen's phone in a parking lot in Christchurch, bearing the tag '18/08/17 15:31.'

'What do you see?' said Lemoine.

'Yeah, I see him,' she said. 'Half past three, he was picking up the rental.'

'All right. Wind it forward, see where he went.'

She wound the timeline forward and saw the icon make its journey south.

'Yeah,' she said presently. 'He got into Thorndike at twenty to nine.'

'And then what?'

'Well, there's a gap,' she said.

'The signal around here is a bit patchy,' he said. 'What's the next location after 8.40?'

'At the lookout,' she said. 'At 11.32. And that's the last one.'

Neither of them spoke for a moment. Then he said, 'Like you said, it might be a glitch. But do you want me to drive up and see?'

'Would you?' she said in a flood of relief. 'Oh, thank you so much. Thank you.'

'I'll go now. Call me if he gets in touch in the meantime.'

'Robert,' she said, 'really, thank you. It's very kind of you to take the trouble.'

'Let's find him first,' said Lemoine.

After she'd hung up, she checked Sir Owen's email and saw one unread message from Robert Lemoine, sent barely an hour ago. It was headed 'RE: FAIRY TERN TAKES FLIGHT!!', and Lemoine had written, 'Owen – apologies, thought I'd sent this days ago. R ≫ Hi Owen, congrats on the launch, wish I could have made it. As you know I'm in California this week, but let's plan to meet at your place this weekend. I'm liking what I'm seeing from the Birnam crew and I think we should progress to next steps. Hope you'll agree. Talk soon, looking forward, Robert'.

Lady Darvish was frowning. What was he talking about? Who were the Birnam crew? She scrolled down to read Sir Owen's original email, sent late on Tuesday afternoon, but it was just a long account of the conservation project launch in Northland; he had embedded a clip from the video segment that had aired on the six o'clock news, which Lady Darvish had already seen. She was about to click away from it when she saw a post-script underneath the video: 'BTW,' Sir Owen had written, 'I'm going to be in Thorndike this weekend, just to check on things. Arrive late Friday night. Maybe I'll catch you if you're there? V best, Owen.' Out of habit, Lady Darvish made a tutting noise. Sir Owen had never quite joined the twenty-first century when it came to formatting his emails. Why on earth had he placed the PS *below* the video, where it might have easily been missed, rather than above it, in the body of the message?

Still shaking her head, she typed the word 'Birnam' into her search engine, but all that came up was a map of a village in Scotland, various high-school exam questions about Shakespeare's *Macbeth*, and, closer to home, a Facebook page for some kind of gardening society in Christchurch that appeared to go by the name Birnam Wood. 'We are a grassroots community initiative,' the profile page stated. 'We plant sustainable organic gardens in neglected spaces, and we are committed to the principles of solidarity and mutual aid.' The photos showed thriving residential gardens, artfully arranged salad bowls and boxes of seasonal produce, smiling young people hard at work digging and pruning and watering seedlings . . . This couldn't be right. Lady Darvish was frowning again as she went back to Sir Owen's email and searched for 'Birnam' in his messages instead. The search returned one result: an email exchange between Sir Owen and Lemoine that bore the subject heading 'Birnam Wood'. It was dated three weeks ago.

'Hi Robert,' Sir Owen had written, 'good to talk earlier. I meant to say, not sure what Jill will make of all this, so perhaps best to keep it just between us for now? Not meaning to deceive as such – just wanting to make a good first impression if and when we do go live . . . All best, Owen'.

A few hours later, Lemoine had sent back a brief reply: 'Fine with me'. That was the end of the thread.

Lady Darvish sat back in pure astonishment. Sir Owen had a secret! The man who had not managed to surprise her in thirty years of birthdays and Christmases – whom she could read better than she could read herself – who lied so badly, so ineptly and implausibly, that his deficiency had long become a family joke – *he* had a *secret*! With *Robert Lemoine*! She read his words again – 'Not meaning to deceive as such' – and felt herself blush. Well, he *had* deceived her. He had done it. She had been deceived. But why? Why would he hide something from her? Why would he hide *anything* from her? What was there to hide? She went back to the Facebook page for Birnam Wood and called up the photo reel again, clicking through the images more slowly now. The members of the group were all in their twenties and thirties; she could see nobody remotely close to her own age. She lingered on a photo of a smiling young woman proudly holding up a gigantic marrow for the camera, and an old saying popped into her head, that there were two things that would always be believed of any man, and one of them was that he had taken to drink. But not *Owen*, she thought, blushing again. Other men, yes, of course – but not *Owen*!

Then she remembered his strange behaviour earlier that week, after he'd spoken with that so-called journalist, Anthony – when he'd been so agitated – and then he'd gone ahead and booked the flight down south without consulting her. Had that been just another lie? She wondered suddenly, crazily, if Anthony was even real. But of course he was. She was being stupid. Sir Owen had forwarded his approach to her – and they'd discussed it on the phone – and she'd visited the guy's website, for heaven's sake; she'd read his writing, or at least, she'd started to. Of course Anthony was real. Lady Darvish drummed her fingernails against the edge of the desk, trying to suppress the sense of dread that was pooling in her stomach and climbing up her throat. Sir Owen had said that Anthony was down in Thorndike. All right: well, perhaps they were together now. That would make sense, since Anthony was the reason he'd gone down there in the first place. (Wasn't he?) Perhaps they'd gone up to the lookout together, for some reason – to talk about that radiometric thing – and then Sir Owen had left his phone there by accident, and then it had run out of battery, and he hadn't noticed, or he'd dropped it, and they'd driven away, and any moment now he was going to call and say, 'Sorry, love, you must have been so worried, look, you're not going to believe what happened to me last night ...'

She could give Anthony a call, she thought; at the very least, it would give her a way to pass the time while she waited for Lemoine to call her back. She searched for his email in Sir Owen's inbox, but nothing came up. Sir Owen must have deleted it. Paranoid, probably, in case it leaked somehow that they'd blabbed to the Mulloys. No matter: she still had the copy on her own phone that he had forwarded to her. She took it out, found the email, and retrieved Anthony's number, feeling a little better that she was taking the initiative, and telling herself, bravely, that if all this *did* turn out to be a storm in a teacup, it might be quite a good story to share at her mental health workshop that afternoon. She could use it as an icebreaker, to illustrate how quick we are to panic, how easy it is to lose perspective and assume the very worst. 'Of course, it turned out he was absolutely fine,' she imagined saying to the group with a laugh, 'but for a moment there, I really thought I'd lost my mind.'

She dialled the number.

'Hi, you've reached Tony, you know what to do. Cheers,' said the recorded voice in her ear. Disappointed, she hung up before the beep, and then thought better of it, and dialled again. 'Tony, hi, Jill Darvish here,' she said, speaking more calmly now. 'I think you spoke with my husband Owen about a piece you were writing? Yeah: he's come down to Thorndike to talk to you, and I'm trying to reach him. I thought you might be together. Or maybe you might know where he is? Anyway, give me a call back,' she said, and then she left her own number and hung up.

The landline shrilled out in the kitchen, making her jump.

She ran to answer it, thinking that if Lemoine had been right and Sir Owen's phone *had* died – and he was certainly due for an upgrade; he'd had the thing for over a year – then maybe he hadn't been able to recall her mobile number off the top of his head – which would be typical, really, since *she* knew all *his* numbers off by heart – and so he was calling the flat to get in touch with her, to reassure her that all was well – and not just that; to tell her about Birnam Wood, to explain what it was, and why he'd kept it from her – and then they'd laugh together over the fact that finally, after all these years, he'd really truly managed to surprise her – and she wouldn't have to confess that she had read his email – and she wouldn't have to doubt him – and she wouldn't have to wonder if he'd betrayed her – and she wouldn't have to grieve—

'Hello,' she gasped.

It was Lemoine.

'Jill, it's Robert,' he said, his voice seeming heavier now, and much further away. 'I don't know how to tell you this' – and that was the last thing she heard.

Lemoine had started strategising from the moment he had seen the body. He had put his arms round Mira not to console her, but to hold her still while he ran through various plays and counterplays in his mind, gaming out his options, bracketing the things he could not change (Darvish was dead; Shelley was tripping on acid that he, Lemoine, had given her) from the things that could possibly be altered or massaged (Darvish had been hit by the van; Shelley had been driving it), and when after a couple of seconds Mira had tried to extricate herself from his embrace, pushing away from his chest with her forearms, craning her neck to turn and look again at the corpse where it lay flung out and staring on the gravel drive, Lemoine had gripped her even tighter, murmuring, 'Trust me – don't look,' until she stopped struggling and began to cry.

It was a bad situation. Darvish was still the legal owner of the property. He had been killed on his own driveway, on his own land, in front of his own house, by a trespasser blitzed out of her mind on an illegal drug that Lemoine had personally imported to the country, and the only reason he'd been walking up his driveway in the first place, alone and in the dark, was because Lemoine had changed the code on his front gate and hadn't let him know. And that wasn't all: in the shearing shed at the bottom of the hill were five other trespassers in the same blitzed-out condition, any one of whom might have seen Shelley drive away into the dark, any one of whom might have heard the Vanette collide with Darvish and then swerve and crash into the poplar at the driveway's edge, any one of whom might be about to appear, at any moment, to ask in psychedelic stupefaction what the hell was going on. Even if there was a way, somehow, of waiting out the collective acid trip, even if Lemoine could think up a reason to delay calling the police until the effect of the drug had subsided, even if the man's death could be made to seem purely like an accident, a misfortune for which nobody could be blamed, not Shelley, not Birnam Wood, and certainly not Lemoine, even then, there was no getting around the trespassing; there was no getting around the fact that the Birnam crew were squatting at the farm without the knowledge or permission of either Darvish or his wife. Their camp in the shearing shed was plainly long-established. Their many beds and plantings were proof in themselves of how long they had been living there, at Lemoine's invitation, with Lemoine's encouragement, and, as Mira's bank records could prove, on Lemoine's dollar. Once all of that got out, Lemoine thought, his mind turning fast, once Jill Darvish learned the circumstances of her husband's death, once she discovered all the ways in which Lemoine had deceived her, had deceived her husband, had caused his death, effectively, and for no better reason than out of malice and for sport, Lemoine could hardly expect that she would want to honour their agreement, proceeding with the sale and subdivision, making him her future next-door neighbour, for heaven's sake, by selling him the greater portion of the beloved acreage where she'd grown up! No: the millions that Lemoine had dangled would now seem offensive and obscene, a slight against the memory of her husband, an outrage against her. She wouldn't just back out of the sale, which was still well within her power; very probably, she would litigate against him. The case would be all over the news. They'd be in and out of courtrooms for years. It would be public; it would be poisonous; it would be louder than loud. And what would happen in the meantime to the extraction site in Korowai, and the mercenaries awaiting his instructions, and all their processing equipment, and the rare-earth motherlode itself? No, Lemoine thought again, shaking his head almost imperceptibly, his chin resting on Mira's hair. No: he couldn't risk Jill Darvish finding out the truth – which meant the truth was going to have to change.

His gaze came to rest on the body. Disappearing it was not an option. He could not afford to invite a Search & Rescue manhunt to the region that might uncover his operation in the national park. Darvish would have to be found, and quickly; but this posed a problem, for the sooner the body was found, the more tools a coroner would have at his disposal to establish both time of death and cause. Lemoine knew already that the CCTV at the petrol station covered the main highway in both directions. The SUV that Darvish was driving would have been clocked by the camera as he drove in, probably around half an hour ago, and of course the onward road over the pass was closed. To drive his body out again and stage his death elsewhere would create a time discrepancy; it would also beg the question as to why Darvish might have left his own property so soon after his arrival, which itself might raise suspicions. Lemoine had no way of knowing how many of the few remaining residents of Thorndike had seen his aircraft coming in to land that afternoon, but even if that number was zero, the plane was still parked up at the airstrip in plain view, and an easy search of the traffic out of Thorndike in the past few hours would prove that he had not left the property by car. What was more, it was a rented plane, and he had called the landing in; his flight log placed him squarely at the farm. To take off now would create another time discrepancy – a memorable one, since small planes did not tend to fly at night.

So his options were severely limited.

Lemoine tried to visualise the man's last movements. Darvish had driven up to his front gate, wound down his window, tried the code, probably several times, without success. Had he seen a far glow of light inside the shearing shed? Had he heard distant music wafting over the fields? Lemoine made a mental note to check if the shed was within sight of the gate. Well, in any case, he thought, Darvish had tried the intercom, and when nobody had answered, he had gotten out of the car and climbed over the gate to walk up to the house on foot, certainly frustrated, possibly even angry, that the code had somehow been changed. Had he called somebody? His wife – to ask if she'd ever had any trouble inputting the code, perhaps – or a neighbour – or even a locksmith? The security company that had fitted the keypad? If he had, then help could be already on the way.

Abruptly, Lemoine let go of Mira and went over to the body. In Darvish's left trouser pocket he could see a flat rectangle:

his phone. He knelt down and eased it out, and then, avoiding looking at the dead man's face, he slid the phone carefully under the lifeless hand and pressed Darvish's thumb on to the sensor button to unlock the screen with his fingerprint.

Shelley was watching him. 'Who is that man?' she said.

Lemoine ignored her. He went to the call history first, to discover that the last call that Darvish had made – to his wife – had been at 3.30 that afternoon; it had lasted one minute and twenty-nine seconds. Relieved, Lemoine opened his messages. The last text message Darvish had received had come in at 5.12 p.m. It was from his son Jesse, and it said, 'hey dad were you and uncle mac invited to kieran's stag do?' At 6.33, Darvish had texted back, 'don't think so when is it?' and that was the end of the thread.

'Who is that man?' Shelley said again.

And then Mira said, from behind him, 'She doesn't know.'

Lemoine looked up, first at Shelley, whose expression was plaintive, both hands clutching strangely at her neck, and then at Mira. 'What?' he said.

'She doesn't know,' Mira said again. Her voice was thick. 'None of them do.'

'What do you mean?' he said. 'None of them know what?'

Mira was crying again. She covered her face.

'Who is he?' Shelley said, stroking her throat with both hands in a strange compulsive motion. 'What's he doing here?'

Lemoine got up, walked over to the van, and opened the rear doors.

'Where did he come from?' Shelley said, still stroking. 'Is he dead?'

'Don't worry,' said Lemoine. 'He isn't real.'

'He isn't?' said Shelley. She looked doubtfully at the body.

'No,' said Lemoine. 'None of this is real. It's a simulation.'

'Oh,' she said, without understanding. 'What for?'

He put his hand under her armpit and hauled her to her feet. 'Get in the van,' he said.

Meekly, she complied.

'I need you to count to five thousand,' he said. 'But you have to say every single number. You can't miss any of them out. All right? It's important. It's part of the exercise.'

'What exercise?' she said.

'I'll explain it at the end,' he said. 'Now let me hear you. One.'

'One,' said Shelley obediently. 'Two. Three. Four.'

'Good,' he said. 'Keep going. Don't stop.' He shut the door on her and looked at Mira.

'What did you tell them?' he said.

She was standing just beyond the red wash of light thrown by the van's tail lights. The indicator was still going – bing-bing-bing – and it occurred to Lemoine that it might be wise not to drain the battery: the hood was dented and steaming, and the windscreen cracked, but there was a chance that the thing could still be driven. He went around to the driver's seat and turned the key, cutting the light and the noise.

Mira hadn't moved when he came back. 'I didn't lie,' she said. 'I didn't make anything up. I just . . . left some things out.'

'What things? The money?'

'No,' she said, looking shocked. 'No.'

'What, then?'

'Him.' She pointed at the body without looking at it. 'And his wife.'

'Why?' said Lemoine.

She took a shuddering breath. 'Because . . .'

He wanted to slap her. 'Why?' he said again, louder. 'Hurry up.'

'Because people might not have come otherwise,' she burst

out. 'They might not have wanted to. We put it to a vote. I didn't want to lose the vote.'

He kept his expression stony – but inside he felt a great relief. So she had something to hide, just as he did. So she was deceiving Birnam Wood, just as he was. That was useful.

The tears were coursing down her cheeks. 'We should call an ambulance,' she said.

'He doesn't need an ambulance,' said Lemoine. 'He's dead.' He tilted the man's phone to wake up the display, but the screen had locked again, so he walked back to the body and knelt down in the gravel a second time to press the dead man's thumb to the sensor.

Rigor mortis would set in soon, he thought; already Darvish's blood would be pooling in his bottom and his back, and the impression of the gravel might be leaving its mark, as well. They ought to get him back in the driver's seat of the SUV as soon as possible.

'What are you doing?' Mira said.

Lemoine didn't answer. He opened Darvish's email app, searching for a clue as to why the man had unexpectedly come home. Scrolling back through his inbox, he found an Air New Zealand boarding pass, purchased on Monday evening, for a return flight from Wellington to Christchurch. The ticket was for a single seat, departing mid-afternoon on Friday and scheduled to fly back on Sunday night; included in the booking was a two-day rental car hire. So the SUV was a rental, then. That meant the engine would be in fairly good condition, Lemoine thought, still running through his options; it also meant that the odometer would have been recorded at the time that Darvish picked it up.

He could find nothing in the man's inbox to explain why he might have made the trip, so he clicked on the sent folder instead. Scrolling down, he saw his own address: this was the email that Darvish had sent to him about the conservation project launch on Tuesday, that he'd deleted without reading. He opened it – and saw the postscript at the bottom for the first time: 'BTW, I'm going to be in Thorndike this weekend, just to check on things. Arrive late Friday night. Maybe I'll catch you if you're there? V best, Owen.'

'Fuck,' he said aloud.

'What?' Mira said, but again he didn't answer.

Darvish had told him he was coming home – and he had missed it.

He turned to Mira. 'I want you to go up to the house,' he said. 'There's a farm vehicle by the kitchen door. I want you to drive it down here. Slowly. Try not to make any noise. And don't turn on the lights.'

'No,' she said.

'Mira,' he said, 'fucking do it.'

'No,' she said again. She stepped back, away from him. 'We should call the police. Put his phone back. You shouldn't be touching it. You should put it back in his pocket.'

Lemoine clenched his jaw tight to control his temper. 'Okay,' he said. 'Is that what you want? I put this back, and we call the police?'

'Yeah,' Mira said, but her voice was high and strange.

'So then the police come,' said Lemoine, 'and they ask what happened. Right? Well, it's homicide, first of all. Right? That's pretty clear. It's manslaughter. That's bad for Shelley. She kills an innocent man on his own property, outside his own front door? That's a court case, that's a conviction right away. But then they find out she's high as a kite, and *that* steps it up a notch. That's drug use, that's reckless endangerment, that's driving under the influence. We're starting to look at years in prison.

And then it turns out she's not the only one tripping off her nut. There's a whole gang of you. So now you're all a part of it, and it's trespassing, and it's theft, and it's destruction of property, and it's vandalism, because this guy *did not know that you were here*, Mira, and his widow doesn't either. What do you think *she's* going to think about it? And his kids? And this is a big story by now, it's all over the news, and up and down the country people are starting to say, hey, you know, I came home that one time and my back yard was all dug up, *that* was pretty spooky, or they're saying, you know, I had that water bill a while back that was *way* too big to make sense, and it all starts coming out of the woodwork, how you guys have been doing this for years, creeping round behind people's backs, stealing, lying, cheating the taxman, breaking the law. This is the end of Birnam Wood, Mira. You're done. *Shelley's* fucking done. She's more than done. She's going to jail, no question. And she's got you to thank for it.'

Mira was sobbing now. 'But you gave her drugs,' she said. 'And you changed the code on the gate. And you didn't hear the intercom.'

'You and me,' said Lemoine. 'We did this to her together. This is our fault. A man is dead because of us, Mira. But we can make it right.'

'We can't,' she said. 'Everything is fucked. We're fucked.'

'No,' said Lemoine. 'We can take care of this.'

'Oh God,' she said, sinking down to her knees. 'Oh Jesus fucking Christ.'

Lemoine crouched down next to her and gripped her shoulders in both his hands. 'This was an accident,' he said. 'Do you hear me? It was an accident. We can't bring this man back to life. We can't change the fact he's dead. But we can change what happens to Shelley. We can save her from spending the rest of her life in jail. And we can save Birnam Wood.'

'No,' she said. 'Stop talking. Stop it.'

He gripped her tighter. 'Mira, look at me. We're not killing anybody. He's already dead. He died in an accident, in a
terrible accident, and all we're going to do now is change the
circumstances of that accident. That's all. And then we'll call the
police. Of course we will. Just not until we're ready. All right?
Not yet. Mira, you need to trust me. I've got this. I know what
to do. I can take care of it. But we're in this together. Do you
understand? This is a decision we need to make together.'

She took a deep breath and held it, her eyes shut tight. In the
van, Shelley was still counting: 'A hundred and twenty-one, a
hundred and twenty-two, a hundred and twenty-three . . .'

'For her,' said Lemoine. '*We* got her into this mess. We're
going to get her out.'

Mira opened her eyes again, but she wouldn't look at him.
She nodded at the ground.

He helped her to her feet. 'Go and get the four-wheel drive
and bring it back here quietly,' he said. 'Make sure nobody sees
you.'

Every limitation could be turned to his advantage, he thought,
as he watched Mira walk away into the dark; every weakness,
seen differently, could become a strength. Darvish had let him
know that he was coming home. Well then – Lemoine had been
waiting for him. They had been planning to discuss what they
had hoped would be a joint financial venture, a lark cooked up
between them, an idea that Lemoine had first brought to Darvish's attention weeks ago, that Darvish had kept secret from
his wife, perhaps, for reasons of his own . . . except that Darvish
never made it home. He'd driven past his own front gate – for
what reason, nobody would ever know – and kept going, up to
the lookout, up to the barricade, where, mysteriously, he'd lost
control of the car – damaging the fuel line as the SUV crashed

down the cliff, perhaps, so that his body burned. Lemoine was nodding. No witnesses, no one to blame, and it was plausible that Lemoine would wait until the morning before he started wondering if anything was really, truly wrong – by which time the others would have sobered up, and he'd have had a chance to clean up the driveway and disappear the van.

He went back to Darvish's body and pressed the man's thumbprint to the sensor button for the third time, guessing that Darvish was not the kind of man to have disabled his location services out of any fear his information would be stored and used against him. Sure enough, when Lemoine accessed the map, he saw that the phone's present location was clearly marked. He was just about to disable the function and wipe the man's location history completely when it occurred to him that perhaps Darvish and his wife kept tabs on one another this way; many couples did, and it might arouse her suspicion, he thought, if Darvish were to stop using the location service on the very night he died. Lemoine knew already that they knew all each other's passwords; Darvish had mentioned it once in the kind of offhand boast that married people make, with false self-deprecation, rolling his eyes. Well, perhaps that could be turned to his advantage too. Lemoine checked for any linked devices, but found none; instead, he erased Darvish's movements over the past half hour, and then disabled the service temporarily. Then he took his own phone out of his pocket, keeping the thumb of his other hand on Darvish's home screen to prevent the display from going to sleep again.

It was simple enough to make an email appear as though it had been sent and received some time ago: all one had to do was set one's clock to a time and a date that had already passed, send the message, and then reset the clock to the present. The recipient's device would file the email as if it had really been received on that prior date. It would be marked unread, of course; but that was easily fixed if one had access to both devices. In fact, if one had access to both devices, one could insert an entire thread into the past. With a few keystrokes, Lemoine could make it seem as though Darvish had known about Birnam Wood from the beginning. But he wouldn't overplay it. Less was more. He tapped away, holding his own phone in one hand and the dead man's in the other.

Up at the house, he heard the distant cough of an engine coming to life, and a few seconds later the farm vehicle came coasting down the hill, the engine much quieter than Lemoine had expected it would be; he realised that Mira must have put the gearshift into neutral to coast down the hill, and this fact alone was enough to reassure him that she was with him, that she had made her decision, that she was in.

'See anyone?' he said, putting both phones away.

She shook her head.

'This next bit is going to be horrible,' he said. 'But it's the only thing you have to do, all right? And once it's done, I'll take care of everything else.'

She nodded.

'We need to get him down to the gate and put him back in his car,' said Lemoine. 'In the driver's seat. Do you think you can do that?'

She nodded again.

'He can't have any gravel on him,' said Lemoine. 'We'll have to dust him off.'

But she was already dismounting from the vehicle, going to the body, crouching down. Her face had a steely, vacant look, like a sleepwalker's.

Lemoine said nothing more. They knelt on either side of Darvish and lifted his torso until he was sitting upright, and then they lugged him to the four-wheel drive, Lemoine carrying his head and shoulders, Mira his feet. Staggering slightly, they folded him into the back seat and Lemoine got in beside him to make sure he didn't topple out. Mira got back into the driver's seat and started the engine. Keeping the car in neutral, she released the parking brake and coasted down the hill to the gate, only jamming the gear stick into second when they approached the inner keypad, so she could lean out and press the button that opened the gate from the inside.

They only had a few seconds to exit before the gates closed again. Mira drove neatly through the gap and pulled up beside the SUV. It was locked, and Lemoine had to fish for a moment in Darvish's trouser pocket to find the key. They opened the driver's door and lugged his body from the four-wheel drive into the SUV, first dusting him down for any gravel that might have caught in his clothing and checking the treads on the soles of his shoes. Lemoine had just strapped him into his seatbelt and was backing out of the SUV to shut the door when his elbow jostled the car horn, and it blasted out into the night, causing both of them to jump.

'Sorry,' he said.

Mira said nothing. Her jaw was moving weirdly from side to side, as though she were chewing the inside of her cheek.

'I can take it from here,' said Lemoine. 'Go back and be with Shelley.'

'What about the van?'

'This first,' he said. 'Go.'

'You've still got his phone.'

'I'll put it back.'

'You were touching it with your bare hands. Your fingerprints—'

'I'll wipe it down,' he said. 'Don't worry. Go.'

But she didn't move. She stared at him, barely an outline, her face a dark void. 'What are you going to do to him?' she said.

'It's better you don't know,' he said. 'We're wasting time. I need you to go back and be with Shelley.'

'You might need help,' she said.

I have help, Lemoine almost said, but didn't. Aloud he said, 'Look, here's the story. You and I are going to meet with Owen Darvish tomorrow morning to talk about funding going forward. And Shelley, too. All three of us. You're excited. It's going to be the first time you meet this guy in person, this guy *who knows you're here, who has known about you all along*. You're looking forward to showing him what you've all been doing on his property these last few weeks. All right? Now go and practise that. Just say it over and over until you believe it. You're meeting Owen Darvish tomorrow to talk about funding Birnam Wood.'

'What about the others?'

'Don't worry about the others right now. We can deal with them later. Just go.'

She walked over to the keypad to let herself back in, reminding Lemoine to change the code back to what it used to be before the night was over. But then she hesitated, her hand outstretched, her index finger pointing.

'Mira,' he said, 'we don't have time.'

She turned to face him. 'This is why we were fighting,' she said. 'Me and Shelley. She wanted to tell the others about meeting up with Darvish tomorrow, and I didn't. I wanted to keep it secret.'

'Good,' said Lemoine. 'That works.'

'That's why she came after me,' Mira said, sounding inexpressibly relieved. 'Yeah, that works.'

Lemoine nodded. He watched, hands on hips, as she punched the numbers into the keypad and the iron gates swung wide to admit her.

The numbers were anthropoid, marching single file, each digit rearing up out of the darkness and then colliding with her bodily in the instant that she counted it aloud. Over and over Shelley felt the bump and clump beneath her wheels, felt herself swerve, felt the van slam into the tree, heard the indicator, heard the swish and drag of the windscreen wipers, the rubber catching on the crack; over and over she saw, too late, the stranger's shocked expression, the heels of his hands, the flex of his torso as, too late, too late, he had tried to jump out of the way. And then the next integer appeared, and the next, and the next, and there was nothing she could do, she had to keep counting, had to keep killing, had to keep crashing again and again into the tree, still sitting, she imagined, in the driver's seat, her feet on the pedals, her hands in the ten-and-two position on the wheel.

And then, all at once, she lost her place. She forgot which number she'd just intoned aloud into the darkness. She forgot if she was meant to be counting down or counting up. She forgot what number she had started from, and how long ago, and why. And then she wasn't in the driver's seat. She was in the back, and it was quiet, and everything was still, and she felt a profound and unutterable relief, for the silence and the stillness could only mean that the stranger in the driveway hadn't happened yet, that the tree and the steering wheel and the cracked windscreen hadn't happened yet, and she lay on the floor of the van in perfect gratitude, feeling the night ferment around her, black currents washing over her, stirring her hair and tugging at her clothes, for a length of time that seemed to loop around itself so that each moment was prefigured in the one that followed it, and Shelley knew that if she moved an inch, if she shifted her weight or moistened her lips or even altered the rhythm of her breathing, the simulation would be over, and the future would become the past. When she became aware of a steady lightening, an incremental greying of the blackness, she shut her eyes to try to stave it off, and when she heard footsteps crunching on the gravel, and low voices, she willed herself not to hear them, not to accept that there were other people in existence, that there were strangers in existence, one stranger, one solitary stranger, who was real, who was flesh and blood, who lived, who had lived, and who could die.

The driver's door opened and somebody got in, rocking the suspension. Shelley heard the key going into the ignition: a tick-tick-tick, and then the engine coughed and turned over. Then came the scraping sound of the gearshift being put into reverse, and the van pulled back, and then from beyond the bonnet there was a rustling, and then a creaking noise, and then a snap, and then whoever was driving pulled up the handbrake and cut the engine and climbed out, rocking the suspension back the other way. Shelley's eyes were still shut tight. She heard Mira say, 'I understand.' Then footsteps, and then she heard nothing for a long time.

She must have drifted off, because the next thing she knew it was dawn, and the van was moving. She opened her eyes to see telegraph poles striping past, and beyond them, angled corrugated-iron roofs suggesting tidy bungalows on quarter-acre sections, with elevations in weatherboard and Oamaru stone, and polite front gardens, and carports, and low chain-link fences painted white and pink and baby blue. The van came to a stop at a four-way intersection and then turned left, and Shelley saw the ridge of the Korowai ranges high above her and realised that they were in the back streets of Thorndike. Whoever was driving must have turned off the highway before the main drag, which was how Shelley had come to think of the little strip of road that comprised the petrol station, a row of souvenir shops, and two shuttered-up roadside cafés. The van turned left again, and then right, into a driveway, and finally came to a stop beside what appeared to be a stuccoed single-storey house: through the van's side window Shelley could see a mossy drainpipe and a frosted bathroom window that was speckled black with mould. The driver cut the engine and got out and walked away, and about a minute later, Shelley heard footsteps coming back again, and then the rear doors of the van were thrown open, and there was Mira, still dressed in the jeans and patched woollen sweater she'd been wearing the previous day.

They stared at each other.

'Where are we?' Shelley said at last.

Mira didn't answer right away. Then she said, 'Somewhere we can talk.'

Shelley sat up, peering out at the deserted residential street over Mira's shoulder, all the colours soft and liquid in the early-morning winter light, and for a brief second she allowed herself to hope that the stranger in the driveway had only been a simulation after all. She turned to look over her shoulder at the windscreen – but it was cracked all the way across.

'Come on,' Mira said.

Shelley got out of the van and Mira shut the rear doors quietly behind her and locked them. The house was painted yellow, with lace curtains at the windows, and three ascending panes of glass in the front door. Mira opened the door with a key and then stood back for Shelley to enter first, looking up and down the empty street before following her in.

Inside, the place had a deserted feeling. A tattered vinyl sofa faced a dated television. The alcoves on either side of the electric fireplace were stuffed with jigsaw-puzzle boxes and peeling paperbacks with broken spines. Beyond a rounded arch lay a kitchenette with a hot plate and a microwave; a second rounded arch on the adjacent wall was curtained off. Above the sofa hung a framed reproduction of Van Gogh's 'Sunflowers', and opposite, above the fireplace, hung a boxy canvas that read 'Home for the holidays' in a red italic font. The room was cold and smelled of bleach and air freshener.

'It belongs to a friend of Robert's,' Mira said, and the thought was so unlikely, that Lemoine would have a friend who owned a house like this, that Shelley laughed. 'Sorry,' she said. 'Just – weird.'

Mira rounded on her furiously. 'What were you doing in the van?' she said. 'You dropped a tab of acid and then, what, you thought you'd go for a *joyride*? In the middle of the night? *Alone?* What the fuck is wrong with you? Where were you even going?'

Shelley opened her mouth to answer, but she found she couldn't speak. She saw the stranger in the dark, his eyes, his mouth, his hands—

Mira gave up and went through into the kitchenette. She began setting out mugs and filling the kettle, still furious, wrenching open the cupboards, slamming shut the drawers. Shelley watched miserably as she opened the cupboard over the worktop and took down a box of UHT milk and a jar of instant coffee.

'I got an interview,' Shelley said.

Mira turned.

'I applied for this job at the Charities Services,' Shelley said. 'Last month, when you went away. I applied for a whole bunch of jobs, like, basically anything that I was remotely qualified for. But this one I was really keen on. They emailed yesterday to say that I've been shortlisted. I found out just before we all sat down to dinner. They actually rang while we were up at the airstrip with Robert, and I didn't hear the call because my phone was on silent, but it was fine, because they emailed all the details anyway. The interview's next week. It's on Thursday.'

Mira's face was taut with rage. 'What the fuck are you talking about, Shelley?'

'I'm answering your question,' Shelley said. 'It wasn't a joy-ride. Last night. I was leaving. I mean, I *am* leaving. This is me leaving. I'm leaving Birnam Wood. Okay? This is me telling you: I'm out.'

'Are you insane?' Mira said.

Shelley tried to laugh again. 'I mean, you're right,' she said, 'it was really stupid and dangerous to get behind the wheel when I was in a state like that, and obviously I'll pay for the damage, I mean, it's your van, I totally had no right to take it and I'm really sorry I drove it when I was fucked up, but actually, to be honest, I mean, maybe it was a good thing I crashed. You know? I mean, I never even made it off the property – maybe that was just as well. I might have really hurt someone. And it's fine, right? I mean, it still drives. You obviously drove it here. So it's not like I totalled it. You know?' Her voice was getting higher and higher. She felt that she might be on the verge of hysterics.

'And look,' she added wildly, fishing her phone out of her pocket and waving it in Mira's face, 'I can show you the email about the interview. Let me show you. It's a pretty cool job, actually. The starting salary is decent, and it's totally a foot in the door for lots of other things I want to do. It's only a desk job, like, in a cubicle or whatever, but working in the non-profit sector, that's exactly what I—'

Her phone was dead. She depressed the power button and shook it slightly to wake up the display, but nothing happened.

'Stop it,' Mira said. 'I can't handle this. You have to stop.'

'Did you bring a charger?' Shelley said. 'I'll go get the one in the van. Can I have the keys?'

'No, Shelley,' Mira said, 'you can't have the keys.'

Again, the stranger rearing up; again the windscreen; again the bump and clump under the wheels—

'Look, Mira, I gave this a shot, all right,' Shelley said, speaking very loudly now. 'I came down here, I gave it a shot, I really wanted this to work out, I really did, but I'm sorry, it's like what I said last night: I just think we might be doing this for really different reasons. And maybe we always were, or maybe it's just Robert, and you've got to see where that goes – and I get it, like, I'm human too – but I've got to think about my future, you know? So that's what I'm doing. I'm thinking about my future, and I really want this job. Look, no hard feelings. Honestly. It's just time for me to move on.' Desperately, she shook her phone again. 'If I could just charge it,' she said, 'I can show you the email. I just need to charge my phone.'

There was a pause. Then, very quietly, Mira said, 'Do you really not remember?'

'Of course I *remember*,' Shelley said, laughing again. 'How could I forget? It's been an incredible four years. Of course I remember. I always will. I've loved this experience with Birnam Wood. It's taught me so much about myself, and about the world, and about everything. And we've really made a difference, you know? I'm proud of that.'

'Oh God,' Mira said. 'Oh God.' She turned away, gripping the kitchen counter with both hands.

Shelley looked down at her phone and saw her own image reflected blackly back at her. She tilted it away.

Then Mira said, thickly, 'I have to tell you something.'

'Okay,' said Shelley, relieved. She put her phone back in her pocket. 'Sure.'

Mira's head was bowed. 'Robert hasn't bought the farm yet.'

'Okay,' Shelley said again. She was nodding.

'He's put down a deposit. The offer's been accepted. It's going to happen. They just haven't quite closed on all the contractual stuff. There was this sideline thing, this conservation pr ... – it doesn't matter. The owner—' Mira took a ragged breath, looking down at the worktop. 'The owner's name is Owen Darvish.'

Shelley was still nodding. She saw the man's corpse in the red tail lights of the van.

'I was going to tell you,' Mira said, still without turning. 'At the hui. But then Tony was there, and I guess he just made me nervous, and I forgot to mention it, and then afterwards ... I don't know. It felt like it was too late.'

'It's fine,' Shelley said. 'Honestly, don't worry about it,' and in her mind she heard Lemoine saying, 'Don't worry. He isn't real.'

Mira turned to face her at last. 'I didn't know that he was coming home,' she said. 'Nor did Robert. And the gate – Robert changed the – I mean, there was something wrong with the gate. So I guess he – he climbed over.'

Shelley was still nodding. 'It's fine,' she said again. 'It's totally fine.'

'Shelley,' Mira said. 'Stop.'

They were both quiet. Shelley fixed her gaze on the cupboard over the worktop, which was still open. She ran her eye across the labels of all the jars and cans. All the items had been neatly arranged, and bizarrely she registered the observation that nothing had been opened yet: there were no rubber-banded bags of pasta, no ripped tabs on any of the cereal boxes, no sticky drips down any of the bottles; there was no mess, no residue, no Tupperware.

'What are we doing here, anyway?' she said.

'Robert's going to tell the others that he staged an intervention,' Mira said. 'He's going to tell them that he told us to go away for a few days and have it out. Like, just, sort our shit out, one on one. For the good of the group.'

'For the good of Birnam Wood,' Shelley repeated, in a false, hearty voice she didn't recognise.

Mira closed her eyes. 'I mean, it makes sense,' she said, 'after how you acted last night at dinner. Everyone knows there's something going on.'

'For sure,' Shelley said, 'it's just that I don't know if I can do a few days. I told you, I've got this interview—'

'Jesus, Shelley,' Mira burst out, 'you're not going to a fucking interview! You killed somebody! All right? You killed a man and Robert's out there right now cleaning it up, so whatever the fuck kind of fucking fantasy world you're living in right now, just fucking snap out of it. You are, like, *this* close to going to jail for the rest of your life! Do you understand that?'

Shelley opened her mouth to reply, then shut it again. She sat down on the vinyl sofa, and Mira went back to the kitchenette to make them both a cup of coffee.

'So where is Robert?' Shelley said, carefully, when Mira came back.

'He said it was better if we didn't know,' Mira said, speaking carefully as well. She sat down cross-legged on the floor. 'We're just supposed to wait here, and I think someone's going to come and fix the van, but he said just stay inside and he's going to sort everything out. And then I guess in a few days we'll go back to the farm and just – carry on.'

Shelley said nothing for a moment. She looked down at

her coffee in silence. Then she said, 'Whose house is this?'

'Jesus, Shelley, I don't know! He said it belonged to a friend.'

'It's a bit weird,' Shelley said. 'Don't you think? Like, it's probably not even seven yet. It's super short notice, we're in this insane situation, and suddenly there's this house, and it's totally available, and there's food in the cupboard, and it's, like, a perfect place for us to hole up and hide? With everything we need? It's, like, who is this "friend"?'

'I told you: I don't know.'

'And it's not even a *nice* place,' Shelley said. 'It's not, like, a place that *he* would ever stay in. Like, can you imagine Robert coming here for—'

'Shut up!' Mira shouted. 'Shut up about the fucking house! It's all we've got, all right? It's this or the back of a cop car, Shelley. It's this or a fucking concrete jail cell with a metal toilet in the corner, and no windows, and some psychotic fucking child molester on the top bunk making a shiv out of a spoon! All right? This is your life now. *This is our life.*'

'I need to charge my phone,' Shelley said.

'No way,' Mira said, and this time she was the one who laughed. 'No fucking way.'

'You know, this is exactly why I wanted to leave,' Shelley said.

'What is?'

'This,' Shelley said, gesturing at the space between them. 'Do you realise that I never actually make any real choices? Like, ever? I know you don't respect me. Maybe you don't even like me. I mean, you make it pretty clear that the only reason you bother to keep me around is because I'm useful. I do all the little things that you can't be bothered with, all the chores, all the admin, all the boring stuff – but when it comes to the actual big decisions, about the actual future, you act like I don't even exist. You act like Birnam Wood is your property, Mira, like it's your baby, like everybody else should just be grateful that you're even allowing them to be involved. Except Robert. Right? *He* can do no wrong, *he's* so fascinating, *he's* such a mystery, *he's* so terrifying, ooh, what could it all mean? Well, it's pretty obvious, actually, what it means. *He* can see it. That's how he's got you in the palm of his hand. He knows you don't really give a shit about anyone except yourself, which is perfect, right? No wonder you want to fuck each other. You've got so much in common.'

Mira was quiet. Then she said, very coldly, 'Well, I guess this whole intervention story isn't a lie any more: we actually *are* having it out.'

Shelley couldn't stand her suddenly. She got up and wrenched back the curtain that led to the rest of the house. Beyond the arch, a short hallway opened on to two small bedrooms and a bathroom. She went into the smaller of the bedrooms and shut the door and climbed under the covers and lay wishing she was brave enough to kill herself as the sun traversed the sky above the ranges and filled the room with slanting yellow light.

Mira was afraid to switch on the TV in case she chanced upon a police drama by accident, and she didn't have the will or strength of mind to read. After Shelley shut the bedroom door, she sat for four and a half hours without moving, her back against the sofa, her knees drawn up to her chest, and then abruptly she got up and took down one of the jigsaw puzzles from the shelves beside the fireplace. The image on the box was of three golden retriever puppies playing in a wicker basket, and the pieces inside were still sealed in plastic, together with a flyer that advertised the dozen other puzzles in the product range. She ripped open the bag and tipped the pieces out over the coffee table, turning them over one by one, dusting off the fine grey powder left by the machine that had cut the interlocking tabs and sockets, and setting aside the odd pair or row of three that had not been properly separated when the puzzle had been broken up and bagged. After the pieces were all picture-side up, she began to sort them into categories, discovering to her contentment that the texture of the retrievers' fur and the repeated weave of the basket made the puzzle much more challenging than she might have expected for a thousand-piece. She had found all the edges and two of the puppies' faces by the time she heard the bedroom door opening quietly behind her, and then footsteps, and then a jointed squeak as the curtain to the hallway was pulled back.

She didn't turn. Several seconds passed in silence, and then she felt a disturbance in the air as Shelley let the curtain fall again. A door opened and closed, and a minute later, Mira heard the water going on. She continued with her puzzle, concentrating on the handle of the basket, which was tied with a tartan bow. Presently the water shut off and Shelley re-emerged, wet hair wrapped in a towel, smelling of Imperial Leather soap and toothpaste. She came around the sofa and went through into the kitchenette, keeping her back to Mira as she opened and closed all the cupboards and drawers, eventually taking down a box of risotto, a can of mushrooms, a jar of dried herbs, and a bottle of oil. When the meal was cooked, she divided the food into two equal portions and brought the bowls into the living room, setting them down among the puzzle pieces on the coffee table.

'Thanks,' Mira said.

Shelley didn't answer. She sat down cross-legged on the floor and picked up her bowl to eat, her eyes on the puzzle as she chewed, and presently she put down her fork and reached out to try a connection that Mira had already tried. Mira said nothing.

She kept her eyes averted until Shelley realised the pieces didn't fit and put them back where she'd found them. But the next piece Shelley tried was a match, and after her bowl was empty, she stayed seated, puzzling in silence until the basket handle was complete and the finished patches had taken on a cobbled shine that begged to be stroked and smoothed with the flat of a hand. The afternoon began to wane. Shelley switched on the floor lamp and dragged it close to where they sat. Mira took their bowls into the kitchen to be washed. She made them both a cup of tea and opened a sleeve of ginger nuts, working in the fading half-light, grateful that the lamp in the living room had been fitted with only a low-wattage bulb. By midnight the puzzle was done. Shelley laid the final piece, then stood up at once, avoiding Mira's gaze, and went to bed, shutting the bedroom door quietly behind her. Mira ran her hand over the completed puzzle one last time, pressing down to feel it flex and shift beneath her finger pads and the bones of her palm, and then she got her phone out of her pocket and turned it on.

There were two messages waiting, one from Natalie and one from Katrina, each saying much the same thing: thinking of you both, take care, good on you for taking some time out to work on your relationship, looking forward to seeing you when you get back, x. She contemplated sending a reply but then decided against it. Instead, she opened her browser and called up the local news, aware that her mouth had gone dry and her breathing was becoming shallow. Her phone took a long time to load the page – over the last few weeks it had been getting slower and slower; she really ought to get on a better contract, she thought, maybe shop around a bit, maybe get a quote from a different company and see if her current provider would match it – and it would also be a good idea to clear out all the files she didn't need any more, delete all the apps she no longer used that were just taking up space and memory – the one that tracked the tides, for example, which she'd never opened since the day she'd first downloaded it – or the one that published daily chord progressions for practising the guitar, which, if she was being really honest with herself, she was never actually going to learn how to play. She wiped a sweaty palm on the knee of her jeans and tried to swallow, but she couldn't muster the spit.

At long last, the website loaded. 'Fatal Crash at Korowai Pass Lookout' was the headline, above a photo taken late that afternoon: it showed a stripe of POLICE KEEP OUT tape in close-up, and beyond it, in soft focus, a police car and a huddle of six or seven men. She scrolled down to read the article. It was brief. A rented SUV had crashed near the Korowai Pass lookout late on Friday night. The driver, who was male, had not survived and was yet to be formally identified. There were no passengers. It appeared that the SUV had driven through a gap in the guard rail and rolled down the cliff. Locals were being asked to assist the emergency services by keeping away from the area while the wreckage of the vehicle could be cleared. And that was it. Mira was expecting that the article would end with a plea for potential witnesses to come forward with information, but the final sentence only reiterated that the road over the pass had been closed since March that year, following a landslide in which five people had been killed.

Her phone started buzzing in her hand, startling her. The article on the screen had been replaced with a notification for an incoming call from a blocked number. She swiped to accept the call and put the device to her ear.

'It's Robert,' said Lemoine. 'How are you?'

'I'm okay,' Mira said, feeling a lump in her throat suddenly.

'Shelley gone to bed?'

'Yeah.'

'How's she doing?'

'Not great. Flipping out a bit.' To steady herself, Mira spread her free hand over the completed puzzle, spanning her fingers as wide as they would go. 'She got an interview for this job. Next week, at the Charities Services. Like a desk job. She was leaving Birnam Wood. At least, that's what she was planning to do, anyway.'

'Why?'

'She's wanted to for ages. Just sick of it, I guess. Sick of me.'

There was a pause, and then Lemoine said, 'Okay. Good to know.'

'How about you? How were the others?'

'Fine. Concerned about the two of you, relieved that you're sorting it out. A bit embarrassed, too. I got the sense they didn't even realise she'd taken off last night.'

'Well, that's good, I guess.'

'And you've seen the news,' he said. It was a statement, not a question.

For some reason she didn't want to admit that she had. 'Not yet,' she lied. 'Too scared.'

Another pause. 'Of what?' he said.

'I don't know,' Mira said. 'I don't know! I really don't know if I can do this, Robert.'

'There's nothing for you to do,' he said. 'It's done.'

They were both quiet for a moment. Then Mira said, 'Does his wife know yet?'

'Yes. We've been in touch all day,' said Lemoine. 'She wanted to fly down, but I persuaded her against it.'

'Really?' Mira said. 'How did you manage that?'

'I told her I'd been through what she was going through. I said, "I know it's hell, and there's a part of you that just wants to be tortured right now, but trust me, you do not want to see that crash site. You do not want those images in your brain." I said, "Take it from me. Be with your family. Be with your kids. All that you'd be doing down here is punishing yourself. Don't do it."'

'And she listened to you?'

'Yes.'

'Won't there be a funeral though?'

'They'll have it up in Wellington, I think.'

Mira was quiet again, thinking of the Darvish family portrait in their living room, two proud parents, three happy children, all with their father's broad brow, their father's cheekbones, their father's wide mouth, their father's grin.

She shut her eyes tight. 'Robert?'

'Yes?'

'How did he die?'

Lemoine sucked in a breath and then expelled it very slowly. 'He drove up to the barricade,' he said. 'He got out of the car and walked around a bit and then got back in again. From the tyre tracks it would seem that he then tried to make a three-point turn to head back home, but he cut too wide, and the car went past the end of the guard rail and over the cliff. It rolled a couple times on the way down, and the fuel line was damaged, so by the time he was found, which wasn't till this morning, everything was pretty badly burned. His phone was in his pocket; between that, the odometer, and the highway cam in Thorndike, they'll be able to come up with a pretty good sense of his last movements. Of course they'll do a post-mortem, but I doubt they'll find any alcohol in his system. Certainly no sign of tampering on the car. Sure, there are a couple of unknowns. We don't know why he drove up there. We don't know why he lost control of the car. But there was nobody up there last night.

No sign of struggle. And he had no enemies to speak of. So I can't see they'll have any reason to investigate.'

Mira's eyes were still shut. 'What about Birnam Wood?'

'I don't see how that's relevant. The satnav on the car will show that he never made it home. He's never had any contact with any of you before. There's now a paper trail to show that he was coming down to meet with you this morning, but we were all at the farm last night, and he wasn't. Seems pretty straight-forward to me.'

'But his wife,' Mira said, eyes still closed. 'She'll know.'

Lemoine didn't answer at once. Then, speaking deliberately and clearly, he said, 'All I know, Mira, is that her husband was wanting to surprise her. I know that he was excited to meet you all today. I know that he and I had talked about providing you with bootstrap funding. I know that we were giving you the chance to prove yourselves, that you were staying at the farm from now till Christmas, and we were going to have a formal conversation all together after that. I don't know why he didn't tell his wife about you, any more than I know why he drove up to the barricade last night. Whatever his reasons were, they died with him. Okay?'

'Okay,' Mira said. She opened her eyes, and almost screamed: Shelley had come into the room and was standing at the end of the sofa, staring at her.

'Is that Robert?' she said.

Mira nodded, horror-struck.

'Tell him that we want a million,' Shelley said. 'A hundred grand isn't enough.'

There was quiet.

'Did you hear that?' Mira whispered.

'Yes,' said Lemoine, and then the line went dead.

*

He had learned three things that pleased him. First, it was plain that Mira still had no idea that he had compromised her phone. Although Lemoine had not yet exercised his power to delete or change her messages, he knew that the device would be taking longer to perform basic functions than it used to, and it would only be a matter of time before Mira began to suspect that something was amiss. He had been alerted, as usual, the moment she had turned it on, and had logged in to his own device and called up her user interface in time to watch her inputting the name of a national news website into her browser, followed by a forward slash and then 'southcanterbury' and then another forward slash, from which he had deduced, correctly, that Shelley must have gone to bed, and Mira must now be indulging in some covert online searching in order to alleviate, and also to inflame, her guilt. Mira was a proud person, and Lemoine was sure she would not have yielded to temptation in such an ordinary way if she had known that he was watching, not so much over her shoulder, as through her very eyes: together, they had read the article twice through, the first time quickly, and then again at quarter speed; together, they had checked for a comments field at the bottom of the page, found nothing, and then scrolled back up to scrutinise the photograph a second time; together, they had enlarged faces of the huddled figures in the background to try in vain to make them out. He had felt a strange affection for her then, and had dialled her number out of impulse, half-expecting she would ask him how on earth he'd chanced to call at just that moment, since her phone had been off all day, and she'd literally only just turned it on. But she hadn't seemed in any way suspicious that he'd called. The opposite: she'd seemed relieved to hear from him. That was good news. She was even more gullible than he had thought.

The second thing that pleased him was the fact that she had lied to him. Lemoine loved to make a study of deceptions, no matter how insignificant or glancing they might seem; in fact, he had often found it was the inconsequential-seeming falsehoods that tended to betray the most about a person's character, exposing their petty vanities, their hubris, their blind spots and soft spots and individual styles of self-mythology and self-exception, all of which could be gathered as intelligence and played to his advantage down the line. As lies went, of course, Mira's had been a fairly innocent one – arguably, it wasn't even so much a lie as an exaggeration, for she probably *had* been scared to read the news, just not *too* scared – but it was telling, nevertheless. She seemed to want to appear to Lemoine both stronger than she really was, and weaker. Her pride would not permit her to concede that she'd indulged in a spot of furtive late-night googling about a death she'd helped to cover up; that was ordinary enough. But her pride would not permit complete dishonesty about it, either, for she hadn't told him she *hadn't* seen the news about the crash; she'd said she hadn't seen it *yet*. That was more revealing.

There was a parental side and a childish side to Mira, thought Lemoine, as he disconnected from her interface and put his phone away. Sometimes when she was under pressure the child came out, and she became stricken, desperate, even self-destructive, as she had when she'd blown her own cover on the day that they'd first met; other times, it was the parental side that rose to the occasion, and she turned lofty, projecting an air of disappointment and impunity, as if to say that she would have preferred for the social contract to have been upheld by all, but since it had now been broken – or, perhaps, since it had never been properly instituted in the first place – then *she* wasn't going to waste her time by abiding by it either, and if anybody had a problem with that, well, they could only have themselves to blame. This was the exacting side of Mira, the forbidding, distant, morally demanding side – but it too had the capacity to undermine her. If Mira were to turn herself in to the police, Lemoine realised, it would not be helplessly, hopelessly in a state of anguish, like a child; it would be gravely, even sternly, having decreed it was the right and only thing to do. It was the child in her who had lied to him, the child who craved his good opinion, the child who could not bear the thought of being ordinary or underwhelming, even for a moment, even in a time of stress. But it had been the parent who had told him that she hadn't read the article about Sir Owen Darvish *yet*. He could manage the child. The child wanted to be managed. The parent he was going to have to watch.

Which brought him to the third thing about their conversation that had pleased him. Lemoine was smiling now. He had been entirely wrong about Shelley Noakes. He had taken her for a dogsbody, a beta fish, a bridesmaid, a ride-along; he had looked right past her, as likely many people did. Even when she'd drunkenly confronted him at the dinner in the shearing shed, he had shrugged it off as mere hysteria, mere sexual jealousy, merely an emotional display from an underling who didn't know she was an underling and who needed to be brought to heel. He saw now how wrong he'd been. Shelley possessed a ruthlessness that Mira simply lacked – and for which Mira, this time, only had *herself* to blame. For Shelley had cultivated her resentment, thought Lemoine. Being perpetually overlooked had deadened her, had sharpened her determination to prove to everyone around her that she was not just a mediocre also-ran, not just a middle manager, not just Mira's understudy always waiting in the wings. Mira's ambition had a limit. She wanted to suffer for the things that she'd done wrong, not to get away with them, and bury them, and profit from them, and triumph over them, and shame the world by her success like him – and like Shelley. Shelley had seen a chance to capitalise, and she had seized it. Shelley had turned a handicap into a strength. Shelley was the asset here. Shelley was the one he could depend on. Shelley was the one he could use.

It was late, but before Lemoine undressed and got into bed, he sent an email instructing his PA in Palo Alto to courier a file of paperwork to the Darvish farm as soon as possible, with the envelope made out to Shelley Noakes. He checked the Korowai surveillance feeds one last time before powering his laptop down and turning out the light, calculating as he drifted off to sleep that he had been awake for almost forty hours.

Lemoine had not stayed in Thorndike a moment longer than he'd needed to. After Shelley and Mira had departed for the safe house early that morning, he had walked down the hill to the shearing shed to check on the rest of the group. They were all still asleep. He woke them up and told them with mock gravity that he had been compelled to carry out an intervention. Any further conversations would have to wait until Mira and Shelley returned, hopefully on better terms, from their enforced retreat. The good news, he said, was that as soon as they *did* return, he could pretty much pull the trigger: he had drawn up a package of fiscal sponsorship already, and his lawyers had begun drafting articles of incorporation and applying to register the group as tax-exempt. They had officially registered the name and purchased a domain online; the website was being built, and a designer he liked was working on options for a logo and a typeface. The main tasks now were to come up with a vision statement, a mission statement, and a five-year plan; to decide how the organisation would be structured and administrated; to open a bank account; and to appoint a board – but as he said, all that would have to wait for Mira and Shelley to return. Before leaving the group to their collective hangover, he asked them how they had enjoyed their acid trip. Had it been hard out? Extremely hard out, they assured him, laughing, still bleary, still grainy-faced – and they thanked him again for the gift.

He went back to the house, sent Darvish the brief message that he pretended he'd thought he'd sent already, waited an hour, and then called his widow. Together they established the last known location of her late husband's phone, as Lemoine had planned; then he drove up to the barricade, as he had also planned, in search of what he already knew he would find there. He parked up at the lookout, got out of the car, inspected the tyre tracks in the gravel and the broken branch at the edge of the cliff, and said, 'Oh God,' for the benefit of anybody watching – though he knew that nobody was. He walked slowly to the guard rail, looked over, saw the burned-out chassis of the SUV, called out 'Owen?' in a fearful voice, shook his head in horror, ran his hands over his face for good measure, and finally – almost moved by the realism of his own performance – he took out his phone to dial 911.

There was a click in his ear, and then the hissing sound of the connection changed perceptibly in quality, signalling that the call was being forwarded to another number. Lemoine tensed – and then remembered that the number for emergency services in New Zealand was actually 111: there must be a forwarding service in place for Americans who didn't know any better, or, more probably, for Kiwis who watched too much American TV, he thought, as the call was answered, and he was invited by a deep-voiced woman with a thick New Zealand accent to state which emergency service he required.

He made several more calls as he waited for the first responders: first to Jill Darvish, and then, when she fainted and their call was disconnected, to the emergency services in Wellington, to direct an ambulance to her address. Next, he called his PA in Palo Alto and told her to find accommodation somewhere within a two-hour drive, to check him out of both hotels in Queenstown, and to tell his entourage to meet him at the new address; after that, he called the aero club in Kingston and informed them that he was going to need to rent the plane a little longer than he'd planned. He would leave it parked up at the airstrip for a while, he decided; he didn't like the optics of flying off into the blue while firemen winched the wreckage up the cliff and bagged and tagged the body, and he didn't much like the optics of staying on at the Darvish farmhouse either, freeloading while the dead man's family mourned. Fifteen minutes later, his PA emailed to say she'd found a place near Lake Tekapo that was available, an eight-bedroom villa with a hot tub and a heated indoor pool, and he'd just sent back a note of confirmation when a police cruiser appeared around a curve in the highway and pulled in next to him. He stood up off his car's rear bumper, put his phone away in his pocket, and squared his shoulders as a sign of respect.

'Forgive me for asking this,' he said to the officers, after they'd taken a statement and begun gingerly assessing the wreckage at the bottom of the cliff, 'but – do you know who I am? I'm sorry I'm even asking that question – just that I have a good deal of money at my disposal – and maybe I can be of service in some way.'

The officers exchanged a doubtful glance.

'Look, I'll just come out and say it,' said Lemoine, 'I'm a billionaire. Money is not an issue for me. So, if there's any equipment that you need, any backup, anybody I could speak with, anything at all to make your jobs easier in any way, please, let me know. I mean, Jesus, if that really is Owen down there

... he was a friend. We were in business together. I know his wife. I've been staying at his house, for God's sake. It was me he was coming to see last night. So – whatever it takes. Yeah? Please tell me. Anything that I can do. Anything.'

Their expressions had softened. They took his contact details, touched his arm, gave him privacy when he checked his watch and told them he really ought to call Jill Darvish back again and see how she was getting on. By noon, the fire department had shown up, followed an hour later by a transporter recovery vehicle and a truck-mounted crane hoist, and as the men milled about debating how best to scale the cliff and whether to extract the body from the wreck at the bottom or to wait until it was winched up, Lemoine drove back to Thorndike to buy a round of Cokes and burgers from the chip shop on the highway frontage. Everyone was patently delighted when he returned – even more when they saw that he'd ordered for himself as well. A billionaire in the Thorndike chippy! A billionaire standing in the gravel verge beside them, shoulder to shoulder, eating a red-meat, white-bread, full-fat, added-sugar lunch, a proud lunch, a workman's lunch! Lemoine stayed sombre, and made a private toast to Owen with his can of Coke, and after they had eaten, he asked the officers quietly if he could be excused. He would have stayed to identify the body, but they'd told him already that that would be a job for someone else; and they had his statement, and his number if anything came up. As he shook their hands and thanked them for their service, he reiterated his offer to assist with the recovery of the vehicle, or the post-mortem, or anything else, in any way he could. 'Call me anytime, day or night,' he said. 'I might be up in Wellington with the family. Depends on what they want. But I'll be reachable.' He put his hand on the car door, and then pretended to hesitate. 'You know,' he said, his eyes sliding off into the distance, 'it's strange; I've got no religion, never had it, never going to have it – but just now, I thought of Owen, and I felt this urge to cross myself.'

He woke late the next morning and turned at once to his surveillance feeds. It was raining in Thorndike, so his visibility was compromised, but he made a low pass over the lookout and saw that the wreckage of the SUV had been removed and the gravel verge beside the barricade was clear. Perhaps that meant the body had been formally identified already; he checked the news, but the article had not yet been updated from the version that he and Mira had read, as one, the night before. He switched to the feed over the shearing shed – nothing; the rain had driven Birnam Wood inside – and then to the feed over the safe house, which told him little more: he could make out the rear bumper of Mira's van, protruding beyond the roof of the carport, and nothing else. Out of habit, he checked the feed above the leaching pits in Korowai, but it was raining harder there, and it took him several minutes even to confirm what exactly he was looking at. He could see no human movement anywhere.

He went for a swim, made a smoothie, and then called Jill Darvish.

'Day two,' he said when she picked up. 'In some ways, not as bad; in some ways, much, much worse.'

'The kids are here,' she said. 'I'm grateful for that. I just feel like nothing's real.'

'I know.'

'I keep thinking about things I was meaning to tell him.' She sounded hollow. 'Just little things. Something I saw last week that would have made him laugh. Something I read in the paper. Stuff I just forgot to say.'

'It's hell what you're going through,' he said.

'Yeah, it is,' she said, and then neither of them spoke for a while.

'Jill,' he said at last, 'I've got to be honest with you. I don't do funerals.'

She gave a strange bark of laughter. 'Jeez,' she said. 'Who does?'

'If I came, I'd bring the press, it would be a story – *I* would be the story. I wouldn't like it. I doubt Owen would have, either. So I won't be at the service. I just wanted you to know.'

'Where are you?' she said suddenly.

'What do you mean?'

'I mean, what room? Where are you in the house?'

'I'm not at the house,' said Lemoine.

'Oh,' she said. 'I thought you were.'

'I was only there to meet Owen,' he said. 'I didn't think it would be appropriate to stay on.'

'When did you leave? Today or yesterday?'

'Yesterday.'

'Oh,' she said again.

There was another pause.

'Would you like me to go back?' he said.

'No,' she said. 'Robert, can you tell me something?'

'What?'

'What's Birnam Wood?'

He sucked in a breath. But he had been expecting this.

'It was in your email,' she said. 'The one you sent yesterday, that you thought you'd sent already.'

'I know,' he said. 'Jill—'

'I looked it up,' she said. 'The only thing I found was this gardening collective.'

'You shouldn't be reading his emails. You're torturing yourself.'

'Down in Christchurch,' she said. 'He's never really been to Christchurch. Well, except on Friday, but that was just passing through.'

'This is not the time to talk about this,' he said, 'but yes, they are a gardening outfit. Owen and I were talking about putting up some bootstrap funding. But really, it doesn't matter right now. The important thing—'

'Funding?' she said. 'Like investment?'

'This is really not the time to talk about this,' he said again, more firmly. 'Jill, it was all just an idea. It was just something we were thinking about. We hadn't—'

'What kind of investment?' she said. 'How much money?'

'Well, it's a non-profit, so more of a donation. A philanthropic kind of thing. After the project up north, it seemed like a natural next step. The image is right, the values are right. Good green credentials. But as I said—'

'I don't understand this,' she said, cutting over him a second time. 'Robert, I have to say, I just do not understand this at all.'

He was losing patience. 'What don't you understand?' he said, trying to keep his voice even.

'Any of it,' she said wildly. 'The conservation label.'

'What conservation label?'

'I mean, we laughed about it,' she said. Her voice was getting higher. 'Not like, *ha-ha-ha*, but it was funny. Owen's not a *conservationist*. He's pest control. He's had clients from all over. He's a hunter. His dad worked in an abattoir. He's never been that kind of hippy-dippy type at all. He doesn't care about the – I mean, he does, of course, I do too, but not . . . This project with the drones. He only dreamed it up when he met you. Because that was your line of work, and he'd seen how they . . . in other countries . . . And it was supposed to be in Korowai, remember. It was just a pet idea, a way of . . . It wasn't this whole . . . And then they turned around and gave him a knighthood for services to *conservation* – when the project hadn't even bloody launched yet! We were stunned.'

Lemoine's free hand was clenched into a fist. 'Well, I can't speak to any of that,' he said. 'They don't do knighthoods where I'm from.'

'And now you're talking about green credentials, and funding, and philanthropy, I mean, it's just not *him*. I don't understand it.'

He saw that he was going to have to backtrack. 'Jill,' he said, 'this is not political. It's just brand management. He's been celebrated as a conservationist; this was on brand. It's reputational. That was the way that we were talking about it.'

'Not with me,' she said. 'He never said a word to me.'

'Well, I can't speak to that either. I don't know why he wanted to surprise you. I never asked.'

She drew a breath. 'Will you be completely honest with me?'

'About what?'

'Was there—' He heard her swallow. Then she said, thickly, 'Was there a girl involved?'

He was so surprised he almost laughed. 'Oh, Jill,' he said. 'Oh, no. No. Jill, listen: Owen hadn't even met them yet. He was coming down to meet them all this weekend for the first time. That was why I was down there waiting for him, so we could have a conversation all together the next day. Honestly. He'd never even spoken to them on the phone before. That is not what's going on here. I promise you.'

'Okay,' she said, but she didn't sound reassured.

'Jill,' he said, 'I understand this impulse, I really do, but you can't do this to yourself. You can't do it to him. Trust me: it will make your grief last longer and it will make it worse.'

He heard a distant clatter on the other end of the line, and then voices.

'Sorry,' she said. 'Someone's just arrived. I've got to go.'

'Take care of yourself,' he said. 'Call if you need to.'

'Thanks, Robert,' she said. 'Really, thank you. Thanks for calling.'

He hung up, frowning, and then swore aloud into the empty room. He'd miscalculated. Badly. He had taken Owen Darvish at face value. More to the point, he'd taken the knighthood at face value. He had been so bored by all the endless talk of orange-fucking-fronted parakeets and fairy terns that he'd failed to see that Darvish had never been moved by any deep environmental passion or ideal. The conservation project had just been a way for him to profit by association, to raise the profile of his business, to play around with gadgets, and to bask in a billionaire's reflected light. Darvish hadn't been a conservationist. He'd just been an ordinary self-serving opportunist who had been knighted for no better reason than political expedience and plain dumb luck.

And now Lemoine had a serious problem. Jill Darvish didn't believe the story he had told her. It wasn't *him* she disbelieved – he still had her trust, at least – but she was already suspecting Birnam Wood. The splinter was beneath her skin; it was in her bloodstream; it was travelling. Sooner or later, she was going to want to meet the group, the young women especially, those attractive, energetic, vital young women, all fit and tanned from all the time they spent outdoors – and then she'd learn that Mira had been at the farm the longest – and then she'd learn that Mira was the founder of the group – and then she'd want to talk to Mira – and then she'd start asking Mira questions – and then Mira would crack.

As soon as the body was identified, he decided, he would contact Darvish Pest Control with his condolences. He'd say what a tragic loss it was, so young, so much left to give, a giant in his field, a family man, an inspiration to us all, blah blah blah. He'd mention that Darvish had been coming home on Friday night to meet with him about another project they had in the offing, another environmentalist endeavour very dear to both their hearts. Maybe he would even mention Birnam Wood by name. The email would undoubtedly be leaked – that was easily arranged – and once Jill Darvish began to learn about her husband's legacy from other sources, to hear his virtues repeated, over and over, to read them in writing, and see them broadcast on the news, she'd start to wonder if maybe it was she who was mistaken. Memory was tractable, and never more than in a time of grief. He would use her doubt against her. He could do that. He could change her mind.

And Birnam Wood? Well, they were going to have to earn that million, thought Lemoine. He was going to drown them in homework. Leadership training, anti-bias training, media training, fundraising workshops – all the ridiculous time-wasting courses he could dream up. He'd send them round the country on reconnaissance tours. He'd set up meetings with potential donors, strategic partners, politicians, influencers, whoever he could think of. Community leaders. Minority interest groups. He'd bore them to tears.

His third phone started ringing in his duffel bag. He fished it out.

'This is Weschler,' he said, and then he listened for a minute. His free hand clenched into a fist again. Then he said, 'Where?' and then, 'How long ago?' Then he hung up.

He accessed the feed over the Korowai leaching pits again, downloaded Friday's archived footage, and waited tensely while it rendered. Then he opened the window, dragged the cursor all the way to the right-hand side of the timeline, and pressed rewind, watching the image flutter and shudder as the feed unspooled backwards in quadruple time. He had been watching for almost fifteen minutes, barely blinking, before he saw a little flare of movement on the side of the screen, and he reached out and tapped a key to freeze the frame: a man, wearing dark gloves and a balaclava and a jacket zipped up to his throat, was captured mid-stride, with one leg extended and a bright rectangle in his hand. Lemoine rewound the video a little further and then pressed play, hunching forward to watch as the figure picked his way around the leaching pits, bending down to lift up the edges of what Lemoine knew were vast sheets of camouflage netting, but what seemed from above to be merely contours of the earth; the effect was a strange kind of optical illusion, almost as though the guy were casting shadows with his hands. He straightened, holding the bright rectangle up to his face with both hands, and then he dropped his hands to the level of his chest and stroked his right thumb across the object in a gesture that Lemoine hadn't seen anybody make in years. Lemoine's blood went cold. The bright rectangle was a camera. The guy was taking photographs, and then winding on the film.

Tony had been waiting for the rain. It had come on all at once, a lowering bank of cloud, a few drops, and then a downpour, but even before the skies had really opened, he had zipped up his jacket, donned his backpack, and clambered out of his hiding place beneath the totara to run and crawl and slip and slide his way out of the Korowai Basin, zigzagging through the bush, hand clapped over the precious roll of film in his pocket, pack jouncing on his shoulders, listening out for a siren, or a shout of warning, or a gunshot, or the now unmistakable sound of a drone. But none came. He kept running for hours, knees and ankles screaming, breath spiking in his lungs, back to the track along the ridge, past the cairn he'd built above the farm, cloud filling the valleys to his left and right. The rain began to ease and then finally stopped altogether as he was descending into Thorndike. He set his jaw and ran faster, determined not to stop until he'd reached the visitor centre car park where he had left Veronica's car.

Tony had breached the fence in Korowai two days ago. He couldn't put a name to most of what he'd found there, but he knew environmental devastation when he saw it; he could recognise the signs of toxic, rapacious, unconscionable, imperial-stage-capitalist industrial disgrace. He had taken photographs of everything: the vast sheets of camouflage-style netting spread over the ground, which could surely have no scientific purpose other than concealment, and which he'd lifted up to see dozens, maybe hundreds, of manhole covers sunk into the ground in a massive grid; and beyond them, also concealed and camouflaged, piles of PVC piping, coiled hoses, empty drums, heaps of rubble, and a tractor-sized piece of equipment he couldn't identify – some kind of pump perhaps; its flank was studded with valves and dials like the side of a fire engine. Everywhere the plants were dead or dying, trees wilting, dead ferns with black and withered leaves, dead branches dusted white, husks of dead insects crunching underfoot, even dead birds, riflemen, wax-eyes, fantails, a kererū, some still plump and glassy, others desiccated and flattened with decay. He had moved swiftly, not wanting to stay a moment longer than he needed to, and when he'd used up his roll of film the last thing he did before he left the area was to try to shift one of the manhole covers aside so that he could see what lay beneath it. It was very heavy, but when he braced himself, it moved. He slid it aside and saw a cylindrical borehole, a little under a metre in diameter, drilled into the bedrock; how deep, Tony didn't know, for the hole was filled to the brim with an evil-smelling chemical solution that had made his stomach rise into his throat. He'd replaced the cover almost at once, but the smell had lingered. It was a toxic, malignant stink, and he had felt it not just in his nose and in his lungs, but in his veins and in his gut and in his fingertips. He recalled it now as he fumbled, weak with exhaustion, for the keys to Veronica's car and clattered to unlock the door, feeling a wave of nausea and the stinging onset of a headache. He got into the driver's seat and shut the door, but he could still smell it. He put the key in the ignition and cracked the window to refresh the air.

Then he sat shivering, still soaking wet, still breathing hard, his pulse still throbbing in his neck.

The government's proposal had not been scrapped at all. They hadn't caved in the face of public pressure. They hadn't respected peaceful protest. They hadn't capitulated to the public mood. They had simply begun mining the country's national parks in secret, against the will of the people, without the *knowledge* of the people, illegally, immorally, without environmental oversight, or oversight of any kind – *and*, given the Autonomo connection, in collusion with a foreign company, to boot. It was a theft of historic proportions – it was conspiracy and corruption at the highest level – it was an offence against democracy – it was the gravest conspiracy, the most shocking lie, the most egregious rape of nature and abuse of power, in the entire history of his country – it was treason. *Treason*, Tony repeated dumbly in his mind, thinking how antique and even fanciful it seemed.

He was so staggered that he started to laugh, but his laughter subsided almost at once, and in its place he felt a wave of fury and despair roll over him at the sheer inexorability of late-capitalist degradation not just of the environment, not just of civic institutions, not just of intellectual and political ideals, but worse, of his own expectations, of what he even felt was *possible* any more – a familiar surge of grief and helpless rage at the reckless, wasteful, soulless, narcissistic, barren selfishness of the present day, and at his own political irrelevance and impotence, and at the utter shamelessness with which his natural inheritance, his *future*, had been either sold or laid to waste by his parents' generation, trapping him in a perpetual adolescence that was further heightened by the infantilising unreality of the Internet as it encroached upon, and colonised, real life – 'real life', Tony thought, with bitter air quotes, for late capitalism would admit nothing 'real' beyond the logic of late capitalism itself, having declared self-interest the only universal, and profit motive the only absolute, and deriding everything that did not serve its ends as either a contemptible weakness or a fantasy.

Then that subsided too, and he was left trembling, heart pounding, chest brimming with a feeling that was very like euphoria. Aloud he said, 'Jesus Christ,' and then again, 'Jesus *Christ*,' and then, hushed, in wonderment, he said, 'I am going to be so fucking famous.'

Wanting suddenly to put some distance between himself and Thorndike, he put his seat belt on and turned the key to start the engine. The nearest town was about an hour's drive away; he'd treat himself to a night in a motel, he thought, somewhere with a stable Internet connection, where he could have a hot shower, get his thoughts together, and plan what he was going to do next. His laptop was under the passenger seat beside him – he reached down a hand to check; still there – and his phone was in the bottom of his backpack, not only powered off, as it had been all week, but wrapped in the foil emergency blanket that he'd carried with him on every tramping trip since adolescence and – until now – had never had a reason to use. That was probably overkill, especially since the photos he had taken weren't digital, so weren't thievable or trackable, and weren't even visible, yet, to anyone but him. But he knew he wouldn't be able to rest until he'd got them back developed from the lab – no; until he'd got them back, *and* they'd been copied, *and* the duplicates had been secured, *and* his article was written, *and* he'd sent it off to multiple publications in multiple countries, the *Guardian*, the *Süddeutsche Zeitung*, the *New York Times*. He wouldn't be able to rest, he told himself, until his byline was on front pages all around the world.

He put his indicator on and looked over his shoulder to pull out on to the highway when something thumped hard against the bonnet of his car. Tony whipped around – and saw that the guy from the chip shop was standing by his left headlight, grinning stupidly and waving at him.

'You a journalist yet?' he said.

Tony stared at him.

'You told me to ask you,' the guy said, strolling round to the driver's window. 'You said, "Next time you see me, ask me again." And I'm seeing you. So.'

'Oh,' Tony said. 'Yeah.' Almost as a reflex – wanting an outlet for his nervous energy, perhaps – he shut off the engine and pulled the handbrake up hard, and then sat gripping the steering wheel with both hands, as if the guy were a policeman and had pulled him over in a traffic stop.

'So?' said the guy. 'Are you?'

And in the second of silence before he answered, Tony heard it again: a distant roaring noise, almost like the sound inside a seashell, a putter curving up into a whine.

'Could you do me a favour?' he said to the guy. 'Could you look up and see if there's a drone overhead?'

'Right now?' said the guy, but he was already craning his head back, turning in a circle, scanning the sky. Then he stopped and pointed up. 'Hey,' he said. 'Yeah. Look at that! Oh – now it's flying away.' He turned back to Tony, grinning now. 'That was cool! Whose is it?'

Tony's guts felt like they had turned to water. He released the handbrake, turned the engine on again, and put his finger on the button to shut the driver's window. 'I'm pretty sure that it belongs to someone from the government,' he said, trying to keep his voice normal, 'and the answer to your question earlier is yes.'

Speeding out of Thorndike, hunching over the wheel to be able to see as much of the sky through the windscreen as he possibly could, he was reminded of an old story that his mother liked to tell, about the first time she'd had Tony's grandparents over for dinner as a newlywed. She had been anxious to make a good impression, and when she had gone into the kitchen to dish out the first course, she had discovered, to her dismay, that the soup had curdled on the stove. She'd grabbed a sieve to strain it, and in her panic, she'd put the sieve into the sink and dumped the contents of the pot into it – only to realise her mistake: the soup, of course, had gone down the drain, and she'd retained only the lumps. Tony had heard the story so many times it was as if the memory had become his own, and although the story had a punchline – something caustic that Tony's grandmother had said – he never remembered it; the detail that captured him was the lumps in the sieve, and the soup running down the drain, and his mother's horror as she realised that she had rescued the wrong part of the meal.

Mira didn't know. That was the thought that resounded in his head as the road unspooled past the tip of the lake and down through the foothills and on towards the plains, over one-lane bridges, through stone cuttings, and over crossings of abandoned railway lines, into sudden shadows, and then out again.

Mira didn't know. None of them did. Tony was sure of it. He'd have been sure even if he hadn't watched them working through his binoculars from the ridge, even if he hadn't gone to the hui and heard Mira describe Lemoine's offer with such naked excitement and desire. Mira may have sold her soul, but at least she *had* a soul to offer up, Tony thought. She didn't know what was happening in Korowai. She couldn't. Mira didn't know.

He needed to pee, but he kept driving five minutes more, then ten, then fifteen, until he was desperate; at last he couldn't wait any longer, and he pulled off the highway into a gravel lay-by that looked out over a ravine. Experimentally, he turned off the engine and cracked the window, listening hard, but he could hear nothing but birdsong and the wind in the trees. He got out of the car and shaded his eyes and looked up. The sky was a liquid cyan, high and clear after the rain, white clouds scudding in the north and in the west. He scanned the horizon until his eyes began to water, and then he relieved himself as quickly as he could and got back in the car. He checked the clock on the dashboard: he had been driving for forty-five minutes at an average of roughly eighty k's an hour. Say sixty kilometres, then, maybe a little less, as the crow flew – as the drone flew – to account for the curves in the road. Call it fifty. Could a drone fly that far that fast? And how long could it go before refuelling? Tony didn't know, but he felt fairly certain that he'd left the thing behind.

He was about to resume his journey when two SUVs with dark-tinted windows screamed past him in the opposite direction, heading for Thorndike. Barely a second later, he heard the squeal of tyres, and the second of the two vehicles reversed back past the lay-by at high speed and then careened sharply sideways to block the bridge over the ravine. The first wasn't far behind: it also reversed past Tony and made a screeching handbrake turn, scorching the tarmac, and coming to a hard stop beside the other. Then nothing. They waited, engines idling, suspension trembling, tinted windows dark.

Tony felt like he was going to be sick. They were boxing him in. The road back to Thorndike was a dead end – if he could even get as far as Thorndike. These were clearly highly skilled defensive drivers. They had been dispatched to find him. Perhaps they had been dispatched to run him off the road. His phone was at the bottom of his backpack – though even if he could get it out and turn it on, he might not get a signal – and even then, help would take some time to reach him. He'd seen nobody at all in the last forty-five minutes, no other drivers, no farmers, no cyclists, no road workers. No witnesses, he thought, and felt even sicker.

He looked to his left. There was a low guard rail around the edge of the lay-by, and beyond it, a gravel slope that led steeply down to the ravine. Downstream, the creek fanned out into stony shallows, and the hills beyond were densely forested in native bush. If he left the car, skidded down to the edge of the cliff, and jumped, he could swim with the current, under the bridge and into the trees. He'd have a head start, and they probably wouldn't be expecting him to leave the car, much less throw himself into the water. Could he chance it? Tony glanced at his backpack on the seat beside him, and then again at the SUVs. Carefully, he released his seat belt, trying to move as slowly and unobtrusively as possible, and ignoring the pulsing red light on the dash that told him to buckle up again. He turned the key in the ignition, put the car into first, and then drove right up to the guard rail, making a neat curve in the gravel as though he were preparing to execute a three-point turn to return to Thorndike. He heard their engines rev slightly in response. He put the car into reverse and completed the second point of the turn. Now he was facing back the way he'd come, still in the lay-by, but on the wrong side of the road; the driver's door was right next to the guard rail. He felt strangely calm. The SUVs were nosing forward, ready to pursue. He could see nothing behind the tinted glass. Tony touched the roll of film in his pocket for luck. He counted to three under his breath, then he grabbed his backpack and threw open the door. He didn't look back. He leapt over the guard rail and flung himself down the slope towards the water.

Late on Sunday evening, Mira was standing in the kitchen of the safe house waiting for the kettle to boil when a mud-spattered SUV pulled into the driveway and a man got out. He walked into the carport, passing out of Mira's line of sight, and a minute later he returned to the SUV and took a large tool-box and a caulking gun off the back seat. He carried these into the carport and returned to his vehicle, opened the boot, and lifted out a large parcel wrapped in bubble wrap and packing tape, which could only be the replacement windscreen for the van. He set the parcel gingerly on the ground, shut the boot, and then picked the parcel up and passed out of Mira's sight again, turning sideways to fit through the narrow gap between the van and the side of the house. Soon she heard the snick of a box-cutter blade being opened, and shuffling as the bubble wrap was cut away, and then the click of the latches on the toolbox, and a scraping noise, and rustling movements punc-tuated by the occasional rasping sound and the clink of broken glass. Lemoine had warned her not to interfere or to identify herself if she could help it, and so she stood very still beside the lace curtain, remaining there long after the kettle had boiled, wondering who the man was, and where he'd driven in from, and how much money he'd been offered, and what exactly he'd been told. Less than half an hour later, he reappeared, carrying his toolbox, the caulking gun – now emptied of its cartridge – and a heavy-duty bin bag full of broken glass. He stowed these in the back of the SUV, shut the boot, climbed back into the driver's seat, reversed out of the driveway, and drove off without a backward glance.

Mira had once read an article about a special butler service for the ultra-wealthy, where any whim could be satisfied, any desire met, any commodity supplied, to any location in the world, at any time of day, with no questions asked; all one had to do was press a button on a special gold-plated (had she made that detail up?) device, at the other end of which a dedicated concierge was always waiting. She wondered now if Lemoine had something of that kind. 'I need a safe house for two fugitives in Thorndike, New Zealand,' she imagined him saying into a golden walkie-talkie, 'and it needs to be accessible from 1606 Korowai Pass Road without passing by the CCTV on the main highway, and it needs to contain a week's supply of food and toiletries, and it needs a carport that is shielded from the street, and it needs to be top secret, and I need it right away.' It sounded crazy – but then, so did the alternative, which was that the house had already been fully stocked and waiting for them at the time that Owen Darvish had been killed.

Shelley was right: their present circumstance was weird. The house was weird. The food in the kitchen cupboards was weird. The unopened toothbrushes in the bathroom cabinet, the unwrapped bars of soap, the stack of fresh clothing in the bedroom cupboard, in a range of sizes, no labels inside any of the collars or on the waistbands, every item either army green or black – and this man who had appeared, at less than forty-eight hours' notice, with a replacement windscreen for a 1994

Nissan Vanette; it was all desperately, horribly weird. Lemoine could not have done this all on his own, she thought. He must have people. But what kind of people? Who were they? And what else did they do?

The water in the kettle had cooled. Mira put it on again, and when it had boiled a second time, she poured out two mugs of Milo, adding a sticky spoonful of sweetened condensed milk to each mug, and stirring until the little clumps of malted powder burst and sank below the surface and dissolved. She carried the mugs back into the living room, where she and Shelley had spent the day working on a second puzzle – this time, of the Venetian Grand Canal – expecting to find Shelley working on the final patch of water that was still eluding them. But Shelley wasn't there. Mira set the mugs down on the coffee table. She peered around the hallway curtain. Both bedrooms were empty. The bathroom was, too. Mira's heart had plunged into her gut. Her breathing had quickened, and her peripheral vision was turning dark and telescoping – and then a second later, the front door opened and Shelley came back in.

They looked directly at each other for the first time that day.

'The van's fixed,' Shelley said. 'The glass looks really clean and shiny though. We might want to drive on a gravel road or something for a bit before we head back. So it gets dusty.'

'Good idea,' Mira said.

There was a pause, but neither of them looked away.

'I didn't hear you go out,' Mira said.

'Yeah, just now,' Shelley said. 'Just to look at the van.'

'Yeah,' Mira said. 'I didn't hear you.'

Another pause.

Shelley came forward and picked up one of the mugs. 'Well, thanks for the Milo.'

'Shelley,' Mira said.

'Yeah?'

'This . . . intervention that we're on.'

'Yeah.'

'Did it work?'

Shelley frowned at her. 'What?'

'I mean, when we go back tomorrow, what do we say? Did it work?'

'Yeah,' Shelley said. 'We say it worked.' She hesitated a moment, seeming on the verge of saying something else. But in the end, she just raised her mug slightly in a kind of toast, and said, 'Goodnight.'

'Goodnight,' Mira said.

Shelley took the mug into her bedroom and closed the door, and Mira looked down at the unfinished Grand Canal. She stared at the toothy vacant patch in the middle of the picture for a while in silence, and then she sighed, sat down, and began to fit the final pieces.

The next morning, they washed their bedsheets and towels and took out the recycling. Mira found a spray bottle of bleach in the kitchen and wiped down the surfaces, including the light switches and the jigsaw-puzzle boxes, and Shelley set aside the open bottles and packets of food to take with them back to the farm. She hadn't asked to charge her phone since the day that they arrived, but when they got into the van, she reached automatically for the charger that fed into the cassette converter, took her phone out of her pocket, and plugged it in. Mira said nothing. She put the van in gear and reversed out of the driveway, and a few seconds later, Shelley's phone lit up and she began scrolling through the waiting messages. 'Oh cool!' she said.

'What?' Mira said.

Shelley turned the phone around, and Mira took her eyes off the road to squint at it: on the screen was a photo of a courier bag, addressed to 1606 Korowai Pass Road, attention Shelley Noakes. 'It arrived for me this morning,' Shelley said. 'Katrina said they opened it just in case it was important. It's all the paperwork for Birnam Wood.'

'What paperwork?'

'I guess like the incorporation papers and stuff.'

'Oh right.'

'Robert sent it,' Shelley said. She disappeared into her phone, texting a reply. Soon they reached the T-junction that fed on to the main highway, and as they came to a halt, Mira looked down at the dash and noticed that the tank was almost empty. She briefly considered turning right, to fill up at the petrol station before heading back to the farm, but Lemoine had been insistent: no detours, no pickups, no drop-offs, no idling. They were supposed to go straight back to the farm. Anyway, she told herself, the van probably had at least fifty k's of mileage left – the orange light had only just come on – and it might be nice to have an excuse to run an errand in the days to come; she might relish the opportunity to be alone. She turned left, and five minutes later they were pulling up at the iron gates outside the Darvish property.

'Wait,' Shelley said, looking up from her phone. 'The windscreen.'

'Oh yeah. I forgot.' Mira backed out again and drove on, up to the gravel service road that lay beyond the southern fence. 'I'll just drive up a bit and then come down again,' she said.

'Cool,' Shelley said. Her eyes were on the highway that led up to the lookout and the barricade, curving round the mountainside and out of sight. Though neither of them spoke, Mira could tell that her thoughts had gone to Owen Darvish. She changed down to second gear and the van juddered and rattled over the stones and up the hill.

They reached the farm gate that led across the hill and through the shelterbelt of pines to the airstrip. Already the windscreen was looking passably worn in, so Mira cut as wide an arc as she could to turn the van around. But as they nosed into the gully at the side of the road and she put the van in reverse, she was startled by a sudden movement in the forest up ahead, and she jumped, stalling the engine. A man was making his way through the trees towards them. He was wearing a boxy communications vest and carrying a semi-automatic rifle, and all the clothes that he was wearing were either army green or black. Evidently he had heard the engine coming up the hill and had mistaken it for someone else, for he had been hurrying to meet them, but when he glanced up and saw the van, he pulled up short and his expression faltered. He hesitated for a moment, seeming unsure whether to come forward and explain himself, or run away. He decided on the latter, turned, and disappeared into the trees.

Mira and Shelley sat frozen. 'Who the hell was that?' Shelley said.

'I don't know,' Mira said.

'Is there an army base near here?'

'I don't think so.'

'He had a gun, right?'

'Yeah.'

'Like, *that was a guy with a gun.*'

'Maybe he was hunting,' Mira said without conviction.

'Is this private land?' Shelley said.

'No – on this side it's national park.'

'But you can't hunt in national parks, right?'

'No, I'm pretty sure you can.'

'Really?'

'Yeah, I'm pretty sure. In certain areas.' Mira's vision was telescoping in again.

'Call Robert,' Shelley said.

But Mira didn't move. Her heart was clutching in her chest.

'Call him,' Shelley said. 'Now.'

'I can't.'

'What do you mean?'

Mira was shaking her head.

'What do you mean?' Shelley said again, more forcefully. 'Mira!'

Mira couldn't look at her. 'I don't know his number,' she said.

'Bullshit. You called him the other night.'

'No. He called me.'

'But in your phone, you'll have his—'

'It was blocked.'

'What?'

'It was a blocked number.'

'*What?*'

'It was the first time he's ever called me,' she said. 'All the other times, he's always just – shown up.'

'Fucking hell, Mira,' Shelley burst out, 'this is kind of a crucial piece of information, don't you think? Like, maybe when you were setting this whole plan up and, like, making these massive life-changing decisions—'

'I know,' Mira said. 'I'm sorry.'

'Like, what if something goes wrong? How the fuck are we supposed to get a hold of him?'

'I don't know!' She was almost shouting. 'I don't know! I don't know! I don't know!'

Her phone began buzzing in her pocket. She pulled the handbrake up and took it out. She glanced at the screen, and then tilted it to Shelley: it was an incoming call from a blocked number. 'That's creepy,' she said.

'Answer it,' Shelley said.

She answered it.

'What are you doing?' snapped Lemoine in her ear. 'What's going on?'

'We're heading back to the farm,' Mira said. 'We just saw—'

'Don't lie to me,' he said. 'Don't fucking lie. I know where you are. I'm looking at you right now. What are you doing?'

Stupidly, Mira looked out the windscreen at the native bush. 'What?' she said. 'What do you mean?'

'We agreed you'd go straight back. No detours, no nothing. What the fuck are you doing heading into Korowai?'

'We were getting the windscreen dirty,' Mira said. 'So it didn't look so new. It was Shelley's idea.' There was a pause, and then she said, 'Robert, we just saw this guy, just now, like a soldier, maybe, with a gun, like a rifle—'

'Go back to the farm,' said Lemoine. He sounded furious. 'Right now. Go back and do what we agreed and shut your fucking mouth and stay there.'

'Wait,' Mira said, 'Robert—' but he had already hung up.

She and Shelley looked at each other.

'Something's wrong,' Shelley said.

'He didn't seem surprised about the soldier,' Mira said.

'We don't know it was a soldier.'

'Well, whoever it was.'

'What did he mean, that he was looking at us?'

'I think he's watching from a drone,' Mira said. 'On the night that – I mean, on Friday night, I saw him looking at, like, a live feed on his phone, like in a bird's-eye-view type of thing. I think he's been watching us the whole time.'

They were quiet.

'We better do what he says,' Shelley said. 'We better go back.'

'Yeah,' Mira said. 'I guess we better.'

But then her phone started ringing again. She picked up.

'Put me on speaker,' said Lemoine.

She did as he asked.

'Is Shelley there?' he said.

'I'm here,' she said.

'Okay,' he said. He sounded calmer now and more controlled. 'I don't want you to freak out, so I'm going to tell you both what's going on. I've been notified of an active threat against my life. This happens sometimes. I have security. They're taking care of it. You don't need to worry. It's one guy, he's on foot, and he's in the national park. He'll be some wack job, some revolutionary wannabe who drank his own Kool-Aid. I don't know who he is and I don't care. My guys will find him. They always do. But if you see anyone, a man, alone, call me immediately. Don't approach him, don't engage. He might be armed. Just get as far away from him as possible and call me right away.'

'She doesn't have your number,' Shelley said.

There was a pause. Then Lemoine said, 'Okay. I'll get that to you. Now, I want you to go back to the farm and tell the others the story we agreed. All right? Not this. This is just between us. I don't want anybody freaking out.'

'Where are you calling from?' said Shelley.

'Somewhere safe. You're safe too. Don't worry. My guys are going to find him.'

'The man we saw,' said Mira. 'Was that him?'

Lemoine hesitated. 'No,' he said at last. 'That was one of mine.'

'Robert,' Mira said, 'what if this has something to do with—'

'It doesn't,' said Lemoine.

'But how can you be sure?'

'I'm sure,' he said. 'I promise you. This has nothing to do with

Darvish and it has nothing to do with Birnam Wood and it has nothing to do with you.'

Tony had tried to land feet first, toes pointed downward to break the surface tension of the water, one hand clapped over his nose and mouth in case the shock of the cold caused a reflex inhalation, the other clutching the pocket that held his roll of film. But the weight of his pack had thrown him off, tipping him forward as he fell so that one of his knees had hit the water first, his body following almost in a belly flop, his pack rolling underneath him, sucking him under, and then bobbing him back up a few seconds later as the current carried him downstream. He was swept under the bridge and round the bend to where the creek descended over shallow rapids, kicking his legs, flailing and gasping, colliding with boulders and branches, grappling for purchase anywhere he could, cold seizing at his testicles, pain shooting up and down his legs and arms. His body bumped and bashed its way over the stones and into the shallows, where he managed to scramble out of the water and into the trees, limping, falling to his hands and knees, pulling himself up, stumbling again, his waterlogged boots and clothes and backpack dragging him down. He didn't stop. He lurched and hobbled through the bush, not daring to look back, not knowing where he was going or in what direction he was headed or whether they were coming after him, aware that he was heavily favouring his right leg, aware that his jaw had begun to chatter, aware that he was holding his left arm tight against his breastbone, aware of his molars pulsing with his heartbeat and a strange tightness in his skull and an ache in his tailbone and most of all, unbearably, aware of the nauseating pain that was coursing through his wrist and shattering his ankle every time he took a step. Broken arm, broken ankle. And both on the same side.

To distract himself from the pain, he made a mental inventory of his belongings. The roll of film was still safe in his pocket, and he thanked God that he'd had the foresight to seal the plastic cylinder in two ziplock bags before he'd left his hiding place beneath the totara that morning. The bin bag that he used as a pack liner would have kept the contents of his backpack fairly dry – what little he was carrying, at least: after his weeklong stake-out up in Korowai, his food supplies were almost spent, and he'd drunk the last of his water that morning on the long trek back to Veronica's car. Mentally he unpacked the emergency kit that he always carried in the topmost compartment of his pack, with its familiar white piping and chunky big-toothed zip. It contained a blister pack of antihistamines, probably long expired; a blister pack of paracetamol, half-used; a tube of antiseptic cream; a roll of yeasty-smelling bandage; a paper accordion of sticking plasters; a sachet or two of electrolyte powder; and a roll of medical adhesive tape. What else? Tony lost his footing and stumbled to his knees. His Swiss Army knife, he thought, getting to his feet again, still hugging his broken wrist against his body. His sleeping bag. A canister of butane, still three-quarters full. A plastic barbecue lighter. His camping stove. His bivvy bag. A change of clothes. His balaclava – no; he'd taken it off when he got back to the car and tossed it into the back seat. No balaclava, then. His vision was starting to blur. Two empty water bottles. His reporter's notebook and his Dictaphone. His fountain pen. His camera. His binoculars. His phone, if he ever dared to use it, wrapped in the foil blanket and stuffed inside his cooking pot. A bag of instant coffee. A bag of milk powder. However many teabags he had left. Some dried apricots – no; he'd eaten those already.

A Peanut Slab. His breathing was rasping in his throat. He thought about his laptop, abandoned under the passenger seat of Veronica's car. He thought about Veronica's car. He had left the keys in the ignition. Stupid. He should have thrown them into the ravine when he jumped.

He wondered if he should try turning on his phone. Service was patchy out in the bush, but it was possible that he might get a signal; he remembered his first night out in Korowai, and how oddly disappointed he had felt to find that even in the wilderness he still had ready access to the Web. He wouldn't be disappointed now. Maybe he should just do it, he thought, his vision blurring again. Maybe he should just get out his phone and turn it on and call the police. Or Search & Rescue. Or his mother. He could call his mother and spell it out to her, the whole conspiracy, the drones, the call with Darvish, everything he'd seen, so that even if they used the signal to locate him, even if they came with guns and killed him, even if they found the roll of film in his pocket after he was dead and exposed it to the light and then cut it into little pieces, even if they burned his notebook and took apart his Dictaphone and smashed his laptop and his phone, even if the police and Search & Rescue and all the emergency services were all complicit with what was going on in Korowai, all bought by the government, all bent, all bribed and blackmailed into silence, even if the whole conspiracy was covered up, even then, his story would be safe, because his mother would know the truth. His mother would know that he wasn't paranoid, or delusional, or mad. His mother wouldn't believe whatever lies they told to explain away his murder. His mother wouldn't rest until she'd come to Korowai herself, until she'd finished what her son had started, until she'd uncovered—

He tripped over a tree root, and this time his injured ankle gave way and he fell forward, on to his broken wrist. He screamed into the earth, writhing, arching, starting to cry. His nose was running, snot and tears mingling with the dirt and turning to mud on his face, and when he took a great, shuddering breath to try to calm himself, he inhaled a mouthful of dirt and choked. He lay gagging and spitting and hacking on the forest floor until the pain from the coughing made him start to cry again. Maybe he had a broken rib as well. At length he forced himself to swallow down his tears, and with tremendous effort, he eased his broken arm out of the strap of his backpack, rolled sideways, and managed to sit up. Using his good hand, he unbuckled his backpack and pulled out the cooking pot where he had stowed his phone. He took out the foil bundle and was about to unwrap it when he hesitated, arrested by a memory from the very early days of Birnam Wood. Mira had drawn up a roster of chores, he remembered, and he'd been trying to wriggle out of it. 'I'm not much of a green thumb,' he'd told her, hoping there was something more intellectual that he could do instead of weeding. But she had laughed. 'No such thing,' she had replied. 'Anyone can garden. It's just a few basic principles and time.' And then, anticipating his objection, she'd added, 'Most plants are actually pretty hard to kill. They're living things. They want to live.'

He left his phone where it was, unzipped the top pocket of his pack, and took out the emergency kit, tearing it open with chattering teeth and upending the contents over the ground. He fished out the blister pack of paracetamol. There were only four tablets left. He swallowed two, bit a corner off the Peanut Slab for sustenance, and then took out both his water bottles to make absolutely sure that they were empty. One had half a mouthful of water sloshing at the bottom; he poured this out into the cap, added one of the sachets of electrolyte powder, and stirred it with his finger to make a grainy orange paste.

He leaned back and scanned the sky above the canopy to try to find the sun, wishing he had packed a compass or, at the very least, a map. Something to remember for next time, he thought, and almost laughed. The electrolytes and the bite of chocolate had revived him. He wondered what he could forage to stretch out his meagre food supply. He knew that horopito leaves were edible, and he might get a bit of nourishment from chewing manuka or kanuka leaves. He'd recognise puha if he saw it; but beyond those few plants, he had no idea what was poisonous or not. He'd be too frightened to try a mushroom in case it was deadly. It wasn't the season for berries, but he'd be too afraid to try those too. He could try robbing nests for eggs, he supposed, but that would involve climbing trees. He didn't know the first thing about fishing. Or hunting. He wouldn't even know where to begin.

The light was thinning – it was probably getting on for four or five in the afternoon – and it seemed to him that the sky was a little brighter to his right than to his left. Sunset was in the west; he'd head towards the light till darkness fell, and in the morning he'd keep going with the sun behind him. He'd listen out for running water in the meantime; the creeks would be swollen after the rains. He wanted to live. Tony buckled his backpack tight around his waist and set off, grunting in pain with each limping step, and as he moved on, a fantail swooped to land on the patch of earth where he'd been standing, dipping and hopping and looking for the tiny bugs that he'd stirred up.

Rosie Demarney was starting to feel uneasy. She had texted Tony over a week ago to tell him about the strange phone call she'd received from the guy pretending to be his workmate, describing, with humorous exaggeration, the blocked number, the slightly staticky connection, and the flat American accent of the voice on the other end of the line; 'just what are you investigating down there anyway???' she'd asked, followed by the frowning monocled emoji and two staring eyes. Then, not wanting to seem as though she'd taken anything too seriously, she'd added, 'love me a conspiracy!!! already a #believer as you can see lol'. The truth was that the call had deeply unsettled her, but she was worried that to tell him so would only spook him; she liked Tony much more than anyone she'd tried to date in recent years, and the last thing she wanted was to blow her chance with him by coming off as paranoid or needy.

But she'd heard nothing back. He didn't have his read receipts enabled, so she had no idea whether he'd seen her messages or not, and when she'd tried to call him a few days later – 'I've honestly gone full dark web on this,' she imagined saying, with a laugh, 'Tony, mate, you've gotta talk me down' – she hadn't been able to get through. Of course, he had told her that he was going to be out of range for a few days; but she felt foolish that she hadn't pressed him at the time to explain exactly what he'd meant by 'out of range'. Was he going somewhere with no mobile coverage? Or was he in the kind of company that might require him to surrender his phone? She knew that his article was about the super-rich; maybe he had an invitation to some sort of select gathering, some retreat, some inner circle with people who might have privacy concerns . . . Or maybe he used a different phone when he was working . . . Or maybe, Rosie thought, disgusted now, he had just wanted a bit of time to himself, and 'out of range' was just a tactful euphemism, and she *was* paranoid, and she *was* needy, and she *was* coming on too strong. She scrolled back up through the string of messages she'd sent him – eight since the last text he'd sent to her

– and sighed. He was probably just ghosting her. She'd probably already blown it, she thought, and despondently put her phone away.

She went to the gym to run it off, telling herself that although, yes, Tony's sister Veronica *did* go to the same gym that she did, and they *did* sometimes see each other there on weeknights, it was hardly likely tonight would be one of those nights, since, as Rosie knew, Veronica was a registrar at the Christchurch Women's Hospital, and so her hours varied from week to week – *and* she had a boyfriend of her own, actually a fiancé, who was a doctor as well, so *his* hours were long and unpredictable as well, which made it even *less* likely that she would be there, especially as he was building up to a marathon and preferred to do his training out of doors, often – Rosie had seen them once or twice – with Veronica cycling beside him.

'Rosie?'

It was Veronica.

'Oh, hey,' she said, switching off the treadmill and hopping down. 'How are you?'

Veronica had a sly look. 'So, you and Tony, eh?' she said.

'Yeah,' Rosie said. 'Well, I mean – maybe. You know.'

'I am so mad at him right now,' Veronica said.

'Why?' Rosie said.

'So, you know he's down in Thorndike?'

'Yeah.'

'Yeah, well, he asked to borrow my car to get down there, and – sorry,' she said, pulling herself up, 'you're like – and I'm being all like, raah!'

'It's fine,' Rosie said.

'I mean, I'm not actually mad at him.'

'Tell me the story.'

'It's not even a story. He's just a shithead.'

'Oi,' said Rosie, feigning a right hook to Veronica's shoulder. 'Finish what you start, already!'

'Okay,' Veronica said, 'so, yeah, he asked to borrow my car, because he said he was interviewing this confidential source for this article that he was writing, and I was, like, of course, thinking I was doing him such a good turn or whatever, but then yesterday I ran into Katie Vander – do you know her? From Birnam Wood?'

'I guess,' Rosie said. 'I mean, I don't *know her* know her, but yeah.'

'Yeah, same,' Veronica said. 'Anyway, I asked her about Tony, because he told me that he'd been chucked out of their last meeting and I wanted to know why, and *she* said, first of all, *that never happened*, and second, they're down in Thorndike! Birnam Wood is down in Thorndike! Right now!'

'What?' Rosie said.

'I know!' Veronica said. 'He totally lied to me! Just to get my car! And he *knows* I'm pissed at him, as well, because he's stopped answering my—'

'Wait,' Rosie said. '*What?*'

Veronica took a half-step back. 'Oh,' she said. 'Now I feel like I'm stirring.'

'He didn't tell me any of this,' Rosie said.

'Oh shit,' Veronica said. 'Okay, I'm – um, sorry – I don't want to—'

'He told me he was writing an article about billionaires.'

'Maybe he is,' Veronica said, now looking unsure. 'I mean, yeah, Katie said the whole reason they went down there in the first place is because Mira Bunting met this billionaire, you know, the Autonomo guy, the one whose wife—'

'Mira Bunting,' Rosie said.

There was a pause.

'I'm totally messing this up,' Veronica said. 'Look, just forget I said anything, all right? Sorry. Sorry, sorry, sorry.'

'No, wait,' Rosie said. 'What was this about the meeting?'

'I'm really not trying to start anything,' Veronica said. 'Honestly. It's not even a big—'

'What happened?'

'This is, like, totally second-hand information anyway—'

'I know that,' Rosie said, cutting over her. 'What happened?'

'Katie just said there was a disagreement,' Veronica said.

'Between who? Tony and . . . ?'

'I guess . . . everyone else,' Veronica said.

'What was it about?'

But Veronica was backing away. 'You should really ask Tony,' she said. 'Sorry. I shouldn't have said anything. And he's really not a shithead. He's just my brother. And I'm actually really happy you guys hooked up, I really am. Sorry, Rosie. Sorry!'

Red-faced, she scuttled down to the other end of the gym, where she put her earbuds in and climbed on to the elliptical and began straining at the handles and the pedals with greater vigour than the machine's settings would permit, and although Rosie had only been on the treadmill fifteen minutes, she gathered up her towel and her water bottle and headed to the locker room to change.

She knew that any self-respecting person in her situation would just delete Tony's number and move on. The whole dreary picture was in focus now: the fact that on the night they'd got together, he had come to the Fox and Ferret straight from Birnam Wood; the fact that when they'd gone out for dinner a few nights later, he had seemed strangely defensive about the article that he was writing, deflecting her questions, not looking her in the eye when he spoke about it, and changing the subject as soon as the opportunity arose; the fact that he'd left for

Thorndike with such urgency, and yet hadn't seemed to have an answer when she'd asked him how long he planned to be away; the fact that he'd now stopped answering her messages. It all felt unbearably tawdry suddenly, a story that had been read and seen and heard and written too many times to count; and as Rosie let herself back into her flat, poached a chicken breast, dressed a salad, and poured a glass of wine, she told herself resolutely that she was *not* going to play the role that he had cast her in; she was *not* going to spend the evening in her sweatpants, getting drunk and stalking him pathetically online.

But hell. Nobody was watching.

She opened her laptop and searched for Mira Bunting, but despite combing through the contacts of all their mutual friends and plausible acquaintances, all she could find was a few old photos on the Birnam Wood Facebook page, none of which were tagged. Either Mira considered herself to be above social media – which would certainly square with Rosie's impression of her, having known her very distantly at school – or, more likely, Rosie thought, now with a haughtiness of her own, Mira *pretended* that she was above social media, but trawled the sites every day in secret, using an avatar, never posting anything, and never risking anything, either. Rosie poured herself another glass of wine and searched for Birnam Wood + Thorndike, and then, opening a bar of chocolate, for Birnam Wood + Thorndike + billionaire. A news article popped up. The result had matched 'Thorndike' and 'billionaire' but not 'Birnam Wood', but she clicked on it anyway and read that on Friday night, a local businessman and conservationist had been killed in a car accident near his home in Thorndike. Sir Owen Darvish, who had been knighted less than a month before his death, had been recognised for his conservation work in partnership with American tech giant Autonomo—

Rosie had been about to click away. She sat forward.

—establishing a project to monitor endangered native birds by drone. In a letter of condolence, Robert Lemoine, Autonomo's co-founder and former CEO, vowed to carry on Sir Owen's legacy—

She scrolled down. A link at the bottom of the page directed her to a related article: a video clip from 2015 that showed Lemoine introducing a new model of Autonomo drone. Rosie clicked on it and maximised the window. At first, she thought she was looking at a screensaver. Dissolving tracking shots from overhead of jungles, urban centres, white-sand beaches, and snowy mountain slopes gave way to a revolving close-up of the drone itself, presented on a plinth and shot from below to give a sense of majesty, the camera housing gleaming, the skids and the propellers sparkling in the turning light. Then the camera pulled back and a man in his forties appeared out of the dark. He pressed a key on a control pad, and the machine hummed to life, lifting off the plinth and out of sight. The picture changed again to the drone's perspective, now circling the man, now climbing higher and higher and veering off through a window and out over roofs and steeples and suburban lawns and swimming pools; now climbing up a mountainside; now passing over a savannah, the grasses and acacias shimmering with heat; now banking out to sea and passing over the flukes of a whale. As the drone flew, a voice-over described its features: the camera specs, the wireless charging capability, the conditions it could fly in, the speeds it could reach. Now it was approaching the Manhattan skyline, where the same man was waiting on the rooftop of a skyscraper, another plinth in front of him, controls in hand. The drone alighted on the plinth and the propellers stilled, and then the image faded out and was replaced by a head-and-shoulders interview with the man with the control pad, who was identified on the screen as Autonomo co-founder Robert Lemoine. 'It would not be an exaggeration,' he began, 'to say that this technology has the power to impact every sector of every economy of every country on the planet. The applications in agriculture, in law enforcement, in wild-life protection, in traffic management, in supply chain security, in border security, in peacekeeping and humanitarian aid, even just in personal peace of mind ...'

He kept going; but Rosie was sitting open-mouthed. This was the man who'd called her on the phone. She was certain of it. The timbre of his voice, his accent, his intonation, the style of his address – she had no doubt whatsoever.

She sat back in her chair, utterly bewildered. Why would *Robert Lemoine* – one of the world's richest men – ring *her* in search of *Tony* – and pretend that he was someone else? Shaking her head, she clicked back to the article about Sir Owen's death and reread it more carefully, and then, frown-ing even deeper, she went back to her phone to revisit the last messages that she'd exchanged with Tony. 'Are you winning?' she had texted him on Monday last. 'Well, I just had my first "no comment",' he'd texted back, 'so I guess that means I'm onto something.' 'Definitely,' she'd replied. She scrolled down. 'I might be out of range for a few days just fyi,' he'd written next. 'Following a hunch ...' And then he'd signed off, 'xxx'. Rosie stared at the conversation, biting her lip, shaking her head. She tried calling him, but as she'd expected, his phone went straight to voicemail. 'Hi, you've reached Tony, you know what to do. Cheers,' said Tony's voice in her ear. She hung up, thought for a moment, and then texted one of her indoor netball teammates who sometimes volunteered with Birnam Wood: 'Hey girl,' she wrote, 'do you have a contact number for Mira Bunting by any chance?' A reply came barely twenty seconds later. Rosie pasted

Mira's number into her contacts, and before she'd had time to second-guess herself, she'd typed a message out. 'Hi Mira,' she wrote, 'this is Rosie Demarney from school, long time no see! I'm trying to get in touch with Tony (Gallo) but his phone is off and I wondered if you might be able to help me out? I know that he was down in Thorndike with you all. Sorry to ask like this but it's urgent. Thanks, take care, Rosie x'.

She sent the message. Unlike Tony, Mira had her read receipts turned on, and Rosie watched as the message tag updated from 'delivered' to 'read', marking the date and the time: 24/08/17 21:49. A second later, a grey bubble appeared, the three animated dots showing that Mira was composing a reply. Then Rosie saw something strange. The grey bubble froze, and then a second later, it disappeared, and the tag changed from 'read' back to 'delivered'. Rosie blinked. She was sure she had never seen that happen before. There must be a bug in the system, she thought, and exited the app; but when she opened it again, the tag still said 'delivered'. She checked again several minutes later, and then again before she went to bed, and then again the next morning when she woke up, but the read receipt never altered, and Mira never replied.

The return to Birnam Wood had been easier than Shelley had expected. She and Mira had rehearsed answers to a range of possible questions about their ersatz intervention, but luckily the others were too polite, or too embarrassed, to press for details, and after an awkward round of how's-it-goings and glad-to-have-you-backs, it was a relief to be able to change the subject to the file of paperwork that had arrived by courier that morning. Opening it, Shelley had been even more relieved to discover that quite a lot of writing and planning and budgeting needed to be done, and they had all fallen into a discussion of five-year plans and vision statements and the dos and don'ts of non-profit messaging so naturally that for a time she had forgotten all about Owen Darvish, and the creepy house in Thorndike, and the active threat against Lemoine. Even Mira seemed roused by the discussion, though after an hour or so she stood up to stretch her back and announced that all this corporate-speak was giving her a headache; she was going to bike up the northern fence line to check on how the crops were faring after the rain. Shelley looked up from her laptop and smiled, and Mira smiled back, and for a moment their friendship felt the way it used to, easy, affectionate, no doubt or blame, no hidden hurt, no overthinking. 'I'm *so* glad you guys sorted out your shit,' said Natalie quietly after Mira cycled off, and almost without artifice, Shelley put her palm against her cheek and said, 'Me too.'

The others had spent an uneventful weekend. Saturday had been a wipeout, they said, and on Sunday the rain had kept them all inside. That was it. Nobody mentioned having noticed any unusual traffic on the highway to and from the barricade, and nobody, it seemed, had read the local news – which was not in itself surprising: like Shelley, they probably got most of their world news online from sites like the Guardian, and relied on social media and Radio New Zealand for news closer to home. Shelley had been refreshing the article about the crash every chance she got, but the body must not yet have been formally identified, for the headline was yet to be updated with the dead man's name. Once that happened, she knew there would be a decent chance that RNZ would air the story, given that Darvish had been a man of some consequence, and that the accident was unexplained; for the moment, however, she reassured herself that the rest of Birnam Wood remained unaware that Owen Darvish had ever existed, let alone that he had very recently been killed.

They spent the rest of the day brainstorming a mission statement. In the late afternoon, Aaron put on a pot of miso broth and noodles, and Jessica went out to cut some baby spinach and spring onions from the hotbeds in the livestock pens. Hayden hard-boiled seven eggs and peeled them, and Katrina began slicing them in half. Suddenly she screamed: one of the eggs had fallen open to reveal a double yolk. 'Twins!' she cried. 'My first-ever chicken twins! Oh my God! I feel so chosen!'

The others gathered round to look, and Shelley took the opportunity to slip out to the loo and refresh the article again. This time, it had been updated. The casualty of the crash had been identified as Sir Owen Darvish, aged 58, a proud Thorndike local, knighted just two weeks before his death. She skimmed down through the broad-stroke details of his life and the description of the conservation project for which he had received his title. Autonomo was mentioned, as was Lemoine; but Birnam Wood, thankfully, was not. She checked social media. None of the accounts she followed on Twitter or Instagram had picked the story up. Quite possibly, they never would; but it was just after five, around the time that someone might think to tune in to *Checkpoint* on Radio New Zealand, and so, just to be safe, she went back inside and put on *The Courage of Others* by Midlake, a wistful, warm, and entirely inoffensive album that couldn't possibly put anybody in the mood for quarrelsome interviews about current affairs. After Midlake, she queued up *Boxer* by The National and then the Fleet Foxes debut, by which time *Checkpoint* would be over, and she would propose to spend the evening playing cards.

'God, I love this album,' she said, positioning her speaker to project out over the room. 'It's one of those albums where you

can't just listen to one track; you have to hear the whole thing.
You know?'

Mira came back in just as they were sitting down to dinner.

'Hey, so, everybody,' Jessica said, 'now that we're all here, I
want to make a toast. Actually, I'm going to stand up.' She got
to her feet, picking up her can of beer and holding it aloft. 'I just
wanted to mark this moment,' she said, 'because, I mean, let's
be honest, we all came down here thinking that maybe this was
going to work out and maybe it wasn't, but it's *happening*, Birnam Wood is fucking *happening* on a major scale, and I know
we're supposed to be all horizontal and leaderless and yah di
yah di yah, but I just want to raise a glass to Mira, because really,
I think we all know, we're here because of you. You're the one
who found this place. You found this crazy fucking billionaire,
and you had this vision for – am I saying something wrong?'

Shelley had been avoiding Mira's gaze; now she glanced at
her and was alarmed to see that she was blushing.

'No,' Mira said, turning even redder. 'It's all good. It's great.
This is great.'

Quickly Shelley raised her can. 'To Birnam Wood,' she said.

'I was toasting *Mira*,' Jessica said peevishly, but the others
were already toasting Birnam Wood.

'And to Mira,' someone added. 'Our *raison d'être*.'

'Our *joie de vivre*.'

'Our *coup de grâce*.'

'Our *pièce de résistance*.'

Everyone was laughing, but Mira's smile was very strained,
and after she'd clinked cans with everyone around her, she put
her beer back on the table without taking a sip.

Shelley sat forward. 'Aaron, this is super yummy, by the way,'
she said.

'It's really easy,' Aaron said.

'I mean, you *say* that,' Shelley said in a jolly voice, but her eyes were on Mira, who was chasing her egg around her bowl with her spoon.

'*Plat du jour?*' someone said. 'Or are we done?'

Jessica was still frowning. 'I feel like I'm missing something,' she said, looking from Mira to Shelley and then back again. 'Is it just me, or are you guys being kind of weird?'

Shelley forced a laugh. 'I mean, yeah,' she said, 'things *have* been kind of weird. I think we're all aware of that.'

'Let's just have dinner,' Natalie said, flapping her hand. 'Let's not drag anything up.'

Jessica drew back. 'I wasn't *dragging anything—*'

'Hey guys,' said Katrina, cutting over her, 'could we all keep talking about my amazing double yolk please? Because I think we all moved on from that topic just a *little* bit too quickly.'

'Actually,' Mira said, 'I want to say something.'

Shelley's heart swerved when she saw the expression on Mira's face, calm despite the high colour in her cheeks, and grave, and deadly certain. She tried in vain to catch her eye, terrified suddenly of what Mira might be just about to tell the group, wondering what she could possibly do to prevent it. Upend the table? Start screaming? Stage a fit? She felt as though her mouth had filled with sand.

Mira had taken a moment to collect herself. Now she looked up.

'Earlier today,' she said, 'when we were talking about all the legal stuff and public messaging and all of that, I had a kind of moment of clarity about myself. I had to go off and be alone and think about it, but now I have, and I've made up my mind.'

'You're totally right,' she said to Jessica, 'I *was* being weird just now. I've been weird all day, I've been in my head, and I'm sorry about that, but what I've decided' – she took a breath

– 'is that when we incorporate, I don't think that I should be Executive Director. I think it should be Shelley.' Her blush was subsiding; her gaze was clear and level now. 'I realised today that I just don't have the head for it,' she said to Shelley. 'You do. You've been right at the heart of Birnam Wood since almost the very beginning, and God knows you've put in more blood, sweat, and tears than anyone. All those words you were using earlier, you know, like, public-facing, client-facing – I mean, what I realised was, you're doing all of that already. And I've been super snobby about this stuff, I know I have, I've taken you totally for granted, and I haven't pulled my weight, and so I guess this is partly my way of saying sorry – but also, it's just obvious that it's the right thing to do. You should be leading Birnam Wood. You'd be really good at it. You'd be better than me. And I mean, of course we'll put it to a vote and everything, but I'm just saying, when we do, I'm going to vote for you.'

There was a pause; everybody turned to Shelley, waiting for her to respond. Somehow she managed to smile and crack a joke – 'Um . . . we're not still on acid, are we?' – and everybody laughed and toasted her as well, and somehow the conversation carried on, and *Boxer* by The National came on, and someone said, 'Now *this* is an album where you have to listen to the whole thing,' and somehow she managed to keep smiling and laughing, and somehow she ate her dinner, and somehow she got up to take her empty bowl to the washing-up tub, nodding along with the music, joining in at the chorus, doing her best to look happy and optimistic and grateful and relaxed and satisfied, and not like she knew exactly what Mira was doing, not like she'd known it from the moment that Mira had begun to speak. Mira was saving herself. Mira was making sure that if the truth ever did come out, if anybody ever did discover what they'd done, it would be Shelley who would have to answer for it, Shelley who would be the leader of the group, the figurehead, the mas-termind, the architect, the one to blame. Mira would just be a follower. Not Executive Director; not a power player; maybe not even a part of Birnam Wood any more. Mira was going to bail. She was already preparing for it. This promotion wasn't an apology, Shelley thought, trembling, livid, almost sick. It wasn't an act of loving kindness, or a way to make amends. It was a getaway plan.

Mira got up and came to join her at the washing-up tub. 'You okay?' she said. 'Boss?'

Shelley couldn't look at her. 'Yeah, fine,' she said in a normal voice, drying her hands. 'Hey, has Robert sent over his number yet?'

'No,' Mira said.

'Will you forward it to me when he does?'

'Sure. But his plane's still here; I'm sure he'll be back soon.' Mira frowned. 'Do you need to get a hold of him?'

'No,' Shelley said. 'It would just be good to have his number, that's all.'

'Maybe it's in the file,' Mira said.

'Oh yeah,' Shelley said, knowing that it wasn't. 'Yeah, good thought. It probably is,' and she excused herself to go and fetch her pack of cards.

For a long time, Shelley had assumed that Mira was an excel-lent and fluent liar simply because she herself was not. Since the beginning of their friendship, she had been accustomed to think of Mira's qualities and talents as diametrically opposed to hers, and certainly on any of the occasions when they'd been caught trespassing or stealing or flouting regulations in some flagrant way, it had always been Mira who had kept a cool head, who had spun elaborate and brazen falsehoods while Shelley shrank mortified beside her. As the years had gone by, however, Shelley had come to see that in fact Mira was only a good liar under certain circumstances. She had to have a lie prepared, first of all; she had to believe, at some level, that she was morally justified in telling it; and she had to be able to retain a measure of control, to feel free enough to relish in the flex and possibility of her own inventive skill. Shelley had also observed that Mira found it exceptionally difficult, for some reason, to pay a compliment she did not mean, and if she ever felt shamed or trapped into saying something emotionally dishonest, she would become a very bad liar indeed – flushing scarlet, avoiding all eye contact, and seizing the soonest chance to flee. That was how she had behaved tonight; but as Shelley split the deck and shuffled and tapped the cards into a pile and bent them back to shuffle them again, it occurred to her with a flat kind of fury that tonight might not in fact have been an instance of Mira lying badly, but an instance of her lying frighteningly, sickeningly well.

She woke early the next morning and refreshed the article about the crash. It was now featured on the national section of the website, and a new final paragraph advised that Sir Owen's funeral was to be held in Wellington that coming Friday. In lieu of flowers, the family had asked for donations to be made, in Sir Owen's memory, to his flagship conservation project, the swansong, as it had become, of his career. Evidently this request was honoured, for apart from a single plastic-sheathed bouquet of flowers that Shelley found propped against the Darvish gate later that morning – she moved it discreetly out of sight – nobody came calling at the farm with cards or sympathy. No friends or family descended on the house. No journalists turned up looking for a scoop, no policemen following a hunch, no neighbours with a funny feeling, no accidental witnesses Lemoine had overlooked – and the rest of Birnam Wood stayed none the wiser.

They were all treating Shelley as though the role of Executive Director was hers already, without any need for a vote, and although Shelley knew it was a poisoned chalice, she could not help but feel a little thrill each time one of them sought out her permission, or deferred to her judgment, or came to her with problems and solutions and ideas, and when the Charities Services sent an email on Wednesday afternoon to confirm her interview for Thursday morning, she experienced only the smallest twinge of apprehension when she replied that she had received another offer in the meantime and had decided, after much deliberation, to accept it. Mira, for her part, was putting in longer hours than anyone, rising early, forgoing her lunch break, and working as late as the daylight would allow, as if to underscore the fact that she had ceded her role as the brains of the operation once and for all, and wished to be regarded purely as a labourer. She was spending most of her time on the terraces above the farmhouse, out of sight of the shearing shed, and Shelley had resorted to using the location-tracker app to check up on her, sometimes as often as a dozen times a day; she was afraid, each time she opened the app, that the map would lurch sideways and locate Mira somewhere unexpected, walking into a police station, or at the departures desk of an international airport, or even just travelling down the highway at a hundred k's an hour. But so far, the yellow dot had always located her exactly where she'd said that she would be.

Late on Thursday night, Shelley had just zipped herself into her tent and was climbing into her sleeping bag when her phone lit up with a message from an unfamiliar number. 'This is Robert,' it read. 'Are you up?'

'Yes,' she texted back.

'I want to talk to you,' he wrote. 'Come up to the house in half an hour.'

Surprised, Shelley sat up, unzipped her tent, and poked her head out to see if Mira's tent was lit – but the canvas dome was dark: she must have already turned in. Only Jessica and Aaron's tent was faintly glowing, though even as Shelley watched, the light inside winked out and she heard distant murmuring and shuffling as they settled down to sleep. There was no line of sight from the shearing shed, where they were camped, to the front gate, but even so, she felt a chill to think that Lemoine had come home without any of them knowing. She lay down again, waited half an hour like he had asked, and then got up and fumbled for her boots, which were already cold and wet with dew. She pulled on a woollen beanie and a head torch, climbed out of her tent, zipped up the vestibule as quietly as she could, and scurried up the hill towards the farmhouse, not turning on the torch until she was well clear of the campsite and facing uphill. Her torch had been angled down for reading; she reached up and adjusted the setting until it cast a long ellipsis out in front of her that frosted the grasses and bobbed and loomed with every step.

The windows of the house were dark. When she reached the front door, she turned off the torch again and knocked. Nobody answered; but a few seconds later she heard the rumble of the garage-door motor, and she came around the side of the house to see the door rattling up. A dark SUV was parked inside, and beyond it, Lemoine was standing in the doorway to the laundry with his finger on the switch.

'Hi,' she said.

'Come in,' he said, and pressed the switch again so that the door rattled down behind her. She followed him through the laundry and down the hall into the living room, where he turned on a lamp and sat down on one of the couches, gesturing for her to do the same. She took off her beanie and her head torch and stuffed them into the pocket of her fleece as she sat down.

'So,' he said. 'How are you?'

Out of habit, she was about to answer, 'Fine'; but for once she decided to be truthful. 'Actually,' she said, 'a little overwhelmed, to be honest.'

'By what, exactly?'

Shelley looked away. 'Well, I guess, by Mira, a little bit.'

He nodded. 'Talk to me.'

'She doesn't want to be Executive Director any more,' Shelley said. 'She told everyone she doesn't want it. She says she's not right for it. She thinks it should be me.'

'Fuck,' he said.

'Is that bad?' she said.

'It wasn't what we agreed,' he said. 'I told her, no big changes. She shouldn't be going off-script. This really pisses me off, actually. This is exactly what I told her not to do.'

Shelley felt a tug of guilt. 'We kind of had it out over the weekend,' she said, 'and I unloaded all sorts of shit on her about how she'd never respected me and stuff. So maybe she's trying to make it up to me.'

He shook his head. 'You don't really think that.'

'I don't really know what I think,' Shelley said.

'You don't think that, either.' He studied her. 'Do you want the job?'

She tried to laugh. 'Does it matter?'

'Of course it matters. If you don't want it, you should say so. Now.'

Shelley plunged her fists into her pockets and twisted her fleece into a figure of eight on her lap. 'Yes,' she said at last. 'I want it.'

'Good,' he said. 'What about the others? How are they?'

'Fine,' Shelley said. 'Normal.'

'Anything I need to know?'

'I don't think so,' Shelley said. 'Just the Mira thing.'

'All right, good,' he said. 'Shelley, I wanted to apologise to you. The last time we spoke, I was stressed out, and I let my temper get away from me. I shouldn't have told you about the active threat. You and Mira had enough on your plate. You still do.'

'Did you find the guy?'

'We will,' said Lemoine. 'Don't worry about that. The point is that you were already going through a lot, and I probably made it worse. I'm sorry.'

She was touched. 'It must be pretty scary,' she said. 'To have to deal with stuff like that.'

'You'd think so,' said Lemoine. 'The first few times it was, I guess, but now—' He shrugged. 'Anyway: we'll find him. The main thing is that you don't need to worry.'

'Are *you* worried?'

He paused. 'There's no such thing as absolute security,' he said. 'You always have to remember that. But we're in a good place. We're going to survive this.'

She nodded, her hands still twisted in her lap.

'One more thing,' he said. 'I wanted you to know that I'm pulling the trigger on the bunker. I've brought everything forward. I've got a crew arriving in the morning to start prepping the site, and you're going to start seeing a lot of traffic on and off the property over the next little while. They'll stay out of your way. I just wanted to give you a heads-up.'

'But tomorrow's the funeral,' Shelley said. 'Isn't it a bit insensitive—'

'I agree the timing's not ideal,' he said, 'but I'm solving a problem. Jill Darvish wasn't buying what I told her about Birnam

Wood. I don't want her asking questions, and by moving fast, I can change the narrative to something else. Do you see?'

Shelley was frowning. 'What do you mean, she wasn't buying it?'

'She got paranoid,' said Lemoine. 'She thinks one of you was fucking her husband.'

Shelley was so astonished that she laughed. '*What?*' she said.

Lemoine wasn't smiling. 'It's a problem,' he said. 'We need to get ahead of it. Give her something else to think about. Something unrelated. This is a way to do that.'

'Mira said you hadn't even bought the land yet.'

'I hadn't. Now I have. Like I said: I'm moving fast.'

'But don't you need, like, planning permission, and—'

'Too slow,' he said. 'I'd rather pay a fine than a fee.'

'Okay,' Shelley said. 'I think I get it.'

'Good,' he said. 'The guys won't bother you. Just stay away from the building site and let them do their work. All right?'

It sounded like a dismissal. Automatically, she nodded and stood up to leave, but he said, 'Shelley,' and something in his voice made her sit down again.

'Yes?' she said.

He sat without moving for a second. Then he said, 'Stay.'

Mira woke early the next morning and went at once to the terraces above the house, feeling a grim kind of gladness that the flask of coffee she'd prepared the night before was barely tepid by the time she reached her planting site and sat down on a stump to drink it, looking out at the dawn-tipped mountains above the steely surface of the lake, and imagining herself in jail. She imagined a cell without a window, and an open toilet, and bars worn shiny-smooth in the places that a pair of grasping hands would go. She imagined clockwise laps around a concrete yard, and maggots in her food, and eczema and chilblains and a new hacking cough, and a dead-eyed cellmate with a buzz cut and a nasty grin. She imagined her parents on visiting day, huddled together behind a pane of glass, her mother putting her hand over her mouth in shock when Mira was escorted out to them between a pair of guards, thin, broken, her complexion dull and waxy, her hair hanging lank over one eye, her father saying, 'Oh, sweetheart, not again,' as she sat down and they saw the bruises on her face that she'd been trying to hide from them, bruises from where her cellmate had—

'Stop it,' Mira said aloud, shaking her head to dispel the fantasy, ashamed that yet again she had caught herself indulging in imaginary scenarios where *she* was the one who'd been injured, where *she* was the one who'd been wronged, this time by an invented cellmate in a fictitious future circumstance in which her parents were not only weirdly back together, but united in expressing their concern and helpless tragic love for her, and not their unmitigated horror, not their loathing, not the unspeakable revulsion they would feel when they discovered what their daughter, their little girl, had done.

What she was still doing. What she'd been doing all week, and all weekend, as the corpse of the man whose death she'd helped to bring about, whose death she'd helped to cover up, had been cut from the wreckage of the burned-out SUV, and zipped into a body bag, and put on a plane, and unloaded at a morgue, and pumped full of chemicals, and wheeled into a fridge, and wheeled out again to be formally identified, by his wife maybe, or by one of his children, or using his dental records, if his face had been too badly burned in the crash that never really happened, the crash he'd never caused, the crash that Lemoine had somehow staged, at short notice, apparently successfully – and surely not entirely on his own? Mira thought about the empty house in Thorndike, and the man who had come to fix the windscreen on the van. She thought about the soldier up the service road, and how Lemoine had said, 'That's one of mine.' She thought about Lemoine's late wife. And then she thought: *You're doing it again.* She shook her head, disgusted at herself. She was still looking for a villain. She was still trying, desperately – and uselessly – to find somebody more monstrous and despicable than her.

The funeral was at eleven. She'd observe a minute's silence, she thought, or say a prayer, if she could think of what to pray. She poured the last of the coffee into the dirt and shook the empty flask till it was dry. She had brought with her a banana and a snack bar for her breakfast, but it gave her a penitential feeling to be hungry, and so she left them on the stump beside the empty flask and went to fetch her fork and trowel, telling herself that she'd spend the morning weeding the pumpkins and courgettes, and the afternoon constructing trellises for the several crops of beans that were coming up and would soon become top-heavy. Stomach growling, she began shuffling along the row on the old hot water bottle she used as a kneeling pad, stopping every now and then to stretch her back and shake the stiffness out of her hands.

She had reached the end of her second row of pumpkins when she felt the air go still and smelled a sudden minerally-earthy-dusty scent that seemed to clarify the leaves and shoots of all the living things around her. It was about to start chucking down, she realised, cursing inwardly, for she couldn't bear the thought of returning to the shearing shed to spend the rest of the day in cosy company, chatting about nothing in particular, and laughing at other people's jokes. Would she draw too much attention to herself if she continued working in the rain? She looked directly upward. The sky was lowering even as she watched.

Maybe she could head out in the van and run some errands, she thought, as the earth around her darkened with a few splashing drops that thickened and then intensified into a deluge. She could make a day of it: head out to the nearest hardware store to fetch a few more bales of pea straw and a load of blood and bone and whatever else they didn't really need. 'Might make more sense if I go alone,' she imagined saying to the others casually, swinging the keys; 'I can fill the front seat that way.' She remembered that the petrol tank was almost empty. Even better, then. Even more reason to leave.

The rain was really pounding now. Mira put up her hood and dashed back to the stump to collect her breakfast and the empty flask, bent almost double, pulling off her gardening gloves and reaching out a hand even before she got to the place she knew the flask would be – except it wasn't. The stump was clear, the surface dark and slick. She circled it, thinking that she must have knocked it into the grass somehow when she got up. But she couldn't have disturbed the banana and the bar as well; she would have noticed. And she was positive she'd left them all right there. She could visualise them perfectly: the banana, the snack bar, and the flask. All three. She looked up, squinting through the rain – and there at the edge of the field, standing partially concealed behind a tree trunk in the shelterbelt of pines, was Tony.

Mira was too surprised even to speak. He put his finger over his lips, and then made the sign for 'phone', putting his thumb to his ear and stretching his little finger down to his mouth. Then he turned his hand palm-up to indicate a question. 'Where's your phone?' he mouthed to her. Dumbly, Mira reached into her pocket to pull it out and show it to him, but he signalled violently for her to put it back again, then put his finger over his lips a second time, and beckoned. He was performing all these actions with the same hand, and as Mira came closer, through the rain, she saw that his other arm was in a kind of sling. He looked desperately unwell. His beard was ragged, and there were purple hollows under his eyes. She came closer still and saw that he was holding her flask beneath his broken arm; now he pinned it underneath his elbow, unscrewed the lid with his free hand, and held it out to her, gesturing for her to put her phone inside.

'Tony, what the fuck?' she whispered, but he shook his head, not speaking till she had dropped her phone into the flask with a clunk and he'd replaced the cap and screwed it tight. He was leaning heavily against the tree. She looked down and saw that his left foot was swaddled in a bandage that was soaking wet and black with dirt.

'I got lost,' he said at last, his voice rasping in his throat. 'I was heading for the other side of the park, but they've been hunting me, and I got turned around. I didn't mean to come here, but I'm out of food, and my arm is broken, and my foot – and you have to help me, Mira. Please.'

Mira was bewildered. 'What?' she said. 'What are you talking about? Tony—'

'Listen to me,' he said, hopping slightly to adjust his weight against the trunk. 'Robert Lemoine is not building a bunker. That's not what he's doing here. He's mining the national park. He's mining Korowai. It's collusion. It's him and the government, and Darvish, Owen Darvish. They're doing it in secret, and they're breaking like a thousand different laws, and you have to get me to a lab so I can get these photos printed and I can blow it all wide open. We can't go to the police. We can't involve anybody else. It's too – Mira, this is the biggest fucking – listen. Just listen. Just listen to me. Please.'

'What photos?' Mira said.

He dropped the flask, then took a ziplock bag out of his jacket pocket and held it up. The bag unfurled to show a stubby grey-capped cylinder at the very bottom: a roll of film. Thrusting it at her, he said, 'Mira, listen. There is a massive, totally secret, *totally illegal* mining operation going on right behind these mountains, right now, *inside the national park.* Do you hear me? I found out about it. I broke in and took these photos' – he shook the bag – 'and now they're trying to kill me to shut me up. I had to jump into a river, and I left the car, it's Veronica's car, I left it with the keys in the – it doesn't matter. I just need to get these photos developed. I need to get this story out, because this is a fucking international conspiracy at the highest fucking level, and the whole park is like crawling with drones—'

Mira wondered if he might be going mad. 'Slow down,' she said. 'Just slow down a second. I don't understand. What are you even—'

'They've been hunting me,' he said. 'All week. They have to fly low because of the trees. I've heard them combing back and forth. I can't move at night because the air's too cold, the contrast with my body heat, they'd see me. But when it rains, they don't work as well. There's guys too, guys with guns, I mean, this is – and you can't use your phone. You have to stop using your phone, because that's – listen. Just listen.'

'I'm listening,' Mira said.

'Listen to me,' Tony said, seeming almost on the verge of tears. 'I spoke to Owen Darvish. To interview him. About the bunker. About Robert Lemoine. But he wouldn't talk to me, and then he must have told Lemoine that I'd called, and he had my number, and I realised, that's how they knew that I – Mira, listen. Everything you said at Birnam Wood, at the hui, like, about the bunker, and how he'd bought this place, this whole farm – he hasn't. The property never sold. Because Darvish is in on it. Do you see? It's all a fucking front for this other massively illegal thing they're doing, in the national park, *and they're in on it together.*'

'But Robert hated Owen Darvish,' Mira said, realising only after she'd spoken that she'd called Lemoine by his first name. 'He told me. He said he was a little prick.'

'Mira, you can't trust him,' Tony said. 'That's what I'm telling you. You can't trust a word he says. He's lying to you.'

'He said he'd put down a deposit. And he was slow-walking the deal because of—'

'No,' Tony said. 'Mira. No. Everything he's told you is a lie.'

'How long have you been out here?' Mira said, meaning Thorndike generally, but he answered as though she meant the farm.

'Since yesterday,' he said. 'I saw you working in the early evening, and I was about to come down, but then I saw the SUV and I chickened out. He's a bad fucking guy, Mira. They tried to run me off the road with that thing. And it's not just him, this is what I'm saying, it's Darvish, it's the fucking *government*, I mean, this mining site, these chemicals, when you see—'

'Stop,' Mira said. 'Slow down. What SUV?'

'The one that drove up to the house last night,' said Tony.

'What?' she said.

'And then I saw somebody with a head torch,' he said. 'Walking. Later on.'

Mira was shaking her head. 'Wait,' she said. 'I don't—'

'Why do you think they gave Darvish the knighthood?' Tony said wildly. 'Mira, this goes all the way to the – I can show you the photos. This mining site – the scale of it – and there are soldiers – guards, and – please, just get me to a lab and I'll show you the photos, and you'll see. I know I sound insane. If

I were you, I'd be thinking – I don't know. But if there was ever a moment in your life when you had to make a choice, Mira, it's right now, it's this choice, right now, right here. Please help me. I'm not crazy. I'm telling you the truth. I swear to God.'

Mira opened her mouth to say something – but she couldn't speak. A weird sensation was building inside her. She had never considered that Owen Darvish had been anything other than an innocent. But if what Tony was saying was the truth, then maybe he'd actually deserved to die. Maybe he'd been a terrible person. Maybe he'd been a criminal. Maybe he'd been a traitor and a thief. Maybe Lemoine had helped to cover up his death not because of Shelley, not to save her – nor Birnam Wood – nor to protect himself, but to protect something else entirely, to hide some vast conspiracy that Mira hadn't known about, that she couldn't possibly have known about, that nobody had known about. She felt as though her chest was about to burst. For this would mean there really *was* a villain; there really *was* someone more monstrous and more despicable than her. This would mean that she was safe. She could tell the world the truth. She could say she'd been coerced into doing what she did. And people would believe her. People would forgive her. Because Lemoine was worse than she was. And Darvish had been worse than she was. And the government was worse than she was. It was all a huge conspiracy. Everything was going to be all right.

'Mira,' Tony said. 'Say something.'

Almost without thinking, she said, 'He's dead.'

'What?' Tony said.

'Darvish,' she said. 'He died on Friday night. His car went off a cliff.'

Tony gaped at her. 'Oh, Jesus,' he said, clutching at his hair. 'Mira. That's what they tried to do to me. They tried to run me off the road. This is – oh my God. Jesus, fuck! *This is exactly what I'm telling you!*'

And all at once, Mira knew that she was going to help him.

'Stay here,' she said, picking up the flask. 'I'm going to go and get the van. I need to fill it up anyway. I'll come back to get you, and you can hide in the back, and I'll drive you out and I'll just say I'm going to fill it up and nobody will know. All right?'

'Don't use your phone,' he said. 'They can't track you if it's in metal. Don't take it out. And don't say anything to anyone.'

'I won't,' she said. 'Wait here. I'll be back.'

'Wait,' he said, reaching for her. 'Just wait a second.'

She was already backing away. 'Don't move,' she said, starting to run. 'I'll be right back.'

'Wait,' he called out. 'Mira.'

She stopped. 'Yeah?' she said.

He seemed much smaller suddenly. He took a breath.

'What?' she said.

'I'm sorry,' he said. 'About my leaving party. I never wanted—'

'Never wanted what?' Mira said, when he didn't go on.

'I just—' His nose was streaming; he wiped it with the back of his hand. 'I just feel like I fucked it up,' he said at last.

She felt a rush of benevolence towards him. 'You didn't fuck it up,' she said. 'I fucked it up.'

Tony tried to smile. '"No, you hang up first,"' he said.

She laughed aloud, buoyed by a crazy feeling of impunity. She felt she might explode with relief and gratitude. 'Tony,' she said, smiling, coming back to take his hand, 'we're fine. Honestly. We're totally fine. We were just – young.'

'Yeah,' he said, looking down at her clean hand in his dirty one. 'We were young.'

She squeezed his fingers and released them. 'Stay here,' she said. 'I'll be back.'

'Bring some food,' he said. 'And painkillers. And be careful.'

She set off running down the hill, still smiling; but when she came around the house and the valley seemed to open out before her, she faltered and the smile fell from her face, for in the few short hours that she had been weeding in the upper paddocks, the lower fields had been transformed into a work-site. The main gate at the bottom of the hill was standing open, and crawling up the driveway was a train of heavy vehicles: eighteen-wheelers loaded with shipping containers, diggers, earth movers, kitset mobile offices, RVs—

She heard engine noise through the rain and turned in bewilderment to see Lemoine's dark-tinted SUV driving across the field towards her, windscreen wipers flashing, the suspension bouncing on the uneven ground. It drew level with her, and the passenger window slid down.

'I came to rescue you,' said Lemoine. 'Some rain.'

She stared at him.

'I think your phone must have died,' he said. 'I was trying to call. What's wrong?'

Mira couldn't speak. 'What is all this?' she said at last, gesturing around her.

'It's my bunker,' said Lemoine.

Shelley often woke up the morning after a sexual encounter with a feeling of manifest exposure, as though she'd been secretly recorded in the act of having sex and the recording was now being screened, at high resolution, on her body and across her face. It was a sensation not of shame, but of transgressive near-exhilaration, and that morning she had felt it even more acutely than on the day that she'd had sex for the first time. She was positive that Mira would only have to glance at her to know exactly what had happened in the night, and where, and when, and in what way – and so she'd waited until the yellow dot on her locator app was well out of sight of the shearing shed before going to join the rest of Birnam Wood for breakfast, where she was greeted, incredibly, as if it were just another sexless morning, as if she were just the same sexless person who had bid them all goodnight nine hours before.

Lemoine had been a surprisingly attentive lover, more focused on her pleasure, seemingly, than on his own. The one thing it was very clear that he enjoyed was commanding her to look at him. When she obeyed, he met her gaze eagerly, seeming suddenly greedy, suddenly selfish, moving faster, and breathing harder, and repeating the command the moment that she closed her eyes or turned her face aside into the pillow, such that she'd begun to disobey him, sensing, correctly, that this would please him even more. Afterwards, lying naked in the dark in the Darvishes' spare room, he'd surprised her a second time by nuzzling into her companionably and asking in a sleepy voice if she wouldn't mind lightly raking her fingernails up and down his back, which was something that his grandmother had done when he was very young to help him fall asleep. She had rolled on to her side to face him and slipped one arm up the warm smoothness of his back like he had asked, and he had pulled her closer and sighed into her clavicle and closed his eyes and seemed to be asleep in seconds. She eased herself away from him and then lay watching him for perhaps a half an hour more, wondering why he and Mira hadn't slept together, and if they ever would, and what it would be like, similar to this, or very different, eventually reaching down for the duvet that was puddled at the bottom of the bed and drawing it up over them both. He didn't stir. Some hours later, she'd woken up and found him gone. She fell asleep again, and when she woke next, it was morning.

She dressed quickly, wanting to get back to the camp before the others got going for the day and realised that she wasn't there, and made the bed, double-checking that he had taken with him not only the condom and the wrapper, but also the little strip along the wrapper's edge from where he'd torn it open with his teeth and then spat it out. But both the bedside table and the space beneath the bed were clear. She came out into the living room and found him sitting at the dining table, working on two laptops simultaneously. Seeing her, he shut both devices, got up, and came around the table to clasp her by the upper arms and kiss her firmly on the cheek in a gesture that made her feel both younger than she was, and older.

'I'm going to keep my distance for a while,' he said. 'I don't want the others wondering about us. If I come down to talk to you, it'll be only in the context of the group. All right?'

'Sure,' Shelley said. 'Yeah. Of course.'

'And I warn you, I'll probably be very matter-of-fact with you, and very short, and to the point.'

'Don't worry,' she said. 'You don't need to explain.'

'But you should call me if you need to. Any reason, any time. I know this is going to be a tough day, so if you feel overwhelmed in any way, don't hesitate. Find a quiet place and call me.'

For a moment, Shelley felt offended. 'Why would today be tough?' she had just been about to say, defensively, before she realised that he wasn't talking about the fact that they'd slept together; he was talking about the funeral. 'Thanks,' was all she said. 'I should be fine.'

He put his thumb against her chin and tilted her face towards him. 'That was a pretty good time last night,' he said.

'Yeah,' she said, blushing.

'Yeah,' he said. He smiled thoughtfully and stepped away, but then seemed to remember something. 'Oh – just before you go,' he said, 'I've been running some background checks, just routine security stuff, and there's this name that keeps coming up: Tony Gallo.'

'Tony?' Shelley said, laughing slightly. 'Oh God.'

'I want to know about him,' said Lemoine. 'Who is he?'

'God,' she said. 'I mean, you should really be asking Mira.'

'I don't trust Mira,' he said. 'So I'm asking you.'

She was startled to hear him say as much so plainly. 'God,' she said again, stalling for time. 'What exactly do you want to know?'

'When was the last time you saw him?'

'Not since the hui,' Shelley said.

He frowned. 'What's the hui?'

'The meeting. When we took the vote on coming down here. Tony was, like, really opposed, and he and Mira had this big fight about it.'

'So he's a part of Birnam Wood.'

'He was,' Shelley said. 'Right back at the beginning. Then he went overseas. He's been gone for ages. Like, years.'

'Tell me about the fight. Why was he opposed? What was the argument?'

'I mean, he's political,' she said. 'You know, he's super . . . and, well, he didn't like the idea of getting involved with you. He thought it went against our values. And also, I think he was a bit jealous. Because he and Mira have this history.'

'They were together?'

'Sorry,' Shelley said, laughing again, 'is this really a security issue, or—'

'Answer me,' said Lemoine, sounding as he had the night before when he'd said, 'Look at me,' and despite herself she felt a stirring of arousal. 'They were together?'

'Kind of,' she said. 'I mean, yeah, once. But they were super close. And everyone always kind of thought they'd probably end up married one day. It was like a will-they-won't-they kind of thing.'

'Tell me more about the fight,' said Lemoine.

'Well,' Shelley said, 'Tony kind of lost before it even started, because Mira was late, and he'd been having this whole other argument with this girl called Amber, whose café we were meeting in, and he was doing the whole mansplainy, Berniebro-type thing with her, and so when Mira finally got there, things were already kind of tense.'

'What happened?'

'He just flipped out, I guess,' Shelley said. 'He said we were betraying everything that we believed in, and then obviously he lost the vote, and he left.'

'And then what?'

'Nothing,' Shelley said. 'Like I said: he left. That was the last time I saw him.'

'What about Mira?'

'Same as me,' Shelley said. 'I'd be pretty surprised if they've been in touch since then. I mean, I don't even think they have each other's numbers. The hui, that meeting – that was the first time she'd seen him since he got back from overseas. But they never really got a chance to talk, and then we left the next day to come down here, so.'

'Okay, Shelley,' he said, after a pause, 'that's helpful. Thanks. Let me see you out.'

He led her to the front door this time, and as he opened it to usher her through, he said, 'Keep your phone on tonight.'

'Okay,' Shelley said, her stomach plunging again. 'See ya.'

'Take care of yourself,' he said.

Her feeling of hypervisibility persisted all the way through breakfast and throughout the morning. A little before midday,

Hayden came in from one of the planting sites to say that a parade of eighteen-wheeler trucks and heavy vehicles was pouring in through the front gate. 'Must be the construction starting on the bunker,' Shelley said, looking up from her spreadsheet. 'Robert said that was going to start today.' The others all wanted to go and look, but just as they were setting off across the hill, it began to rain, sending them all back again. As Shelley watched them all dash for shelter, laughing, soaking wet, she realised that Mira would probably be returning shortly, too; the rain was really hammering, and it showed no sign of letting up. She saved the spreadsheet she was working on and put away her laptop, announcing to no one in particular that she was heading into town to fill the van – and maybe, she said, she'd do a run to the hardware store while she was out. They could use more pea straw, and another load of blood and bone.

'Thanks,' she said, when Natalie asked if she wanted company, 'but it might be easier if I go alone. I can fill up the front seat that way.'

She hadn't driven since the night she'd killed Owen Darvish, and as she put the key in the ignition and the clock on the dashboard winked to life, she saw the time and realised that his funeral was probably almost over, approaching the final hymn perhaps, the hearse standing by, the pall-bearers coming forward to grip the brassy handles and hoist the coffin up – his sons; his brothers, if he had brothers; maybe a nephew; maybe a best friend. She put her seat belt on and turned the van around to head across the field towards the gate, and she had just changed into second gear and was stepping on the gas when Lemoine's dark-tinted SUV appeared over the crest of the hill, coming in the opposite direction. It slowed to pass her, close enough for them to nod at one another through two sets of flashing windscreen wipers, and for Shelley to see, with a jolt, that Mira was beside him. The two friends locked eyes for barely a quarter of a second before both vehicles drove on, but it was long enough for Shelley to read in Mira's expression something entirely different from the hurt and disappointed judgment she had expected she would find there: Mira was wide-eyed, and looked almost plaintive, almost despairing, as if she were desperately trying to communicate a message that she knew Shelley had not received, and would not receive in time. Shelley drove on across the field to the line of poplars by the driveway, where she met the train of heavy vehicles arriving at the farm to prepare to break the ground. She slowed to a crawl, passing by the container trucks, the cement mixers, the earth movers, and the RVs, and tried to imagine, for the life of her, what that message might have been.

Tony had waited all afternoon for Mira to return, his eyes fixed on the place she'd disappeared over the brow of the hill that morning, willing her to reappear there now, now, now, as the rain eased off into a drizzle, and then into a mist, and the clouds lifted, and the daylight faded into dusk, and evening fell, and he knew he couldn't leave his hiding place among the pines until the dawn. It seemed an age since he'd eaten Mira's breakfast, an age since he'd gone back to the banana skin that he'd discarded, brushed it free of dirt and eaten that too, an age since he'd cut away a piece of bark from the pine tree under which he sat and placed it on his tongue to suck the resin, eyes closed, tasting turpentine, recalling that willow bark was an effective pain reliever, envisaging willows on the shores of Lake Korowai, and then wondering if the vision that he'd conjured of those heavy-shouldered trees around the placid lake was a memory or a desire. His exhaustion was making him delirious. The night before, he had spent hours trying to remember whether he had told his mother yet about the Korowai conspiracy; he'd felt sure that he had, until he played out the memory in his mind and realised that he himself was not present in any of the scenes that he remembered. He could see his mother on the telephone to him, and he could see her standing alone in the living room after she'd hung up, and he could see her a few days later receiving the news that Tony had been killed by accident in unsuspicious circumstances, and he could see her expression as she disbelieved it, and then as she decided to avenge him, her middle child, her oldest son. He settled down to try to sleep, focusing on the gnawing pain in his belly as a way of distracting himself from the pain in his ankle and the pain in his arm, his consciousness flickering and fluttering, the movement of the branches above him seeming to be whispering his name:

'Tony . . . Tony . . . *Tony!*'

He jolted awake. It wasn't the branches. It was Mira, crunching through the shelterbelt, feeling her way through the darkness, looking for him. In the moment that he saw her, she saw him. She hurried over, breathless, slipping one arm out of the backpack she was wearing and slinging it down to unbuckle the clasps.

'I'm so sorry,' she whispered, releasing the drawstring and reaching both her hands inside. 'Shelley took the van. She went to fill it up like I was going to, and then she took fucking ages at the hardware store, and Robert came, and I couldn't get away without it being obvious. Here, I've brought you—'

She shoved the contents of her bag towards him: a first-aid kit, a box of paracetamol, a bar of chocolate, a sandwich, an apple, a box of snack bars, a bag of nuts.

'It's a fucking carnival down there,' she said. 'There are like a thousand people on the property all of a sudden. I'm going to try to bring the van up here tomorrow, but obviously I'll need a reason. I thought I could maybe break something. Like, put a hole in the hose, or something, so it has to be repaired – or, like, make it seem as though we've got a pest problem? I don't know. I'll think of something. But this is just to tide you over in the meantime. I'm so sorry it took me so long to get back.'

She was talking very fast, her features all but obscured in the dark.

'Can you think of something?' she said. 'Like, I even thought, maybe I could pretend my mum was sick or something, so I'd have to leave in a hurry. But then I thought, it can't be too much of an emergency, or Robert would offer to fly me out in his plane. I mean, maybe he'd do that. I don't know. Aren't you hungry?'

Tony was staring at her in pure horror. 'Mira,' he whispered, 'I told you. *You can't travel at night.*'

'No, it's okay,' she said, reaching out a hand to reassure him. 'It's okay. I don't have my phone. It's still inside the Thermos, like you said. I left it in my tent. I didn't take it out all day. It's fine.'

'No,' Tony said, still horror-struck. 'No. I'm talking about the drones. If you move at night, they can see you better. Because of the contrast. The heat of your body contrasts with the air. It makes you more visible. I told you that.'

'Oh,' she said, seeming to deflate a little. 'Yeah. Shit. But we're probably okay. Right? I mean, it's not like they're going to be watching everywhere at once. It's probably fine.'

'Or it's not fine, and we're fucking dead.'

She drew back. 'Hey, Tony, I'm actually risking quite a bit to help you here, you know, so—'

'Sorry,' he said quickly, fighting down feelings of despair. 'Thanks for the food, really, and the help, I'm just—'

'No, I know,' she said. 'I'm sorry.'

'I've just been so careful.'

'I know,' she said. 'I know. I'm just – I'm freaking out. You know?'

He nodded. 'What do you mean, there are like a thousand people?'

'They're digging the foundations for the bunker,' Mira said. 'It's like a whole construction site. It's crazy.'

'No,' Tony said. 'No. It's a front. It's a fucking front. I'm telling you.'

'Robert said he bought the farm,' Mira said. 'He paid the balance, like, this week. And then his guys came, and they started working right away. Everything's happening, like, right now.'

'You have to believe me,' Tony said, clutching her. 'You have to.'

'I believe you,' Mira said.

'You do?'

'Yes. But Tony, listen—'

Tony heard a slither in the trees nearby, the synthetic sound of a jacket sliding past a branch. He shot out his hand to cover Mira's mouth – but it was too late: now he heard footsteps too, patient footsteps coming straight towards them, and in the next moment, the darkness seemed to thicken and took on a shape that crouched down to peer under the branches of the tree where they were sheltering. A second later came a click and then a blaze of yellow light so bright that Tony winced and snatched his hand off Mira's mouth to shield his face.

'Well, hello,' said a voice on the other end of the torch. 'You must be Tony.'

'You seem surprised,' Lemoine had said that morning, sitting in the driver's seat, watching Mira take in the scene that filled the field below the paddock where she stood.

'I mean, yeah,' she'd said, rain beating down on her and plastering her hair against her head. She gestured limply at the excavation site. 'I thought this was still, like, months and months away.'

'It was,' he said. 'Get in. I have something to tell you.'

'Can you tell me here?' she said.

'I can, but I don't want to,' he said. 'Get in.'

'It's just, I've got a lot of work to do,' she said. 'I want to keep moving.'

'What's the matter with you? Get in the car.'

'Nothing's the matter, it's just—'

'Mira, it's raining. You're soaking wet. Get in.'

'I'm fine,' Mira said. 'I'm used to it.'

'What the fuck is wrong with you?' he said, and this time she turned fierce.

'Oh, let me think,' she snapped. 'What could possibly be happening today to stress me the fuck out? Nope, can't think of anything. Sorry, Robert. Drawing a real blank there.'

The show of temper reassured him. 'Get in,' he said again.

She glared at him for a second longer, then wrenched open the door and climbed in.

'What?' she said.

When Lemoine had intercepted Rosie Demarney's message late on Thursday night, he had decided instantly to cut his losses and give the order to his soldiers to pack out, ending the leaching process prematurely, but salvaging, with luck, the better part of the value of his operation in the park. Yes, he would lose a lot of money in the process – but that was better than losing every cent. Mira was already a liability. The fact that she and Tony had been known to one another after all had been a catastrophic oversight on his part – all the more since Tony, together with his roll of film, was still at large. Lemoine had been hoping he might be able to dispatch Tony quietly, in some innocent and accidental-seeming way; reading Rosie's message, he saw that this would be impossible, since Tony's death would connect automatically to Mira, and through her, to him, throwing the death of Owen Darvish into doubt, and calling into question Lemoine's entire involvement with Birnam Wood, which had turned into a million-dollar hush-up job, to boot. There were too many variables in play, Lemoine had thought, as he'd deleted Rosie's message, logged in to the Korowai comms unit, and given the order, as Lt Col Weschler, to strip the site and bring the mission to a close. It had all become too messy, too multiple. Lemoine didn't like messy. He didn't like multiple. He liked single, he liked swift, and he liked clean.

As far as anyone could prove, Lemoine was still sitting in his rented house in Tekapo, sending emails, browsing websites, and even making purchases online. In reality, he'd been driven back to Thorndike late the previous night by one of his bodyguards, hidden under a blanket in the back seat of the dark-tinted SUV. If anything went wrong during the pack-out operation, he wanted the option of denying that he'd been present at the farm at all, and to that end, he'd told the guard to pull into the Thorndike petrol station, go up to the store, and try the front door; he knew that the station would be closed already, but he wanted to give the CCTV camera a good few seconds' look into the car. The guard had taken the deception even further, taking his time coming back, ambling across the forecourt, inspecting the pressure in the tyres, even getting out his phone and scrolling through his messages a while – just a few mindless little actions to make it clear that he was off the clock and there was nobody else in the car. The guard was good. He was better than good, in fact. He'd been in the house the whole time that Lemoine had been with Shelley, and she'd never had a clue.

'You said you had something to tell me,' Mira said.

'It's about the threat against my life,' he said. 'I found out the guy's name.'

'Okay, what is it?' she said, when he didn't go on.

He turned to her. 'I think you already know,' he said.

She scowled at him. 'Why would you think that?'

'Because he's a friend of yours,' said Lemoine calmly. 'Or he used to be.'

Recognition dawned across her face. 'Oh my God,' she said.

Lemoine said nothing.

'But . . .' She put her hands up to her temples. 'Wait,' she said. 'I don't understand.'

Ever since Lemoine had seen the footage of Tony taking photographs in Korowai – days before he learned who Tony really was – he had been looking for a way to ruin him, to destroy his credibility pre-emptively, just in case those photographs got out. It had taken him until that morning to circumvent the password of the laptop he'd discovered under the passenger seat of what he now knew was Tony's sister's car, and once he'd finally broken in, he'd been rewarded beyond his wildest expectations when he'd discovered, in Tony's 'Recent' folder, a Word document that bore the file name 'eattherich' – created, not incidentally, the morning after the controversial vote at Birnam Wood. Reading it, Lemoine had laughed out loud. The guy had no credibility to start with. The job was already done.

'I don't understand,' Mira said. 'How?'

Lemoine got out his phone to quote a passage. ' "These tax-dodging economic parasites," ' he recited, ' "cannot be allowed to retreat into a private sphere of luxury so well-insulated from the lives of ordinary people, and so well-defended against them, as to amount to a form of secession – an obscene evasion of social, moral, and environmental responsibility that would be condemned, and likely prosecuted, if practised by any other interest group or social class."'

'What is that?' Mira said.

'Well, I don't know about round here,' said Lemoine, putting his phone back in his pocket, 'but where I come from, it's called a manifesto.'

'What?' Mira said. 'You mean – that's Tony's? Tony wrote that?'

'Yes.'

'Where did you get it?'

'I hacked into his laptop.'

'What?' she said. 'When?'

'About an hour ago,' he said.

'An *hour* ago?' she repeated, looking shocked. 'Why?'

'Because he's dangerous, and he wants to kill me.'

'No, he doesn't,' Mira said. 'That's crazy.'

'How is that crazy?'

She was shaking her head. 'Because – because – I mean, lots of people on the left write things like that. It's not even – I mean, it's just an opinion. Right? It's a point of view.'

'This manifesto makes it very clear that Tony Gallo thinks that I should not exist.'

'Yeah, but as a billionaire, right? Not as a human being.'

'Oh good, so you've read it, then?' he said, trying to catch her out, but she was still shaking her head.

'Look, I know Tony,' she said. 'And I promise you, this does not make sense.'

'It makes perfect sense,' said Lemoine. 'He came down here to find me. He knew where I'd be, because you told him. He was staking out the farm, my security got nervous, they tried to talk to him, he bolted. People don't run if they've got nothing to hide.'

395

'They do if they're scared.'

'This is a serious situation, Mira. I have the best security on the planet, and they're telling me that this guy is a credible threat.'

Mira was quiet. 'But you don't know where he is,' she said at last.

He didn't move. 'Do you?'

To his surprise, she laughed. 'You just said you had the best security on the planet,' she said, shooting him a scornful look. 'Why would I know something they don't?'

'Answer the question.'

'Jesus, Robert,' she said. 'No, I don't fucking know where Tony is. This is crazy. I can't believe this. Everything you're saying to me right now is fucking mental.'

He studied her. If she was lying, she was lying well. 'Has he tried to contact you?' he said.

'Like when? Like recently?'

'Since you've been here.'

'No,' she said, not looking at him. 'And he wouldn't. Like you said, we're not exactly friends any more, so.'

He watched her for a moment longer, and then said abruptly, 'Okay. Let me drive you back.' He reached over his shoulder to put his seat belt on, and automatically she reached over hers to do the same – and as she moved her body, there came a muffled thunk from inside the Thermos she was holding on her lap. Lemoine glanced at it. 'What's in there?' he said.

She looked down at the Thermos as though she couldn't quite remember what it was. Eventually she said, 'My phone.'

'Your phone?'

'Yeah,' she said. 'I didn't want it to get wet.'

'Oh,' he said. He released the parking brake and they drove off across the hill.

Did she know that putting a phone inside an aluminium flask would block the signal? Of course she did. Everyone knew that. Didn't they? Lemoine kept his eyes straight ahead. Why would she not have simply put the phone in her pocket? Her jacket was waterproof – and she was wearing a zippered fleece underneath it, which would have pockets too – and anyway, it was an iPhone; she had to know that they could handle getting wet. Lemoine thought about Tony's obfuscation tactics, his insulated clothing, his analogue camera, the way he'd timed his escape from the park to coincide with the rain. He thought about the fact that it was raining now. He thought about Mira saying, 'An *hour* ago?' in a tone of shock. Why had that been the detail that alarmed her? The Vanette appeared over the crest of the hill and Lemoine slowed to let it pass; but he hardly saw Shelley sitting in the driver's seat, hardly caught the look that passed between the two young women, hardly noticed as the van went rattling by.

A solution was before him. It was so perfect he could hardly believe it hadn't been his endgame all along; he felt as he had in the days after the landslide on the pass, when he'd first dreamed up his survivalist disguise, and he had thrilled in the knowledge that the contingency had delivered him something even better than the plan. For who wouldn't believe this story? A disaffected, sexually frustrated, isolated young man, socially downgraded and rejected from a group he once belonged to, tracks his old friends down to Thorndike, stalks them as they work, convinces himself that they've betrayed their very nature, and then massacres them all. Who could doubt it? And who could doubt that this malevolent sub-creature, this toxic trend, this hateful vector of societal decline would then kill himself, leaving no survivors at the farm – none except Lemoine, who, as far as anybody knew, was safe in Tekapo, a hundred miles away?

Birnam Wood was going to prove a better form of camouflage than he had ever dreamed. For after they were dead, after Tony had committed this unspeakable atrocity, he, Lemoine, would have the perfect reason to terminate the whole construction project and recall all the heavy vehicles, the containers, and the crew. The bunker would never be unloaded, let alone interred – but after such an evil deed, how could it be? Who could blame Lemoine for wanting never to be near that wretched place again? And who would guess that when the cement mixers and the earth movers and the containers and the trucks and the RVs all left Thorndike, they would be loaded to the gills with a trillion dollars' worth of sludge? The precious minerals would leave the country. Lemoine would put the subdivision up for sale again. He would detonate the site in Korowai, settle his debts, and fly home.

It was single, it was swift, and it was clean.

He dropped Mira at the shearing shed and returned to the farmhouse, deciding as he bumped his way across the fields that he would bring his bodyguard on board. He couldn't carry out his plan alone. The mercenaries answered to Lt Col Weschler, not to him, and Lemoine could think of no conceivable reason why Weschler, who had never had any dealings with any member of Birnam Wood, would want or need to be rid of them. Besides, the PMCs had enough on their plates with the packout in the park – they were already having to extract the stolen minerals in suboptimal conditions and at speed – and Weschler had leaned on them once already. He'd spun the death of Owen Darvish as an accidental security breach that had required a simple clean-up job; he couldn't use that explanation twice. Better to keep them separate. Church and state, thought Lemoine, smiling slightly as he pulled into the garage, cut the engine, and got out of the car. Anyway, the bodyguard was desperate to see some action; he'd been chafing at the bit for months. And he was good. Lemoine opened his laptop, transferred a stack of cash into the guard's account, showed him the balance, and promised him ten times that amount when the job was done. The guy didn't even hesitate. 'What do you need?' he said.

'I'd rather pay a fine than a fee,' Lemoine had said to Shelley the night before. This was a maxim that he had held through his entire career; what he might have added was that in most situations, he usually avoided even being fined. He knew that once the rare-earth elements were in his hands, no government of any country in the world was really going to care how he had gotten them – and that included New Zealand. Sure, there might be a bit of knuckle-rapping, a few warm words. Tribunals might be formed, activists might strut about, legislation might be passed, politicians might be voted in and out, et cetera; but so long as there was a phone in everybody's pocket, so long as there was a screen in front of every face, so long as there were bat-teries and satellites and cameras and GPS, so long as there was avarice, so long as there was loneliness and envy and ambition and boredom and addiction, he, Lemoine, would be untouch-able. The value of the minerals was just too great. What they made possible was just too vast. Too important. Too desirable. And nothing would incriminate Lemoine. He would even be hailed as a liberator: the man who bravely faced down China and secured technological independence for the West.

'Well, hello,' he said, shining the torch into the trees. 'You must be Tony.'

He waited for their eyesight to adjust.

Tony was the first to find his voice. 'You're going down, you piece of shit,' he said. 'You're going to rot in hell. You're fucking done, you motherfucker. You lose. I know what you're doing out in Korowai. You and the fucking government. I know it all. I saw the fucking mines. I saw your drones. I saw what you did. I took photos. I sent them all around the world. They're gone. I sent them to every fucking paper I could think of. All around the world. They're being published any minute. You're fucking done, man. You're fucking destroyed, you little bitch.'

Lemoine said nothing. He shone the beam of light down Tony's body, noticing that his arm was in a sling. He was going to have to work with that. A guy with a broken arm couldn't carry out a massacre, still less with a bolt-action hunting rifle that probably only held ten rounds. As far as Lemoine could remember, in the gun locker in the Darvishes' garage there was nothing semi-automatic; he remembered Darvish saying that he didn't own a handgun, nor even any kind of shotgun, as he showed Lemoine the rack of hunting rifles arranged in order of ascending calibre, most of which were only meant for shooting rabbits, and none of which could be operated with one hand.

'This is getting blown wide open, man,' Tony said. 'You're going to fucking fry. You're fucking done.'

Lemoine was still thinking about rabbits. 'You need medical attention,' he said, almost absently, taking out his phone to send a text.

'What are you doing?' Mira said.

'Sending for help,' said Lemoine.

'Don't fucking talk to her,' Tony said. 'Don't even fucking look at her, you fuck!'

Lemoine ignored him. He sent the message and then put his phone back in his pocket. 'All right,' he said. 'Let's calm down.'

'You killed Owen Darvish,' Tony said. 'You were in on it together and then you fucking murdered him. Didn't you.'

Lemoine looked at Mira, who looked away.

'You fucking psychopath,' Tony said. 'You fucking piece of shit.'

'You need to calm down,' said Lemoine.

'Or what? What are you going to do? Kill me? What? You're going to kill us both, you little prick? Just like Owen Darvish? You're going to run us off the road?'

'Tony,' said Lemoine, 'look.' He turned the flashlight around and lifted up his shirt to show them his torso and the waistband of his pants, using his free hand to pat his pockets down. 'See? I'm not armed. I have no weapons.'

'Fuck you,' Tony said. 'You lying piece of shit. Fuck you.'

'I am alone,' said Lemoine. 'I haven't threatened you. I haven't tried to hurt you. You're the one who is the threat here. You're on my property, without permission, in the dark, making God knows what kind of plan to move against me. You're the one cursing me out. The only action I have taken is to send a message to my driver to come and take us all back to the house so you can get some medical attention and we can talk. Okay?'

'Bullshit,' Tony said. He was trembling. 'You're lying. Everything you say is a lie.'

Lemoine shone the light on Mira. 'Mira,' he said. 'Would you please—'

'Don't fucking say her name! I'll fucking kill you!' Tony shouted.

But Mira reached out her hand. 'Don't,' she said, gripping Tony's knee. 'Don't threaten him.'

Good. She was wavering.

'Listen to me, both of you,' said Lemoine. 'Here is the truth. Yes, there is something going on inside the national park, and yes, I am involved. But this is not the deep-state conspiracy you think it is. No laws are being broken. This project has top-secret applications in defence that are a matter of critical international security. I am fulfilling an entirely legitimate contract in the full knowledge of all the Five Eyes governments, including yours, and you would know this already, Tony, if you hadn't jumped into the river like a fucking lunatic the first time my guys tried to talk to you. Okay? You have put me in a very difficult position. I can't let you go, because you pose an active threat to my personal safety, and because those photos in your pocket are highly classified images that need to be disposed of securely. If you come down to the house, we can get you some help, I can make a few calls, and I can explain to you, as far as I am able, what is going on here. I did not kill Owen Darvish, as Mira very well knows, and if she has told you otherwise, Tony, then she is the one who is lying to you, not me. I am not going to hurt you. I have no interest in hurting either of you, but what I *am* going to do is detain you, as peacefully and respectfully as I can, so we can have a conversation and figure out what to do about this incredibly complex and delicate situation we are in. You are badly injured, and quite frankly, you dying on my property is a mess I would rather not clean up. All right? My driver is going to be here in a minute. Just come with me back to the house and talk to me. That's all I'm asking.'

'Bullshit,' Tony said again, but he didn't sound as sure.

They heard the engine of the SUV coming up the hill towards them, and Lemoine waved the flashlight to signal to his driver where they were. The SUV drove up to the trees and stopped. The driver's door opened, but nobody got out.

'I'm going to get in the car now,' said Lemoine. 'I suggest you follow.'

He shut off the light and walked out of the shelterbelt, blinking away the reddish bloom that filled his vision in the sudden dark.

His phone was vibrating in his pocket. He took it out and saw that it was Shelley calling. He walked a little further to the edge of Mira's planting site and then answered the call.

'Mira's gone,' Shelley said, sounding out of breath. 'She said she had a headache and she went to bed, but I just checked and she's not in her tent and her backpack's missing too, and on the app her location is the same as it was this morning, like it hasn't updated, like it still says "Last Seen" about eleven something this morning and then nothing after that. She must have disabled it. She's never done that before. She's gone. I don't know where she is.'

'She's with me,' said Lemoine.

'What?' Shelley said. 'With you?'

'She was trying to make a run for it,' said Lemoine. 'I just caught up with her. I'm going to need to stay with her for a while, I think. Talk her down a bit.'

'Is she okay? Like – how is she?'

'She's just scared,' he said. 'Don't worry. She's not going anywhere. I promise.'

'Do you think that I should—'

'No,' he said, 'let me handle this.'

'Are you sure?'

'I'm sure,' he said. 'I'm just sorry it means I probably can't see you again tonight.'

'Oh,' she said. 'I guess I didn't realise that was … maybe going to happen.'

'I've thought about you all day,' he said.

'Me too,' she said. 'I mean – you. Not me. Obviously.'

'Can we rain-check?'

'Yeah,' she said. 'Of course. I'm just a bit worried about Mira.'

'I am too,' he said. 'But I don't want to spook her. I just need her to see that everything is fine, and the hard part is behind us now. She'll come around.'

'I hope so,' Shelley said. 'Good luck.'

'Oh – Shelley? One more thing.'

'Yeah?'

'I want to call a meeting for tomorrow morning. Just to draw a line under all of this. Could you round everybody up? Say eight o'clock?'

She seemed to hesitate. 'What kind of meeting?'

'Well – the others are going to find out about Owen Darvish sometime. I was the one who found his body; the longer I wait, the stranger it's going to seem.'

'Okay,' Shelley said, still sounding doubtful. 'But what about Mira? I mean, aren't you worried that she might—'

'She won't be there,' said Lemoine. 'I'll leave her at the house.'

'But what if she—'

'I have security,' he said. 'They'll be here. They'll make sure she doesn't leave.'

'Yeah, but won't it—'

'Shelley,' he said firmly, 'she's going to be fine. I know she will. I just don't trust her around other people right now. I don't trust what she might say, what she might do. You know it your-self: she's in a fragile state.'

'Yeah,' Shelley said, 'but how will you explain—'

'I'll tell them the truth,' he said. 'I'll say that this has been a hell of a lot to take in, she's having a bit of a breakdown, and soon it'll all be absolutely fine.'

'Okay,' Shelley said. 'Okay.'

'Make sure everybody's there tomorrow. Eight o'clock.'

'I will.'

'I'll bring breakfast,' said Lemoine.

'I want you to run,' Tony whispered, as Mira helped him out of the shelterbelt and into the back seat of the SUV. 'Don't worry about me. Okay? The first chance you get, just run.' The door to the back seat was standing open. He gripped the handle, set his teeth, and swung himself up into the car with his good hand. Mira helped to lift his injured leg in after him, seeing the blackened bandage up close for the first time and smelling dirt and sweat and urine.

Lemoine's driver patted Mira down and then escorted her around the back of the vehicle. She could barely make his face out in the dark, but as he opened the door for her and stepped aside, she smelled him too, a soapy fragrance of rose water and patchouli that almost made her sick. She climbed in beside Tony and the driver shut the door behind her. Lemoine was talking on his phone nearby; Mira watched through the tinted window as he paced back and forth. Experimentally, she tried the handle to see if the child lock was on. It was: the door wouldn't open. She glanced over at Tony, but his head was lolling back against the headrest, and his eyes were closed. She reached for his hand.

'Where are the photos?' she whispered. 'The roll of film. Where is it?'

Tony's eyes didn't open. 'I sent it to Mum,' he said.

'No, Tony, the roll of film. You showed it to me. It was in a plastic bag.'

'Yeah,' he said, eyes still closed. 'Mum's got it. It's fine. She knows what to do.'

'Tony,' Mira said. She gripped his hand and shook it, trying to rouse him.

'I'm just so tired,' Tony said.

'Don't give up,' she said. 'You can't give up.'

'I think I did already,' he said. 'A little while ago. Back there.'

Lemoine ended his call and came back to the car. He spoke to his driver in a low voice for a moment, and then they peeled apart, opened their respective doors, and got in. The driver put the key in the ignition, lighting up the dashboard, so that Mira got a partial glimpse of his features for the first time. He was handsome, with high cheekbones and thick lashes and dark eyes, and somehow this was even more sickening to her than the smell of his soap. She held on tight to Tony's hand, wondering what he had done with the roll of film. Had he hidden it back at the shelterbelt? Maybe he had buried it. Or maybe he'd stashed it in a tree – up high, because anyone who came looking for it would probably be looking on the ground. He would have been clever like that. He would have been careful. They had left all his gear behind, along with Mira's backpack and the food that she had brought to give to him, and the box of paracetamol he'd never opened, and the first-aid kit she'd taken from her bicycle pannier. He wouldn't have walked away from all his stuff unless he'd had a plan. He wouldn't have come to the car so willingly. And he was probably pretending to be more delirious than he was, Mira thought, to give them the advantage of surprise later on. He was probably just pretending he had given up. It was a strategy. He had a plan.

They pulled up outside the Darvish farmhouse and the driver and Lemoine got out. Lemoine went into the house, and the driver came round to Tony's door and waited until Lemoine reappeared again and nodded. Then the driver opened the door and reached into the back seat to help Tony out. Mira let go of Tony's hand and Tony put his arm around the guy's neck and allowed himself to be lifted out of the car. Mira scooted across the back seat to slip out after him, but before she made it to the edge, the driver said, 'No,' and shut the door on her. She tried the handle, but it, too, was locked from the inside. She watched through the tinted glass as the driver held Tony up by the armpits and Lemoine reached into Tony's jacket pocket and pulled out the ziplock bag that contained the roll of film. In the light from the porch Mira could see that Tony's face was white with pain and exhaustion. His eyes were dull. Lemoine checked his other pocket and withdrew a Swiss Army knife that was opened at the blade. He folded it shut, then patted Tony's trouser pockets and felt around his waistband and down his thighs and between his legs. Tony stayed limp. He had no expression on his face at all. Mira had never seen him look like that before. She had never seen anybody look like that before. At last Lemoine stood back and nodded again to the driver, who put Tony's arm across his shoulders and half-carried him into the house.

Lemoine and Mira looked at one another through the tinted glass. Then, to Mira's surprise, he opened the door to let her out.

'Go take care of him,' Lemoine said. 'I wasn't kidding: I don't want him to die.'

'So call an ambulance,' Mira said.

'No,' said Lemoine. 'I'm not going to do that.'

'His bones are broken. What am I supposed to do?'

'We'll see what we can find in the bathroom cabinet.'

'No,' Mira said. 'No way.'

'Mira,' said Lemoine, 'he did this to himself. All right? *He* broke into a top-secret research facility. *He* did that. *He* saw what he wanted to see behind the fence. *He* went on the run. *He* jumped off a cliff. He did that all on his own. I am the innocent party here.'

'Prove it,' Mira said.

'You're not listening to me. I can't. Mira, the clearance on this project is way above top secret. I can't just take him to a hospital. I need time to sort this out.'

'Prove it,' she said again, hating how weak and pathetic she sounded.

Lemoine made an impatient noise. 'I don't have time for this,' he said. 'Go take care of him. I've put him in the master bedroom. There's some water in the room already. We'll get him to a doctor, but tonight you're going to have to make do with what we can find in the house. My guy's name is Daniel. He'll be right outside the door all night.'

Mira's chin puckered. She felt like a stupid child.

'We'll talk in the morning,' said Lemoine. 'Go.'

She went. She found Tony laid out on the Darvishes' bed. His eyes were open, and he watched her as she took down a bottle of water from the dresser and broke open the seal around the cap. She sat down on the bed beside him and tipped a little into his mouth.

'I told you to run,' he said, when he had swallowed.

Mira said nothing. Her chin was still puckered. She was trying not to cry.

'You should have run,' Tony said, and closed his eyes.

The driver – Daniel – came in with a New Zealand Red Cross first-aid kit. He set it down on the end of the bed and then reached into his pockets and dumped a handful of prescription bottles on to the lid. Then he went out again, shutting the door behind him. The tin was dusty and rusted at the rivets; it was the same standard-issue kit that Mira's parents had kept when she was growing up, and she guessed that it must have come from the Darvishes' garage. That reassured her. She went over to it and picked up each of the bottles in turn: amoxicillin, hydrocodone, tramadol, extra-strength acetaminophen, each almost empty, the labels made out to Mr Owen Darvish, Mr Liam Darvish, Miss Rachel Darvish, Mrs Jill Darvish . . . She looked at the dates. They were all expired, but the tramadol was the most recent. She opened the bottle and shook out four pills.

Tony's breathing had turned shallow and regular: he seemed already to be asleep. 'Tony,' she whispered. 'Take these.' She pressed the pills to his lips and got him to swallow them along with a little water. He was lying on top of the duvet, and there didn't seem to be any spare blankets or comforters around, so she got up, moved the first-aid kit and the bottles over to the dresser, and then folded the other half of the duvet over him, wondering, as she turned out the lamp and lay down next to him on the bare sheet, which of them was sleeping on Sir Owen's side, and which on Lady Darvish's.

She didn't know how long Tony slept – it might have been minutes, or it might have been hours – but a little while later he awoke with a yelp. She sat up and turned on the light. His face was shining wet.

'What do you need?' she said. 'Water?'

'Hurts,' Tony said.

There was no more tramadol, so she chose the extra-strength acetaminophen this time, praying that she wasn't overdosing him, and that the pills in the bottles hadn't been switched for something else. She shook out four more pills into her hand and fed them to him, one by one. In the first-aid kit she found a roll of glucose tablets. She added them to the water bottle and shook it up. But when she tried to offer it to him again, he tasted it and immediately turned his face away. 'Poison,' he mumbled.

'It's not poison,' Mira said. 'Look, it's from a packet. Look. Tony. It's a brand.'

He craned his neck to look. Beads of sweat were running down his face and into his beard. 'Hurts,' he said again.

'I'm going to wrap up your arm,' Mira said. 'Okay? I'm going to wrap it up really tight. You'll sleep better.' He nodded, crying out in agony as she eased his arm out of the dirty bootlace he was using as a sling, and then again as she peeled off the sock that he had wrapped around his wrist as a cushion. His forearm was mottled and inflamed, but as far as she could tell, the skin wasn't broken. That was good: probably no infection, then; it was just a broken bone, or, if he was really lucky, a sprain. She found a roll of bandage and wound it tight around his arm, starting at his hand and working up towards his elbow, wincing every time he gasped, and she was concentrating so hard on trying not to hurt him that she only noticed belatedly that he had fainted. She sat back on her heels and watched his eyelids flutter for a moment, wondering if she ought to take the opportunity to bind his leg as well, but then she decided that she'd tortured him enough. He needed sleep.

'Mum,' he muttered, shifting on the pillow. 'Tell Mum.'

She vowed to watch over him all night, but at some point she must have nodded off; she woke and found that it was morning. Tony was asleep, breathing softly beside her, still very pale, but seeming peaceful. She felt his forehead. His skin was dry and cool. She got up and went to the door, expecting to find the driver standing right outside as Lemoine had told her he would be, but when she peeked out, the hallway was empty, and the house was silent and still. She went to use the bathroom, and on the way back, she saw the landline receiver in its cradle on the hall table. She picked it up and turned it on, but as she'd expected, it was dead. She put it back, and then sensed movement behind her and turned to see Lemoine standing in the kitchen doorway with his hands on either side of the frame.

'How is he?' he said.

'I'm not a doctor,' Mira said. 'I don't know.'

Lemoine studied her. 'I'm going to make some coffee,' he said at last.

She followed him into the kitchen and watched as he took the glass jug out of the Darvishes' electric coffee maker, filled it at the tap, poured the water into the back of the machine, and then spooned coffee into the filter. He shut the lid and turned it on.

'I thought you didn't drink coffee,' Mira said.

'I don't,' said Lemoine. He leaned back against the worktop and folded his arms and gazed at her thoughtfully, cocking his head. The machine began to hiss and burble. 'What's the deal between you two, anyway?' he said after a moment. 'I mean, the guy's nothing. He's a punk. What am I missing here?'

'What are you missing here?' Mira echoed, hearing the idiom as though for the first time.

'Yeah,' said Lemoine. 'What's the appeal? I don't get it.'

She stared at him, hating him suddenly, and wanting to spite him with the truth.

'I guess,' she said slowly, 'I guess . . . it was the possibility.'

'Will they or won't they?' he said in a mocking tone.

'No,' Mira said, surprising herself, for she had never described this aspect of herself to anyone before. 'Not that. Or at least, not only that. I meant the possibility of everything. Our whole lives. And our ideas, and the future, and the whole world. Tony made me feel like things were possible. Like I was possible. Like there was time.'

Lemoine said nothing. His gaze slid sideways over Mira's shoulder. Tony was hobbling down the hall towards them, still heavily favouring one leg, but moving well despite the blackened bandage around his swollen foot. He was clearly feeling better: his eyes no longer had the dull and hopeless look they'd had the night before, and there were spots of colour on his cheeks. Lemoine uncrossed his arms and went over to the pantry. He found the sugar crock and then took down two mugs from the shelf above the coffee maker.

'There's no milk,' he said. 'You'll have to have it black.'

Tony looked at Mira. 'What are you doing?' he whispered,

seeming disappointed with her almost to the point of disgust. 'What the fuck are you doing, Mira? Why are you still here?'

And in that moment, she hated him as well. She shrugged and looked away.

Lemoine was smiling at them. 'We'll have a bit of break-fast,' he said, 'and then we'll head down to the construction site. There's something there you need to see.'

The Eagles' 'Desperado' was the song that Sir Owen had want-ed to be played at his funeral. 'Ooh, this is going to be a tear-jerker,' he'd always said when it came on the radio. 'Ooh boy. This is going to be a doozy. I don't know how you're going to make it through this, Jill. Oh man oh man oh man. You'll be a puddle on the floor.'

'*You'll* be a puddle on the floor in a minute,' she had respond-ed, or, 'Don't talk about your funeral, it's bad taste,' or, 'Stop it, Owen, it wasn't funny the first time,' or, 'I told you, I don't like to think about that,' or, 'I won't have time to cry; I'll be too busy snogging my new boyfriend,' or, 'Owen, will you just shut up for once, and let me hear the bloody song?'

But he'd been right. She cried from the first chord. She cried from the first melancholy lyrics, and she cried at the way the background strings swelled up to meet the piano, and she cried when the drums came in. The screen beside the casket lit up with cross-dissolving shots of him, as a boy, as a teenager, as a young man, on their wedding day, with each of their children, at the hospital, guiding first steps, blowing out candles, giving horse rides on his hands and knees, asleep in bed one lazy morning, wearing a paper crown on Christmas Day, and on through the years, as his chest broadened and his shoulders thickened and his hair turned grey, saluting from the driver's seat of a convertible, digging a hole for a fence post, hunting with her father, show-ing off a pig on a rotisserie, grinning by a waterfall, giving away Rachel at her wedding, dancing Gangnam Style. The final shots were crisper and held on a little longer than the rest: the photo of the two of them that had been published in the *Thorndike Times* when he'd first received the news about the knighthood,, after which, she remembered, he'd picked her up, laughing, in a fireman's lift, and carried her inside and straight to bed; and then, finally, an official portrait from the day of his investiture, just him alone, all scrubbed and sashed and starred and suited up and looking fit to burst with pride. This image held on a little longer after 'Desperado' reached its end, as a shifting silence filled the room, and Lady Darvish wiped her eyes and blew her nose and heard Sir Owen's voice: 'Now *that's* how you end a song,' he said, or would have said, or used to say. 'None of this fade-out crap. None of this just-turn-down-the-volume-and-let's-call-it-a-day kind of carry-on. *That* is a *song*, Jill, that *knows* when *it* is *done.*'

The wake was held at the Mulloys'. Mark was waiting with a glass of Chardonnay, but when Lady Darvish excused herself to go and freshen up, she poured it down the drain and refilled the glass with tap water instead. She drank it without breaking eye contact with her reflection, and then refilled the glass and drank that too, and then refilled it a third time and poured it out again for no good reason, a habit that had used to drive Sir Owen mad, and then she sat down on the toilet seat and breathed and thought about Lemoine and Birnam Wood. Her thoughts went round and round. Cathy tapped her fingernails against the door and whispered, 'Jill? Sweetie?' and all at once she heard Sir Owen in her head again: '*That* is a *song*, Jill, that *knows* when *it* is *done.*'

She would know when this was done, she thought. This

wasn't done. She wasn't done. She, Jill Darvish, devoted wife of Owen Darvish, mother of his children, was not done.

'One minute,' she called through the door. She took out her phone and opened the Air New Zealand app and searched for a flight to Christchurch. There was one that left Wellington at 9.05. She booked a seat without a bag and paid for it, and then went back into the living room and did the rounds, thanking everyone for coming, accepting hugs and clutching hands and agreeing that Sir Owen would have been so happy with his send-off, agreeing it was all so shocking, so abrupt, so unbelievable, so sad, agreeing that he was a wonderful man and a wonderful father, agreeing that her life would never be the same. Cathy had made her up a plate of finger food, and she ate purely so that nobody could tell her they were worried that she wasn't eating, and then she gathered up her kids and held their hands and told them all she was exhausted; she had barely slept all week, she said, and it was finally catching up with her, now that she'd made it through the funeral and reality was hitting home. They had each offered to come back to the flat with her, just to stay a while, just to keep her company, just so there'd be someone in the house when she woke up; it had been very sweet of them to offer, she said, but the sooner she got into a normal routine the better – and really, all she needed now was sleep. Jesse and his girlfriend drove her home. She hugged them both and said goodnight and went inside the flat and shut the door and waited thirty seconds and then called a taxi to come and take her to the airport right away.

In Christchurch she hired a rental car and set off south, but she had barely left the airport car park when she began to cry again, and soon her vision was so blurred by tears that she had to pull over and hug the steering wheel and sob. It was past eleven. She cried until her eyes were swollen shut, and then she sat with her forehead pressed against her folded arms above the horn and told herself that she *was* exhausted, that it was true she hadn't slept all week, that she was really in no fit state to drive, least of all a five-hour trip to Thorndike *in the middle of the night*. The last thing her children needed was to lose both their parents in the space of a week. Chastened, she went to a motel instead, and let the night clerk draw his own conclusions from her puffy face and the lateness of the hour and the fact that she was carrying no luggage, not even a handbag, just her phone and her keys and her driver's licence and a credit card. She paid for the room in advance, let herself in, got under the synthetic comforter, and slept.

It was still quite dark when she woke, but even so, she stared at the digital clock on the bedside table without comprehension for almost a minute, trying to figure out if it was 4.15 in the morning or 4.15 in the afternoon. Both seemed equally implausible, as did the bed that she was lying in, and the flat-screen television mounted on the wall, and the darkened window, and the plastic kettle, and the shiny comforter, and everything else in the room; but at last she managed to locate herself in space and time, and with great effort, she clambered out of bed, left the room, put the key through the slot of the after-hours check-out box, and got back into the car.

'What is it that you think you're going to find down there, exactly?' she had said to Sir Owen, when he'd so uncharacteristically gone behind her back to book his flight. 'If I knew that,' he had replied curtly, 'I wouldn't be going down. Would I.' Lady Darvish replayed the conversation in her head as she drove. 'Owen,' she had said, pressing him, 'I told you, Anthony probably just made a mistake.' 'Yes,' he had shot back, 'I heard you.' She thought about the fact that Anthony had not returned her call. She had left a message on his answerphone a week ago, and he had never called her back. Why not? In his email to Sir Owen, he had said explicitly that he was writing an article about Lemoine. So why would he not have called her back? She knew as much as her husband knew. She was a source as much as he was. She was a party to the land sale, just as he was – in fact, she was now the only party to it – and Sir Owen's death had not exactly been a secret; it had been broadcast and published in the news. So why would Anthony not want to speak to her? It made no sense. Lady Darvish felt her thoughts returning to a furrow. Why had Sir Owen driven to the lookout after dark? Had he really been in talks to fund a not-for-profit? And why had he never mentioned Birnam Wood to her – not once?

Dawn broke as she left the coast and headed inland, feeling, as she always did the closer she got to Thorndike, a deep sense of rightness, of things existing in their proper places, in their proper order, for all time. She drove on, past the shuttered shops along the highway frontage, past the petrol station, past the edge of town to the bottom corner of what was now Lemoine's property, and along the fence to what was now their shared front gate. She could see the vast mound of gravel in the lower fields that she and Owen had intended for the new road that would have fed on to the subdivision, before the landslide caused the closure of the pass, before they'd met Lemoine, before he'd made his offer; glancing over at it, she was surprised to see a great many heavy vehicles clustered in the field around it, cement mixers, eighteen-wheelers, mobile offices, RVs . . . Surely Lemoine could not have started work so rapidly, Lady Darvish thought, frowning, slowing down, and craning for a better look; he'd need planning permission, obviously, and that process would take months, or even years. What was going on? Did the construction site have to do with Birnam Wood somehow? She had reached the front gate. She was about to pull in, but at the last moment she changed her mind and decided to keep driving, up to the unsealed service road that ran up the southern fence. It was a Saturday, and Lemoine had told her on the phone that he wasn't staying at the farm right now; but even so, some instinct told her to be cautious.

When she reached the farm gate at the top of the hill, she got out to unlock the padlock and unwind the chain around the fence post and saw that there were deep tyre tracks in the mud, running up the hill and out of sight. In her head she heard Sir Owen's voice again: 'It's that Anthony specifically said the word "radiometric",' she heard him say. 'That's what doesn't make sense. There wouldn't *be* an on-the-ground testing site for that, because nowadays they do it all from the air. They use high-flying drones. That's what I'm telling you.' She pushed the gate open, trapping it behind a tuft of grass to stop it swinging shut again, and then got back in the car and drove through. On the other side, she stopped again and got out again to shut and lock the gate behind her, taking her phone out of her pocket to check the time – but the battery was dead. She got back in the driver's seat and looked at the clock on the dash. It was coming on to half past nine; her children would probably be calling the flat in Wellington pretty soon to see how she was doing. They'd panic if they couldn't reach her. They might be panicking already. She hated the thought of having to explain to them where she was, and what she was looking for, and why; maybe when she got to the house, she thought, she'd send an email to all three of them at once.

She put the car in gear and drove on, off-roading down through the fields below the shelterbelt and cutting a wide arc to avoid the seam of limestone that formed a kind of shallow cliff above the house. As she came back around across the hill, she got another view of the heavy vehicles clustered by the

417

mound of gravel in the field below. She stopped and shaded her eyes to see if she could spot anybody moving, but the site appeared to be deserted. She drove on, parked beside the back porch, collected her phone from the cup holder between the two front seats, and let herself in the back door.

'Robert?' she called out, just in case, but the house was still.

Coming down the hall, she knew at once that something was wrong. The front door was standing open; and when she came through into the kitchen, she found the glass jug from the coffee maker smashed across the floor. One of the dining chairs was lying on its back; looking down at it, she saw that the middle section of a jagged splash of coffee had been disturbed. Something – or someone – had been dragged through it and towards the door. Lady Darvish stood very still, looking around her, listening hard, and then she went quickly to the hall table and picked up the landline. It was dead. Adrenalised, she ran on quiet feet down the hall to the garage, fearing that she was going to find the gun cabinet looted, the door pried open, the rack of rifles gone . . . but it was shut and locked as always. She went across to open it and reassure herself that the guns were all accounted for, before she realised that – of course – Sir Owen had the key; it was up in the flat in Wellington, his keyring having been returned to her after it was found on his body following the crash. She turned on the spot, feeling light-headed, feeling electric, feeling weirdly potent and alive, and then she saw that something else was missing: the plastic drum marked DANGEROUS POISON and SODIUM FLUOROACETATE and RESTRICTED CHEMICAL PRODUCT and 1080 BAIT FOR THE CONTROL OF RABBITS, with an authorising label made out to Mr Owen Darvish of Darvish Pest Control.

She heard a scream. It was distant – she guessed it issued from the fields below the house – but it was unmistakably a scream of pain, an abject, full-throated, terror-stricken cry for help. It sounded like a girl. Lady Darvish felt her heart constricting in her chest. She couldn't move. She waited for the ghastly sound to stop, and eventually it did – but only long enough for the girl to draw another breath – and then she screamed again.

Lady Darvish ran down the hall to what they'd always referred to as the front room, even though it was strictly speaking on the side of the house, and not at the front; it had been the living room before they'd built the extension and put in the picture window, and since the renovation they had hardly used it. On a low bookshelf against the wall was the special presentation case that she'd had made for Sir Owen's fiftieth birthday, where his .22 air rifle and his skinning knife were displayed on velvet behind museum glass. She opened the case and took out the rifle, jamming the stock against her hip, gripping it just beyond the trigger guard with her left hand, and with her right, smacking it to break the barrel open. She pulled the barrel down until she heard a click, looked down the length of it to make sure that it was clean, and then hooked it over her arm and scrabbled for the tin of pellets that Sir Owen kept in the top drawer of the desk. She opened the tin, selected a pellet, inspected it for imperfections, then slipped it head first into the breech and snapped the barrel shut again. She shoved the tin into her pocket and was about to leave the room when she thought better of it and grabbed the skinning knife as well.

The same instinct that had warned her not to drive on to the property through the front gate told her to leave the rental car behind the house, where she had parked it, and proceed quietly on foot. She shoved the skinning knife into her back pocket, put the rifle stock against her shoulder, and ran in the direction of the sound, stepping lightly, scanning the fields around her as she ran. All the doubt that she had suffered over Birnam Wood had left her. All her grief had left her. All the confusion and second-guessing doubt that had brought her to the farm was gone. Someone was in trouble. Someone needed to be saved. She felt as she had in the last stage of childbirth, animal and yet primordial, emptied-out and yet invincible, unstoppable, incredible, alive—

She came over the crest of the hill.

Lemoine was standing with his back to her, one hand in his pocket, scrolling through something on his phone. The person who was screaming was on the ground in front of him. It was not a girl, but a young man, a hippy type, Lady Darvish thought, bizarrely, with a beard and tangled hair. His left hand was band-aged; his right was bound at the wrist to a young woman whose other hand was bound to the chassis of a truck. Lady Darvish watched in horror as the young man tugged desperately at the tie that bound them, stretching the woman's arms out as far as they could go. Her head was slumped forward, and there was vomit down her front. She was dead, or at the very least, uncon-scious. The young man was still screaming. Horrified, Lady Darvish tore her gaze away, seeing more bodies, more vomit, all young people, all dead, fanned out across the site and contorted where they lay, as if they had discovered all at once that they'd been poisoned, and had tried, too late, to run. Lady Darvish felt her vision start to blur. She saw that the vehicles had been defaced with slogans, the sloppy letters trailing rivulets of paint. She saw the words THIS IS YOUR FUTURE and she saw the word JUSTICE and she saw the word SHAME.

The young man stopped screaming: he had seen her. Lem-oine glanced up from his phone, alerted by the change. He saw where the young man was looking, followed the direction of his gaze, and turned around.

Lady Darvish said nothing. She advanced towards Lemoine,

holding the rifle level, breathing through her mouth, lifting her knees high and rolling each step from the heel to the toe like she'd been taught, and as she drew nearer, she felt, suddenly, a transcendent sense of calm. Lemoine had killed her husband. Lemoine had done it. Lemoine was capable of evil. Now she knew.

And she had always known. That was the sad thing. Neither she nor Owen had ever been under any illusions that Lemoine was a *good person*, Lady Darvish thought, as she advanced. They'd known that he was bad right from the start. And still they'd courted his business. Still they'd courted his approval, his respect. Still they'd courted *him*.

Her thoughts alighted on a scene from her early twenties, when she and Owen had first been going round together; he'd given her a lamb that wouldn't suckle, and she'd raised it on a bottle and kept it as a pet for a few months, and then they'd killed and butchered it together. He'd given her the stunner. 'Right in the middle of the forehead,' he had murmured, standing a few steps behind her with a boning knife concealed behind his back, ready to slit the lamb's throat as soon as the animal went down. 'Don't spook him. You can take your time. Wait until he turns to look at you, and then imagine there's an X in the middle of his forehead, and shoot for the middle of the X.'

She was still advancing. Very slowly, Lemoine put up both his hands, extending one arm and dropping his phone into the dirt, throwing it away from his body, as if he were giving up a gun.

'Breathe out before you shoot,' Lady Darvish heard Sir Owen say. 'At the bottom of the breath you're steadier than at the top. You're doing fine, Jill. Just wait for him to look at you, then breathe.'

Lemoine was looking at her. She breathed. She visualised an X in the middle of his forehead. And then she shot him right between the eyes.

The report echoed in the hills around them. Lady Darvish barely heard it. She drew Sir Owen's skinning knife out of its sheath and ran forward with it to cut the cable tie that bound the dead girl and the boy.

'Is there anybody else?' she said, as she sawed at it, and the plastic snapped, and he was free. 'Is there anybody else alive?'

But he was already scrambling away from her, crying, rasping, hobbling away.

'Wait,' she said, reaching for him. 'Wait. Is there anybody else here?'

He was running now. 'The driver,' he said, his voice cracking, 'behind you,' and she was already half-turning when she caught a spray of bullets in her back.

Tony knew that he was just about to die, and he wanted to die in the bush, in Korowai, in a place that was green, and forgiving, and alive, and as far away as possible from the horror he had left behind him, the horror that the world would think he caused. He kept moving, hearing gunfire behind him, hearing it echo in the hills, wishing that he'd stayed, wishing he'd picked up the skinning knife, wishing he'd picked up the rifle, wishing he could say that he'd died fighting, which was stupid, since that was something that nobody could ever say, since they'd be dead. He didn't stop. He kept moving till he reached the border of the national park, then he climbed the fence and dropped down into the service road, and it was only as he fell, and his bad leg gave way beneath him, that he remembered the barbecue lighter that he had placed against his broken ankle as a splint. He tore off the dirt-soaked bandage and drew it out and fumbled it as he tried to test the trigger. He picked it up again. He tried again. It worked: a little dancing flame appeared. He clenched the lighter in his fist and began to move again, faster now, dragging his broken body through the undergrowth, and through the bush, and across the hill, and into the basin, and when at last he reached the fence with the lichen-spotted signs that read 'RESEARCH IN PROGRESS – PLEASE KEEP OUT', he put the aluminium wand between his teeth and clambered up and over, feeling that the end was very close now, that any minute now, it would happen: he would die. On the other side, he pulled his body forward in an army crawl until he reached the nets that camouflaged the leaching pits, and then he put his good shoulder against a manhole cover, and with the last of his strength, shoved it aside. He pushed one of the nets into the evil-smelling hole and then pulled it out again, and then he drew a breath and held the trigger down with both his thumbs and thrust the lighted wand against the sopping fabric, praying that the flame would catch, praying that the fire would send up smoke and burn away the nets so that the scale of the destruction would be visible from overhead, so that somebody would see it, so that somebody would notice, so that somebody would care, and as the fire began to blaze and crackle up the ancient trees around him, Tony prayed that somebody would come to put it out.

Acknowledgements

The town of Thorndike, the Korowai Pass, and Korowai National Park are all invented. In my imagination, the Korowai region combines elements of Tititea/Mount Aspiring, Aoraki/Mount Cook, and Arthur's Pass National Parks.

The name Finn Koefoed-Nielsen appears in this book as the winning bid in a Freedom from Torture Immortality Auction. Thank you to Christian Koefoed-Nielsen for his generous donation to the cause.

I am fortunate to have worked with extraordinary editors and publishing teams. My deep thanks to Jenna Johnson and Bella Lacey for vital editorial feedback and advice; to Christine Lo, Mandy Woods, and Kate Shearman for copyediting and proofreading the manuscript; and to Jon Gray for his brilliant cover design. Deep thanks also to Lamorna Elmer, Simon Heafield, Anne Meadows, Noel Murphy, Sigrid Rausing, Pru Rowlandson, and Sarah Wasley at Granta; Rodrigo Corral, Lianna Culp, Nina Frieman, Hannah Goodwin, Debra Helfand, Na Kim, Spenser Lee, Isabella Miranda, Caitlin O'Beirne, Sheila O'Shea, Nicholas Stewart, Hillary Tisman, Daniel del Valle, Sarita Varma, Amber Williams, and Jonathan Woolen at Farrar, Straus & Giroux; Tonia Addison, Jared Bland, Anita Chong, Sarah Howland, Ruta Liormonas, Kim Kandravy, and Kimberlee Kemp at McClelland and Stewart; and Fergus Barrowman, Craig Gamble, Penny Hartill, Tayi Tibble, and Ashleigh Young at Te Herenga Waka University Press.

Thank you to my very dear and very patient agent, Caroline Dawnay, and to Kat Aitken, Anna Watkins, Lucy Joyce, Georgina Le Grice, Amy Mitchell, Alex Stephens, Jane Willis, Georgina Carrigan, Gemma Bicknell, Natasha Galloway, and Talia Tobias at United Agents, and Rich Klubeck and Geoff Morley at United Talent Agency.

Thank you to the Amsterdam Writers Residency where I first encountered the ideas that would germinate this book.

Thank you to the New Zealand Arts Foundation Te Tumu Toi for their incredible and very generous support.

Thank you to Christine Poole for giving me time to write.

Love and thanks to all my friends and family, especially Glen Maw and Steven Toussaint for many energetic and inspiring conversations about politics, philosophy, and art; my parents Philip and Judith Catton; my crucial cats, beloved Laura Palmer, and dear departed Isis, sorely missed; and, last and first, my little one, A.D.